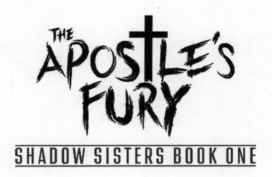

SHADOW SISTERS BOOK ONE

QUINN NOLL

In Memory of Lisa
Animal whisperer, keeper of secrets, and a better friend than I
deserved.
Love you, puddin'.

"For he is the servant of God, an avenger who carries out God's wrath on the wrongdoer."
Romans 13:4.

CHAPTER ONE

June 25th, 3 a.m. Dulles Airport, Chantilly VA

"Apostle": an ardent supporter; a person who initiates great moral reform; one sent on a mission.

The man shifted the blade from one hand to the other, testing its weight, the glint of moonlight bouncing off the steel. He'd never much cared for knives. As a weapon, he'd found them far too messy and much too quick. Still, they had their uses in covert operations. Silent and smooth, a precisely placed thrust could kill in an instant. He would need that kind of efficiency tonight.

Genuflecting, he closed his eyes and inhaled. The acrid scent of jet fuel collided with the sweet smell of summer blooms. Above him, aircraft equipped with blinding lights and flashing red beacons peppered the sky. It was a beautiful evening, a 'good to be alive' kind of night, and he reveled in it.

Pity he could not bask for long.

Meditating, calculating the risks, he prepared for this evening's task. It mattered little to him who died tonight. The world had become a shitshow, an affront to God, and

1

all those created in His likeness. The inferior continued to breed, leaving an untold number of weak-minded fools happily infecting the planet. It was enough to drive a sane man mad.

Darwinism, he knew, was a myth. Brain-dead scholars, spewing their evolutionary theories ad-nauseum, were full of shit. The concept of natural selection had one fatal flaw —too many half-witted creatures had somehow found a loophole. And so, it was up to him to weed out the parasites who contributed nothing to society.

Even a slight imperfection can ruin the canvas of a masterpiece.

He grinned, impressed with his profound insight. While weaker men were floundering in idiocy, here he was, creating life lessons destined to be embroidered on pillow tops.

C'est la vie.

His eyes swept the Dulles Airport parking area, searching for activity. Fate had carried him from the dust and heat of Laredo, Texas, to the crisp, clean air of Northern Virginia. His mission? To close a chapter in his life that remained opened, unread, stained.

But first, he needed a vehicle.

In the shadows of a dilapidated shuttle bus, he crouched low, tracking two beams of light coming his way. An airport vehicle, sans passengers, headed toward him on its way to the terminal. Every ten minutes, bleary-eyed employees driving courtesy buses would make the loop from the main terminal to short-term parking. Circling the lot like vultures circling the dead, the drivers dutifully searched for wayward travelers needing a lift. Tonight, arrivals were scarce; the parking lot a ghost town.

He checked his watch and sighed, irritation settling around him like a heavy cloak. He hated waiting. A familiar gloom, like a black hole with no beginning or end, moved through him. He shook his head, trying to claw his way out of the ugly mood threatening to drown him, but the darkness remained. He needed a distraction.

Opening the button on his shirtsleeve, he rolled up the cuff, tightened his grip on the knife, and dug the tip of the blade into the flesh of his forearm. Pain, then disbelief, rocked him as he followed the steady stream of red that flowed from his elbow to his wrist.

Blood? But... how?

He'd trusted that God would protect him, keep him from harm. Even self-harm. Could he have been wrong all these years? Is it possible that, somewhere in his journey, he'd lost his grace?

"Even a penitent man must be tested," a soothing voice whispered in his ear.

"Yes!" he croaked, spinning around, seeing no one. "I understand! To gaze upon the spirit's journey, I must first show piety!"

He blessed himself for the second time that evening and adjusted his sleeve. If all went well, tonight he would witness what had eluded him all his life—the transition of a soul. He called it 'The Splendor,' the precise moment during death when the spirit fled the body. It was only the purest, the truest of God's servants who could behold such glory.

He was that servant. He was the Apostle.

Gathering himself once again, he stretched and brushed a hand down the front of his thigh. This operation was taking too long. The clock was like a feral dog, nipping at his heels, and he was running out of time. The words of a cleric he knew, a distant time ago, echoed in his brain.

"You stand still long enough, boy, even a cripple will pass you by."

He'd hated that preacher man, but the words of

caution rang true. Sunrise was coming, and the longer he lingered, the greater the danger of failure. If captured, he would become just another statistic in the archives of criminal history: a has-been, a wannabe, one who never quite made it—loathed, ordinary, forgotten.

Oh, he'd no doubt there'd be an article or two written about him in the local papers. He could envision it all in his head; narcissistic, true-crime authors, smoking endless cigarettes and downing gallons of black coffee, opining on his checkered youth. Amateur sleuths with a degree in nothing would label him a lone wolf, an outsider, and a freak who 'kept mostly to himself.' And their readership would devour the details, gossiping amongst themselves and marveling at how he tried to mirror the world's most prolific serial killers. He could almost hear their conversations now:

"Did you know he studied Dahmer and Bundy?"

"Yes. Gein and the BTK killer, too. It's so creepy!"

"You want creepy? I heard he refused to eat anything but human flesh!"

Which, of course, was ridiculous—only the insane resorted to cannibalism. Still, the images in his mind rang true; if he were not careful, he'd end up just like all those killers he'd revered.

He deserved so much more. He deserved immortality.

Shoving his canvas bag beneath the ancient shuttle bus, he resumed his surveillance. To his right, the closest parked car was a speck in the distance. Fifteen feet to his left sat a luxury car, its driver commandeering two spaces, as if their existence held more value than anyone else's.

He smiled. *Some people were just begging to die.*

The sound of laughter jerked him from his reverie, while the rattle and clank of luggage wheels atop the pavement lent promise that the target was near. He huddled closer to the ground, his 6 foot, two-hundred-pound frame screaming in protest. Concentrating on the sounds around him, he anticipated at least two, possibly three people walking his way. He lowered his body further still, peeking under the bus. High-heeled shoes and penny loafers appeared in his view.

Two pairs of legs, not three.

The rhythmic cadence of his heart pounded in his ears, muffling the sound of his breathing. Goosebumps peppered his skin, and his pupils swelled. The thrill of the hunt—dangerous and electric—was nearly as satisfying as the kill.

Grabbing his bag, he skirted around the bus, mirroring their movements as they passed in front of the vehicle. The contact with the shuttle, virtually fossilized with rust and grime, left his palms damp and gritty. Someone had written 'wash me' on a side window, ostensibly pointing out the obvious. Repulsed, he continued to track them. They were nearly in range now, a petite female in her forties, and a frail-looking man of about seventy. He almost laughed aloud, giddy that the hand of fate had somehow divined that he would triumph.

They stopped behind the trunk of the fully-loaded, brand-new Silver Lexus LS. The female cradled her purse in one hand while digging for the car keys with the other.

Too easy.

Tucking the knife into his waistband, he positioned his jacket over his belt. He had no desire to scare them immediately. Maintaining control of his subjects, his students, was less about savagery and more about presumptions. The illusion of survival was a powerful tool.

A check of his watch showed he had just seven minutes left until the next shuttle passed. Unflappable, he stuck to his plan and, in three long strides, came upon them.

"Begging your pardon, folks," he began, his smile dazzling, "but do either of ya'll have the time?"

Startled, the woman looked up from her bag to find a rather tall man, broad in the shoulders and about thirty-five years of age. He wore a blue shirt under a light denim jacket, Levi jeans, and a pair of well-worn cowboy boots. His voice was silky smooth, with a deep Southern drawl. He was attractive, in a rugged kind of way, save for his cold, blue eyes and the scars lining the edges of his face. Slightly guarded, the woman glanced down at her wrist. It was late, and it was dark. There was no way she would paw through her purse, searching for her phone.

"I'm so sorry, I don't," she said sheepishly. She held up her arm as if to prove that her wrist was bare. "No jewelry this trip. I get nervous traveling with it, especially late at night. Feels as though I'm advertising." She offered a weak smile and waited for some sign of approval. He merely grinned back, enjoying the game.

"Well, a'course. I understand completely," he said. "Can't be too careful nowadays. More sinners on this here earth than what's found at the gates of Hell, I expect." He gave her a quick wink and continued to play his role.

Eyeing the Lexus, he whistled in appreciation. "Lord, have mercy," he said innocently, excited by the ruse. "That's a mighty nice ride you have there. I reckon that automobile had to set you back a pretty penny. Ya'll fixing to go on a trip?"

The woman tensed. She had become suspicious of this encounter and was scrambling for a way to end it quickly. Something about his smirk and the way he said "automobile," sounding out each syllable, unnerved her. She rubbed her hands together, as though it were the middle of January rather than late June.

"Um, no trip for me. I was just picking up my dad from

his red-eye." She paused for a second, searching for the words that would best get her point across without offense. Instinct told her it was necessary not to offend this man. "Well then," she said, chuckling in self-deprecation, "now that we've established that, embarrassingly, I have no idea of the time, I guess we will be off. Enjoy the rest of your night." Clearing her throat, she continued hurriedly. "Dad? You ready?" With a wave to the old man, she took a tense half-step, turning to advance toward the front of the Lexus.

In one quick motion, the Apostle pulled out his Bowie knife and maneuvered around her. Pointing the blade in her direction, he spoke crisply.

"Hold on there, little lady," he commanded, his voice devoid of inflection. "I'd be much obliged if you'd stay right where you are." The words, which might have sounded polite, almost charming, if spoken by another man, were robotic and indifferent to her escalating panic. "I'm thinking I'd like to see you place your hands in the air, nice and easy." He turned to address the man. "You too, old-timer. Do as I say, and everyone gets home tonight."

Swallowing a scream, the woman experienced a moment where her brain refused to process what was happening. Terrified, her eyes darted from left to right in search of a savior. The lot was empty, the vacant cars distant and scattered like bones in a graveyard. Her mind raced as she gave herself a mental kick for parking in such an isolated area.

What did he want? Would he kidnap them? Steal the car and kill them both? Dear God, would he rape her?

And the biggest question of them all loomed largest in front of her—should she fight? Could she?

Paralyzed by fear, her mind was an empty slate; an abyss wiped clean of any strategies of self-defense.

7

Everything she'd ever learned, ever read, about protecting herself in the face of an attacker escaped her. Shaking, she did the only thing that came to mind and raised her hands. The old man glanced at her, then followed suit.

The Apostle took the keys, and using the key fob, opened the trunk. "What's your name, baby?" he asked, moving between her and the elderly gentleman. His voice remained detached, toneless.

The woman paused for a second, debating whether to give him a false name. Then, seeing the dangerous glint in his eyes when she hesitated, thought better of it.

"My-my name is La-Laura Dixon," she stuttered, "an-and this is my dad, Henry. Please. We-we will do whatever you want, just please, don't hurt us. Take the car. Really. It's worth a lot." She licked her lips nervously. "How about money? Is that what you want? We have a lot of money." When he continued to stare blankly, she said, "I can get it for you. There's an ATM in the terminal." She swayed, a light sheen of sweat lining her upper lip and dampening her underarms. Sending up a quick prayer that she did not faint or lose her last meal, she resumed scanning the lot, this time looking for the next shuttle. Her arms, still pointed skyward, felt as though they were made of lead.

"It's a right pleasure to make your acquaintance, La-Laura Dixon." He smirked and glanced down at the keys in his hands. Lifting his head, eyes boring into hers, he said, "If'n you don't mind, Laura, I'd like you to get behind the wheel of this here vehicle." He gestured with the knife towards the front of the car.

He was so calm, as if he had done this thing every day. Laura would have preferred a raving lunatic to the emotionless man in front of her. Knees weak and stomach lurching, she somehow found the strength to speak. "Hold on. Wait. J-Just wait a minute. Why are you doing this? I don't understand. Just take the damn car, take our money. We won't tell. I swear!" She cringed at the wicked look he gave her, a look that told her he would not walk away. Defeated, throat dry as dust, she croaked, "What about my d-dad?"

The Apostle smiled, a smile that never quite reached his eyes. "Well, he surely puts a different spin on the situation, don't he, baby? But don't you fret." He nodded toward Henry. "Your Pop over there will ride in the trunk. Long as you do as I say, he'll be just fine. Right as rain, I expect.".

A fresh wave of anger began building inside of her. Was he planning on stuffing her father into the trunk? Like a spare tire or a sack of groceries? She was livid. But she also understood both her limitations and the danger this man presented. Brutality, even evil, seemed to roll off him like fog rolling over a wave.

Desperately clinging to hope, her mind explored all the potential outcomes of the situation and hated every one of them. Crushed, she decided there was but one viable option; cooperate and live. All they had to do, she reasoned, was follow his instructions. If he raped her, so be it. If they lived through tonight, she would deal with it.

She stood still for a moment, unsure of what to do next. Was she supposed to wait for her father to crawl into the trunk? Or should she get behind the wheel of the car first? Just what *was* kidnapping protocol, anyway?

The Apostle decided for her, gesturing impatiently with the knife, a communication that clearly said, 'get moving.' Repeating the mantra inside of her head, 'Do what he wants, live to see tomorrow,' she made her way to the driver's side and, legs trembling, got in and shut the door.

He turned his attention to Henry. They stood at the rear of the car, trunk open, both obscured from Laura's view. Checking his wrist, the Apostle noted the time. Three minutes left.

Henry's heart slammed against his chest. He had never known such savage fear. Hyperventilating, bowels threatening to loosen, he took one last look around. There were no shuttle buses, no police officers. No Superman swooping down to save the day. Like a blast of ice water to the face, his mind finally accepted the ugly truth.

They were on their own.

Resigned, he mumbled an act of contrition and made peace with the world. If destiny decreed he would die here, then he would die with his dignity intact. He swallowed, placed his hands at his side, and pushed his chest out in defiance.

The Apostle stared in disbelief. Why wasn't the old bastard shaking with fear? How could he learn his lesson if he did not believe in the power before him? Irked and somewhat offended by his student's lack of dread, the Apostle leaned forward, whispering into Henry's ear. Immediately, the older man's jaw dropped, and the stench of sweat and urine saturated the air. Henry spun, ready to flee, all thoughts of 'stand your ground' abandoned.

The Apostle smirked. "Shit just got real, Hank."

The ensuing attack was vicious, calculated, and effective. Laura's dad fought valiantly, but it was a fight he could never win. Mind whirling, out of time, Henry barely registered the muscled bicep that shot out or the sharp tug at his collar. Pulled nearly off his feet, his vision swam as his head slammed painfully into his attacker's chest. Impossibly strong fingers clawed at his forehead, yanking his head back to expose the tender flesh of his neck.

Eyes skyward, Henry gazed helplessly at the night sky. In his periphery, he saw the sudden flash of metal, felt the cold, sharp steel as it dragged cleanly across his throat.

Horrified, eyes wide, he grabbed frantically at the wound, a feeble attempt to stop the spurting fountain of blood. Silenced by a severed voice box, the only sounds that split the night were the throaty gurgles and wet whistles of a dying man.

Behind him, the Apostle studied the bloody, gaping hole that was once Henry's neck and felt a pleasure and satisfaction near-orgasmic.

This!

This was his purpose, his calling. He lifted Henry by the waistband and unceremoniously dumped him into the trunk. Impassively, he stared into the dead man's vacant eyes, searching for a sign, a light, a soul. He found nothing.

One target neutralized, he closed the lid and strode to the passenger side of the vehicle. He had much to do and very little time to do it. He despised deadlines. Deadlines meant rushed work, and rushed work was sloppy, amateurish, and beneath him.

But the world, as they say, was his oyster. He was powerful, smart, determined. He owed a very special someone a visit, a visit that was long overdue. But first, he needed a car.

And Laura Dixon needed to die.

CHAPTER TWO

December 2nd, Sugarloaf Mountain, Dickerson Md, Thirty-five miles north of Washington, DC

"Callahan! Over here! Jesus, Mary, and Joseph, I found something!"

Quickening her pace, Katie Callahan yawned and pressed forward. She was so damn tired. She'd give anything for a few hours of peaceful, uninterrupted shuteye. Four hours would be great. Six? Heaven. Sleep was an illusion for her; insomnia, a chronic affliction that even the finest whiskey would not remedy. And so sweet, dreamless slumber came only on the heels of total exhaustion.

And Katie was okay with that. If she was honest, most nights she dreaded closing her eyes. The things she saw, the intensity of her dreams, were much too vivid. Disturbing and nightmarish, the visions revealed themselves in rapid flashes of three-dimensional pictures or snippets of a movie reel. She knew there was a meaning behind every image, every sliver of information. She had only to decipher it.

Easier said than done.

She picked her way through the wooded path, the

distant sounds of conversation becoming clearer. Lieutenant Francis Blake, Maryland State Police, bellowed her name a second time, an undeniable urgency in his voice.

Resisting the urge to run toward him, she continued at her current pace. In her left hand, she wound the leather lead tighter while Chance, her seven-year-old Golden Retriever, tugged impatiently at the sound of voices ahead. The possibility of finding new friends, of getting cuddles and kisses and peeing on virgin trees, sent him huffing and pulling in their direction. Katie administered a sharp correction and rolled her eyes.

"Calm down, Lassie. Timmy isn't going anywhere."

The discovery of possible human remains brought Katie and Chance, a trained cadaver dog, to Sugarloaf that morning. The park, owned and operated by a non-profit organization, offered hiking trails, gorgeous vistas rife with wildlife, and Sugarloaf Mountain. Small compared to most mountains in the region, it nonetheless was popular with tourists. Geographically, it was an outlier of the expansive Blue Ridge Mountains.

The December morning was overcast, the temperature hovering at a bone-chilling 38 degrees. An overnight freeze had left a slick coating on the ground and moss-covered rocks. Stepping carefully to avoid a fall, her hiking boots gripping the slippery turf, she spied Frank facing the base of an ancient red oak tree. He was in a low squat, hands on his thighs, head bent in concentration. His olive uniform pants stretched tightly across his buttocks, threatening to split the seam down the middle. Mumbling to no one in particular, he repositioned his legs.

The years had not been kind to Frank Blake. While she had known him, he'd suffered a heart attack, been diagnosed with diabetes, and had several cancerous lesions removed from his face and neck. Despite all of that, porterhouse steaks and Twinkies remained a huge dietary favorite, and he continued to bake in the sun, unprotected. The man was a ticking time bomb, a stroke waiting to happen, an advertisement for a Living Will.

None of that mattered to him, though. Frank remained Frank; an overweight, beer-guzzling guy cursed with both a sweet tooth and a penchant for the beach. He was a man's man, a tough but loyal cop who could be abrasive, short-tempered, and jaded. Still, he treated Katie with the utmost kindness and respect. And he loved her dog. What more could she ask for?

She paused for a second, enchanted by the scenery. The trees of Sugarloaf, graceful and stately, had shed their greenery for winter and now produced a haunting landscape. Branches, unclad and slumbering, transformed the mountain from a world of the living to a stagnant, napping, 'between' world.

Like purgatory, she thought, *only for trees.*

As far as the eye could see, birch, hemlock, and poplars stood shoulder to shoulder, their rough bark and scarred surfaces a testament to their strength. Katie found an absolute serenity in being cocooned amid such sleeping wonder. She held her breath for a moment and listened. Preternaturally quiet, she wondered where all the animals had gone. Did they stay away, cowering, fearful of the evil that lurked in these woods and beckoned her to this mountain? She tilted her head back, searching the treetops and sky above.

Nobody ever looks up.

A friend in the U.S. Park Police taught her that, concerned for her safety during a spate of particularly violent rapes in the area.

"No one looks up, Kate," Patrick had told her. "Bad

guys can climb as well as run. Always check your surroundings, above and below. Too many people, too many good cops, have lost their lives because they failed to look up."

And so she did. The treetops were sparse, the skies a bland and cloudy canvas.

No bad guys so far.

She noted a scenic overlook south of her position. Protected by just a few large boulders and a puny fence, she estimated the drop from the edge to be one hundred feet, easily. And with so few barriers, it wouldn't be hard to toss a body into the abyss. She shuddered, an icy chill running down her spine. When had she become so macabre? So morbid?

She brought her focus once again to Frank and the two uniformed officers that surrounded him. As a group, they had been searching these woods since 5 a.m. Now, two hours later and miles from the marked trails of Sugarloaf Mountain, it appeared as though they had finally found something.

"I'm here, Frank," Katie said, trying to look over his broad shoulders or around his ample waist. She was standing behind him, unsure of the find or if it required a secure perimeter. Chance, to her left, halted and sat still, as he was trained to do. "Good dog," she said, giving him a scrub behind the ear. "Rest."

She stepped closer, apprehensive about what she might see. Bending, she spied the object of Frank's interest—a human skull, covered in dirt, leaves, and a few stoic beetles scrambling for breakfast. Its mandible dislocated, the jaw hung eerily to its side as if secretly telling an off-color joke. Nearby lay a shredded piece of clothing, possibly the last three-quarters of a shirt sleeve.

Frank took a deep breath and, still on his haunches,

scanned the area. "Well, I guess the little bastards were right. I was hoping those kids that reported this were high or just some assholes fucking with us. I mean, this is a public place, right? Off the trails, but still out in the open? Like a gay guy at a Pride Parade?" He wiped his brow and adjusted his hat. "It's an active park, for Christ's sake. Who the hell would just dump a body like this, Katie?" It was a rhetorical question.

Katie shrugged. "Could be bodies, Frank. Plural. That bone those boys brought to your station? The length and thickness of it suggest femur, probably male. This skull appears to be female. The ridges are less pronounced, and the bone thinner than that of a male."

Frank stood and stretched his back, testing his hips and knees after squatting for so long. He turned to face Katie.

"A dog handler and a forensic anthropologist. Damn, I'm like a proud Papa over here. Good on you, Katie. And on us. We lucked out." Sighing, he rested his right hand atop his holster, subconsciously ensuring contact with his service weapon. "Swear to God, baby girl, this is gonna be a cluster. An investigative nightmare, and I'm getting too old for this shit." He wiped his hands on his dirty pant legs, then followed with a swipe to his face. The residual dirt on his palms left a line of mud down the side of his cheek. Katie ignored it.

She studied that face now, mud streaked and well-worn at the edges, his straw Stetson perched on top of his balding head. He had seen more in his sixty years than most people would see in two lifetimes. But beyond the grooves and pastiness of his skin, his was a comfortable face; a face to take to ballgames and cookouts and birthday parties.

She had grown to adore that face and the man who wore it.

"Easy, pal, don't kill the messenger," she said with a smile, taking a step back and away from the skull. The last thing she wanted to do or have her dog do was contaminate evidence. "We will need to search this entire area for the rest of the remains. It may be that animal activity is the reason the skull is out in the open. Scavengers, mountain cats... anything could have carried this skull here. The actual dump site or burial could, conceivably, be miles away."

"You got any good news, Missy?" Frank said, frustrated. "Be just my luck that the bones are scattered all over this mountain." He slowly scanned the area. "Goddammit!"

After a moment, his mouth voiced what his mind had been fearing. "We may be looking at a multiple here, a serial, and we just don't have the manpower to scour this mountain alone." He paused for a minute, a thoughtful expression plastered on his craggy face. "So, tell me, Professor Callahan, what does your gut say? Will we be digging somewhere close by, or are we gonna be fiddle-fuckin' fifteen miles away?"

She hesitated before speaking, sure that the victim's bones were not in this area of Sugarloaf. In her experience, most killers will attempt to conceal their crime, and their victims, from discovery. Yet, they had bones from two different people, a male and a female, unburied and accessible. Embedded within the skull was a considerable amount of packed dirt and debris, leading her to believe it had been underground, at least for a brief period. Someone, at some point, had tried to conceal their crime —they just did a crappy job of it. There were no signs of disturbed earth here, no evidence of a grave present. It stood to reason, then, that the bones they discovered were transported from the burial site by animals.

17

Most importantly, though, there was Chance. Working similarly to a Search and Rescue dog who used scent, Chance's specialty was HRD, or human remains detection. Training involved teaching him to locate human remains using air currents, known as air-scent, rather than following an odor to the ground as a tracking dog will do. It took hundreds of hours of practice to get this specially trained dog to the working stage. Successful programs produced canines that would ignore distractions, only alerting when they scented human decomposition. Yet, there sat Chance; unperturbed, happy, waiting for the all-clear signal to let him know he had completed his work. She studied him a moment, eyes narrowing as he chomped at an invisible insect.

"Hey, Chance," she whispered, her voice playfully stern, "get your head in the game, man. You look ridiculous." In response, he yawned, turned his back, and casually licked his groin. "Perfect," she muttered.

Addressing Frank, she said, "I'll give you my thoughts if you promise not to box my ears. I think we are looking at a burial site, somewhere in the vicinity, but not here. The amount of ground material covering the skull's crevices and contours show that it was underground at some point, unearthed, and carried away by scavengers weeks, or maybe months, ago."

Frank clasped both hands behind his neck and groaned in frustration. "Great. Fuckin' awesome." Rolling his eyes toward the heavens, he gave her a weak smile. "Well, I guess I better make some phone calls. We will need more than four of us searching this grid." He ground out some orders to the other officers silently standing by, instructing them to set up a perimeter to preserve the scene. Next, he pulled a cellphone out of his side pocket and scrolled through his contact list. He knew exactly who to call.

~

Katie picked up the end of Chance's leash and quietly slipped into the background while Frank made his calls. She walked south, eyes downcast, slowly scanning the ground cover for depressions or disturbances that could indicate recent digging. The mountain remained eerily silent, determined to divulge none of its secrets. She could faintly hear Frank's side of the conversation as he spoke with an FBI agent—strained, confrontational, angry.

Typical Frank Blake school of communication, Katie thought, shaking her head.

She raised her eyes from the ground and looked up at the trees and beyond, waiting. Chance seemed to be waiting, as well, but there was nothing. No one stepping forward, begging to be seen; no translucent beings with flickering torsos and imploring eyes. No ghosts. And no deep emotions, fears, or regrets assailing her mind.

Glancing over her shoulder, she watched the men as they huddled together by the oak tree. Frank was off the phone, his callused hands gesturing in a circle around him. She began the walk back, then hesitated a moment. She needed to be sure the area was clear.

Of spirits, of souls. Of death.

Throughout her life, she struggled to believe that God had given her this ability for a reason. But the truth was, it was a gift too painful for her to think it divine.

She could trace its beginnings to the summer of 1996, a summer that would change her life forever. It was a time when innocence was lost, and she learned that there was more to the universe than bicycles and cartoons and ice-cream cones with sprinkles.

It was the summer that she drowned.

Tragedies, they say, occur closest to home. In Katie's case, it found her in the family swimming pool. Clinically dead for several moments, she was resuscitated and placed into a medically induced coma. When she finally awoke from her deep sleep, it was with the ability to perceive the emotions of others. A psychic Empath, capable of experiencing what other people felt, sensed, imagined. It was a heavy load for anyone to bear, but the burden on a six-year-old child was enormous.

But there was more. Katie's visit to the other side gave her yet another gift—the ability to see the dead. Wandering spirits came to her, caught in an endless loop while searching for individuals just like her. Individuals who, bright as lanterns illuminating the darkest night, emitted an inner glow that only the dead could see. This near-celestial inner light could identify to the departed a living, breathing being who could both see and communicate with them.

Except, in Katie's case, she hadn't quite figured out how to open the communication channel. It was like talking into a one-way radio or cell phone where only one party had reception. But, although she could not converse with them, they remained undeterred—a parade of spirits who seemed not to notice the fright in her eyes, or to grasp that the child rocking in place, eyes squeezed shut, was terrified. Day and night, whether through emotions or sight or smell, they came.

In the end, Katie Callahan learned at a very young age that she neither coveted nor embraced her ability. Instead, she merely felt a strong obligation to use it.

As she got older, the visits could often be disabling and intrusive. Clairsentience was an explosion of thoughts, pains, hopes, and dreams that molested your senses simultaneously. Encounters with strangers could be raw, intimate. She'd yet to discover a discernible pattern to the process, so was blind to when it would strike. Her Nana, long since gone now, had called her ability a blessing; Katie thought of it as a cross. One that, at the age of twenty-eight, she had yet to control.

Which brought her to the ultimate reason for believing the burial site on Sugarloaf Mountain was elsewhere. Here, as she scanned these woods, she felt... nothing.

Giving herself a mental shake, she threaded her way through the unmarked path, dodging uplifted tree roots and green moss, to make her way to the State Police group. Frank was pacing, head down, hand still on his Glock .40 caliber pistol. He reminded her of a sick animal trying to claw its way out of its skin. Picking up on his anxiety and frustration, Katie stepped back a bit and took a deep breath. Absorbing the emotions of others was exhausting, mentally and physically. Thankfully, Frank stopped moving when he noticed her and waved her over.

"I've reached out to the FBI headquarters in D. C.," he began, face scrunched up as if he smelled something foul. "They are sending us an Assistant Special Agent in Charge from the Washington Field Office, a guy named Devereaux. Who has a name like Devereaux, anyway? Sounds like a pansy to me. Like a French chef or a hairdresser." He shrugged. "But what's in a name, right? Anyway, he and his team will be over here tomorrow morning. MSP will provide some people on our end as well." He looked down and once again scrubbed his hands over his face, vigorously this time. Eyeing the skull before him, he continued, "So, what are the chances..." he stopped speaking and smiled, his mood lifted. Grinning slyly, he quipped, "Get it? Chances?" At the sound of his name, Chance wagged his tail and pulled at the lead. Katie let him go as, almost dancing, he finally got to his mark. Frank grabbed him around the neck and hugged him fiercely. "He's a good boy, isn't he? Yes, he is!" Frank looked up at Katie and asked, "How did you come up with the name Chance, anyway? He's a rescue, right? You give him a second chance or something?"

Katie shook her head, a soft smile on her pretty face. "He's a pure-bred Golden, actually, with championship bloodlines. When he was four months old, I adopted him from a family who decided they didn't want a dog after all. So, in that sense, I gave him a second chance. But life has a funny way of turning things around. When I accepted him as my own, I was in a dark place." She bent over and kissed Chance's nose. "So, it turns out that I didn't give him his second chance; he gave me mine."

Frank nodded. He understood all about second chances and had been on the receiving end more times than he cared to admit. Standing, he brushed the dog hair off his pants and got back to his original point. "Let me rephrase," he said, "What are the odds you are available to come back out tomorrow morning with my furry friend here?"

Katie looked down at Chance, who was utterly content under Frank's tender hand. "That won't be a problem for me. George Mason University is on break, so there are no classes. And, as an Adjunct Professor, even if class was in session, I could easily get someone to cover me."

"Excellent. Does 7 a.m. work for you? I figure by the time the polite introductions and unnecessary bullshit is over, we will be ready to start by then."

She nodded. "That works."

"Okay. So, what about a starting point for the grid?

Should we cover everything within a ten-mile radius of where we found the skull, or do we go farther out?"

She gave it her best guess. "I would begin southwest of here, to the right of that overlook. The easiest, most efficient way to dispose of a body up here in these mountains would be to toss it over the edge of the highway. The suspect could then hike in by foot, dig a shallow grave close by but still beyond prying eyes, and drag the body to the grave. These woods provide a lot of cover, even in winter, so getting caught wouldn't be a concern. If we scent with the dog from just before the overpass, we can follow it to the end." She thought for a moment. "Maybe add an extra two miles in either direction, just to be thorough. I don't think anyone could drag a body, let alone two, farther than that."

Frank grinned. "Damn, girl! You've given this some thought, haven't you?" He wiped his face once again. "You're a cool customer, Katie Callahan. Smooth as glass. Not sure if it's the freckles or the Irish roots that make you so tough, but I'm sure as shit glad you're on my side." Beaming with pride, he snickered softly, "Toss 'em over the edge! That's my girl!"

Smiling, she took one last look around. Her eyes landed once again on the mountainside, and she shivered. Something terrible had visited these woods. Something dark, something dangerous, something ugly.

And, God help them, she feared it had just gotten started.

CHAPTER THREE

"The faithless will be fully repaid for their ways, and the good rewarded for theirs." Proverbs 14:14.

Katie drove down I-95 south in her red Denali, her thoughts drifting toward home. The traffic was light now, as light as the interstate could be at 9 a.m. this close to Washington D.C. After leaving the crime scene, she headed for the nearest coffee shop, practically drooling at the thought of a gooey chocolate chip muffin and café mocha latte. Admittedly a junk food junkie, she made up for her dietary failings with a vigorous gym routine three days a week and a five-mile run every other day—except for Sundays. Sunday was her Sabbath, her 'me' day when she would laze around the house with Chance and her black Labrador named Blue. In the heat of summer, you could find her on the deck, reclining with a cold drink in one hand and a trashy novel in another. During the colder months, she would sit at the expansive window seat in the sunroom, enjoying a cup of cocoa and the breathtaking scenery. The view overlooking the magnificent Rappahannock River in Virginia was unequaled.

The Fredericksburg's log cabin she lived in was a quick commute from both her teaching position at George Mason and her consulting job at the Smithsonian Institute. The house, situated parallel to the great river, was bequeathed to her by her paternal grandfather upon his death. It was larger than most homes in the area, with an expansive second-floor master bedroom and adjoining bathroom, two additional bedrooms upstairs, and a guest room/office on the main floor. There was a living room with a stone fireplace that climbed to the second floor, a fully equipped and updated kitchen, and three full baths. Her favorite place in the house, the sunroom, boasted floor to ceiling glass panes and French doors that opened to the oversized, two-tiered backyard deck. A detached three-car garage, with an apartment above, housed her best friend of over twenty years, Darby Harrison. A twenty-seven-year-old golden-haired, blue-eyed beauty, Darby was the only person in Katie's world that understood the extent of her abilities.

Privacy and silence were rarities in the life of an Empath. But here, in this place, the soothing sounds of the Rappahannock and the sweet smell of wildflowers left her calm, centered. Not a simple task, considering she still could not control her talent, could not turn on the mute button. Hours of meditation and volumes of self-help books–gifts from Darby–had proven useless.

Still, there had been days when she'd embraced the ability to connect with the dead. Her grandad, Rory Callahan, visited her frequently. He had died a wealthy man, leaving her siblings a charitable trust and her, the cabin he loved. It was that love, Katie believed, that brought him to the house again and again.

She pulled out of the Starbucks parking lot, mocha latte and muffin beside her, and contemplated what she would do today. George Mason, where she taught Physical Anthropology, was closed for winter break. She was too tired to run, and yesterday, she'd spent an hour in the gym. Sighing, she checked the dashboard clock. There was still an hour left on her commute back home. Her thighs ached, her eyes felt gritty, and she had the beginnings of a wicked blister on her right heel.

"Buck up, Princess." she scolded herself aloud, "Maybe next time you'll spend a little more money on your hiking boots."

Skills practice with Chance and Blue, both Search and Rescue dogs, required patience, physical agility, and hundreds of hours of free time. It also demanded proper footwear. Being a volunteer for many years with A.R.R.F., or Air-scent Rescue and Recovery Foundation, she knew better. But she was nothing if not an avid bargain hunter. Now, her feet were paying for her thriftiness.

Based in Falls Church, Virginia, the rescue group utilized canines specially trained by their owners to find missing persons, detect buried survivors, and recover remains. Since Chance was the lone cadaver dog in the company, they were the only resource available for recovery situations.

Hoping for a diversion from the monotony of the drive, she peered into the rearview mirror and clicked her tongue, waiting for the dog to look up. "Hey Bud," she said, voice soothing, "what do you want to do today? Shopping? Pedicures? I would suggest ice cream sundaes, but your hips are looking a little chunky monkey lately." Chance gave a shake of his head and put his snout back on his paws, bored with the conversation.

"C'mon, that was funny!" she whined. "Get it? Chunky

monkey? It's an ice cream flavor!" When he continued to ignore her, she shrugged and dialed the radio to a smooth jazz station, tapping her foot to the beat.

Fifty minutes later, she turned down a secluded side road, best known to the locals as a detour around the headache of I-95. Half a mile in on the right, an ominous yellow sign warned travelers of fresh oil and loose gravel.

She groaned. *Perfect.*

Carefully navigating the road, she winced at the steady ping of stones that bounced off the undercarriage. Lowering the radio volume, as if that would ward off the potential damage, she adjusted her grip on the steering wheel and began an odd, yet somehow soothing, mental conversation.

Why the hell did I take this road?

Because it's a shortcut, dummy!

Yeah, a shortcut that will cost me hundreds of dollars in car repairs!

No need to be so rude, pal.

Engrossed in a one-on-one conversation with her brain, she initially didn't hear the rev of an engine from behind. Checking the rearview mirror, she spotted a battered white pickup truck barreling toward her.

"Slow down, buddy," she muttered, "I'd like to make it home in one piece."

She continued to drive at a slow pace, eyes alternating between the mirror and the road ahead. The pickup driver continued to advance, flying through the freshly laid gravel as if it were polished glass.

What the hell is his issue? She thought nervously. Had she cut him off without realizing? She checked once more and saw, to her horror, that the driver was right on her tail.

"You know," she said aloud, trying to maintain calm,

"if you want to get that close to my ass, you best be buying me dinner first."

She increased her speed to fifty mph, seriously pushing the speed limit, and hated herself for it. Accelerating for a tailgater was like giving a bully your lunch money or paying off a kidnapper.

Never negotiate with a terrorist! Maybe I'll slow down to a crawl… that'd piss him off!

But something about this didn't feel like your average tailgating or road rage incident. It felt increasingly threatening and hostile—like targeting. Despite believing in never giving in, Katie continued to speed up. The slick, oily pavement made it impossible to pull over without significantly slowing down. She attempted to let him pass, but whenever she backed off the gas pedal, the truck got closer

"Think!" she commanded.

She tapped the brakes, hoping the guy would get the hint and back off. If anything, he got closer. Her fingers were white against the steering wheel as her hands held a death grip on the leather. She couldn't remember ever being this scared.

Seconds later, a loud bang, followed by a jolt, pitched her forward. Her eyes flew to the mirror and, terror-stricken, she finally understood his intent; he was trying to force her off the road. He bumped her again, and, gripping the wheel tighter, she screamed.

"Son of a bitch! What the hell are you doing?"

Fumbling with the dashboard, she tried to dial her phone via Bluetooth. Her fingers were wooden and clumsy as, panicked, she stabbed randomly at the screen. Seconds later, a robotic voice informed her that her phone was not connected.

Dammit!

Nearing hysteria, she looked for a mile marker or house number to report her location as she manually dialed 9-1-1. Just as the call went through, he rammed her again. Hard.

She screeched as she lost control and braced for impact, watching helplessly as the car veered toward a drainage ditch. The vehicle bounced and dipped, finally landing with a thud into a gaping chasm at the road's edge. The momentum threw her head back and forth as her torso slammed forward, stopped only by her seat belt. In her periphery, she saw something fly off the dash, flip through the air, and strike her hard across the browbone.

Sunglasses?

An eternity later, the Denali jerked to a stop, shuddered, and stalled. Katie, eyes wide, dropped the steering wheel as though it were a ring of fire. In contrast to mere minutes ago, the air was deathly still. Distantly, she heard the muffled voice of the 9-1-1 dispatcher coming through her cellphone, now lying face down on the passenger floor mat. Beyond shaken, adrenaline spent, a single tear found its way down her cheek. Then another. She laid her head back on the seat, closed her eyes, and worked to calm her racing heart.

A moment later, she reached back and stroked Chance. "You're okay, boy." Taking a few seconds to inventory her injuries, she noted that, aside from where the glasses struck her head, she felt no pain. Again, she heard, "9-1-1, what is your emergency? Hello?" echoing in the background. Unbuckling her seatbelt, she bent over, picked up the phone, and dutifully reported the accident to the dispatcher. When the conversation ended, she tossed the phone onto the passenger seat and took a calming breath. Her head throbbed in synchrony with her racing heart. Peering into the rearview mirror (*had she ever used that mirror so much?*), she noted a small laceration on the right side of her head, just above the brow. Relieved to see a tiny gash, rather than the crater she imagined carved into her forehead, she turned once again to console Chance. He appeared physically fine, although his anxiety and tension were evident in his respirations and posture. She didn't need to be an Empath to sense that.

"It's okay, buddy," she said sympathetically, "I know. That was scary, right? That was a nasty man." Pausing a beat, she added, "Can you say 'asshole'?" Chance nuzzled her hand, his enormous eyes watching her intently. "I think you're all right, pal. That jerk can't..." Suddenly, she remembered the truck.

Oh, God, she thought, heart pounding once again. *Where is he now? Could he be hiding somewhere, waiting for us to get out of the car?*

She rotated her entire body, wildly searching the street behind her. There was no sign of the pickup or its driver. He must have kept going when she went off the road.

Idiot.

Still rattled, she pocketed her cellphone, grabbed at the door handle, and pushed. The door was at an odd angle, forcing her to heave it open with her shoulder and then hop up and out. The entire front end was nose down in the shallow ditch, while the back end remained solidly on the road. There was no way she could get out of that hole unassisted. Resigned, she stood at the edge of the trench and pulled open the back door. Chance sat up immediately, and she gave him a big hug. "I'm sorry, sweetie," she said tenderly, "but you're okay. It's okay, baby." She unbuckled him from his harness, picked up his leash, and guided him out of the Denali. They both stood by the car for a moment, two weary travelers dazed and stranded on a sticky, lonely road. Leaning against the trunk, she pulled out her cellphone and dialed a number. Waiting for the party to answer, she muttered softly, "Who the hell was that guy?"

~

Twenty minutes later, Darby Harrison pulled up behind the Denali, blind panic distorting her pretty face. Jumping out of her Volkswagen before it was barely in park, she hurried over to Katie and Chance.

"Jesus, Kates, are you okay? Your head is bleeding. You could have internal injuries or something. Should we call an ambulance? Yes, I think we should. I think we should call an ambulance." Darby was pacing now, talking more to herself than to Katie. Notorious for her inability to remain calm in an emergency, she would never be a cop. Or a doctor. Thankfully, she aspired to be neither.

"Oh shit," Darby continued, "I don't know what the hell to do here! Is Chance okay? Maybe you should sit down. What the freak happened?" Katie waited for her friend to take a breath before she spoke.

"I wish I knew, Darbs," she said. "One minute I'm driving home, listening to Kenny G and minding my own damned business. The next? Some dick starts riding my bumper, hits us, and runs us off the road." Katie dabbed at her head again and, lacking a tissue, wiped the blood on her pant leg. "All I know is that he drove a trashed white pickup with Virginia tags, and he seemed royally pissed."

Darby reached out a hand and gently brushed a strand of hair away from Katie's big, green eyes while taking stock of her physical condition. The ponytail holding her friend's auburn hair in place was failing miserably. Her face was paler than usual, making the light smattering of freckles across her nose look more pronounced. There were flecks of mascara in the hollows of her eyes and faint tear tracks on both cheeks. Darby could not recall a time when her friend seemed so muddled. She grabbed Katie's hands in hers and spoke as if she were soothing a skittish foal.

"How 'bout the cops, Kates?" she murmured. "Did you call them yet?"

Katie nodded, releasing the breath she was holding. "Yes, I got in touch with the local P.D. right before I called you. When I said I was uninjured and would contact a friend, they requested that I file the report at their station. Guess they are short-staffed today." When Darby made a face, Kate continued, "No, really, it's fine. I would much rather do that than have to wait for hours on this creepy road." She looked at Darby for a minute, concern lining her forehead. "So, about the Denali. You got in touch with your tow guy, right?" she asked hopefully.

"Yep, we are all set," Darby said, a little too cheerfully. "Although Pete, my usual guy, was not there, so they are sending someone else. Same garage, though, and these guys are cool. Won't rip you off for the repairs you might need."

Twenty minutes later, a tow truck with 'Pete and Sons Towing' painted brightly on the passenger side drove towards them. The driver pulled up and parked to the left and just ahead of the Denali. Getting out of his rig, the mechanic did a quick inspection of the car. Whistling, he walked back toward the women standing next to Darby's vehicle.

"Gud mawnin, ladies," the man said, "Look to mi like some ting wen wrong den, huh?" His tone was friendly, his smile infectious. Katie smiled despite the circumstances. His name was Aman, a short and solid fellow with vibrant, dark skin and a crisp Island accent.

"Nu worries, Mon," Aman said, "Mi git ya outta heya in no dime."

He walked back to his truck, and Darby turned to Katie with a questioning look. "You think he's fakin' the Jamaican?" she whispered conspiratorially.

Katie laughed and shook her head. "Nah, he's legit. I've seen him on campus before. He seems to show up whenever the kids at the school need a hand. Likable guy."

They watched as he hooked the chain to the axle, then pushed a button to tighten the slack. In minutes, the Denali was free of the ditch and ready to tow to Pete's garage. Aman assured her he would take care of the repairs needed personally and ended with another "Nu worries, Mon."

After settling with Aman, Katie watched as her only means of transportation was being hauled away, a sick feeling in the pit of her stomach.

Was any damage done to the frame? Any major lines severed? What the hell am I going to drive tomorrow to the search site?

As if reading her mind, Darby put an arm around her shoulder and pulled her close. "Don't worry, Kates," she said affectionately, "I'm working at my store all week. If you drop me off in the morning, you can use my wheels to get around. Just pick my ass up at night, and we'll go back home together."

Katie's shoulders relaxed a little, and she hugged her friend back. "And this is why," she said with a grin, "you get to be my very best friend!"

~

Katie threw her purse in the Volkswagen, then took a second to admire Darby's unique sense of style. The car looked as if it could have toured with The Beatles. Bright flowers adorned the exterior, and beaded necklaces draped the rearview mirror. Every outfit Darby wore, every song she sang, every expression she referenced harkened back fifty years. Katie teased that she was born several decades too late. Even her store, Time and Time Again, was a place that sold retro items. The inventory centered on apparel worn in the '60s and '70s, toys of yesteryear, and jewelry found during that era. Her biggest sellers, though, were items related to the paranormal. Crystals, mood rings, and Ouija boards were, apparently, in outrageous demand in Virginia. Darby, fascinated by anything beyond the five senses, spent countless hours researching ways to help Katie control her abilities.

Opening the back door, they loaded Chance carefully into the backseat. Packing a seventy-pound Golden Retriever into such a compact space was not a simple task and, limbs stiff, he was not shy about displaying his displeasure.

"It's only for a little while," Katie purred. "You can do it, tough guy."

As she circled to the passenger seat, a familiar tingle flashed through her scalp. Like an electrostatic charge, it started at her skull and sped to the nape of her neck. Brain chills, she called it; her very own 'Spidey sense.' Unoriginal, but the term certainly expressed the physical sensations that ripped through her body when tuning into something otherworldly or malevolent. At the moment, although she could see nothing, she felt a powerful presence.

Something was there, watching.

Apprehensive, she scanned the street and the surrounding woods. There were few homes on this road, and the ones she could make out were just dots in the distance. Still seeing nothing, she put her hand on the passenger door and opened it.

And there it was again. The tingle. *Shit!*

Only now, it covered Katie's entire body; the gooseflesh rising on her limbs, causing her to shiver.

He was here.

She couldn't explain how she knew it was him, or even where he was, but she was confident that he was spying on her. Noting Katie's sudden tension, Darby's eyes widened.

"You've got that look, Sis," Darby whispered. She circled slowly, her eyes squinting in concentration. "That 'I see dead people' look you get. Holy Hannah, you're lousy with it! Is it him? You got a bead on that prick?"

Sometimes, it was as though Darby was literally inside of Katie's body, inside of her mind. They were as close as two people could be, often finishing each other's sentences or calling each other simultaneously. But, despite their bond, Katie could not bring herself to answer honestly. Instead, defeated, she just shook her head and hurriedly climbed into the passenger seat.

Today, this man had won. He had so wholly unsettled her, she could not confide in the one person who truly understood the darkness enveloping her.

And the evil that lurked behind it.

~

I see you, bitch.

Everything was going according to plan, to design. He'd followed her from Sugarloaf Mountain, waiting for just the right moment. He knew she would use this shortcut. His research over the last six months told him as much.

Watching from behind a copse of trees on some

unknown's property, he tensed as the tow truck pulled up. The male mechanic greeted the women with a smile, and that irritated him. A slow burn began in his belly.

This was all wrong.

He wanted this lesson inconvenient, unsettling. Curious to see if the scare produced its desired effect, he strained to hear the trio's conversation. The target seemed quite rattled. Excellent.

In time, she and all those complicit in her sins would witness his wrath, hear his message. She would learn about fear, would experience pain and sorrow so deep, it would scar her mind and crush her spirit.

And he would rejoice.

He would savor the moment she would kneel before him, stripped naked of dignity. She would weep and barter and beg for a forgiveness that would never come.

For his was a mission of vengeance, not mercy.

He was the Apostle.

CHAPTER FOUR

There are two glaring truths thrust upon a person in the process of dying. The first truth is how greedy, how desperate, how utterly frantic they are to survive. No matter how painful the process or how much life they have lived, they will always leave wanting more. And the second truth? The shocking realization of how easy it is to die.

Water surrounded her—deep, cold, endless. The young girl bobbed up and down, her screams for help dissolving into little more than hushed, pathetic gurgles. Panicked, arms flailing wildly, she tried to wave, to signal her older brother.

Finn would protect her! Finn always came through!

Her legs kicked feverishly, silently, beneath the water. The slapping of her palms pounding the smooth surface reverberated in her ears. Why couldn't he see her? Hear her? Her eyes jerked back and forth, following him as he paced the patio. Phone tucked under his chin, his back to the pool, he remained oblivious to her distress.

Drowning, they say, is a silent death. They were not wrong.

Desperate for something to cling to, she clawed, and she scratched, watching helplessly as fistfuls of water raced through her hands.

"Ffffiinnn!" she choked, chlorine scorching her throat. *The cascade of water filling her mouth was relentless, while the steady drone of a neighbor's hedge clippers succeeded in further muffling her cries.*

Clinging to hope, she continued the fight, struggling for headway, inching forward. She'd nearly convinced herself that she'd made progress to the ropes, the thick braid of cord that floated mid-pool. The ropes signaled the dividing line between the shallow end and danger—between life and death. If she could just get there, she knew she would be safe.

Oh, please, she prayed. Get there!

Her lungs burned, her limbs ached, and exhaustion threatened to overtake her. Despite her tenacity, she remained where she had started, amid depths of over eight feet. In truth, she hadn't moved at all.

Coughing, gagging, spitting, she continued the maddening loop: dunk, surface, repeat. Her arms flapped unnaturally, mimicking an injured bird in flight. Terror gripped her, fear sending waves of cramps to her belly. She couldn't swim, couldn't even float. How on earth would she save herself?

Momma, help me! Please!

She dipped underwater once again, resurfaced, and instinctively threw her head back, greedily gulping precious air. The sky above was clear, a beautiful blue canvas.

Sky blue, like her favorite crayon.

In quick order, shock began its insidious assault on her body. Blood diverted from her extremities to perfuse her vital organs. The diving reflex kicked in, slowing her heart rate to conserve oxygen and making her mind grow fuzzy. Unable to stay afloat, she fell beneath the water for what would be the last time.

In drowning, there is always a last time.

Underwater and hypoxic, the respiratory centers of her brain finally surrendered to the desperate need for air. She took that inevitable breath, and immediately, her larynx began to spasm, and her vocal cords tightened. Once fully constricted, additional water would not enter her lungs, and she would, mercifully, lose consciousness.

Beaten, she began her descent, the water cradling her in a final, graceful dance to the bottom of the pool. It was quiet there. Peaceful. And although the icy hand of death restrained her, kept her bound to her fate, she remained calm and accepting. Her red hair floated like tangled seaweed around her shoulders, and a rainbow of colors flashed before her eyes. Her last conscious thoughts were of her parents, of how angry they would be with her for venturing beyond the safety of the ropes.

And then, at the tender age of six, Katherine Callahan died.

Katie awoke with a start, the veil between sleep and consciousness, a muddied line of perception. It took her a moment to realize she was safe, in her bed, and twenty-two years older than that little girl in the pool. The dream was always the same. It was eerie how the details never changed, perhaps because the nightmare was rooted in memory, not fantasy. She wiped her brow and tried to slow her respirations. Chance and Blue, curled on the floor beside her, gave a sympathetic glance. It was as if they understood the emotional cost paid each time she relived her death. The clock on the table read 4:45 a.m.

Three hours of sleep. Outstanding!

She had to get moving if she wanted to be on time for the search. It was an hour and a half drive to Sugarloaf, but first, she needed to bring Darby to her shop. Willing her legs to move, she wondered what Aman would find wrong with her car. Yesterday, after watching him tow the Denali, she and Darby drove to the local police station. The officer who took the report was sympathetic but concluded that the incident was most likely a case of road rage. Apologetic, he explained that the chances of finding the other driver were slim. His suggestion? Avoid such isolated roads in the future.

Thank you, Captain Obvious.

Still, he'd convinced her it was just some pissed off

asshole having a foul day. However, knowing that wouldn't change the fact that she still had no car. She debated getting a rental, then tabled that decision until she had the damage report on the Denali. Sitting up, she swung her legs over the edge of the bed. Her entire body ached as if every bone and muscle in her young frame were in a vice. She let out a groan, and both dogs whipped their heads around, more curious than alarmed. They were, after all, trying to sleep.

"Thanks for the concern," she said, frowning. "Don't mind me… I'm just dying over here." She stood slowly, unsure if the pain was because of the accident, her exercise regime, or the thirty-plus miles she had hiked with Chance and the A.A.R. F group over the last few days. Slipping her sleep shirt over her head—an image of Winnie the Pooh demolishing a jar of honey—she hobbled over to the master bath and turned on the shower. Just then, her phone rang.

Who the blazes would call this early? She wondered. *Frank, maybe, to reschedule?*

Naked, she padded back over to the side of the bed, thankful that, for once, her shades were drawn.

"Hello?" she said, aching bones causing her to ground out the word.

"Hey, Katiebug! How are you?" Her twin sister's voice, too lively and chipper at this hour of the day, came over the line. Callie had never been a morning person. She communicated in grunts and monosyllables until she was on her third cup of coffee. Something was up.

"Callie? Is everything okay? Grams? Ryan?" Her maternal grandmother lived an hour away from Fredericksburg with Callie and their youngest brother, twenty-three-year-old Ryan. Their oldest sibling, Finn, made his home in Leesburg.

Margaret Kelly, aka Grams, left Florida many years ago to start a new life in Falls Church with the children. Widowed in her youth, she became the sole guardian of the Callahan children when they lost their parents through a series of unfortunate events. Katie knew it was her grandmother's love and guiding hand that reversed the children's fate and made them all decent, successful people. Callie, a psychology major who also minored in foreign language, was just a few weeks short of completing her dissertation and getting her doctorate. Ryan, hands-down the brightest of the bunch, was a first-year medical student and top of his class. Finn ran a profitable horse farm and cattle ranch in Leesburg. And, of course, Katie had authored her own success story.

"No, sweetie, Grams is fine. Everything is fine here," Callie said. "I was just worried about you. I called you a few times last week, but you never returned my calls. Then, yesterday, I felt crazy anxious. Well, more anxious than usual." She clucked her tongue. "What is it they say? Like someone was walking on my grave? Anyhow, whether it was our twin E.S.P. or some kind of Vulcan mind-meld, it felt like you were in danger."

Katie smiled at the reference. Callie had always been a huge Star Trek fan.

"Odd. Anyhoo, since I can never seem to reach you at a normal hour," Callie teased, "I figured I'd wake your ass up."

Katie laughed. Ever since they were kids, they had a unique psychic bond that seemed to come only to those who shared a uterus. Womb mates, they called themselves. They were not identical, but there was no doubt they had similar D.N.A. Callie had the same auburn hair and dusting of freckles, but her face was rounder, her eyes a brilliant blue rather than emerald green. Shorter than her twin, she had a figure that leaned more toward voluptuous than athletic.

After the drowning incident, the temporary lack of oxygen caused Katie's brain to swell. Doctors had little choice but to place her into a drug-induced coma. For seven days, Callie rarely left her sister's side. The nurses in the unit took to calling her Katie's 'shadow,' and the nickname stuck. Even when Katie was well enough to go home, the girls remained inseparable. It was as if Callie feared that leaving Katie alone would open a door, allowing fate another chance to reap her sister's soul.

Aware of her twin's dizzying propensity to worry, Katie deliberated on how much to divulge about the car accident. Although she loved Callie dearly, she could be a hovering, clinging pain in the ass.

"I know I've been a slacker, Cal. No excuse. Well, no excuse good enough for my forgetfulness. I'm an idiot: a simpleton, a jackass, and a boob." Katie sighed. "No, worse than that. I'm a crusting, weeping sore on the end of a—" Callie, laughing, cut her off.

"Okay, enough, already. I get it. You're a bozo," Callie joked, "I just worry about you, ya know? And when you don't call me back, I think the worst. Like fire and brimstone and Hannibal Lecter-type shit. But it's all good." Hesitating, she added, "You are fine, though, aren't you? That feeling of gloom and doom that I had? Just me being my paranoid self, right?"

"I am fine. Truly. You know, Cal-Pal, you're gonna wind up prematurely gray. With crinkles around your eyes and a furrowed brow at thirty. Seriously," Katie lied, "I'm peachy keen. Nothing to see here. I've been busy working on a case with the locals. We are excavating a site that may be a body dump."

Well, she thought glumly, *at least that part is true.*

42

"Jesus, Kate," Callie said, annoyed. "I will never understand why you do what you do. Can't you just, like, let them bring the remains to you? Like a normal anthropologist?" She paused. "Is it safe, at least?"

"I'm sure it is," Katie stuttered. She was hedging now, as she was getting into dangerous territory and disliked lying to her sister. The road rage incident, or whatever it was, happened off the mountain, far away from the crime scene. It would be difficult to find a definitive connection without more proof. She had no idea why that lunatic seemed so angry or tried to force her off the road.

Karma's a bitch, though, she thought.

For now, whatever his reasons, she would keep her sister in the dark. Eventually, she would explain everything. It would be cruel not to tell her that her twin sense was on target.

She glanced at the clock, eager to end the conversation before she tripped over her tongue and said too much. "I'm fine, really. Please don't worry about me. I have to run, though. I'm supposed to meet Lieutenant Blake at the search site in less than two hours, and I'm standing here totally naked, decidedly unwashed, and woefully unfed. Everything's fine, though, Shadow. I will call you back later, 'kay?"

"I'm gonna hold you to that, Katherine Mary. You need to promise me you'll tell me the truth about what's going on. And, um," Callie hesitated, "we need to talk about Finn. I called him again, but he has returned none of my calls. It's been months since he's checked in on Grams. I'm starting to worry." Callie's words tumbled out in quick succession, her voice soft and reflective. "I know he still feels responsible for what happened, Kates, but jumping Jehoshaphat, get over it already! It's been over twenty years. Christmas is coming, and I have an image of us all drinking bad eggnog and decorating an ugly ass tree."

Chuckling, Katie pledged that they would have a nice long talk later to include the proverbial elephant in the room. Finn was a sore subject in so many ways. No matter how much she pleaded, petitioned, or cajoled, he couldn't seem to get off the pity train. He had an uncanny ability to take the air out of the room.

She hung up the phone and rushed back to the bathroom to check the shower. Just as she feared, the water temperature was freezing.

Dammit!

Throwing a towel around her body, she hurried to the kitchen and put on a pot of coffee while the water heater caught up. Then, she fired off a text to Frank to let him know she was running late.

It was going to be a long-ass day.

~

Sugarloaf Mountain, 7:56 a.m.

"Where the hell is your cadaver dog, Lieutenant?" Assistant Special Agent-in-Charge Jake Devereaux planted his feet firmly beneath him, annoyed. "I was under the impression that our start time was 7 a.m. It's almost 8." He raked a hand through his hair. "No offense, but when I dragged my ass out of bed this morning, I assumed it was to work. Never once did I figure I'd be scratching my nuts, dicking around on this mountain for an hour."

Frank Blake rolled his eyes. "That's funny. I wouldn't have pegged you for a guy who even had nuts to scratch."

Glaring, Jake shook his head. "Christ, I hate wasting time. Can't you call him or something?"

Beside him, Jake's partner, Agent Ian Sullivan, watched the exchange with amusement. Clearing his voice, he said, "Well, boss, not to make excuses for the guy, but traffic was a bitch this morning. You couldn't buy a clear path down I-95 in either direction. Could be he's just stuck behind a slow-moving pack." He grinned, flashing his perfect white teeth. Women, all women, adored Ian. His charm, warmth, and impeccable manners, courtesy of his southern upbringing, made many a young girl swoon. Wavy hair as bright as the sun, large hazel eyes, and dimples that went on for days didn't hurt his chances with the ladies, either.

His boss, on the other hand, was an enigma. Few of the women Jake Devereaux dated were around long enough to discover the real man behind the handsome facade. Stony and distant, he had a limited social circle. Rumor was that, following his involvement in a fatal shooting a few years back, he had become an introvert and selective in the company he kept.

Physically, he was an imposing figure at 6'1" and one-hundred-and-eighty pounds. His commanding presence gave an air of confidence and expertise. Not the slave to the gym that Ian was, he, nonetheless, had a frame of solid muscle. Thick, raven-colored hair complemented his olive skin, but it was his piercing, violet eyes that fascinated most people.

Frank watched those eyes, recalling what he knew of the man. Although not friends, the stories he'd heard were legend. The thin blue line was a powerful force, the band of brothers, unbreakable. Law enforcement officers traveled in the same circles, and Frank had learned a great deal about Jake Devereaux. The cop grapevine painted a picture of a stand-offish perfectionist and workaholic, who, as far as the intel went, never married.

Jake unbuttoned his suit jacket and rubbed his bristled chin. Addressing Frank again, he said, "You realize this is on you, right? Obviously, you picked the wrong dog handler." He folded his muscular arms across his chest, eyes flashing. "This guy, this 'professional,' is pissing me off."

Annoyed, Frank snapped back. "Too fuckin' bad." Turning to Ian, he deadpanned, "How embarrassing for you, forced to watch as your partner constantly steps on his dick." Eyes finding Jake again, he hitched up his pants and added dryly, "Out of thousands and thousands of sperm cells, you were the fastest? Seriously? For your information, Einstein, this *guy* happens to be a..."

He stopped mid-sentence when he spotted Katie and Chance plodding toward them, heads down in concentration. This morning was much warmer than yesterday, but the rocks were still dew-covered and slippery. Seeing the men, she gave Frank a smile and a wave, and then made eye contact with the man standing beside him.

Time stood still.

Frank heard the FBI Agent's breath hitch and almost laughed aloud. Katie was strikingly beautiful, and Frank was used to the visceral reaction men experienced in her presence. But to witness Devereaux, the bane of his morning, breathless, was just too perfect. He enjoyed the reaction a second time when Devereaux's partner elbowed Jake in the ribcage.

"Damn," Ian whispered, "are you seeing this, boss? I think I'm in love."

Devereaux shushed him and, adjusting a tie that needed no adjusting, stood a little taller. Frank rolled his eyes for the second time that morning.

Jake had never seen a more graceful creature in his life. She still hadn't taken her pretty eyes off him and, as she got closer, he noted their color—emerald green, brilliant and gleaming, like the sea after a summer storm. His thoughts drifted, wondering how it would feel to get lost in those eyes. He'd never had such a physical reaction to a woman before and didn't much care for the feelings of helplessness it gave him. His last romance was a disaster, leading him to swear off relationships for a while. When he noticed her captivating smile and shapely legs, he decided a hiatus from dating was a stupid idea.

Hypnotized, he watched her. Her hair coiled in a neat bun at the nape of an exceptionally long, very feminine, neck. It's color, deep and warm, shimmered like a fine Cognac. She had a heart-shaped face with a dusting of freckles that graced her nose and cheeks. Dressed in jeans that hugged in all the right places, hiking boots, and an anorak jacket, he guessed her height to be around 5'7". His gut clenched, and he tensed when she stopped in front of them.

She addressed the group, a slight smile of apology on her face. "Sorry I'm late, guys." Katie was sure those four words were about all she could muster right then. In front of her were two drop-dead gorgeous men, and the testosterone flooding the air was staggering. The blond, a man about her age, wore a beautiful smile that made her weak in the knees. He was, as Darby would say, a 'fox.' But it was the other fellow that had her heart fluttering faster than a hummingbird's wings. His jet-black hair and high cheekbones spoke of a Native American descent. Faint lines around his eyes told Katie he was a few years older than her.

He had the eyes of a warrior. Eyes that had witnessed a thousand horrific scenes yet had also seen a thousand beautiful ones. She felt that the instant she gazed into their rich, violet depths. His face was square, his jaw strong and masculine. He was breathtakingly gorgeous, and she briefly wondered if he was married.

Of course, he's married, she thought. *How could he not be?*

She gathered her wits, a feat difficult to do in his company, and pulled her gaze back to Frank. Noticing her trouble focusing, he plastered a grin on his face and teased, "Well, butter my butt and call me a biscuit! Look who's here!"

Katie laughed lightly at the joke made at her expense. "Okay, okay, I get it. Nobody likes a slacker. I apologize for running late. I had an incident on the road yesterday and had to borrow a friend's car." She looked directly at Agent Devereaux now, thankful that she'd found her voice. "If I may, let me introduce myself, and we can start the search. My name is Katie Callahan, and this beautiful boy here is my dog, Chance." She ran a slim hand down Chance's back. "Chance can lead us, via air-scent, to any bodies buried in this vicinity. He can detect decomposition on remains up to twenty feet underground, although I don't believe we will need to go that deep. If experience tells me anything, any remains we find today will be in a shallow grave. Or graves."

Satisfied that the group remained interested, she continued. "Chance can differentiate human remains from animal carcasses, food, or trash. His training ensures that he will only alert on human decomposition. If there is anyone deceased in this region of Sugarloaf, he'll find them." She exhaled, confident that she'd covered the basics necessary for a successful search. Eyeing Jake again, she mentally gave herself a high-five. She'd managed to stand a mere three feet away from him and still get through the rundown without drooling.

Yahoo.

"I'm looking forward to watching you both work," Ian

said eagerly, glancing at Jake. He bent down and ruffled Chance on the head. "I'm Agent Ian Sullivan of the D.C. area field office, but please, call me Sully. Everyone else does." He grinned, dimples carving craters in his cheeks, and shook her hand warmly.

"Pleasure to meet you, Sully," she said, smiling.

Sully turned to Jake and, with an eyebrow up inquisitively as if to say, "your turn, pal," waited for Jake to introduce himself. A minute passed as Jake stood there, unmoving. Perplexed, Sully took matters into his own hands.

"And this distinguished fellow, who seems to have a cat imprisoning his tongue, is my boss, A.S.A.C. Jacob Devereaux. Jake also works out of the D.C. office." Katie stuck her hand out, waited, and when Jake ignored it, awkwardly put her hand back down at her side.

What the hell is his problem?

Flustered, she watched him eye her up and down as if she were a distasteful dinner or had shown up drunk at a kindergarten recital.

Screw you, she thought, miffed. *Anyone that attractive is probably an egotistical jackass, anyway.*

Acting as though the snub went unnoticed, Katie picked up where she'd left off, explaining how she and her dog worked. "Scene preservation is a part of Chance's training. If he picks up a scent, he alerts using only a passive response. That response means sitting as close as he can to the odor, but he will not roll, urinate on, or otherwise disturb the area. As his handler, I can identify his behavioral patterns and will know when he is on point."

Finished with the background information and uncomfortable in Jake's presence, she was more than ready to get started. As she turned away, a deep, velvety smooth voice stopped her cold. It caused her stomach to flip and revved up her heart rate all over again.

"Fascinating," Jake said dryly, clearly not fascinated at all. With a curt nod at Chance, he added, "He doesn't exactly strike me as a go-getter, Callahan. Are we to believe that this animal can actually locate a body?" She looked down at Chance, who was biting enthusiastically at his haunches, chasing an imaginary flea. As if on cue, the dog looked up, yawned, and scratched an ear.

"No offense, lady," Jake continued, "but how much genuine success has this mutt had, anyway?"

Katie glared at him, open-mouthed, furious at both his poor manners and his reference to Chance as a mutt. Her hands curled into tight fists at her side, and she took a few steps forward. Shoulders squared and cheeks flushed, she tilted her head, just inches from Devereaux's face. Somewhere in the distance, she thought she heard Frank mutter something that sounded a lot like "Oh, shit."

"Mutt? Did you just call my dog a mutt?!" Her lips curled in anger. "Listen here, mister. This *mutt* is a full-blooded Golden Retriever with champion bloodlines. This *mutt* has worked all over the Mid-Atlantic area, racking up two trophies and three Blue Ribbons." Her voice continued to rise with each fact she presented. "This *mutt* has found more people in his seven years than you could find in a lifetime."

Speaking through gritted teeth, a finger pointing at his chest, she continued firing. "This *mutt* is certified as an H.R.D. canine by goddamn F.E.M.A. themselves. This *mutt* recently found the body of a three-year-old, dead in a rat-infested sewer, and saved his family from forever wondering what happened to their child!"

She was shaking with fury, her anger making it difficult for her to speak without stuttering or screaming like a banshee. "And this 'mutt,' Agent whatever-the-hell-your-name-is, can find a pimple on a flea's backside faster than you can find your ass with both hands, so back the hell off!"

She stared him down, breathing hard, waiting for his response. Amusement danced in Jake's eyes, and his lips twitched as his mouth fought off an upward curve. Astounded, she froze. Was that just a smirk she saw?

Seriously? she thought, incensed. *He's laughing at me?*

Fuming, she took a deep breath and turned, speaking only to Frank. "I am going to start about a half a mile behind us, working parallel to the overlook. My opinion, if that means anything," she glared pointedly at Jake, "is that we comb the area from there and move westward, covering the width of the overlook. We can then head north in small increments if necessary." She spun from them, and, in what could only be considered a huff, strode purposefully to the starting point, back stiff.

Incredulous, Sully threw up his hands. "Really, Jake? What the fuck was that?"

Brandishing his first genuine smile since coming to Sugarloaf, Devereaux turned to him and winked.

"That," he grinned lazily, "was my kind of woman."

CHAPTER FIVE

The Bones on the Mountain

"Indeed, under the law, almost everything is purified with blood, and without the shedding of blood, there is no forgiveness of sins."
Hebrews 9:22.

K atie searched alone for nearly an hour. Frank knew her well enough to know she was royally pissed off and needed some space from that FBI agent. Chance seemed to sense it, too. He kept on point, behaving exceptionally well, occasionally looking back at her with sad and knowing eyes. That ability to pick up on variations in mood or nuances in her demeanor was a key reason he was a magnificent service dog and a wonderful friend. As she walked, she replayed the scene that just occurred between her and Devereaux.

What the hell is the matter with me? Why do I always insist on engaging with morons?

Aggravated at him, but mostly at herself, she focused on the task at hand. Chance had shown no interest in anything so far, and that was troubling. Was it because there was nothing to find? Or was it an inability to focus? Could that arrogant son of a bitch Devereaux be right?

"C'mon buddy," she said pleadingly, "that dude called you a mutt! Are you going to let him get away with that?" She gave him a vigorous rub behind the ears. "Let's do this, Chance. Seek!" He lifted his snout high in the air, sniffed a few times, and happily forged ahead.

Ten minutes later, his tail whipping back and forth like a fan, Chance was still chugging and puffing along. Katie took a moment to appreciate the complexity and physiology of his sense of smell. Comprised of millions of olfactory cells, a dog's nose had the ability to experience odors undetected by their human companions. Canine nostrils, by design, will shunt exhaled air to the sides in a circulatory pattern, continuously recirculating the air. Since every scent was virgin and new, they never became desensitized to any smell. Chance was currently enjoying the bouquet of thousands of recycled scents, a veritable smorgasbord in the sniffer for her four-legged pal.

The sound of footsteps rapidly approaching from behind caused them both to turn. Jake Devereaux was heading toward them at a brisk pace, trying to catch up.

Great, pretty boy wants to talk—tough shit.

She turned forward again and kept walking. She wasn't about to make this easy for him.

"Hey, Callahan! Hold up a second," he yelled. Katie continued to ignore him.

"C'mon, Callahan, slow down!" he said breathlessly, adding a desperate "please?" at the end.

She almost smiled. He looked ridiculous, chasing after her in spit-shined shoes and an Armani suit.

Who climbs a mountain dressed like that? Unless, of course, you're an obnoxious, self-important FBI agent!

He trotted in front of her and put his hands out in a

stop position, blocking her route. "Please. I just want a second of your time," he pleaded. "If you don't like what I have to say, I promise I will leave you alone. No harm, no foul, no hard feelings. I probably won't even slap myself silly or jump off this mountain after you've rejected me." He smirked. She didn't.

"What do you want, Agent?" she said stiffly. "As you can see, my 'mutt' and I are working here."

Jake smiled then, a warm smile that seemed to make his eyes shine even brighter. He shook his head. "I know, I know. I crossed a line back there. I'm sorry. Really, I am. I had no right to call your dog names." Eyes twinkling, he continued. "I mean, I don't even know him. For all I know, he's a top-notch pup and a credit to his breed. And all those rumors going around? The ones about his drinking, womanizing, and gambling? Gossip, I'm sure." He gave her a devastating smile, and she struggled not to laugh.

Feigning indignation, she said haughtily, "For your information, Agent, they ARE all rumors." Waiting a beat, she added, "Chance quit gambling two years ago." She smirked, and Jake burst out laughing.

"That's great. Good to know. Um... I just wanted to clear the air. With you both, really. Hard to believe, but there's a possibility that we may have gotten off on the wrong foot back there," he said, adding a wink.

Damn, she thought, *that wink might someday bring me to my knees.*

"Ya think?" she said, her voice dripping with sarcasm. He chuckled again, a deep and hearty laugh. She could get used to that laugh.

"Apology accepted, Agent Devereaux. Shall we?"

They began walking again, eyes scanning the surroundings for disturbed earth, traces of blood, or scattered belongings. Thirty minutes later, they found themselves just below the overlook, the vista much more congested than the previous areas they had searched. The air seemed heavier; the shadows cast by the trees more ominous. Chance, it appeared, sensed it too. His pace picked up, and his tail wagged.

"I think we are close to something," Katie called over her shoulder to Jake, fifteen feet behind her now. "We need to contact Frank and Sully. We will need them, along with some uniforms, to scour this area."

Jake frowned. "Now? Are you sure? I have them searching the outer perimeter, and hate to pull them off the grid unless we are certain?"

Katie nodded, and Jake radioed Sully, filling him in on the situation and their position. As she waited for their transmission to end, she walked Chance around in circles several feet away. She was hoping to keep him engaged as she scanned the scenery, searching for the source of her disquiet. To her left was a flicker, a whisper of smoke, behind the tree line. She turned for a better angle, unsure if it was real or just a trick of the light. In an instant, her heart pounded, and her breath caught.

It didn't matter how many times it happened; she would never get used to the visits. Beneath the shadows of an ancient birch tree, the figure of a middle-aged woman shimmered in the winter sun. Her form was transparent, a glistening row of maples visible far behind her. She looked to be about forty-five years old, with elfin eyes and coffee-colored hair shaped into a bob. Her features were plain, her nose thin and long, her forehead a bit too high for her narrow face. She reminded Katie of an actress from "Little House on the Prairie," a TV drama about life in the Old West. The woman stood with her hands at her sides, looking lost, a beaded chain bunched up in her fist. Katie tore her gaze from the woman and glanced at Jake. He was in a low squat, his back to her, carefully examining the tread from a pair of sneakers. She tiptoed toward the figure, while Chance, spooked but determined, pulled feverishly in the same direction.

Does he see her too? She wondered. *Sense her?*

As they drew closer, Chance barked, the sound sharp and resounding in the hushed surroundings. It was his way of communicating with Katie that they'd found something. But to the specter, the splintering of the quiet was harsh and frightening. The figure faded, vanishing entirely within seconds.

In an instant, Katie experienced a sadness so profound, so intense, that it nearly consumed her. Her vision blurred, and her head throbbed. She felt detached, as if floating yards away from her body. Physically and emotionally ravaged, she cried out, an anguished wail that fractured the landscape. Then, finding it impossible to stand, she collapsed to one knee.

Jake first heard Chance's enthusiastic barking, immediately followed by a heart-stopping shriek. He jumped up, unsure if the sound he'd heard was even human. It was a howl that told of unspeakable sorrow, of unrelenting pain, and it scared the hell out of him. Spinning quickly, he saw Katie down on one knee and rushed to her side.

"Callahan! Are you hurt? What happened?" Jake said, dropping to the ground so they were face-to-face. "Did you fall?" He grabbed her face, hands cradling both sides of her cheeks in concern. She reached to the ground, attempting to rise. Jake stood first, grabbing her elbow and helping her to stand. Her skin, a lovely porcelain on any other day, was deathly pale. Jake's eyes scanned the ground, searching for snakes, spiders, even bullet casings—

56

something to explain such a tormented cry. He found nothing.

"Thank you," Katie stammered. "I'm really not sure what happened. I... I think I tripped and twisted my ankle. Scared me more than hurt me. Sorry if I startled you."

And there it was, she thought bitterly. *More lies.*

She worried that it was becoming natural, that she was getting good at it. Someday, all her deceit would bite her in the ass. But what was she to do? Tell him the truth? She imagined how that conversation would go:

So, um, Jake, about that scream? Funny thing, but it turns out it had nothing to do with physical pain and everything to do with emotional suffering. You just witnessed a cry born inside a dark place, a dimension where a woman, conscious of the crimes against her, remains trapped in a world that is no longer hers. Ain't that a kicker? But here's the best part, Agent Devereaux—not only do I see them, but I can feel them, too. I can sense their sorrow and heartache, their misery, from my front-row seat to the living and the dead.

Oh, yeah, she thought glumly, *that's the ticket.*

"Should I get help here? Do you think you can walk?" Jake said, looking around for Sully or Frank.

Katie shrugged. "It's all good. Really." She turned her ankle in a circle to demonstrate its mobility. "See? No pain. I guess I expected it to snap, so it startled me. Honestly, I'm fine. Let's just keep going. I don't want Chance to lose the scent."

As they started walking again, Katie subtly guided Jake to the area where she last saw the woman. Chance pulled on the lead, trepidation and excitement at war with each other. He was a smart dog. He knew that something wicked had traversed these woods recently. His desire to please was at odds with his innate need for self-preservation.

A few feet later, in front of the very line of maple trees that the translucent visitor once stood, Chance alerted. He sniffed the air, wagged his tail, and sat at attention. Jake raised an eyebrow, and Katie nodded.

Moving carefully to where Chance sat, they noticed a disturbance in the earth, a shallow depression about eight-feet-long. Behind it, somewhat hidden by a massive tree trunk, lay a partially decomposed human skull.

"Well," Jake said soberly, "I guess we found our gravesite."

Within an hour, the woods of Sugarloaf Mountain were swarming with uniforms. State and local police, FBI agents and crime scene technicians worked diligently to ensure that procedural policies were in place. The integrity of the scene, including the preservation of bones and the evidentiary chain of custody, demanded specific protocols. Physical evidence found on this mountain would be bagged, tagged, and cataloged to ensure that it was admissible in a criminal trial. Additional personnel remained behind the yellow caution tape until their area of expertise was required, reducing the threat of scene contamination.

Katie directed the investigators where to dig, how deep to go, and what precautions were necessary to prevent damaging the bones. It was a painstakingly slow process, and by 6 p.m., nearly nine hours from the discovery of the shallow grave, the teams were ready to call it a day. The temperature was dropping; the sun going down. Jake and Sully stood off to the side, making phone calls and checking schedules.

As Jake was waiting to connect to Headquarters, he caught Sully toss a dazzling, dimpled smile Katie's way. He and Sully had been partners for a long time, and Jake recognized the signs.

Fuck me... Sully is interested in Kate.

He pinched the bridge of his nose. Of course, Sully was interested. She was a beautiful woman, and Jake had no claim on her, no right to be angry. Still, an icy dread blanketed his entire body, and an unfamiliar sensation waved at him. It was huge, it was ugly, and it was green.

Jealousy.

Ignoring his irritation, Jake assembled the team and addressed them as a group. "Ok, people, you did outstanding work today," he said sincerely. "I know this has been difficult. Our findings today indicate that this may be ground zero for an unknown killer. You've all remained focused and professional, and I admire that kind of dedication." He snapped off his gloves and stuck them in a pocket. "That said, I would be remiss in my duties if I failed to remind you that this is a criminal investigation. We are obligated to keep confidential any evidence found, or any information disseminated here today." He surveyed the group, maintaining eye contact while he spoke. "It is imperative that we remain objective and that the sharing of any data or info go through the proper channels. We don't want to blow a potential conviction because of sloppy practices." He held up a clipboard. "We're assembling here tomorrow at 6 a.m. and will need as many, if not more, people to continue the dig. If you are interested in working this site again tomorrow, please sign up before you leave. I will reach out to your supervisors to request that they assign you to the team for the duration. Thanks again for your hard work today."

He nodded his head in a combination of both thanks and dismissal. The team dispersed, some mumbling to their co-workers, others trudging back to their vehicles in silence. Katie, standing next to Sully and Frank, approached Jake as soon as he dismissed the others.

"So, what are your thoughts?" she asked. "I'm convinced that this is the only burial site, at least on this part of Sugarloaf. Chance would know if there were more bodies buried nearby, and he is no longer alerting. That's not to say that twenty miles away, there isn't another site. But why borrow trouble, right?"

She paused for a minute, searching Jake's face for any sign of what he expected her to do. He could be infuriatingly impassive. He looked up at the sky, ostensibly looking for the answers in a cloud. Finally, after what felt like forever, he spoke.

"You specialize in forensics, right?" he asked.

"Forensic Anthropology, yes."

Jake nodded. "Frank tells me you sometimes do some freelance work with the Smithsonian?"

"Yes, I've consulted for them several times, mainly to help with bone identification in digs out of the country. Where are you going with this, Jake?"

"Look," he said, "you've been in on this case since the onset. Victim identification will be crucial to give us some starting point in this investigation. You have the experience, a rapport with state and local agencies, and a stellar reputation. Those assets make you an invaluable resource for us. I can think of no better person to see this investigation through than the woman who has been there from the beginning." He gave her a furtive glance, as if he had a spectacular secret and was about to spill it. "As an agent, I have a hook in the FBI Lab Division," he whispered conspiratorially. "I can get you whatever you need. Equipment, personnel, whatever… no questions asked." He gazed at her. "No bullshit here; we really could use your help. Would you consider taking the lead, forensic wise? You'll be working with a lab assistant from the bureau, but I'll make sure you have total autonomy. You know, to do whatever it is that a forensic anthropologist, such as yourself, needs to do." He ended his pitch with another one of those devastating winks.

Katie was thrilled with the offer, and the wink, but played it cool. After all, it wasn't like he was inviting her to dinner; he was asking her to put together the life and death of an unknown individual, or individuals, using a pile of bones. All of which didn't exactly scream romance. Still, the thought of seeing him regularly, even if it was work-related, made her blood sing.

"Well, I suppose I could lend a hand," she answered, drawing out the word suppose while playfully swinging Chance's leash back and forth.

Dear Lord, did I just bat my eyelashes at him?

Horrified by her behavior, she cleared her throat and answered, this time in a more professional tone. "I am between job obligations now, so I have the time. It would be an honor to help identify these victims. Thank you for the offer, Agent Devereaux."

Jake grinned, pretending not to notice her obvious flirtation. "Good to hear, Professor Callahan. I look forward to working with you." As he turned his back to speak to Sully, Katie tilted her head and scanned the tree line. Something long and iridescent was dangling from a lofty branch several yards from where they stood.

Nobody looks up, she mused.

As she inched closer, she spotted what looked like a crucifix hanging from a chain. A necklace, perhaps? Perplexed, head still back, she circled the tree.

No, not a necklace, she realized. *Rosary beads.*

∼

The Apostle sat on a flat rock west of the overlook, looking down at the activity below. Hidden from sight, he surveilled the uniformed police, the personnel from the coroner's office, and the FBI agents in million-dollar suits. He had a cheap pair of binoculars, a police scanner, and a digital camera. As he snapped pictures, he became increasingly irate. They all looked like ants to him, scurrying from one area to another.

Assholes. Did they really believe they were smarter than him? That he didn't plan for them to find his students?

Of course, he did. For what good was a lesson that never reached its audience? He dropped the binoculars, his hands clenched, palms sweating.

Where was she? That spawn of a sinner, that she-devil?

He felt his agitation grow and tamped it down, as he had learned to do. Taking a calming breath, he raised the binoculars once again and spotted her just behind a poplar tree. She was flirting with that FBI guy, the dark-haired prick with the big shoulders.

Whore. He could not wait until he had her alone.

He had worked tirelessly to get to this point. Six months of research, of leg work, just to learn her habits, her routine. There had been many sacrifices along the way, some according to design, others out of necessity. As a rule, he avoided impulsive kills such as Laura Dixon and her father, Henry. But what began as collateral damage became intoxicating, the fear Henry felt as he faced his mortality, exhilarating.

"He despairs of escaping the realm of darkness; he is marked for the sword." Job 15.

Those words, and a whispered promise of what he planned to do to Laura, were the last words Henry would ever hear. As soon as the Apostle uttered them, the old man understood.

But Henry's death was too quick, his pupils fixed and dilated almost immediately. There was no opportunity to witness the grand finale, no time to take part in the Splendor. Once again, the Apostle had missed the transformation, the moment when a person's soul takes flight.

Laura Dixon took longer to die. Pathetically, shamelessly, she fought for her life until her eyes glazed, and the Blessed Mother's gift to the faithful choked her into silence. Afterward, he placed his head on her chest, the absence of sound music to his ears. He waited, but the Splendor continued to elude him. He unwrapped the rosary beads from around her neck and put them in his pocket.

"For all have sinned and fall short of the glory of God," he whispered, quoting Romans 3:23.

He shivered, the memory wrapping around him, its warmth like a lover's arms. And although he did not witness the Splendor with either of them, he nonetheless felt fulfilled. He had sent them, these pawns who stood in the way of his mission, to their final reward.

Raising the lenses to his eyes again, he continued to watch her. She moved with the grace of a dancer; her beauty and poise beacons of light in an otherwise bleak world. She was kind and giving and stunningly beautiful.

And he hated her with every fiber of his being.

CHAPTER SIX

December 10th

"Honor thy father and thy mother; that thy days may be long upon the land which the LORD thy God giveth thee." Exodus 20:12.

A week after it had begun, the excavation on Sugarloaf Mountain ended. The FBI, satisfied they'd collected all the evidence they could find, uncovered hundreds of bones and a third skull, bringing the total victims to at least three. Suddenly, the implication of what they had discovered brought with it a fresh sense of urgency. They were in a race against the clock where every moment that ticked by could bring them one step closer to yet another victim.

The rosary beads Katie found hanging from the tree branch were rugged, well-made, and constructed using a sturdy cord rather than a chain or string. They were heavier than one would expect, with a sterling silver cross dangling at the end. She'd seen nothing like it and wondered where such an item was sold.

Outdoor store? Military?

Until they figured it out, she was hoping to find some

answers in the bones. The study of humans and their physical and cultural development is a complex science. Her specialty, forensic anthropology, incorporates basic anthropology with an in-depth study of the structure and function of bones. Candidates in the field require knowledge in several disciplines, including biology, physics, and chemistry.

Bones hold a myriad of clues regarding a person's genetic composition, gender, overall health, and physical attributes. They can aid in identifying decomposing human remains, unidentified homicide victims, and bodies burned beyond recognition. Learning how to read them was an art. Like pieces of a puzzle, each one was unique, with its own story to tell if you knew how to decipher it.

As she drove Darby's car to Quantico on this chilly December morning, she contemplated her life's work and the choices she had made. The path she'd chosen, although she had grown to despise the word, was all about closure. It was about finding a resolution to the most painful chapter of her life.

The death of her mother.

~

October 27th, 1997

"Callie, knock it off!"

Katie gave her sister the 'death stare,' a clear signal that she was not amused. Her backpack was heavy, loaded down with a Learn your Letters reader, half-dozen math problems, three library books, and a Scooby-Doo lunchbox. The October sky was clear, the sun brutally hot and unforgiving, causing little beads of sweat to dot her upper lip. The last few weeks had been unseasonably warm, with temperatures exceeding the average high for autumn in Falls Church, Virginia. Her mom called it an Indian Summer; Katie just called it hot. Now, as she attempted to climb the long driveway home, Callie kept pulling at the zipper on her backpack. More than once, Katie had nearly toppled over, her sister's tugging causing the weight of her load to shift.

"I said, cut it out, Callie! I mean it!"

"C'mon, Kates, let me see your report card. I'll show you what I got. What did you get in math? I didn't do so good. Second-grade math is hard," Callie whined. "Mom is gonna kill me!"

"I'll show you at home, Cal. I just want to get into the house, okay?" She huffed, wiping her brow. "This backpack is killing me."

Pouting, Callie mumbled, "Fine! I don't want to see it, anyway!"

They continued up the lane in silence, only the occasional pant from Katie breaking the quiet. Callie's respirations were smooth, effortless. Silently, Katie fumed.

Why do I always have a ton of books, and she has none? How does she even do her homework? No wonder she's failing math!

As the two girls scaled the drive, Katie absently wondered where her mother might be. Her mom was always waiting at the end of the lane to escort the seven-year-old twins safely into the house. Brow furrowed, she did a slow spin, surveilling the property. Everything was quiet.

Approaching the front door, Katie paused, uneasy. Ever since that awful day a year ago, she could sense alterations within a familiar environment. Like a kind of psychic Feng Shui, her body knew when things were off balance or out of harmony. Warily, she touched the doorknob and was instantly transported to an alternate reality. Alone, terrified, she found herself spinning through a vortex that twisted and turned and threatened to pull her under. A whirlpool of sensations descended upon her all at once—anxiety, anger, fear. Fear so intense, it stole her breath away.

Standing behind her, Callie saw her sister begin to shake and grabbed her by the arm. "What's the matter? Is it Mom? It is, right? Oh, this is not good! Not good at all!" Whispering, she said, "I'm scared, Kates!"

Callie's respirations grew noisy, an audible whistle evident with each exhalation, compliments of emotionally triggered asthma. Katie had seen this stress reaction before, right after she told Callie about her Empath abilities. Precisely because of that physical reaction, Katie did not reveal to her sister the gift that came a month or so later... the ability to see the dead.

As Katie watched, helpless, anxiety was narrowing the delicate airways in Callie's seven-year-old chest. A full-blown asthma attack now would make a scary situation even worse. Concern for her sister carried Katie back from the black hole.

"It will be okay, Shadow. Honest." Dropping her backpack by the stoop, she said, "Just wait here and let me check, all right? You can do that, can't ya? Easy, peasy, lemon squeezy!"

Callie was technically five minutes older, but Katie had always assumed the role of big sister. Perhaps it was because she was the more mature of the two, or maybe it was because of Callie's sometimes frail health. Regardless of the reason, Katie took control. Somewhere in the back of her mind, though, she knew that once she opened that door, her life would change forever.

Smiling weakly at her sister, Katie twisted the knob and stepped through the front door into the foyer. Pungent air filled her nostrils, its odor vaguely familiar yet somehow out of reach. She quickly probed the recesses of her brain, scrambling to identify it.

Pennies.

The foyer was awash with the heavy scent of thousands of copper coins. Cautiously, she walked through the entryway and into the living room. A strangled sound, somewhere between a heavy sigh and a kitten's mew, escaped her lips. The room was in shambles; couch cushions flipped over, lamps smashed, tables upended. Little flakes of pot-pourri, formerly housed in a crystal decanter, lay haphazardly scattered across the room. The telephone, its cord ripped out of the wall, was upside down on the floor near the fireplace. She paused, confused for a moment. Something else was off in this room. Her eyes focused on the bare spot beneath the overturned coffee table.

No, not off. Missing. Where is Mom's oriental rug?

Eyes widened and gut in spasms, she inched cautiously through the living room.

"Mom? Momma? Are you home? Momm-mee!" She started slowly toward the kitchen, her little legs like lead weights, the sense of doom at a near crescendo. Whatever was wrong, she knew that she would find it in the kitchen.

"Mom, where are you? Oh, please, Momma! Answer me!" she pleaded, her voice fading to a whisper, her throat tight. When there was still no reply, Katie considered fleeing, a booming voice screaming inside her head.

Leave! Go! Get Uncle Tim!

Tim was her mother's little brother and the closest thing to a father that she and her siblings had. Divorced following a terrible union, he lived a few blocks away with his daughter, Trisha. Ignoring that inner voice, Katie pushed on through the living room to the threshold of the tiny kitchen. She could faintly hear a baby crying, the soft sobs coming from somewhere upstairs. The child sounded weak and exhausted, as if it had been weeping for hours.

Oh, no! Ryan!

Her eyes swept the room, stunned, as she took in the scene before her. The sunshine yellow walls, the stainless-steel sink, even the walnut cabinets her mom had refinished herself, were all painted red.

No… not paint, she thought, panicked. *Blood.*

The floor was a river of crimson, with small clots of matter dotting the baseboard. So much blood that Katie had difficulty making out the star-shaped pattern of the linoleum floor. She felt woozy and oddly detached from her surroundings. There was a distant humming in her ears, her palms were damp, and her lower lip quivered. The sting of unshed tears nearly blinded her. Heart pounding, she folded her arms and hugged her chest.

Ryan.

Taking the stairs as fast as her seven-year-old legs could carry her, she headed toward the sound of her baby brother's cries. She found the two-year-old cowering in a hallway linen closet; thumb plugged into his mouth, emotionally spent but uninjured. Cross-legged on the closet floor, his round face tear-stained and snot covered, he reached his chubby little arms out and whimpered, "Tatie."

"It's okay, Ry Ry. You're okay. C'mere little man."

She picked him up and, together, they conducted a frantic search of the bedrooms. Ten minutes later, her mother nowhere to be found, Katie awkwardly carried her brother downstairs. They rushed through the ravaged living room, away from the kitchen that smelled like pennies, and outside to Callie. There, bewildered and numb, the trio sat on the steps, waiting for Finn to come home.

Forty minutes later, Finn, the eldest of the Callahan children, returned from school to find his siblings huddled together, eyes vacant, voices mute. Ryan perched on Katie's lap, greedily sucking his thumb, his congested nose hissing with every breath. Callie, eyes damp and face ashen, picked absently at her shoelaces while furiously bouncing a bony knee.

And Katie, wide-eyed, unmoving. Trapped in a nightmare only she could see.

The investigation into the disappearance of their mother dragged on for almost two years. In the end, the police concluded that Eileen Callahan had walked in on a burglary in progress. The house's condition suggested that the attackers were looking for something, most likely money or other valuables. There were several expensive pieces of jewelry missing, including Eileen's engagement ring. Over the years, the ring had become too tight and sat in a box on her dresser, a shadow memory portending happier times. Someday, she had told Katie, she would get that ring resized.

Someday never came.

Eileen's usual morning routine was regimented. After seeing the older kids off to school, she and Ryan would drive twenty minutes to his pre-school, Kiddie Cove Academy. She had a job there as a teaching assistant while he attended a toddler program. On October 27th, however, Ryan had been running a fever, and Eileen kept them both home. Evidence suggested that she confronted the intruders and, perhaps, protecting her small son, fought with at least one of them before they killed her. The killer or killers wrapped her body in the oriental rug, disposing of it in an unknown location. Authorities never determined whether baby Ryan witnessed the attack.

The science of DNA helped authorities link Katie's mother to the blood found in the kitchen. Although her body was never found, the volume of blood at the scene eliminated any hope of survival. The police identified no suspects, nor found any murder weapon. Several years after that horrible day in October, authorities declared Eileen Callahan dead, leaving the four Callahan children destroyed. And parentless.

The sound of Night Ranger's 'Sister Christian' pealed on Katie's cellphone. "Crap, crap, crap!" she hissed, angry at herself for having failed to call Callie back as she'd promised. Hoping against hope that Callie had forgotten that promise, she pushed the button on her hands-free device and answered with a cheery, "Hello, my Shadow. How are you?"

"Did you forget something, Kates? Like, I don't know, a phone call, mayhaps?" Her sister's voice dripped sarcasm, and Katie inwardly winced.

So much for that plan!

"Okay, I know. I know. But I have an excellent excuse this time. Honest." She paused for dramatic effect. Callie loved theatrics. "We found at least three bodies on that dig I was telling you about. The lead FBI agent working the case, a guy named Jake Devereaux, asked me to join the investigation. I will get to work in Quantico at the FBI Lab, trying to piece together what happened and identify these poor people." She stopped talking, waiting for Callie to congratulate her, advise her to be careful, maybe even tell her to go to hell. When nothing was forthcoming, Katie assumed they lost the connection.

"Callie? You still there?"

"I'm here," Callie replied sharply. "Just trying to wrap my head around why you still insist on pursuing these depressing cases. I mean, murder? Really? Who are you? Columbo?"

Bracing herself, Katie quietly listened as Callie went on. "Katherine Mary, you have a respectable teaching position as a professor of physical anthropology. At freaking George Mason University, for God's sake. Why in the bloody hell would you get yourself wrapped up in this, Kates?" She paused for a moment, then added, "Especially you."

Katie was surprised by how much those words irritated her. *Especially her? What the freak was that supposed to mean?*

"What are you trying to say, Callie? What the hell is the matter with me?"

"Nothing is WRONG with you, sweetie," Callie explained patiently, as if she were trying to teach the alphabet to a slow child. "It's just that we both know how you are, how you get with the whole Empath thing. Being around so much death has got to take a toll on you. Mentally, emotionally, perhaps even someday, physically."

Katie relaxed. Her sister was expressing concern, not judgment, about her empathic abilities.

Good thing she's clueless about my other parlor trick.

Katie's ability to see the dead was a secret she'd shared with only three other people in this world. One, her Nana, was long gone. Of the two still living, one of them was her best friend, Darby, and the other flew out of her life the minute she'd revealed her secret. She carefully phrased her next sentences, mindful that her twin required reassurance, not reprimand.

"I can see how you would worry about that, Cal," Katie soothed. "And, although I have moments when I pick up residual emotions from someone's remains, I have had no major issues. I wish you wouldn't worry so much."

Try telling the truth, Pinocchio. Maybe you'll become a real girl.

"All right, if you're sure? Anyway, the other reason for my call is to talk about Christmas. It's just two weeks away, and I don't even know if you are coming home. Be nice to have a guest list for food and such."

Katie dropped her head and groaned.

I'm such a shit!

"Of course, I will be there! Where else would I go?" she said brightly. "What can I bring? Appy? Dessert? Both?"

"Just bring yourself, Kates. I know how busy you've been. I've got it covered. Uncle Tim is coming with Trish." Smirking, she added, "Oh, and Stacy will be here. Although truthfully, I think the harlot is just coming to see Ryan."

Katie laughed, thinking about how many women her little brother had wrapped around his finger, including Callie's best friend, Stacy. "I've no doubt. It's that Callahan charm." The conversation winding down, Katie mentioned bringing a cheesecake and said goodbye. Just before she hung up, she heard Callie's voice again.

"Kates, hold up. One more thing I forgot to tell you."

"What?" Katie teased, "You can't believe how lucky you are to have me as your sister?"

"Um, yeah. Not exactly," Callie hesitated a moment, then blurted, "Finn is coming."

Perfect.

~

When Katie arrived at Quantico, she received a visitor's pass and directions to the lab Jake had secured for her. Hurrying, tote bag over one shoulder, she followed the instructions given and found the room without difficulty. In her enthusiasm to get started, she stepped too quickly across the threshold, caught her heel, and stumbled forward. Grabbing the door jamb before she fell flat, she looked up, red-faced, praying the room was empty. To her horror, three pairs of eyes watched in amusement. One of those pairs was a beautiful, brilliant violet.

"Good trip?" Jake said flippantly, a gleam in his eyes.

"Ha, ha. Hilarious," Katie said sourly. "No, seriously, you should be in stand up."

Sully, ever the gentleman, walked over to make sure she was okay.

"That doorway gets me every time," he said graciously. "You good?" His smile was warm, the concern in his voice obvious.

What a sweet guy, she thought. *I really must introduce him to Callie.*

"I'm good, thanks. Guess that's what I get for wearing heels."

Jake squinted, scrutinizing her wardrobe. She wore a slimming skirt that emphasized her waist and showcased her long, shapely legs. Her blouse, a pretty Kelly green, complemented her complexion while playing off the unusual color of her eyes. Her hair was gathered in a loose bun at her nape, a few wayward strands cascading down the sides of her face. Inexplicably, he felt possessive and unreasonably territorial.

If he were a dog, he'd have peed on her leg.

"Might want to tone down your outfit next time," Jake snapped, willing himself to shut up, but finding that he was woefully unsuccessful. "You're examining human remains, not…" he faltered a moment, "not going to a disco."

Katie blinked once, twice, then burst out laughing.

A disco? She thought, incredulous. *Who says disco anymore?*

Puzzled, she glanced down at her clothing. She wore a tan pencil skirt to just above the knees *(thank you very much!)* paired with an emerald-colored blouse and low-heeled pumps. She looked more like a librarian than a dancing queen.

"A disco? Um, ohhh-kay," Katie said, drawing out the words. "I think someone didn't get their caffeine this morning. Or are you always this grumpy when you first roll out of bed?" The minute the words left her lips, she wanted to call them back. The thought of him in bed, all sleepy-eyed sex appeal, jarred her. Jake, sensing her discomfort, grinned and looked her up and down.

"Wouldn't you like to know, Professor," he said with a wink. That damned wink again. It would be her undoing. She felt the flush creep up her face and cursed her fair skin and Irish heritage. Luckily, the third person in the room stepped forward.

"Don't you pay him no never mind, honey," the woman said sweetly, a slight southern drawl in her voice. She was in her mid-forties, painfully thin, with short, caramel hair sprinkled with gray. A paisley scarf tied neatly around her neck accented her dull, brown slacks and tan sweater. "Around here, we know Jake as a big softie. Just the sweetest, kindest guy of the lot, except for Sully here." She patted Sully's arm, her smile genuine and kind.

Katie, still stuck on the 'big softie' description, had difficulty concentrating on what the woman was saying.

Boy, has he got you snowed, lady!

"My name is Lydia Jensen," the woman continued,

"and I'll be working with ya'll on this case as a facial reconstruction artist. I promise to do my best to give these poor souls a face if you promise to give me the technical dimensions needed to produce a 3D image." She stuck out her hand, and Katie grasped it, instantly liking her.

"I will do my best. It's a pleasure meeting you," Katie said. She swept the room with a smile, then felt it fall when she made eye contact with Jake. The dark glare he gave her was evidence of how angry he remained.

Why? She wondered. *What was this guy's problem?* Ignoring him, she walked with Lydia to the giant table in the center of the room.

"As you can see," Lydia began, "the apprentices in the Forensic Anthropology Program, or FAP, have set out the remains for us. I believe," she shot Jake a questioning look, "that Agent Devereaux has also lined up an assistant to aid you in your work?"

Jake nodded in agreement. "Tucker Simon, an intern in the FAP program. He will assist us in reconstructing and identifying the remains. He's also an apprentice in Forensic Odontology, which helps when examining the dentition of victims. Since he is on vacation for another week, we will use a rotating list of interns until his return. We called in Lydia," he gestured at the tiny woman, "anticipating that we would need her services to help identify the victims quickly. We may be dealing with a sociopath, a killer without a conscience. If so, time is of the essence." He shrugged. "Unfortunately, we didn't uncover any personal effects with the victims to aid in identifying them, which is why we called in Lydia. The quicker we can put a name to the victims, the faster we can try to discover a pattern or M.O. that can lead us to the suspect or suspects."

Katie nodded in agreement and pulled a lab coat out of her tote bag. Slipping it over her arms, she grabbed a pair of vinyl gloves from the edge of the table and snapped them on.

"All right, then. Let's get to work."

~

Dumfries, Virginia

The Apostle dried his coffee cup and wiped down the kitchen counter. Next, he adjusted the position of the dish detergent that sat nestled neatly on a silver tray atop the sink. He strived to maintain cleanliness and order in all things, for a tidy home was a happy home.

Or some such bullshit.

Several of his childhood homes, although neat as a pin, were not happy at all. His bitterness grew as he relived the misery he endured living in those homes. Squeezing the towel in his hands harder, he twisted it into a rope.

Why should he have been the one to suffer? Bounced like a ball from foster home to foster home, at the mercy of strangers who couldn't give two shits about him? Didn't his mother, the woman who gave birth to him and professed to love him, know what went on in those places?

Near rage now, as always happened when he thought of his mother, he began pacing the kitchen floor. The house he'd rented was a modest-sized, three-bedroom ranch, but it was all the room he needed. He had only two requirements when searching for a place to live in Dumfries, Virginia; the home must afford him complete privacy, and it had to be less than thirty miles from Fredericksburg, Va. He did not relish a long commute while keeping tabs on the target of his obsession.

And it *was* an obsession, he conceded. But a man blessed with the power to receive the Lord's messages, and entrusted to carry out His punishments, should be obsessed with his assignments.

The home, on an acre of wooded land miles from the nearest neighbor, was, indeed, secluded. The large, detached root cellar was virtually soundproof, the perfect place to conduct his lessons. He strolled from his spotless kitchen to a small table in the dining area. Taking a seat, he began thumbing through a photo album, its faded title of 'Our Family,' barely visible on the worn leather exterior. Flipping through the pages, he smiled when he came across an image of his father. He knew his father would understand his mission, even embrace it. But he was gone now, dead, and never coming back.

Turning the page, he came across another photo, one of his smiling mother taken during happier times. He felt the anger build again, a slow simmer threatening to become a furious boil. Releasing the picture from the confines of its plastic prison, he held it up, hands trembling.

Harlot! Bitch! Liar!

She had lied to him his entire life. Treated him as though he were an idiot who could not distinguish the truth from lies. But her deception had cost her dearly. Reminiscing, calmer now, he recalled their last day together.

~

June 25th, six months earlier, Baltimore, Maryland.

He had come a very long way to see her, expecting an explanation, a resolution to the bitter feelings he'd been harboring for years. Taking an immeasurable risk, he had driven nearly sixty miles—in a stolen vehicle containing two bodies—just to speak with her.

He hadn't laid eyes on his mother since he was a boy of eighteen, still intimidated by the power she held over him. Through the years, there had been the annual phone calls comprising small talk and nonsense. Now, more than a decade later, he would face her again, not as a frightened little boy, but as a man.

She had called for him from her deathbed, the years of alcohol abuse and failing health finally taking its toll. Her dying wish was to confess, to reveal to him valuable information that she'd concealed all these years. Information that, she had promised, would change his life forever. And so, the obedient son returned to the woman who had forsaken him. Certainly not out of any fondness or sense of duty, but merely out of curiosity. He wondered what secret she possessed, what knowledge she held, that was so earth-shattering it could alter the direction of his life.

He was the Apostle, after all. His life held a purpose more meaningful than anything she could fathom. His pride would not allow him to beg for the secrets she'd been guarding. He refused to crawl to her, tail between his legs, lapping up scraps of affection like a fucking dog.

He squeezed his eyes shut, reminding himself she was no longer a problem. Once she had unwrapped the mysteries of his life, his path became obvious. And so, using a pink rosary and the very pillow cradling her deceitful head, he choked her into silence. She twisted and bucked, and he squeezed harder, crushing her throat until her tongue swelled, and her eyes bulged. Then, for good measure, he held the pillow over her face. Afterward, he positioned the beads around her neck, replaced the cushion beneath her head, and left. There would be no investigation, no autopsy. She was a frail and dying woman who, sadly, had accidentally strangled herself in bed.

End of story.

He opened his fisted and shaking hand to find her picture, crushed, in the center of his palm. Smoothing it out, he placed it back behind the clear plastic wrapping; the faint creases an ironic reminder of the damage done by his hand.

Rising from his chair, he closed the photo album and headed to the root cellar. His student should be awake by now. It was time. Let the lesson begin.

CHAPTER SEVEN

December 20th, Ten days post-dig

"So how do you determine the age of the skull you're holding?" Jake peered over Katie's shoulder, chest up against her back, his aftershave teasing her nostrils. She inhaled deeply, bathing in his scent.

Lord, but he smells amazing!

Disturbed, she took a slight step forward, pushing closer to the examination table. He was warm and masculine, and oh, so close.

Christ, what am I? Twelve?

"In this case, the environment surrounding the remains is key. I suspect the soil's acidity, combined with insect and scavenger activity, hastened the decomposition process. A body exposed to the elements, buried without the benefit of a coffin or embalming fluids, will decay at an accelerated rate." Voice shaking, aware of his intense gaze, she pointed to various areas of the skull. "But suppose we didn't have that information available? There are several methods we use that give us an approximation of age. One approach is to look at the color, texture, and weight of the bones. For example, remains that have been in the elements for decades will show visible signs of wear, and their color will be dull brown rather than the brilliant white you see here. Nutritional deficiencies and dietary differences, prevalent years ago, make the texture rougher and the weight lighter. Here," she gestured to the skull's forehead, "touch the ridge above the eye socket."

Jake reached over and, using two fingers, gently brushed the brow line. His touch was tender, sweet. She found herself oddly jealous of the recipient of such a caress. Then, like a slap to the face, she remembered that he was examining a dead woman. Ashamed, she carried on.

"Smooth, right? So, the pure white and smooth texture hints at present-day remains. We can also examine the teeth, checking for amalgam, bridges, or other signs of modern dentistry," she explained. "One of the quickest methods we use to determine whether remains found are ancient or modern, though, is to check the surrounding area. If we find a Gucci bag, a debit card, an iPhone— well, that tells us the decedent lived in an era of advanced technology." She stopped for a second, wondering if he was even listening. It looked as though he was too busy examining her face.

What does he hope to find?

"A-and we can use chemical analysis as well," she stuttered, her tongue tripping over the words. "Specifically, isotope analysis, which reveals more about the victim's diet, age, even the geographical locations where he or she has visited or lived. CT scans and x-rays will also provide clues to the age of a bone. We can see growth plates, wear and tear, and evidence of bone disease, such as osteopenia. All of this information combined can help us determine a fairly accurate estimate of age."

"I see," he said, still staring at her. She could swear that he was stalling, looking for another question, another reason to remain this close. Probing her eyes, he asked, "And what else can you tell me, Professor? Number of victims? Weight? Sex?"

Why did it seem like they were slow dancing to a very intimate song? They'd worked side by side for over a week on the mountain. He had visited the lab many times to check on her progress, yet he still captivated her. She felt engulfed by his presence, doused in it, the sensations both welcoming and startling. His lips mesmerized her, and she wondered what it would be like to feel their softness, to taste their sweetness.

Focus, Callahan!

Escaping, at least momentarily, from her fantasy, Katie nodded and swept her hand over the bones before them. "These bones are from a female. Your apprentices did an impressive job keeping all the remains separate. The second victim, a male, is over there." She jerked her head toward a table against the back wall. "I assume that the third victim, also male, is in storage for now. It would be too confusing to have all the remains out at once, like assembling a jigsaw with pieces from three separate puzzles. So far, I can tell you that this victim was middle-aged, petite at 5'3", and maybe one-hundred-and-twenty pounds. Do you see these small, circular grooves here on the inner surface of the pelvis?" Katie turned the bone toward him, pointing them out. When he nodded, she continued. "Those are parturition pits, created when the female pubic bone separates and the ligaments pull away, allowing a fetus to pass. During remodeling, when the bone comes back together, they form grooves." At Jake's questioning look, she said sadly, "Yeah… this lady was somebody's mom."

Thirty minutes later, before he left for his office, Jake asked Katie if she would join him for lunch.

Shocked, she quirked an eyebrow. "Is that a joke?"

He put his hands up in an 'I surrender,' position. "No, no, not a joke. Look, I get it. I do. I may have been an ass when we first met. But give me a chance to make it up to you, okay? Let me buy you lunch."

Katie teased him about the "may have been an ass" remark, but not unkindly, and they agreed to meet in the lab later that afternoon. He started toward the door, turned, and gave her a small salute.

"See you in a bit, Professor."

Making his way to his office, Jake mentally reviewed the dozens of calls and countless computer searches on his to-do list. First, he needed to get into the Department of Justice's database. The National Missing and Unidentified Persons System, or NamUS, was a program that cataloged missing individuals. He hoped to find a recent entry matching the vague descriptors they had: forty to fifty-year-old Caucasian female, approximately 5'3" and one-hundred-and-twenty pounds, who bore at least one child. Unfortunately, with over 600,000 people reported missing in any year, it was like looking for a needle in a haystack.

A more attainable goal, though, was to assemble a Task Force. He had several people in mind for the team, including Lieutenant Francis Blake. Frank would be invaluable if they needed to go back to Sugarloaf Mountain and, hopefully, would bring some additional officers from the Maryland State Police into the investigation. He grabbed his Rolodex, a tool he still relied on, much to Sully's chagrin, and flipped through the phone numbers.

~

Katie, hunched over the table for hours, stood tall, stretching her spine. It was 11:30 a.m., and the work, notoriously tedious, seemed to be dragging on. She checked her watch for the third time that morning and sighed. Typically grounded, her head was in the clouds today.

Geesh, it's just lunch! It's not like he gave you his Netflix password or anything.

Forcing herself to focus, she went back to the bones in front of her. The excavation on the mountain uncovered twenty-one of the usual twenty-seven bones that comprise the human hand. Not bad, considering the evidence of scavenger activity at the scene. Knowing the easiest way to identify what bones were missing was to place the ones she had in anatomical position, she went to work.

Time marched on. Thirty minutes later, head still bent in concentration, she noticed a presence in the room. At first, she believed it to be an actual person. Turning her head toward the door, she instantly recognized the figure before her—brown hair to the shoulders, thin nose, an incredibly forlorn look.

It's the woman from the mountain!

As the figure stood there, looking at the table covered in bones, her bones, Katie's heart ached. Several emotions played over the woman's face, as, finally, her bleak reality emerged.

She was dead.

Katie, fearful of alarming her, whispered. "Hello, my

name is Katie." Seeing the startled look on the woman's face, she explained. "Yes, I can see you. I can sense your pain and suffering, too. I want to help, but I need to know your name. Can you tell me who you are?"

The spirit glanced once again at the remains on the table, shook her head sadly, then vanished.

"No, wait!" Frustrated, Katie kicked her tote bag across the room. "Crap, crap, crap!"

"Temper, temper Professor Callahan! Did that poor, defenseless bag upset our star anthropology teacher?"

Katie snapped her head up at the sound of the unfamiliar, male voice. Searching her brain, she studied his face. Was he a co-worker or student? A caretaker from the Smithsonian? Unable to come up with a name, she took the direct approach.

"I'm so sorry, but I'm afraid I'm dreadful with names. Do I know you?"

Smirking, he shrugged and said nothing.

Oh, please don't be a wiseass. I'm in no mood for it.

Ignoring her question, he said, "What brings a brilliant and beautiful anthropologist to the dungeons of Quantico? Slow going at George Mason? Strapped for cash? Or maybe you heard the news that the FBI has only the best-looking men!" He leered at her, wiggling his eyebrows, and she recoiled.

So much for hoping he wasn't a jackass.

Uncomfortable, she dismissed him. "I'm assisting the FBI in an extensive investigation and not to be rude, but I am swamped here. It was nice to meet you, though, Mr....?" Again, she threw out a not-so-subtle hint, trying to get a name for this strange man.

"Tucker's my name, bones are my game," he said with a grin, as if that line had won him free drinks and desperate women in the past. He was smacking loudly on a piece of gum, the obnoxious chewing showing off a row of rotten teeth. He stuck out his pale, damp hand, and Katie shook it reluctantly.

"Oh, you're Tucker Simon. The man Jake sent to assist me."

"The one and only," he said with a half-hearted bow.

Katie almost moaned aloud. The thought of working with this clown made her skin crawl. Jake would owe her when this case was over. Big time.

Swallowing her distaste for the man, she went about showing him what she had accomplished and suggested he start with cleaning the remaining bones of the upper body. Once cleaned, they would take measurements and x-rays. He agreed, and they both worked in silence for a few moments until, much to her dismay, he began humming. The tune was vaguely familiar, and, after a few lines, Katie recognized the melody.

Sweet baby Jesus, kill me now.

Tucker's deep, nasal rumbling of 'Close to You' by the Carpenters echoed through the air. It was like listening to a dozen honking geese or a stuffy-nosed mouth breather.

God help me if he sings.

As if sensing her misery, he looked up. "Forgive my bluntness, but I can't help but ask, seeing as how we seem to have so much in common. Is there a Mr. Callahan in your life?" He winked, licking his lips.

Gross. Was he hitting on her?

All creepiness aside, he just wasn't her type. He had bad skin and soft hands, and an 'I like to wear women's shoes,' feel about him.

Okay, that last might be a stretch, she conceded, *but he certainly was odd.*

Dishwater brown hair slicked back with an overly enthusiastic amount of hair gel lay plastered to his head.

His physique was lanky—damned-near scrawny, truth be told—making it painfully obvious he'd never seen a gym or lifted more than a triple venti, no-foam latte. His eyes, hooded and in constant motion, were the eyes of a predator. He reminded her of a pet adopted by her third-grade class, an anorexic weasel the children had named Jefferson.

"There **was** a Mr. Callahan," she said stiffly. "My dad. But he died a long while ago and, frankly, I'm not looking for a relationship. Work and all that. I'm sure you understand." She held her breath, praying that he did understand. And that he'd go away.

"Well, you know what they say about all work and no play," he responded, openly ogling her now. Slithering over to the cleaning station, a glib smirk on his face, he said, "Can I be honest here?"

I wish you wouldn't...

He continued. "I look at you, and I see a woman who works all day, then goes home alone to nothing but a glass of wine and her four-legged friends. Lonely and unsatisfied, she is looking for fun, adventure, and dare I say, pleasure!" He winked his beady eye again, thinking it screamed sex appeal.

In truth, it looked like he needed medical attention.

"I'm a man who gets it," he boasted, his voice low. "I know how to satisfy a woman completely, if you get my meaning." Katie, open-mouthed, stared at him.

Seriously? Ew. And how does he know about the dogs?

Just when she felt her stomach roil, aware that he was undressing her with his slimy, Jefferson eyeballs, a deep voice echoed in the lab.

"What's going on here, Tucker? Are you hitting on my woman?" Jake glanced at Katie and dished her one of his sexy, boyish winks.

Yes! she thought happily. *Now there's a wink I can get behind!*

Tucker looked first at Katie, then Jake, then Katie again. It was comical, as though he could not comprehend the two of them together. Katie couldn't wrap her head around that ever happening, either. After all, he'd called her dog a mutt.

Unsettled, Tucker said, "Just feeling out the possibilities here."

When Jake remained silent, Tucker, braver now, cracked his gum and puffed out his non-existent pecs. "Don't get your dander up, Jake. Like I always say, if there ain't no ring, there ain't no thing. You follow?"

Katie held her breath as the room went quickly from a place of light-hearted banter to an atmosphere of animosity and contempt. Jake quickly closed the gap to where Tucker stood, getting within inches of his face.

"My dander? First up, pal, it's Agent Devereaux to you, and my dander is none of your damn business. Second, no, I don't 'follow,' Tuck. At all. In fact, I'll never follow." Talking through clenched teeth now, he said, "Professor Callahan is here as a guest. My guest. She has been kind enough to lend her expertise in a crucial investigation. You'd do well to remember that and show some damned respect." Jake turned his head toward Katie but continued addressing Tucker. "If you can't see your way to doing that, I'm sure I can find someone who can. Do you 'follow' Mr. Simon? Is that clear enough for you?"

Tucker swallowed hard and nodded. "Crystal, Sir." Dropping his head, he tightened his apron and made a show of getting back to work. Katie, turning her back on the assistant, smiled at Jake and mouthed, "Thank you."

Addressing Tucker again, Jake said, "Professor Callahan and I are going out to lunch. I expect that you will have your work completed by the time we get back. Every minute we waste brings some poor bastard closer to becoming the next victim." As Katie gathered her things to leave, she shot one last, furtive glance at Tucker. He was watching her, seething, and Katie felt a familiar sensation rock through her body.

Fear.

～

The restaurant Jake picked was more a pub than a restaurant, but it was charming, cozy, and had a draft beer menu three pages long. They took a corner booth, its scarred oak table and leather seats warm and inviting. Around them, black and white photographs depicting long-ago movie stars graced the stone walls. America's cinema darlings—Bogart and Bacall, Monroe, and Hepburn—forever young, forever frozen in time. An ancient Jukebox sat silently in the corner, while a half dozen TV's played the movie 'Casablanca.'

Katie loved it.

After ordering, they sat in companionable silence, sipping their beers and enjoying the quaint surroundings. Jake was the first to break the silence.

"Hey, I just wanted to say I'm sorry about Tucker. He's a tool, I know, but he's smart. I think he will be a significant addition to our forensic team someday." Irked, he added, "If I don't deck him first."

Katie shrugged. "If you say so. But I would be lying if I told you he didn't scare me, especially after what happened recently. I guess I'm still a little rattled." Jake gave her a blank stare, and she realized he had no idea what she was talking about.

"Oh right, you don't know about that," she said. "Well,

it seems I seriously pissed someone off. Not that I know how, mind you. One minute, I was listening to a sweet jazz station, and the next, I was in a ditch. Forced off the road by some redneck in a white truck."

"Wait. What? Who was it? Why didn't you tell me?" Jake automatically went into cop mode. Katie thought it was kind of cute.

"I didn't tell you because, if you recall, we weren't exactly BFFs when we first met."

Jake had the decency to blush, knowing that he was the reason for the animosity at their first meeting.

"Besides," she continued, "there was nothing you could have done. The police took a report but said it would be next to impossible to find the driver. They think it was just a run-of-the-mill road-rage thing." She sighed, her eyes shuttered, and her shoulders slumped.

"But you don't believe that, do you?" Jake asked, squeezing one of her hands in his. The intimate gesture took her by surprise, and her head popped up, eyes locking with his. "It seems like you feel it's more. More than just an asshole. More personal." He frowned from across the table. "Am I wrong?"

"No, it felt personal. It was like he was angry specifically at me." How could she explain to Jake that she could *feel* the hostility, the rage, coming from a driver she never really saw? If she told him her secret, that she was an Empath, he would never look at her the same way again. The last guy she revealed her secret to had run Mach 10 with his hair on fire, as fast as his sized twelve sneakers could carry him. She didn't want to risk ruining a pleasant working relationship, or possibly even a budding romance, with something as pesky as the truth.

So, she polished up her long, wooden nose and lied.

"I was exhausted, I think. And scared. Now that I'm

calmer, though, I'm sure it was a random incident." When Jake said nothing, she added, "Most likely, the jerk was just in a hurry."

No doubt, rushing to the proctologist's office to find his head.

The waitress, a cute brunette, flashed a brilliant smile at Jake and delivered their order. Blind to the youthful woman's overt flirtation, Jake's eyes remained glued to his lunch mate. He had been in law enforcement a long time and was sure she was leaving out some key details about the accident. He also knew that, if pushed, Katie would shut down. So instead, he teased her about her meal choice.

"You always eat like this? I mean, any idea what the fat content is in that cheeseburger? And don't get me started on those fries," he said, trying to get a rise out of her.

Defensive, she countered, "Hey, just because I don't subsist on bean sprouts and tofu doesn't mean I'm a candidate for the Cath lab. Do you eat like a rabbit all the time, or only on days that end in D-A-Y?"

"Okay, okay," he grinned. "Never mind. Just eat your cow butt, and I'll eat my bunny chow." He unfolded his napkin and draped it across his thigh. "So how about the bones? Anything new you can give me since this morning?"

Katie nodded, dipping a steak fry into her ketchup. "I found a few things. The female victim had a previous fracture to the right distal radius, a rather severe one from what I can see. It looks to be at least three years old, from the degree of remodeling, so we can rule out a post-mortem or ante-mortem injury. I also found a hole at the radial tip that may be from a surgical screw. That means that if we can't identify her in conventional ways, we can start asking around at surgery centers and hospitals." She waited a beat, then rushed on. "Oh, and one more thing," she said, as she popped the fry into her mouth, "our victim was a brunette." That information came from her encounter with the spirit, not from any DNA extraction or phenotyping; those lab results would take weeks to process.

"Outstanding," he said, impressed. "What about the other bones? Any ideas?"

Katie took a sip of her beer and responded, "I got a preliminary look at one of the male victims. I can tell you he was older, probably between sixty-to-eighty years of age. We'll know more when we assemble the remains and get the results of the imaging." She hesitated, reluctant to get anyone in trouble. "Your FAP apprentices did an excellent job of distinguishing between male and female bones. Unfortunately, we have two male victims, one elderly and the other much younger. The interns mistakenly combined all the male remains in one location, so it will take us a while to sort it all out."

Frustrated, Jake shook his head. "Damn. You have my permission to flog them for the screwup; mistakes like that can blow a case." He ripped open a package of saltines. "On my end, I'm waiting for a call back from Frank Blake about the Task Force. I'm eager to get this up and running, but this stuff takes time and miles of red tape and requisition forms in real life. I'm hoping we can get a few guys on loan from the Maryland State Police. Out of my agency, I count myself, Sully, two agents from the Fredericksburg field office, and a Behavioral Analysis Unit investigator. Add in you and Lydia, and we have a decent team." It flattered Katie that he included her.

"The BAU? A profiler?"

Jake shook his head. "There isn't a profiler position, per se, in the FBI. We all profile when working cases, looking at the patterns and characteristics of a suspect's behavior. Our guys at the BAU specialize in the workings of the human mind. They do nothing but study psychological markers and behaviors to help us determine who we are dealing with and where they are, mentally. We all just work in tandem." At Katie's nod, he continued. "I also entered the physical characteristics we have on our Jane Doe into the Missing Persons database, although truthfully, that may be a Hail Mary pass if no one has reported her missing. This afternoon, I'll poke around the ViCAP database and start an entry on our female victim." He shrugged, stabbing a tomato, "Who knows? If someone reported her missing under suspicious circumstances, we might get lucky."

Katie had learned about the existence of ViCAP, or the Violent Criminal Apprehension Program, while searching for a man who was murdered by his business partner. The killer had slain two other partners, using the same technique, over a five-year period.

ViCAP was a program that helped law enforcement correlate the methods and motives of murders, attempted murders, and sexual assaults. In this way, officials could match crime characteristics across the nation, hoping to pinpoint a suspect. Katie knew that the more information they discovered about the manner of death of their victims, the easier it would be to find unsolved cases that mimicked them.

"Sometimes, though," Jake continued, "when dealing with a serial or spree killer, the best clues originate from the minor offenses they have committed in the past. The problem is, there's no way to track those minor crimes unless you know where to look. It's an obstacle that we, as law enforcement officers, need to find a way around."

Their conversation halted momentarily with the ring of Katie's cell phone. It was an unfamiliar number with a Fredericksburg exchange.

"Katie Callahan," she answered.

"Miss Callahan? This is Pete Stanley, from Pete and Sons towing? We towed your vehicle out of a ditch a couple weeks back?"

"Oh, yes, Mr. Stanley. Thank you for calling. How goes the repairs?" She smiled apologetically at Jake and mouthed "car guy," to him.

"Uh, well, ma'am, it seems as though it will take a bit longer than I thought to complete the repairs. I'm sorry for any inconvenience."

Katie felt her heart sink. *Rats!* She was counting on having it by Christmas.

"But I don't understand," she frowned, "Aman said it would be a simple job, that he would get right on it."

"That's the thing, Miss. He was doing the work, but he uh… he stopped. And I don't have any other mechanics working with me right now. I'm in the middle of a transmission job that's turned into a real bitch, pardon my French."

Katie rubbed her head, the skin on her browbone still tender from the accident. "So what happened? Why did Aman stop work?"

"I can't really say, Miss Callahan. Truth is, I think Aman's gone missing."

CHAPTER EIGHT

"What do you mean he's missing?" Katie said, concern creasing her forehead. She was leaning forward in the booth, eyes bright, hanging on every word Pete was saying.

"Just what I said, Miss. Aman was working hard, trying to finish her up. Came in early the day after we got her and stayed late each night. Last I knew, he was working on the suspension. That was Friday the 14th. He left at 4 p.m. that day, fixin' to be back around 5:30 Monday mornin', but never showed up." Katie heard Pete shuffling papers. "I can't recall him taking a day off in all the time he's worked here. He was carrying much of the shop's load, taking extra shifts since both my sons went back to school, and my guy Roger retired. I expect he knows how much I depend on him. Like I say, this dropping a job before it's done? Not the Aman I know."

Katie swallowed hard, her stomach churning. She looked across the table at Jake, held a finger up as if to say, 'just one minute,' and continued.

"But today is the 20th, Pete, which means you've been

out of contact with him for six days. Are there any family or friends you can check with?"

"I'm afraid not, Miss. It's just him. When he didn't show up, I figured maybe he needed a breather. But the more I thought about it, the more it made no dang sense."

Katie drummed her fingers on the table. "Is it okay if I come to the shop and talk with you? Aman may be in trouble, and perhaps, between the two of us, we can figure out what happened." The air around her grew heavy, a chill snaking its way through her body. It was an ominous sign. Discord, a lack of harmony, was once again about to enter her world.

They agreed to meet at closing time, and Katie tucked her phone into her purse. Perplexed, she glanced up at Jake. He was staring at her, patiently waiting for an explanation to her cryptic call.

"Okay, so apparently, Aman, the mechanic who towed my car and was working on the repairs, is AWOL. I've only met him once, but he seems like a lovely man. According to Pete, the garage owner, Aman had been working night and day to complete the job." Her teeth gnawed at her lower lip. "He left the shop on Friday the 14th intending to return the following Monday, but he never showed. No phone call, no text messages, just off the radar. The way Pete describes him, Aman is a hard-working, 'never take a day off,' kind of guy. I don't know, Jake. Call it intuition, but something is off."

Jake listened, riveted, as she relayed the story. She could read him the phone book or a detailed account describing the life cycle of a sea sponge, and he would still be enthralled. The way she worried her bottom lip when she was deep in thought or troubled was enchanting. What was it about this girl that had his stomach flipping and his head in the clouds? She was on his mind constantly, obsessively. When he awoke in the morning, his body tingled with the thought of seeing her. When he closed his eyes at night, her image remained etched in his brain. Her hold on him was like none he'd experienced. It was fierce; it was addictive, and it was frightening in its intensity.

He hesitated a moment, then threw out an offer he thought would serve two purposes. It would help allay her fears about Aman, and it would allow him to spend just a little more of this day with her. It was sneaky and selfish of him, and he knew it.

He didn't care.

"I have an idea. What if we go pick up your friend's car at Quantico, drop it off at her shop, and then take my Suburban to the garage and tag-team this guy? Chances are, Aman is just a sick, or very burned out, employee taking a few days off. If not, we can start a report on his disappearance. Either way, we'll try to piece this thing together."

Katie thought for a moment, then shook her head. "Thank you, it's a kind offer, but I don't think that will work. Unfortunately, I have a full plate today. I need to do some gift shopping and then grab a cheesecake or something to bring to Christmas dinner." She looked at him, embarrassed that it was so close to the holidays, and she appeared to be one of those last-minute shopping lunatics. It also irritated her that his opinion of her mattered, perhaps more than it should at this point. She'd only known him for a few weeks, although admittedly, it felt as though they had known each other for years.

"Anyway," she shrugged self-consciously, "since it's only five days until Christmas, I'm up against the wall. Normally, I'm not such a slacker. This year, though, I'm scrambling like a one-armed shortstop in the majors." She peeled a piece of the label off her bottle and continued.

"My sister has envisioned a kind of 'National Lampoon's' Christmas dinner, heaven help us, and I have nothing to bring. Nothing. I feel like the Little Drummer Boy, except I have no rhythm, so I couldn't even play for the King." She snickered, shrugged, and took a swig of beer. "I know, I know. I'm pretty lame."

Jake smiled lazily. "Well, I don't know about lame, but you sure are pretty." If he had only one wish, it would be that he wished to spend more time with this woman. How bizarre, how foreign, that felt—like being surrounded by miles of sand, parched and dying in the desert heat, and she was a tall glass of water. He needed to drink her in, for only she could satisfy his thirst.

"Tell you what. We will keep to the original plan, and I, Jacob Devereaux, will take you shopping. Skipping out of work is one of the perks of being a boss, right?" He winked at her. "Besides, I'm a fairly decent bargain hunter. I can teach you tricks you never knew existed."

Katie almost spit out her beer, then snorted. "You? A bargain shopper?" she asked, incredulous. "We are talking about Jake Devereaux, FBI guy, right?" When he tipped his beer bottle at her in assent, she continued. "Really? Why can't I see that? You, pushing a wee little cart, with your suit and sidearm and a body language that screams, 'I'd just as soon kick your ass as look at you.'" She took another gulp of beer and teased, "Your big ol' man hands going through racks and racks of woman's pumps and tiny purses and itsy-bitsy lingerie." Giggling, she inhaled some beer, grabbed the table napkin, and coughed.

"Hey, hey," Jake said, getting up to pat her back, "Jesus, don't die on me here." Smoothing down an errant strand that escaped from the confines of her bun and, convinced she was not, in fact, dying, he sat down again. "Look, I know it sounds weird. And I admit, I wasn't exactly telling the entire truth. Full disclosure? I detest shopping. I would rather lie naked on an anthill, covered in maple syrup, then shop. Anywhere, anytime, for anything." He finished his beer and said candidly, "I just think shopping would suck less if I did it with you." That devastating smile, the one she was sure could bring peace to nations and feed the hungry and power the sun, was aimed directly at her.

Her breath left her momentarily, and the wings of a thousand butterflies beat steadily in her stomach. She was playing it cool, but what he'd said kept echoing in her mind.

He wanted to take her shopping! He thought she was pretty!

When she was sure she could speak without stuttering like an idiot, she said, "Well, I would be lying if I said I enjoyed shopping. I hate it myself. I know that's not the typical, all-American female sentiment, but there it is. And I agree that shopping with a friend is less... sucky." It was her turn to wink, and she immediately felt a change in the air. Licking her bottom lip, she watched his gaze follow her tongue. He leaned forward, his violet eyes boring into hers, conveying a message as old as time.

Oh, my, she thought, spellbound. *This could get dangerous.*

After leaving Quantico, Katie headed for Darby's store in the VW, Jake following in his government-issued vehicle. The Chevy Suburban was on the clunky side, but it offered a smooth ride and was roomy enough to carry his various supplies. The route Katie took was scenic; the sun still peeking around some clouds.

It was a beautiful day.

Fingers drumming a beat on the steering wheel, he sang along to a Garth Brooks tune on the radio. Jake never sang. Well, maybe in the shower or with his roommate, Gus, but never outside the confines of the bathroom walls. He strained for an insanely high note, and his voice screeched like a cat with its tail caught in a door.

He smirked, grateful that he had no ambition to live his life as a singer.

After driving about thirty minutes, they arrived at Darby's boutique, Time and Time Again, in Stafford, Virginia. Stafford was an affluent and friendly community, rich with history. The Stafford Marketplace, an extensive collection of stores in the area, was just a few blocks away from her shop, so her business profited from the crowds it drew. Jake found a spot close to the entrance, parked the Suburban, and met Katie on the sidewalk.

The building was on the smaller side, a ranch design with cedar shake siding and a gable-styled roof. 'Time and Time Again' hung above the door, done in tie-dyed lettering, giving patrons an idea of what they would find inside. On either side of the store name, vinyl albums and musical notes were hand-painted in a glossy finish. Scattered over the small porch stood wooden signs, each of varying heights and etched with symbols and verses one might see during the '60s and the '70s. Engraved on one sign was 'Peace,' with the universal two-fingered 'V' under the word; others depicted the toys of yesteryear—hula hoops, yo-yos, and jump ropes. Still more signs touted popular song titles like 'All You Need Is Love' and 'Daydream Believer.' At the entrance were two green rockers, and four or five hanging baskets, decorated with bandanas and filled with ivy. As he stood taking in the exterior, Jake could hear Janis Joplin belting out 'Me and Bobby McGee' from somewhere inside the building.

"Wow," he said, impressed. "Very cool."

"Isn't it, though?" Katie smiled. "My girl has a knack

for sure. I'm lucky if I can hang curtains, and here she's done an entire store."

A female voice boomed from the front of the building. "Well, ya'll just plan on standing there gaping, or are you gonna come in?"

Jake looked at Katie and said, straight-faced, "Darby, I take it?"

She chuckled and nodded. "The one and only. Let's go on in before she starts hollering again." Katie led Jake up on the porch and through the front entrance, draped with beads.

Looking inside was like staring into a time warp. Jake was amazed at how much stock Darby had fit into the compact space. But even with the amount of merchandise, she made it all look organized and uncluttered. They spotted her behind a counter adorned with more beads and colorful lava lamps.

Jake drew closer to the counter and heard the orchestra of a thousand broken heartstrings—a melody produced by the countless men who undoubtedly pined for these girls over the years. Darby was a stunning woman, a whisper over five feet tall with thick, blonde hair and vibrant eyes of turquoise blue. She wore a multi-colored, ankle-length skirt and a white, off-the-shoulder peasant blouse, both throwbacks from decades ago. Her smile was lovely and genuine, and she radiated optimism and goodwill.

Katie hugged her friend in greeting. "Hello, honeybunch! I'd like you to meet someone." Katie grabbed Jake's hand, and instantly, a jolt of electricity ran up her arm. Jake felt it too, as evidenced by his quick intake of breath and startled expression. The same thing happened, on a smaller scale, when he took her hand in the restaurant.

Ignoring her racing heart, she continued with the

introductions. "Jake, I'd like you to meet my best friend in the whole wide world, Darby Harrison. Darby, Assistant Special Agent in Charge, and FBI phenomena, Jake Devereaux." Katie batted her eyes, saying the last breathlessly as if he were the darling of the hometown football team.

Jake smiled at Darby, winked, and said, "Phenomena may be a reach, but it's a pleasure to meet you. Kate has told me a lot about you—when she isn't being a smart-ass."

Darby laughed and shook his hand. "I'm not sure what Kates has told you," she said dryly, "but whatever it is, try to keep an open mind."

Pulling Jake away from the counter, Katie said, "We're gonna have a look around, Darbs. Be right back."

She dragged him to the back of the store and her favorite section, an area chock full of '70s memorabilia. "I think I was a disco queen in another life," she said, only half-jokingly. "Someone as big as Donna Summer or Diana Ross."

"Really?" Jake replied. "Weird how people always think they were someone famous. I'm fairly certain I was a dog. And not a cool dog, either. Some kind of... mutt." Katie grinned at the inside joke, and he whispered conspiratorially, "Don't worry, though. So far, I've resisted the urge to scratch my ass or pee on a tree."

Katie giggled, covering her mouth with both hands. "Okay, Fido," she said when she'd collected herself, "let's get moving."

When they reached the front of the store, Katie rested her hands on the counter and told Darby about Aman. Then she filled her in on the plan to speak to Pete Stanley.

"Missing?" Darby asked. "How does a grown man, one as physically fit as Aman seemed, just disappear? You don't think something bad has happened to him, do you?"

Worried now, she frowned. "I feel terrible. I was the one who called him. Maybe I should have called AAA instead. I've heard they carry weapons because of all the crazies they encounter."

"C'mon, Darbs, let's not panic. Maybe the guy quit but doesn't have the nerve to tell his boss." She patted her on her hand and said, "Instead of beating yourself senseless, let's just wait and see what we find out."

They headed for the door, Jake in the lead, and Katie turned to wave. Darby blew a kiss, made a heart shape with her hands, and mouthed the words, "what a hunk!"

Katie smiled, thankful that this was the woman who kept her secrets, loved her unconditionally, and was probably the only person on the planet who still used the term hunk.

After stopping in a few little shops in Stafford, Katie found gifts for Grams, her siblings, and Darby. She even found a little something for Uncle Tim and Trish, and gourmet dog biscuits for Chance, Blue, and Tim's ancient St. Bernard, Romeo. Jake, as it turned out, really was a bargain hunter. She ended up saving a good deal of money between his haggling and the coupons he downloaded to his phone.

The only thing Jake gained from the shopping trip was a feeling of satisfaction and a pack of gum.

"I owe you an apology," she said, as they drove to Pete's garage in Fredericksburg. "I admit, I doubted your superior shopping prowess. Because of your ability to haggle, I didn't need to take out a second mortgage to afford these gifts. I am forever in your debt." She grinned, swept her hand down, and bent forward in her seat in an exaggerated bow.

When she sat back up, Jake reached a hand to her face and brushed back her hair. Sighing dramatically, he whispered, "I would navigate through the roughest seas, scale the highest mountain, or haggle with a thousand merchants, just to see that beautiful smile."

She batted her lashes, laid her cheek tenderly in his hand, and quipped, "Eyes on the road, Sherlock."

He spit out his gum, laughing.

They stood in the parking area outside of Pete's Towing, wondering what their next move should be. Pete Stanley could not offer much more information other than what he had told her earlier via phone; Aman had been out of touch and was not responding to phone or text messages. Concerned, Pete even drove to the house and, although Aman's car was in the driveway, no one answered the door.

Katie didn't need Pete to tell her something was amiss. The balance in this precise area of the universe felt disturbed, her Spidey Sense on high alert. It felt like someone was watching her, waiting. But waiting for what? Did it have anything to do with the lunatic in the truck? A disturbing thought popped into her mind.

Could it be Kyle?

She and her ex-boyfriend had parted on less than friendly terms, but she didn't believe he would hurt her.

"What are you thinking?" Jake's question derailed her from that train of thought, and she threw her hands up.

"Honestly? I don't know what to think. Weird, though, right? How does a guy who has been, like, employee of the year, go from Mr. Outstanding to Mr. Irresponsible in days? Makes little sense."

They walked back to the Suburban, each silently pondering the possibilities, when her cell phone began singing 'California Dreamin.'

"The Mamas and the Papas?" Jake said with a grin. "Darby?"

Katie smiled and answered the call. "Hey, girlfriend. What's up?"

"Hey. Um, I need to talk to you about something. It's, it's kind of important," Darby sputtered, her sentences fragmented and cryptic.

Uh, oh, Katie thought. *Something tells me I'm not going to like this.*

"Okay, so I'm at the house and, well, we have a situation. But before I tell you, I need you to promise me you won't freak out," Darby said, hardly convinced her stipulation would, indeed, prevent Kate from freaking out.

"Spill it, Sis. What happened? Did Blue eat another sock or Chance go swimming in the river? Don't tell me the dryer blew up again!" Katie moaned.

"No. No, I wish. I just got home. I was a little later than usual because I was doing inventory, and when I pulled up to the driveway..." Darby stopped, her sudden silence troublesome.

"And?" Katie prodded, "And what? Darby, you're scaring me."

"There was something in the mailbox, Kates. I'm okay. I'm fine, really, just got the shock of a lifetime." She exhaled, resignation in her tone. "Ugly bitch was just sitting there, in the mailbox, staring right at me. A snake, sweetie. A fucking copperhead."

"What? Oh, my God! You sure you are okay?" Katie's heart raced. "You didn't get bit, right?"

Pulling the phone away from her ear, she whispered to Jake, "A snake! In my mailbox!"

"There's more, Kate," Darby said, letting out a long breath. "When I saw the snake, I screamed, and she slid to the ground. Once she made her way out, I spotted something in the back of the mailbox: a shiny red, Snow White quality apple. Someone must have put them in there deliberately." She stopped speaking for a second, then added, "I wonder if I should call someone. Who deals with snakes, anyway? Thank goodness Chance and Blue were not with me. They can be over-protective, you know?" Darby was rambling, but she couldn't stop herself if she tried. After a few more minutes of talking, she reassured Katie again that she was unharmed and promised that her next call would be to the Fredericksburg PD.

Katie stood there for a moment, her head down, stunned into silence. Someone had put a copperhead into her mailbox deliberately. But why? Was it the mystery driver? Or Kyle? She never thought of herself as a person with enemies, yet here she was, immediately spitting out two suspects.

What does that say about me?

She suddenly felt like she did on that October day long ago, when she knew, deep down, that she would never again hear her mother's voice. Something huge, both life-changing and ugly, was coming her way. It was like watching a tornado aim for a sleepy town or a jumbo jet plummet from the sky onto a freeway. Death was coming, and there wasn't a damn thing anyone could do to stop it. Lost in thought, she felt Jake take both of her hands, concern in his beautiful, bright eyes.

"Katie, sweetheart. Look at me." When she looked up, he rubbed his thumbs over the tops of her hands. "Tell me what's going on. What did Darby say?"

Katie gathered her thoughts, then told Jake, verbatim, everything Darby had related. When finished, she said simply, "Could someone hate me that much?"

Jake's mind was whirling, trying to think of a rational explanation, a simple reason that this reptile had found its way into Kate's mailbox. He hated snakes. They were slithering, slimy animals that often crawled into his nightmares. But rather than paralyze him, his irrational fear caused him to study them and find their weaknesses, as he would with any other adversary. Consequently, he knew a lot about snakes.

He supposed that if the mailbox were ajar, the snake might have climbed in there to keep warm. But it was December; snakes should be quasi-hibernating right now.

Okay, he reasoned, *so maybe someone's pet had gotten loose. But what of the apple? A neighborhood pet climbing into the box wouldn't explain the apple. No, someone put it there intentionally. A biblical message, maybe? Eve, the apple, and the serpent?*

"C'mon," he said finally, "I'll take you home. The local PD should be there shortly." He placed his hand at the small of her back and gently led her to the car. The spark from her eyes had vanished, and her feet seemed to drag across the pavement. Quiet and introspective, this was not at all the feisty, sassy girl that he had known for the last few weeks. She seemed almost defeated.

And that scared Jake more than any snake ever could.

CHAPTER NINE

December 20th, 10 a.m., Dumfries, Virginia

"So it will be at the end of the age, the angels will come forth and take out the wicked from among the righteous." Matthew 13:49.

The Apostle wrapped a towel around his waist and stepped out of the shower. Water pooled at his feet as he wiped a hand across the mirror, studying his reflection. Although not handsome by conventional standards, he possessed an undeniable appeal, a magnetic attraction. He had the high cheekbones, straight nose, and strong jawline seen in nobility. His ice-blue eyes could cut through a person's defenses, leaving them raw, vulnerable. Thick, whiskey brown hair curled in a gentle wave at the nape of his neck. Many women had run their fingers through that hair, lost in the rapture and throes of passion. Others had clutched it in desperation amid something much darker—panic-driven hysteria urging them to act, to fight, to save themselves.

He turned his head from side to side, examining his profile with a critical eye. Faint scars lined either side of his face, their dimpled pattern like stones skipped across a pond. Ugly souvenirs, courtesy of a razor-wielding man who no longer drew breath.

The Apostle saw to that many years ago.

Naked, he walked to his bedroom, opened the closet door, and considered his wardrobe. A row of neatly pressed, starched shirts hung on the top half of his closet, arranged by color, light to dark. The bottom half of the closet held his slacks, pristinely hung on uniformly spaced hangers, a perfect crease down the center of each pair. He didn't own many shoes, but those he did sat rigidly on a shelf at the closet's bottom. He chose a plain white Oxford shirt, blue jeans, and loafers. He believed in looking his best.

He had big things in store for his Chosen.

Today, he had followed her from Quantico to the pub where she and that FBI Agent stopped for a meal. He seethed as he watched them, infuriatingly cozy, laughing in the restaurant booth. But it was a pretense, a lie. She was nothing more than a Jezebel, a shameless wench who would chew up that agent, spit him out, move on to the next.

And that asshole cop is too fucking stupid to realize it! Too blind to know that she's leading him around by the dick.

He felt the anger rising again and did his best to tamp it down. He needed to focus, to stay the course. He spotted a Tyvek coverall and a pair of work boots on the top shelf and tossed them on the bed. He would need these later. But first, to the basement, and his student's final lesson.

Sweat forged a steady stream between the man's shoulder blades, the rivulets finding the small of his back and winding their way to the crease of his buttocks. His face, armpits, even his ears were damp. Two wood stoves blazed in the cramped space, making it intolerably hot. His throat felt like sand, his tongue thick and dry. He could not recall the last time that he drank.

He rubbed his face against his shoulder, attempting to catch a droplet of sweat before it reached his eyes. For the thousandth time, he tried to plot a way out of his prison. Naked and bound, forced to kneel for days, his arms ached, and his thighs shook. The skin on his back was shredded and bloody, the result of a cruel lashing by his tormentor. Hopelessness and despair threatened to overtake him.

Ominous footsteps descending the cellar stairs startled him, and he jerked his head up, suppressing the scream on his lips

"Please, God," he cried, "help me!"

The Apostle, hands folded, casually walked over to where the man sat. "Well, good morning, sir. I trust you slept well?" His captive stared at the ground, terrified to make eye contact.

The Apostle continued. "Rejoice, for today, your lessons conclude. And, although your sins cannot go unpunished, I am pleased that you've received your teachings with bravery and grace."

His student listened intently, clueless about the sins his captor spoke of, daring to hope the bizarre words meant his release. He was ready to admit or confess to anything to save himself. There remained a niggling doubt in the back of his mind, though, that caused his stomach to churn. His attacker wore no mask, no cover, to obscure his face. The implication of what that could mean for survival did not escape him.

Fresh fear shot through the man as he watched his captor drift to an old wooden table that held an array of

razors, knives, and whips. Heart threatening to pound
through his chest, his terror turned to confusion as his
tormentor returned carrying only a set of thick, mauve-
colored rosary beads.

Standing before his pupil, the Apostle folded his hands
once again and recited the Lord's Prayer. When finished,
he genuflected, then looked down at the quivering man in
front of him and sneered.

"State your name."

The man gulped, bewildered.

Calmly, the Apostle repeated the command. "You must
state your name for the Lord to hear. It is your judgment
day."

Panicked, the beaten man attempted to stand and
immediately fell to his side. Restrained and in a kneeling
position for hours, his feet had lost all sensation.

The Apostle crouched low, his lips inches from the
man's ear, and ground out, "Your name!"

Sobbing uncontrollably, broken and defeated, the
student complied. At last satisfied, the Apostle kneeled
behind the crumpled man, gripped the beads in both
hands, and coiled them around his throat.

"My friend," he said, tightening the ligature as his
victim struggled in vain, "fear not! For this is the day the
Lord hath made; let us rejoice and be glad in it!"

Dehydrated and weak, the battle was more symbolic
than substantive, and death did not take long. The student
lay at the Apostle's feet, eyes open but unseeing, his
pounding heart forever silenced. There was no Splendor to
witness, no bright light seen ascending to the heavens. The
man had simply... died.

Changing into his coveralls, the Apostle hoisted the
body over his shoulder, carried it to the stolen pickup truck,

and began the trip to its ultimate resting place in Shenandoah National Park.

The park was remote, with secluded trails and winding paths miles from the famous Skyline Drive. Away from prying eyes, it was the perfect setting for both legitimate hiking and nefarious deeds. He whistled a cheery tune as he drove, secure knowing that he had thought of everything.

Hours later, having disposed of the remains without incident, he discarded the Tyvek suit into a random dumpster and congratulated himself. Everything was progressing beautifully. He looked forward to a pleasant drive to Fredericksburg, contemplating his next move and the surprises in store for his Chosen.

Little by little, he would chip away at her life. He only wished he could be there to see her crack.

~

December 20th, 6 p.m.

When they pulled up to Katie's drive, a Fredericksburg Police Department vehicle sat in front of the mailbox. Jake parked behind the cruiser, and they got out, heading toward Darby. She was standing next to a uniformed officer, hands on her hips, looking uncharacteristically irate. The nametag on the cop's blue shirt said Ptl. Lance Jeffries. He was in his mid-fifties, with a sizable belly, aviator sunglasses, and, what appeared to be, a sour attitude.

"It's like I told you, Missy," he said, bored. "I will take the report, but I seriously doubt anything will come of it. You have no witnesses, no security camera on the premises, and no suspects to offer. There have been no injuries, and the owner of the property isn't even home. I don't know what you expect me to do here."

"What I expect," Darby said tersely, "is for you to do your job. Canvass the neighborhood, see if anyone in town has purchased a snake from that exotic pet shop down on Seventh Avenue. I'm certain it was a copperhead." She paused, pursing her lips. "How about checking with the surrounding towns? Maybe somebody reported something like this recently."

When Jeffries gave her a condescending shake of the head, Jake jumped in.

"Hey, how's it going?" he said to the uniformed officer. "I'm A.S.A.C. Jake Devereaux, D.C. office, and this is the owner of the home, Kate Callahan." Jeffries eyed Katie suspiciously but extended a pasty, clammy hand. She shook it, then discreetly wiped her hand on her thigh.

"I would appreciate any extra hustle your department can provide," Jake said. "I think we are all on the same page here; that copperhead didn't just wind its way up the post and crawl through the mailbox door. And it certainly didn't haul an apple up there either, right? So, it's safe to assume someone put them there deliberately."

Jeffries, disinterested, picked at a stained cuticle on his index finger.

Growing annoyed, Jake continued. "Which brings me to my next question. Where are you on the snake?"

The cop stared at him blankly, so Jake took a more direct approach.

"The snake, Jeffries. Have you found it yet? Probably long gone, but we should look for it, regardless."

"The snake?" Jeffries repeated, genuinely dumbfounded. "Nope, haven't seen it. Probably went into the woods or crawled to the river. Anyway, it hardly seems to matter much." He shot an ugly glance toward Darby.

"Unless, of course, the reporting party made the whole thing up."

Jake felt his face flush and his blood pressure climb. Not only was this cop inattentive and lazy, but he was disrespecting a lovely woman—a woman who was important to Kate.

"I will assume that you're having an off day, Jeffries," Jake said darkly. "Otherwise, I might question your skills as a police officer. The first rule of policing is to gather facts, right? And I would think a huge fact to include in this report would be an accurate description of the snake's type and size. You know, in case this has happened before, as Ms. Harrison suggested? We are standing in a civilian neighborhood; a poisonous snake and children are not a pretty combo." He stepped closer, muscles tense. "So, if I were you, I would start acting on the whole 'protect and serve' thing, rather than offering excuses about why you can't solve a case before it's even investigated."

Beads of sweat dotted the patrolman's forehead. "Ok, ok, you don't have to get so pissed about it. I'll look for the fucking thing if it makes you happy."

Jake took a calming breath. "Excellent idea. I would hate to have to explain to your Sergeant why you found it unimportant in this investigation."

Jeffries dabbed his head with a shirtsleeve and hurried back to his police car. He radioed the dispatcher, requesting an animal control unit to his location. Then, adjusting his uniform belt, he started his search.

Jake, Katie, and Darby, eyes downcast, stepped carefully back to the house. Jake believed the animal was long gone by now, but it never hurt to be prepared. Admittedly, he would hate to be the one to find it.

"I appreciate what you did back there," Katie said. "Thank you for jumping in before I said something nasty."

She paused, then said with a grin, "I think you scared the bejesus out of him."

"Understatement of the century," Darby said, "Did you see his eyes? I kept checking his pants, looking for the wet spot." They looked at each other and burst out laughing. Jake smiled and shook his head.

At the porch steps, Darby said goodnight. "I'm just a phone call away, Kates. You've had a rough couple of days. I can stay here with you tonight if you want. I'm supposed to leave early tomorrow for my folk's house, but I can easily take that off the table."

Katie grabbed her friend's hand. "Oh, no, you won't! Look, we know the snake isn't in the house. Besides, I have the dogs—they will bark like mad if anyone, or anything, tries to get in. And you're right next door if there is a problem tonight. As for tomorrow, you get your butt to your parents' place. I'm heading to Gram's in a few days myself, so it's all good. Go, have fun, and kiss the 'rents from me. We will have our own Christmas when you get back."

Katie watched as Darby walked down the brick pavers to her apartment above the garage. Once her friend was safely inside, she looked at Jake and said, "Thank you so much for all you did for me today. From taking me to a lovely lunch, to interviewing Pete and even coming with me as I dragged you Christmas shopping. You are a delightful man, Jacob Devereaux." She wrinkled her freckled nose and smiled. "But don't worry. Your secret is safe with me."

Jake raised his eyebrows. "So that's it, then? Aren't you supposed to, like, feed me or something? Ply me with wine? Ravage me when I am at my most vulnerable?" He grinned boyishly, and her heart fluttered.

Unsure whether he was merely teasing or starving, she

said, "I'm afraid I don't have much. I meant to go food shopping today, but you saw how that crashed and burned." She exhaled dramatically, then brightened. "But I have tons of pasta and some frozen dinner rolls. Oh, and some stuff to make a salad."

Jake smiled and swept out his arm, inviting her to enter first. "You boil the water; I'll toss the salad."

When she led him through the front door and into the foyer, Chance and Blue tag-teamed him with wagging tails and slobbering kisses. After lavishing them with affection, his eyes surveyed the rooms within his view, and he gave a low whistle. "Wow, nice. A lot of room here. Love that stone fireplace."

Katie showed him around the first floor, through the living room with the fireplace he'd admired, to the kitchen, and finally to the sunroom. She, unconsciously or not, avoided upstairs and the master bedroom.

"I can understand why you love it out here," he said, as they took in the view. "Very calming."

"Definitely. I come to the sunroom when I'm stressed out, and all my worries seem to fade away."

His expression darkened. "You get stressed out often?"

"Not as much as I used to. I think with every birthday, I get wiser about what's important and what's just background noise, you know?"

They went to the kitchen, and she pulled out several boxes of penne. "Do you want a beer or something? I think I have some Chardonnay somewhere, too."

"Beer is great, thanks. I can pour us a couple if you point me to the glasses?" he said, shrugging his shoulders.

Damn, but he's cute.

Too bad she wasn't interested in a long-term relationship. The burns that Kyle had given her left long-lasting, skin-graft type scars. She pointed to a cabinet, turned on some soft jazz, and they drank and prepared their meal. As he was chopping celery, he asked her about herself.

"So, tell me about Katie Callahan. I know what you do for a living. I also know that you volunteer with A.A.R.F., which is admirable. But what about you? Any family? Brothers or sisters? A sixth finger or a hidden tail I need to worry about?" He said the last with a frown, poker face in place. Katie laughed, then became solemn.

"I'm afraid my background is not very interesting. I'm the product of a benign upbringing and the normal childhood that goes with it. I grew up in Falls Church, Virginia, with my Grams and siblings. Mom and Dad died within a year and a half of each other, so we became orphaned early on." Why on earth did she tell him she'd had a normal childhood? She'd died at six, became an orphan a year later, and could see the dead before her seventh birthday.

Yep. Boringly average.

"My Dad died in a plane crash, and my mom… well, authorities declared her dead after disappearing under mysterious circumstances."

Jake's knife stilled, and he stared at her, open-mouthed. "Are you shittin' me?" he asked, incredulous. "That is possibly one of the saddest stories I've ever heard."

She smiled wistfully. "We made out okay. There are plenty of kids who aren't so lucky. Grams, my maternal grandmother, took care of us. She moved from Florida to Falls Church, and she and my mom's brother, Uncle Tim, became our legal guardians. Grams is great." Katie turned from the stove and leaned a hip against the counter. "I don't know what we would have done without her. As far as siblings go, I have a twin sister, Callie, and two brothers, Finn and Ryan. And my mom? On the day she disappeared, the house was ransacked, and the kitchen covered in blood." She turned to stir the pasta, addressing him over her shoulder. "Mom was gone. No note, no ransom demands. Mom was declared dead a few years later, leaving Grams free to adopt us. We never found her body." She took a cleansing breath, suddenly feeling as though she'd run a marathon. She hated talking about this stuff.

"And they had no suspects? No idea where her body could be?" Jake thought for a second. "Who was first on the scene? Sometimes, it turns out that the perpetrator is the person who made the original report."

"Not in this case. There was no doubt in anyone's mind that the person who reported her disappearance was innocent."

"You're sure?"

She looked at him pointedly, then said, "I'm sure. I was the first person on the scene." When he raised his brows, she added, "Yep, true story. And I was just seven years old."

Jake blinked twice. "Damn."

~

When their meal was over and the dishes done, they sat on Katie's overstuffed sofa with full bellies and a couple of glasses of Chardonnay.

"So, if you don't mind my asking, how is it you became a Professor at such a young age? You go to college at like, aged ten?" he asked.

Katie smiled. "No, not that young, but I was a nerd. In my junior year of high school, they accepted me to a local college's fast-track program. I took a combination of honor classes and college-level courses for two years. By the time

I graduated high school, I already had an associate degree."

"Wow. Impressive."

Laughing, she said, "Yeah, but my social life sucked."

"Ok. So, back to your family. How about your dad?" Jake asked. "You mentioned a plane crash?"

"It's kind of a long, morbid story," Katie said with a sigh. "Besides, I'm tired of hearing myself talk. How about you? We've spent most of the evening talking about my screwed-up life. Fair is fair and all that. Please tell me you have some pathetic stories about your childhood," she pleaded, the Chardonnay starting to go to her head. She wasn't exactly a seasoned drinker, and her second glass of wine was going down a little too easily.

Jake smiled, remembering the long ago, almost perfect childhood he enjoyed. "I wish I could commiserate with you, sweetheart."

As he spoke, he had one hand resting on the back of the couch and the other wrapped around the stem of his wineglass. She suddenly wished he had a third hand to place in hers.

Yeah... that'd be weird.

"My parents are amazing. They have supported everything and anything my brother and I ever wanted to do, without question or judgment. We grew up, my brother Jed and I, in Montana. If you've ever wondered what state God would call home, look no further than there. The air is crisp and clean, and the sunsets across the mountains steal your breath away. People have a genuine sense of community and compassion, you know? It's a great state to raise a family." He couldn't believe he was so open with her. It had been ages since he shared his family with anyone, let alone someone he'd only met a few weeks ago. As he spoke, his face serene, she found herself rapt.

His eyes reflected the warmth he'd felt for his childhood home.

"You love it." A statement, not a question. "Montana. So why did you leave? What brought you this far east?"

"The job, mostly," Jake explained, setting down his wine. "If there had been a seat at the table anywhere near that state, my ass would have filled it. But unfortunately, I had only two choices at the time for a field assignment. New York or Washington. I chose D.C."

"And your parents and brother? Are they still in Montana?"

"Yep," he said, nostalgic. "Lucky bastards. My parents live on a fifty-acre ranch. Dad is a mason and does things with brick you cannot imagine. They have a few milking cows, some horses, a couple of goats. And an amazing garden, with every type of flower, fruit, and vegetable native to Montana. I don't know how they keep up with it all. Jed lives about twenty-five miles south of them and comes home for dinner every Sunday. I can sleep better, knowing at least one of us is not far away. He owns his own business, a company called Private Investigative and Personal Protection Services, or P.I.P.P.S., for short. Funny. We used to have a Jack Russell named Mr. Pipps. I bust him about that all the time."

"Cute name," Katie said.

He smiled and leaned forward, arms on his thighs. "Jed's business supplies armed guards, security systems, and private eye type investigations. Every time we get together, we talk about me going out there to work with him." Jake picked up his wine and smiled. "Honestly? Sometimes I think it would be nice to get away from the constant ugliness I see every day. So, although the offer is taken tongue in cheek, I could get used to fresher air, honest women, and a steadier work schedule. I'm thirty-five years old. Not getting any younger here." He dazzled her with a crooked smile, and she instantly regretted her promise to herself to swear off relationships for a while.

At 10 p.m., Jake grudgingly got up to leave for the night. For the first time in a long time, like maybe forever, he wished he could stay all night. It wasn't even a sexual thing. Well, ok, maybe that was part of it.

A very big part, he thought, amused. *Huge.*

But he couldn't seem to get enough of this woman. It was too much, too fast. But like a dangerous storm or the taxman in April, you were helpless to escape it.

Katie stood in front of him, a tad bit tipsy, her attention drawn beyond his left shoulder. She froze, eyes wide, and he quickly turned and scanned the room. He saw nothing.

"What is it? Did you hear something outside? See something?"

Katie shook her head, her brain scrambling for an excuse to explain her odd behavior.

"No, no, nothing like that. Just a wicked headache. Too much wine, I suppose." She was talking too fast, almost stumbling over her words.

Not necessarily a bad thing, she thought. It would help cement the illusion that she was trashed, not psychotic.

"Oh, um, ok," he said, unconvinced.

Shit. Leave it to me to get hung up on a guy who can smell a lie at fifty paces.

"I'm sorry you aren't feeling well. Hope I didn't keep you up too late." His playful grin suggested keeping her up too late didn't bother him in the least.

She started walking to the door, hoping he would take the hint. Her top priority right now was to get this tremendously handsome man to leave.

There is seriously something wrong with me!

"Will I see you at the lab tomorrow?" she asked. "I plan on renting a car until they fix the Denali."

"Maybe you should take a breather, Kate. Take tomorrow off."

She shook her head. "No, I'll be there. Lydia is working on the younger male's facial reconstruction, and I'd like to see the process up close. I find that work fascinating."

After practically pushing him out of the front door, she watched him walk to his vehicle. As soon as the engine turned over, she slammed the door, leaned against it, and closed her eyes. Slowing her breathing, she tiptoed back to the living room. A figure sat on the couch, hunched over, rocking herself. It was not the same woman she'd seen in the lab and on the mountain. This woman had long, gray hair pulled back into a braid that reached her waist. Her face was gaunt, her eyes sunken. She looked quite ill.

Of course, she's dead, so...

Katie studied the figure, and, though she was sure they'd never met before, conceded that the apparition felt somehow familiar. As the image waxed and waned, Katie received all the spirit's negative emotions in an unrelenting volley, like hundreds of tennis balls hitting her at once. Cold, menacing fingers of dread, along with sorrow and disgust, wrapped around her chest, constricting her breathing.

For the first time since acknowledging her ability to see and feel the dead, Katie was wholly overcome. The last thought that slammed into her brain before the monstrous headache began and she lost consciousness was an understanding of this spirit's intentions. This woman wasn't there to relive her own demise; she was there to prevent Katie's.

This visit was a warning.

CHAPTER TEN

"For this is the will of God, your sanctification; that is, that you abstain from sexual immorality; that each of you know how to possess his own vessel in sanctification and honor, not in lustful passion, like the Gentiles who do not know God." Thessalonians 4:3-6

When she awoke on the floor, the first thing Katie noticed was the swirling clumps of dog hair and fuzzballs waltzing beneath the couch. Amid the chaos, a desiccated raisin appeared to be making love to a dust bunny.

Ew.

Holding her breath to avoid disturbing the dirt, she took a moment to get her bearings. The clock above the fireplace mantel read 10:32 p.m. Since Jake left around ten, that meant she had lost thirty minutes. Horrified, she tried to piece together the last moments she remembered.

The suffering emanating from her spirit visitor was crippling. Over the years, she had witnessed the darkest hours and deepest pain a human being could endure. Yet, through it all, she had never lost consciousness.

She scanned the room and found the house tranquil; the presence gone. Sitting up, she assessed her body for injury. The stone surrounding the fireplace was a mere two feet away from where she'd fallen. Probing her scalp, she checked for bumps, tenderness, and fresh blood but found nothing.

Head still throbbing, she slowly made her way to the kitchen to tend to Chance and Blue. She planned to settle them in for the night, then brew a cup of tea. Honey and lemon, or maybe chamomile, sounded good.

And a bath. Lord, I could bathe for days.

Her muscles burned; her limbs ached. It felt as though every nerve in her body had fired simultaneously. Exhausted physically and mentally, she doubted that even the spirits of the dead could keep her awake tonight.

Ten minutes later, she carried her tea up the stairs to her spacious bedroom. In the master bath, she turned on the tap, set the plug, and poured in some sweet-smelling bubble bath. As the tub filled, she searched her dresser for her favorite pajamas—the ones that felt soft and cool and right against her skin. She tugged and pulled through her lingerie drawer until she finally found them buried beneath some stockings and a few bras.

Weird. I just washed these. How did they end up on the bottom?

Unsettled, she tossed the nightclothes on the dresser and returned to the bathroom and the promise of a therapeutic soak. Twenty minutes later, her muscles once again fluid and her skin perfectly pruned, she toweled off. Entering the bedroom, she went to the dresser and stared into the mirror. Her mind raced, firing off questions for which she had no answers. Why couldn't she control her visions? Or, more to the point, her reaction to her visions? Entities had visited her since she was a child, so what was different? Why was she shaken by the souls who appeared to her now?

Dressing quietly, she released the pins securing her hair. Without the confines of barrettes, elastic bands, or bobby pins, her hair fell midway down her back in thick waves. She brushed it thoroughly, then turned toward the bed. Just the simple pleasure of closing her eyes excited her.

Geesh, I need a hobby. Or a boyfriend.

Fixated on just one task, to get a fabulous night's sleep, she almost didn't see the piece of paper lying on her pillow.

She smiled. *Darby.*

The thoughtfulness of her friend warmed her heart. She reached out to grab the note and hesitated, brows furrowed. Boxy penmanship and a shaky hand jumped off the page, turning her blood to ice. Katie knew her best friend's writing as well as she knew her own.

Darby didn't write this letter!

Keeping the note at arm's length, as if it were rabid and possessed teeth, she read the message. Bizarrely worded, it was difficult to grasp the threat at first. While Katie's brain scrambled for an explanation she knew would never come, her legs, quivering like jelly, seemed perfectly content to remain nailed to the floor.

A long-forgotten memory surfaced, one of a toy Ryan had as a child; a plastic clown suctioned to his highchair tray, designed to entertain him while he ate his meals. The clown's rubber band legs would bend, collapse, and then straighten when he pulled a string.

Christ, I'm him. I'm Stand-up Man.

Willing her shaking legs to cooperate, nursing an irrational belief that the threatening words could not touch her if they could not find her, she cleared the bedroom door and flew down the staircase. Breathless, she reached for the kitchen phone and called the first person who came to mind.

~

Three minutes later, Darby was pounding on the front door. When the door opened, she took one look at Katie's face, pulled her into the kitchen, and poured them both two fingers of scotch. Then she poured another glass. After a few more sips, Katie appeared calm enough to answer questions.

"Ok, what the hell, Kates? You look like crap. A whiter shade of pale kind of crap, like you saw a ghost or something." Darby considered that for a moment. "Did you, hon? Did you have a visitor tonight?"

"More than just a visit, I'm afraid," Katie replied. "Tonight, I had the most intense experience I've ever…" Voice cracking, she continued in a whisper. "Did you ever feel you were imploding from within? As if your body was collapsing in on itself, like a sinkhole?" Katie paused for a second, head bent, the memory causing her to shudder. "It was as though a thousand pieces of *me* just dissolved. The feelings from this spirit were so raw, so real, that…"

"That what?"

Katie groaned, loathe to say the words aloud. "I folded like a cheap suit, Darbs. I fainted, or at least, I think I fainted. One minute, I'm getting hammered with every horrible event this woman has ever lived through, feeling like I will vomit, and the next? I'm horizontal on the pumpkin pine, out like a light. When I finally came to, I had lost thirty minutes and was counting dust motes on the floor and spider webs on the ceiling."

"Jesus! Are you all right?"

Katie nodded. "Rattled, but functioning."

"What about the woman? Do you know who she is? What she wants?"

Katie threw her hands up. "No, and that's what's so damn frustrating. I have no clue. Something about her seemed familiar, although I'm sure she's no one I've ever met." She took a steadying breath. "That's not all, though. I saved the best for last."

"Of course, you did," Darby said sarcastically.

Katie chewed a fingernail. "When I regained consciousness, I was exhausted and headed upstairs to, you know, have a soak and unwind. But when I got out of the tub…" She stopped and took a breath. She wasn't trying to be dramatic; she was trying to calm her racing heart.

"When you got out, what? What happened?"

A wayward strand of hair made its way to Katie's cheek, and she pushed it aside. "I realized that someone had been in my bedroom. They were kind enough to leave a greeting card on my pillow, a message meant to intimidate me." She sighed, closing her eyes.

God, I'm so damned tired. "And the icing on the cake? I think whoever it was also had a party in my underwear drawer."

Darby jumped up. "Holy macaroni! We need to call Jake. I just knew some bad juju was coming this way!"

Katie frowned. "And just how did you know this, girlfriend?"

"Okay, okay," Darby said, "you hate the cards. So, sue me, I did a reading anyway. Look, don't be mad, ok? I've just been worried, and the Tarot never lies. Wanna know what came up?"

Katie stared blankly, unwilling to take the bait.

Ignoring her lack of enthusiasm, Darby continued. "The Page of Swords reversed. Many people believe that it can foreshadow a stalker." She pointed at herself, expression bland, and cracked, "Wait! This is my shocked face!"

Katie remained annoyingly silent.

Darby forged ahead. "And that's not all. Both the Devil and the Magician came up several times during the reading."

Despite herself, Katie was intrigued. "Meaning?"

"Meaning an individual with ill intent, someone as evil as Satan himself is in your life. The magician card shows manipulation and trickery, which could mean a crafty son of a bitch is playing you." Darby rubbed her temples. "I don't know who, but someone is after you, Kates." She held up her fingers and ticked off the incidents that had occurred. "First, some unknown maniac runs you off the road. Then, we find a poisonous snake in the mailbox, complete with its own damned forbidden fruit. And now, someone breaks into your home, gets creepy with your underwear, and leaves you a note about it. You don't have to be Dick fucking Tracy to see a pattern here." She shuddered, a look of panic on her face. "We need to call the cops. This douchebag could still be watching you."

Head bobbing in agreement, Katie whispered, "You're right. How do we even know that he's gone?"

They both shook at that thought and, working together, gathered the dogs and left for the garage apartment.

"Well, that settles it," Darby said, once they were safely inside her haven. "I was debating whether to stay here or see the folks for Christmas. After tonight, there is no way I'm leaving you here by yourself."

"Oh, no, you don't!! Your parents would skin me alive if I let you back out of seeing them," Katie chastised. "They live for the interrogations. The questions about your love life, like current boyfriends and marriage prospects, so you can, you know, 'give them grandchildren before they're dead.'" She winked and raised her brows. "You aren't getting any younger, you know."

Darby stuck out her tongue.

After double-checking the lock, they walked to the living room and took a seat on the couch. Darby commandeered Katie's cell phone and scrolled through the contact list, searching for Jake's number. "So, what am I to do? Leave you to fend for yourself against a psycho? What kind of friend would I be?"

"A smart one." Katie teased. "Anyway, you're right about one thing. There could very well be someone nearby, watching me."

"But you were in the house tonight with Jake, right? So, I wonder how they got in with you both there?"

"Maybe they broke in earlier. When Jake and I returned, we had dinner and then drinks in the living room. Neither of us was upstairs."

"Why is that, Kates?" Darby grinned. "Didn't want the hot tamale too close to the bedsheets?"

Katie wrinkled her nose. "Hilarious. The truth? I am a little nervous. This wacko intruder may very well be hiding somewhere in my house."

She replayed those last words in her mind, conscious that there was another feeling coursing through her veins —something pulling at her, something other than fear.

Katie Callahan, the reigning queen of human emotions, was thoroughly pissed off.

The Apostle drove home from Fredericksburg, listening to a Christian music station and lightly fingering the dainty, lavender panties lying on the passenger seat. His thoughts were erratic and disorganized, a whirling cyclone colliding with the past and present.

He had spied on her for months, binoculars in hand, a ravenous man starving for just a taste of his addiction. Night after night, he'd slink around the property and peer through her windows, just another voyeur in the woods.

Camera flashing, he took hundreds of pictures, capturing her in every light. The photos sustained him for a time. But his actions were never enough, and soon, he needed more.

He broke in on a Tuesday to avoid dealing with the dogs. His research told him that Chance and Blue accompanied Darby to work every Tuesday. It was a break in the monotony for her and an opportunity for Chance and Blue to get treats from Darby's customers.

Entry was easy, courtesy of an open back window. Her home was orderly and larger than it appeared. Once inside, he'd found himself flying higher than he ever thought possible. Something about a forbidden act was electrifying.

Her room was her sanctuary, and he took great pleasure in defiling it. After bathing in her scent, he disrobed and jumped naked onto her bed, rubbing his body over her pillows. In her dresser, he pawed through her most intimate things, coming across a pair of sexy lavender thongs. He closed his eyes, sniffed them, then crammed them into his pocket. He was disgusted by his actions but fascinated by the feelings they invoked.

Forcing himself back to the present, trying to reorganize his jumbled thoughts, he drove on. His brain had a way of evading his control, traveling down a path of memories he would just as soon ignore. Now, thirty miles from home, he twisted the volume on the radio, an attempt to immerse his mind in the music. Glancing down, he noticed that the delicate lavender panties had made their way from the passenger seat to his lap.

Are they silk or satin? Who the fuck cares?

His groin stirred as a memory teased the corners of his mind, struggling to take shape amidst his fragmented, wandering thoughts.

∼

September 2002

It was the summer of his first love, Samantha Norman; his fantasy, his dream, the itch he couldn't scratch. Every day he prayed (to the Gods and the demons and his favorite Aunt Tillie) that she would fall madly in love with him. They were meant for each other, her very essence twisting around his soul, squeezing him dry. Some days, he could barely breathe.

And so he watched her. Obsessively, compulsively, he imagined that it was him she kissed and stroked and made love to, instead of that pansy-ass boyfriend.

A dentist. Who the fuck dates a dentist?

Still, he persevered. Through his binoculars, he devoured her, knowing full well that she felt his eyes studying her, ogling her. She reveled in it.

Eventually, he summoned the courage to ask her out. And she laughed at him. Not precisely out loud, he conceded, but he could see through the mask she wore. Her sad smile, the gentle shake of her head—she was ridiculing him, a pathetic fool trapped in a fantasy love with a woman who would never be his.

How dare she molest his mind, tease him with her body, then feign innocence and piety! She was a whore and him, no whoremonger. She needed to be punished, to learn the consequences of trampling on his heart.

And he would start by taking all that she loved.

Samantha had no actual children. Her 'babies,' and the single most important thing in her life, were her cats. She had dozens of strays, a kaleidoscope of colors and breeds that she'd collected over the years. They were her life, her purpose, and she loved them all.

One bright and sunny Saturday, Samantha headed down her long driveway to get the day's mail. In one hand, she carried an outgoing parcel; the other held a six-week-old kitten, purring softly against her chest.

Several feet from her destination, she stopped, squinting at a moving mass of black fog that gathered around the mailbox door. Confused, she tiptoed closer, a hum-like vibration reverberating in her ears and growing increasingly louder. Her heart flipped as she caught sight of the large-eyed insects with their wildly beating wings, desperately feeding on... something.

Hesitantly, she walked around to the open door, peeked inside, and covered her mouth. Hundreds of flies blanketed the form of a kitten, its eyes wide and mouth yawning, silently communicating its last screams. A gray tail dangled perversely from the door, limp and matted with blood. There was a cavernous incision in the animal's belly, its abdominal organs providing fodder for a hardy maggot infestation. The smell was intolerable, the sight abhorrent. Samantha vomited on the asphalt driveway.

A few days later, still mourning her beloved 'Ranger,' Samantha opened the front door to discover her tabby cat, Emma, beaten, skinned, and lying stiffly on her

"Welcome" mat. On the low-lying limb of a nearby maple tree, the missing hide waved like a ghoulish flag.

This time, she notified the authorities. The police completed a thorough search of the grounds and the home but found nothing. After taking a full report, they strongly suggested that she keep the animals inside until they caught the culprit. In the meantime, they recommended a security camera and a change of locks, just to be safe.

They didn't have to tell her twice.

She ordered a state-of-the-art security system and contacted a locksmith. She also purchased motion detecting floodlights, an additional layer of protection until they installed her security system. She even thought about buying a dog.

None of it mattered, though, for he would not be deterred. Instead, he would use more caution for his next teaching. He had an especially delicious lesson in mind, one that would both sanctify and purge her soul.

It only required a spark.

Fire had always fascinated him. He loved watching it snake and spiral as it licked its way toward the heavens, a liberated spirit taking its final journey. Its unsullied flames captured the whispered promise of baptism and renewal. Samantha, soiled and impure, needed to know of those cleansing flames.

And so, reverently, humbly, he incinerated her garage. But he wasn't done yet.

The final lesson took place on a chilly Thursday evening. She had just returned from a three-day job convention; the only thing on her mind a quick meal, a glass of Chianti, and a hot bath. Wearily, she climbed the stairs to her bedroom and flicked on the light. In the shimmering glow of a 40-watt bulb, a very young, very shirtless man/boy stood over her bed. She froze, momentarily stunned, until recognition burst through her befuddled mind.

Then, panic.

She knew this kid from her church. After services, he would follow her around like a lost puppy, trying to engage her in conversation. He even asked her out once, though she was several years his senior. He was one of those people you instantly feared but couldn't lay a finger on why. She tried to back up, but before her feet got the memo to move, he pounced.

"Noooo!"

It happened in a blink, a nanosecond. There was no time to strategize, to defend. He was fast, strong, and armed with the longest, sharpest knife she'd ever seen. He grabbed her, and she continued to howl, her voice turning raw. Disgusted, he tossed her on the bed like a rag doll, then punched her square in the face. She watched, horrified, as her blood sailed across the room. The blow was so powerful, her ears hummed, and her teeth rattled.

Enunciating each word between gritted teeth, spittle flying in all directions, he ground out, "Shut... the fuck... up!"

Straddling her on the bed, he ran the steel blade up her cheek, stopping just below her eye. Samantha held her breath, terrified that the rise of her chest would cause the tip of the knife to pierce her eye.

Whistling, the man/boy tied a scarf around her mouth, then secured all four of her limbs to the bed frame. Once immobilized, he savagely cut off her clothes, sending fabric and buttons flying. Samantha was sobbing so hard she feared she would vomit and choke on it. When he finally stood, only one article of clothing remained on her body, unscathed.

He stared at the material laying softly at her

womanhood. The lacy, lavender panties provided little coverage to her genitalia. He removed them carefully, untying and then retying her leg bonds, occasionally slapping her bucking limbs. Once removed, he gently placed the panties on the nightstand. Desire coursed through him, his racing heart marking time to his throbbing erection.

He had never been so turned on.

Samantha was nearing hysteria. Her eyes darted around the room, a trapped animal without an exit. Writhing, twisting, kicking, she fought to escape her restraints. Her screams were nothing more than muted, buffered moans. As she watched, blind with fear, he undressed and sat astride her hips.

He concentrated on her face, looking for a sign, some 'thing' reflected in her eyes, but unsure of what that would be. For a split second, he felt a morsel of regret—not for what he was about to do, but because he could only do it once.

The assault had all the savagery of a predator tearing into its prey. Samantha's pain was an aphrodisiac to him. Her mind continued to whirl, to search for options, even as he violated her in every way imaginable. She kicked, jerked, and willed herself to urinate on the bed, hoping that it would disgust him. When those strategies failed, she bent her legs as far as the restraints allowed and squeezed her thighs together.

It only excited him further.

Out of ideas, her eyes found his, hoping to glimpse compassion or mercy. Instead, his dark gaze revealed a hollow, black vacuum, free of humanity. The only image reflected in those stony eyes was her beaten, horrified face.

Time crawled, the minutes an eternity. He pounded into her ruthlessly, grunting like a pig in rut. He stank of sweat and booze and sex, his hot breath and wet tongue bathing her neck. Searing pain, excruciating in its intensity, ripped through her most intimate places. Each penetration, each brutal thrust, brought with it fresh blood and shredded skin.

Her suffering only empowered him.

It would be hours before he was finally sated. Samantha lay unmoving, her soul crushed, her mind shattered. Near catatonia, her bruised and bloody body small against the queen-sized bed, she began to hum. It was a simple lullaby, one her mother used to sing to her:

"Too-ra-loo-ra-loo-ral,

Too-ra-loo-ra-li,

Too-ra-loo-ra-loo-ral,

Hush now, don't you cry..."

Rocking softly within the confines of the binds that held her limbs, a single tear slid down her face. Her mortality danced before her eyes, mocking her.

He rolled off the bed, interrupting her stupor. Lazily, he circled to her side and removed the scarf from her mouth. A soft smile touched the corners of his lips as he bent down and, reverently, kissed her forehead. Dazed, she watched him, felt the smooth satin of the scarf as it wrapped around her neck. By the time her sluggish mind registered his intent, his knee was on her chest, and the noose was tightening.

It was too late.

Frantic, she yanked hard against her restraints, freeing her right hand. Jubilant, if only for an instant, she clawed at the knot that was crushing her windpipe. Tears blurred her vision, and her lungs spasmed. She tried raking his face, gouging his eyes, pummeling his back.

A twinkle in his eye, tasting his omnipotence, he toyed

with her by alleviating the pressure. She coughed and took a ragged breath, daring to hope.

He squeezed harder, enjoying the game several times.

Eventually, regretfully, playtime was over. Samantha's eyes bulged, and her face contorted, her porcelain skin turning a deep shade of blue. Exhaustion and defeat arrived on the heels of acceptance. Physically spent and emotionally bankrupt, her arm fell to her side as she succumbed to the darkness.

Later that evening, he would torch the home that contained the body of Samantha Norman. She was just thirty-seven years old, and he, a child shy of his seventeenth birthday. It would mark the second time in his brief life that he had killed another human being.

And it would herald the night that the boy ceased to exist... and the Apostle was born.

CHAPTER ELEVEN

J ake was almost back to his home in Alexandria when he got the call from Darby. He made an illegal U-turn on I-95, and, heart in his throat, headed back to Katie's house. Darby sounded terrified. After telling them to sit tight, he notified the local P.D. and asked them to meet him there.

Fifteen minutes from Fredericksburg, his phone rang again.

"Devereaux."

"Hey, Jake. Sully here. I just wanted to give you a heads up about a call I received from Frank Blake over at the Maryland State Police. The Park Police reached out, told him about a body found in Shenandoah National Park. There is an investigative team up there now. It looks like the victim was killed sometime within the last twenty-four to forty-eight hours. The guy wouldn't have been found for weeks, if not for a couple out looking for their missing dog."

"Ok," Jake said. "I'm guessing since you're bringing it to my attention, it's not a routine murder investigation?"

"Doesn't look like it. In fact, it's more than likely directly related to the bodies on Sugarloaf Mountain."

Perplexed, Jake asked, "How so?"

"The manner of death. Medical examiner's preliminary indicates asphyxiation via ligature. And the murder weapon? Well, let's just say I'd bet my left nut and my Granny's booties that it was rosary beads."

"Shit."

"Yeah."

Jake filled Sully in on what happened at Kate's. "I'm on my way over there now. How about you head over to the Shenandoah crime scene and talk to the M.E.?"

"You got it."

"Oh, and Sully? Can you swing by my place and check on Gus? You know how he hates to be alone." Jake sighed. "He's getting old and senile on me. I'm afraid he may get confused and turn on the stove or something."

"Not a problem." Teasingly, he added, "You know, I have no difficulties standing in for you on this one. You sound wiped. Just say the word, and my ass will be over at the Callahan residence forthwith."

Jake snickered. "Mighty generous of you. You're saying I could spend the night traipsing all over a mountain, freezing my stones off and examining a dead guy, or I can spend my evening assisting a beautiful woman in distress. Gee, what do you think, Junior?"

Sully laughed. "I think my junk is gonna get cold tonight. I'll reach out when I know more."

~

Pulling into Katie's driveway, Jake checked the surroundings. Everything seemed quiet. As he started toward the garage, he spied her coming down the stairs from the apartment. They met in the driveway, and he took her hands in his.

"Hey there," she said weakly.

Brushing a stray hair back from her face, he said, "Hey yourself. You ok?"

Shivering, she nodded. It was chilly, and she wasn't wearing a jacket.

"How 'bout you start from the beginning, sweetheart," Jake said, as they walked toward the house. "What happened after I left?"

She filled him in about the note left on the bed and the disturbed drawer. In true Callahan form, she left out any mention of the gray woman.

That'd be a hoot trying to explain, she thought miserably.

"Did you touch the note at all?" Jake asked.

She shuddered. "No, I read it from a distance, then backed out of the room and ran like the wind. It's embarrassing. I swear I'm not such a sissy about this stuff. It just spooked me that some stranger had been in my bedroom and gone through my things. Except now that I've had time to swallow it, keep it down without choking on it? I'm damned angry, Jake."

They entered the main house together, and he searched the home while Katie and Darby waited by the front door. Fifteen minutes later, after ensuring the house was secure, they joined him upstairs.

"So, what do you think?" Katie asked, standing at her bedroom doorway. She really didn't want to enter that room.

He watched her as she chewed her lip, then ran her tongue over the sensitive flesh.

Damn, but that's distracting, he thought.

Talking more to himself than to her, he muttered, "The car accident, the snake, and now, a break-in. What's the connection that we're missing? There is no such thing as coincidence, only design." His eyes pinned hers, his voice grave. "What do I think? I think you have a stalker on your hands."

Darby was nodding like a bobblehead on someone's dashboard. It would have been comical if not related to such a frightening event. "That's what I said! It has to be connected!" Whispering, she added, "I'm scared for you, Kates."

Finding the courage to enter the room, Katie joined Jake and Darby at the foot of the bed. The three of them stood side by side, quietly staring at the block lettering scratched on to a piece of yellow legal paper. Reading such an ugly message left on top of a cream-colored spread— one lovingly crocheted by her Nana—was obscene.

The air felt thick in the confines of the bedroom. The contents of the note repulsed, with no mistaking their meaning. Jake read it silently, trying to calm the storm brewing in his mind.

'Next time, I will take far more than your panties.'

"Fucking scumbag," Jake hissed. He turned to Kate and tipped her chin up. A vein on the side of his forehead bulged, and his jaw clenched. He was livid, struggling for control.

"Did you notice anything missing, love? The lingerie he spoke of, maybe?"

"Honestly? I didn't look. After I saw the note, I got out fast." Katie glanced down and realized, for the first time, that she was still wearing the skimpy pajamas she had put on after her bath. At once, she was both mortified and disappointed. Mortified that she was parading in front of him scantily dressed, and deeply disappointed that he seemed not to notice.

He opened the dresser drawers with a pen and asked

her to check for missing articles of clothing. After several moments, she realized that there was, indeed, something missing from her lingerie drawer: her brand-new, lavender panties. They took inventory of the rest of the house but, finding nothing else missing, huddled together on the first floor.

"How 'bout I run back to the apartment to fetch Chance and Blue while you guys wrap things up here? I'll let them out, too, so I may not be back for a while," Darby said, her brows doing a little jig Katie's way when Jake wasn't looking.

Katie gave her friend a warning glance. She was in no mood for Darby's matchmaking.

"Sure," Katie said wearily, "that would be great. Thanks."

When Darby left, Jake and Katie stood, unmoving, at the foot of the stairs. He was gazing at her intently, an unreadable expression on his face.

Uncomfortable with his silence, she challenged, "What? Do I have spinach in my teeth or something?"

His eyes grew wide, and he chuckled. "Spinach," he said, shaking his head as if that was the most ridiculous response he'd ever heard. Then, eyeing her up and down, he smirked.

"Nice P.J.'s."

She gulped. *Oh, God, he did notice! Be cool, Callahan.*

"You likes?" she asked, her voice sounding thin to her ears. "They're my faves. Comfy."

"Yeah," he said dryly, "I likes. But unless you want a couple of patrol officers from the Fredericksburg P.D. to 'likes' too, I suggest you put on a robe."

"Oh, crap!" she said, sprinting towards her room. "I didn't realize you called them already! Be back in a sec."

He watched her run up the stairs to the bedroom, her

frilly pants riding up her cute backside with each step she took. He wished she would climb a little slower—the view was amazing.

With a devilish grin, he stepped outside to wait for the patrol car.

~

The minute the police car pulled up to the house and its occupant came into view, Jake swore. Behind the wheel was a paunchy, middle-aged man with a doughy complexion and a perpetual scowl.

Jake snorted, disgusted.

Patrolman Lance Jeffries pulled his belly from beneath the steering wheel, hoisted his body out of the cruiser, and scanned the property. He spied Jake and met him halfway across the yard.

"Hello again, Officer Jeffries," Jake said, offering him a hand. "Sorry to pull you back here this evening."

Jeffries grasped the outstretched hand limply and tucked his hat under his arm.

"Let me guess," Jeffries began, "dispatch had the nature of the call all wrong. You found the lizard?" When Jake squinted his eyes at him, he quickly corrected, "Snake, I meant. You found the snake."

"No, Jeffries, we didn't find the snake. Pretty sure that's your job." His expression darkened. "There was a break-in here, sometime in the last twelve hours. The perpetrator left a message on Miss Callahan's bed. We need to consider the likelihood that this break-in, and the incident with the snake, are related."

Jeffries rubbed his chin. His five-o'clock shadow had morphed into a soul patch. "Yeah, I can see that. But why? Lover's dispute or something?"

Jake tensed. "Ms. Callahan is single. It could be an obsession, an angry student, maybe even a revenge thing. Whatever the case, someone is seriously pissed. You have anyone on-call that can come out to get some prints? We may be able to pull some latents off the note. And we'll need pictures."

Jeffries dug into his shirt pocket and pulled out a cigarette. "Really? You want prints on this? It seems to me, we take a few pictures and then question the victim on the men, or women if that's how she rolls, in her life. You know that's how this shit usually goes." The corners of his mouth turned up, showing a row of tobacco-stained teeth peeking out from beneath severely chapped lips.

Jake leaned into the cop's face, eyes narrowing. When he spoke, a tic bounced off the side of his jaw. "If I ask for a detective to process a scene, that means there's been a crime to be processed. Somebody ran this lady off the road, put a venomous snake in her mailbox, and now has graduated to breaking and entering. The perp also left a threatening letter in her bedroom and helped himself to a God-damned pair of panties. I'm willing to bet we are looking at the same fucker."

Jeffries' demeanor never wavered. Flat, impassive, bored.

It was seriously pissing Jake off.

"So, in answer to your question, yeah, I want prints on this." As the patrolman turned to leave, Jake hissed, "Oh, and Jeffries? I better not see your fucking butts all over my crime scene."

The cop returned to his police car, mumbling something about waking up the duty dicks for a shit ass call. Jake jogged back to the house and met Katie, now wearing sweatpants and a long-sleeved T-shirt, at the door.

"You see who caught the call?" Jake asked her. "None

other than our personal hero, Lance Jeffries." When Katie made a face, he added, "It's ok. I told him to kick it down to the duty detectives. That means we can process the house as a crime scene, so Jeffries will have little to do with the investigation. Meanwhile, I think it would be wise if you and Darby stayed somewhere else. You're not safe here." When Katie objected, he held up his hand.

"It's just for a little while until we can get a handle on it. The bottom line is that this asshole has a serious hard-on for you. Figuratively, and perhaps, literally."

Katie frowned and crossed her arms. Her shoulders squared, and she lifted her chin. Suddenly, she seemed taller.

Jake cringed. *Shit, I've seen that posture before—right after I called her dog a mutt.*

"Look, I appreciate your concern. Truly, I do. But I will not let this idiot run me out of my own damn house. I admit that, at first, he unnerved me. Now, I'm just mad as hell."

Irritated, Jake's hands flew in the air. "Jesus Christ, Callahan, do you even hear yourself? What part of 'you're not safe here' don't you understand?"

She shook back her hair, defiance in her voice. "I have my dogs, and Darby is right next door. I'm not afraid of this asshole."

Jake exhaled through pursed lips, trying to quash his temper. "Well, you damned well should be afraid! I have no fucking clue what this guy is capable of doing. Do you understand that you're playing Russian roulette with a loaded gun?" His teeth clamped hard together, threatening to turn his molars to dust. "Be smart, Kate. We need to err on the side of caution and—" She cut him off before he finished his thought.

"Not going to happen. Look, Jake, I'm not an idiot. I've

known pricks like this before. Everything that he's done has been done covertly, in shadows. Whoever he is, he's a flippin' coward. I seriously doubt this guy has the onions to instigate a face-to-face meeting."

There was a heavy silence, an awkward pause, while Jake tried to control his reaction. When he spoke, he fought to choose his words carefully, struggling to keep the sarcasm out of his response.

He failed miserably.

"Thank you for your crackerjack analysis, Miss Callahan. As a man with over ten years of law enforcement experience, I'm so glad that you've cleared that up for me. Good to know that we can add 'Behavioral Specialist' to your impressive resume."

Katie huffed, annoyed.

Ignoring her, he paced the walkway in front of the door, hands on his hips. "And here I foolishly thought, because there were at least two attempts to cause you harm, we were looking for a focused and determined perpetrator." The more he spoke, the angrier he grew. His hands fisted, and his face turned a deep shade of red. He was furious, unreasonably so, and he did not understand why. "It's such a relief to hear that, in your expert opinion, this lunatic, this fuckstick, won't have the balls to come calling on you!"

Katie turned and stormed into the house, Jake fast on her heels. She was fuming and, if honest, a little hurt. His sharp ridicule of her opinion stung more than she cared to admit. They argued back and forth, him about the stupidity of her staying, her countering that she could take care of herself. It was a passionate, steamy quarrel that they knew neither would win. In the end, he raised a white flag.

"Ok, fine." Rubbing his neck in frustration, he couldn't

resist one last dig. "Despite the genuine danger, I can see that you are determined to stay here."

"Ya think?" Truce or not, she was still mad. "It's my call, Jake. Not yours, not the FBI's. Mine. You're not my father, not my brother, not even my…" She stopped, mid-sentence.

"Your what?" he whispered. "Boyfriend? Lover? No, I'm not any of those, but give me time. I'm workin' on it." He delivered a classic Devereaux wink.

Her eyebrows raised, incredulous. His arrogance was showing, and she wasn't a fan.

Is he joking? What makes him think I'm even interested? Just because I flirt shamelessly, hang on his every word, and fantasize about jumping his bones whenever he gives me that damned wink? That doesn't necessarily mean I'm interested.

She stewed for a second. *Ok, I'm interested… but I'll be damned if I give him the satisfaction of knowing that!*

"In your dreams, G-Man. The men I date treat me as an equal, an independent partner. Not as some damsel that needs rescuing."

Jake eyed her as she stood there, all puffed up and pissed off. Her eyes shone greener and brighter than the finest emerald. Her hair looked alive, a gorgeous river of red cascading down her back. Heat colored her cheeks, giving rise to a faint blush. She was stubborn and reckless and, perhaps, the most beautiful woman he'd ever known.

"Let's make a deal, Red," he said, attempting to placate her. "What if I stay with you, on the couch, until I can get a lead on this dirtbag? That way, you get to stay here without me hassling you, and I get to feel better knowing that you're safe."

She tilted her head to the side, mulling over the offer, eyes narrowed suspiciously.

"Not that you need anyone to protect you, of course,"

he said, ever the wise guy. "Or that you couldn't handle things yourself. It's just strength in numbers and all that. Wouldn't you agree?" With a dazzling smile, he added, "Slugger?"

Despite herself, she chuckled. "Ok, fine, but just for tonight. You can stay down here in the guest room. Tomorrow, if we don't know more, you can bunk at Darby's while she is at her parents' house." Katie needed distance—she couldn't guarantee she wouldn't throw herself at him if he stayed more than one night.

Harlot.

"Agreed." He put his hand out, and she grasped it, the handshake sealing the deal. They held hands for much longer than what was customary, each of them unwilling to be the first to ruin the moment and break contact. Jake's cell phone shattered the spell.

"What's up, Sully?" he asked, walking back outside.

"Latest update on the body, boss. I'm wrapping things up with the M.E., but it looks like the vic, a male in his mid-thirties, was killed elsewhere and dumped a few miles from Skyline Drive. The rosary beads found with him are large, bigger than any I've seen, and that's coming from a guy who went to Catholic school. Custom made, maybe?" He took a breath, then said, "They were wrapped around his damned hands, Jake, as if he were praying. Ligature marks on his throat suggest those beads were around his neck at some point, although the M.E. isn't committing to C.O.D. yet." Sully paused, and Jake waited patiently, knowing there was more information coming.

There was always more.

"After we processed the front of the vic, we flipped him to check his posterior. There were deep lacerations, lash-type marks all over his back. According to the coroner, someone beat him with a whip or belt; not deep enough to kill him, mind you, but deep enough to add to his pain and suffering. Someone tortured the poor bastard, probably for days."

"Damn. Any luck with the I.D.?"

"We found a wallet near the body. Hard to make a positive I.D. from his face, but the physical description on the driver's license seems to be a match." Sully read the information on the license, and Jake's blood ran cold. After confirming the name once again, Jake filled his partner in on what was going on at Katie's.

"We need to figure out how this all relates to her. I feel like we are missing a colossal piece of this puzzle." Glancing toward the house, he added, "Keep on top of it. I'll call you in the morning."

He walked back inside and headed to the kitchen. Katie stood at the stove, the piercing tones of a whistling teakettle fading as she turned off the flame.

"Can I get you something? Tea or coffee? I'm afraid I only have instant, though. Another thing on my grocery list," she said with a pout.

"No, I'm good. Listen, Kate, that was Sully on the phone." He stopped for a moment, trying to find the easiest way to break the news to her. "They found another body, this time in Shenandoah National Park." He hesitated, gaging her reaction. "The victim's been dead for at least a few days. Sully and the Medical Examiner are trying to pin down the time of death."

"Ohhh-kay. So what's the catch? A body only a few days old doesn't require a forensic anthropologist. Does this have something to do with the bones on the mountain?"

Jake cleared his throat. "It might. They are processing the scene as we speak. The um, the deceased is a male, mid-thirties." He faltered. "Dark-skinned."

Katie's stomach dropped, and she prayed that she was wrong.

She knew she was right.

"They found him holding a set of rosary beads, sweetheart. And his physical descriptors match the identifiers on his driver's license. Guy's name is Bailey. Aman Bailey."

CHAPTER TWELVE

"Then when lust hath conceived, it bringeth forth sin: and sin, when it is finished, bringeth forth death." James 1:15.

Bright sunlight shone through Katie's bedroom window, and she stirred.

Please, don't let it be morning, please don't let it be morning. She cracked open an eyelid and groaned.

Dammit. It's morning.

Stretching, she felt her muscles lengthen and her bones pop. Her waking mind was a crazy quilt, a dizzying collage of memories and events that bled together. The scientist in her believed in facts, not conjecture. Unfortunately, guesswork and speculation were the only weapons in her arsenal at the moment. Someone had targeted her, but who? What did they wish to accomplish? A possibility jumped at her, and she ran with it.

What if I dreamed it all? Could the memories be false ones, the result of a severe injury? Yes, a concussion would explain everything.

Some creep ran me into a ditch, and I bumped my head. There is no bogeyman, no crazed maniac, no stalker.

She paused for a moment, the impact of her thoughts finally hitting home. If that were true, if it was just an illusion or a head injury, then Jake was a mirage as well. She rose and slowly shuffled to the bedroom window, afraid of what she'd see.

Please be real!

Jake's suburban sat as she remembered, an imposing presence in the driveway. Happiness and dread both jockeyed for position as she acknowledged the implications. If these events were not a nightmare, a delusion, or the result of a concussed brain, then someone was watching her, stalking her. And that sweet man who had helped her was gone—not on vacation, not playing hooky, not home sick with the flu.

Aman Bailey was dead.

She flopped down heavily on the bed, exhausted. The crime scene technicians processed her home until the wee hours of the morning. Some dusted for fingerprints, asked questions, and examined doors and windows for points of entry. Others collected trace and other evidentiary materials and took hundreds of photographs. Katie understood that this unit was going above and beyond what was routine for a usual breaking and entering crime. She suspected it was because of Jake's influence as an FBI Agent and the discovery of Aman's body.

As Jake had mentioned several times, he was not a big believer in coincidence. Aman was connected to her, albeit remotely, and he was dead. Rosary beads played a role in his death, and she was working on a case involving the rosary. In fact, from the first day she'd joined this investigation, someone had run her off the road, left a nasty surprise in her mailbox, and burglarized her home.

Call me crazy, but I'm beginning to feel unloved.

Deciding she needed a diversion, she pulled her hair into a ponytail, threw on some sweatpants and a tee-shirt, and grabbed her Nikes.

I'll do five miles. Nothing distracts the mind like leg cramps and swamp ass.

Creeping down the hallway, not wanting to disturb Jake in the guest room, she let Chance and Blue out the back door. After starting a pot of coffee, she did some stretching and called the dogs back inside for breakfast.

Giving them each a scratch behind the ears, she said, "Sorry, guys, but I have to go solo today. This will be a serious run, and I'm afraid you two fleabags won't be able to keep up." Ignoring her, they greedily inhaled their kibble. "I can see how broken up you are," she deadpanned. "Next time, though. Promise." She snagged a sweatshirt off the back of a chair, donned her Ravens football cap, and went out the front door.

Halfway down the drive, she heard a voice boom from inside the house.

"Just where the hell do you think you're going?"

Katie turned. Jake was leaning lazily against the doorjamb, bare-chested and in faded jeans. His eyes were bright, his hair tousled from sleep. As she stared at him, half-naked, abs ripped, she could think of only one word.

Damn!

Ok, two words. *Yum!*

"Beg your pardon?" she said, walking towards him.

"I said, just where the hell do you think you're going? There could be a psycho stalking you. You can't just up and go for a run without telling me first."

She stopped, her eyes narrowing as she processed what he'd just said.

She can't go for a run? Without telling him first?

"For your information, Agent Devereaux," she spat, incensed but trying not to sound like a shrew, "I am an American woman. An adult citizen, one without a criminal history or mental deficits. As such, I can go anywhere I damn please." Nose in the air, she added haughtily, "And since we're just getting to know each other, I'll let you in on a little secret. Want to know the fastest way to get me to do something?"

He shrugged.

Eyeing him up and down, she whispered, "Tell me I can't."

Jake smirked from the doorway and raised his hands. "Ok, lady. You win. But if you're going for a run, I'm coming with you. Give me two minutes to change and get my sneakers."

Impatiently, she tapped her foot as he ran back inside. His audacity annoyed her. Several moments later, her irritation changed to unease.

No, not unease. Fear.

A familiar tingle marched down the back of her head, found its way to her shoulder blades, then coiled like a serpent in the pit of her belly. Dozens of emotions, all profoundly negative, peppered her senses—hate, disgust, and pure, unrelenting evil.

Oh, God, she thought, her stomach in knots. *He's here.*

She did a slow 360 degrees turn, scanning both the road in front of the house and the trees along the property line. Distantly, she heard the soft click of a lock as Jake secured the front door. He jogged toward her, the slap of his sneakers bouncing off the smooth pavement. She wanted to scream at him, yell out a warning. But what would she say? That she *felt* her stalker? That her Spidey sense had gone ape shit?

She scurried back up the lane toward Jake, her mind

racing. Seconds later, an earsplitting crack echoed off the trees. It was a blast so loud, so fierce, that her heart skipped a beat, and her teeth clacked together. Something impossibly fast whizzed by her left ear, lifting a strand of her hair in its wake.

Dear God, what the…

Time ceased to exist. It didn't grind slowly to a halt or wind delicately to a stop, as they claimed in the movies. It merely… slammed shut.

"Get down!" Jake yelled, zigging and zagging towards her. "A shooter! Six O'clock! Get down! Get on the ground!" He dove forward and, with what seemed like a superhuman leap, tackled her. She grunted as their bodies slammed hard on the turf beside the driveway, the breath hissing out of her lungs. Ten feet away, the bark from a poplar tree cracked and splintered as another burst surrounded them. Jake's body covered hers, his hands shielding her head.

Curled in a fetal position, palms over her ears, Katie was too terrified to move. She could feel his heart reverberating against her back, his face nestled into her neck. A volley of thunderous rounds rained around them, punching into the ground, the earth puffing up like smoke with every strike.

When several moments passed without fire, Jake rolled to the side, drew his Glock from his belly-band holster, and looked around.

"Are you hit?" he whispered, his lips at her ear.

She shook her head.

"Ok. On the count of three," he instructed, still in a whisper, "I want you to run, as fast as you can, to the house."

His gut clenched at seeing the fright in her beautiful eyes, and he vowed to rip apart the man responsible for putting it there. Voice low, he coached, "I want you to run like the wind, Callahan. Run like a fat man running towards an all you can eat buffet." Adjusting the cap on top of her head, he winked, "Run like Forrest, Kate."

Whispering back, throat dry and voice unsteady, she said, "What about you?"

"I'll be right behind you. Don't worry about me." He smirked. "I'm the FBI guy, remember? Bulletproof."

He flipped to his stomach, knees slightly bent, and said, "Ready? One, two… three! Go, go, go!"

Katie jumped up and ran. Her legs felt heavy, as though she were moving through mud. Awkwardly, she propelled forward, confident she'd either fall flat on her face or catch a bullet in the back.

Just when she feared she could no longer stand, Jake magically appeared at her side. Supporting most of her weight, they ran toward the house in a serpentine pattern of dodging and evading. Katie reached the front door ahead of Jake, turned the knob, and felt resistance.

Shit, shit, shit!

It was locked. The key sat securely, mockingly, in a corner pocket on Jake's sneakers. Another crack sounded, this time followed by the shattering of glass as the bay window in the guest room imploded.

"Fuck!" Jake bellowed. He pulled the key from his shoe, unlocked the door, and they spilled into the foyer. Breathing hard, legs still weak, Katie ran in a crouch to the kitchen. Both Chance and Blue lay under the dinette, unharmed but frightened. Remaining low, unsure if the shooter could see them, she made her way back to the living room sofa and sat down. Adrenaline spent, she covered her face with her hands, hiding the tears as they fell.

Jake kneeled beside her. "Are you hurt?" When she

shook her head, he said, "Aww, honey, don't cry. Please?" Heart still racing, he raked his hand through his hair. "Fucker is a piss-poor shot, thankfully." When she continued to sob quietly, he took her hands away from her face, tucking them both inside his. "Kate, please, you're killing me."

She looked up at that, saw the desperation in his eyes, and softly smiled. "Killing you? I don't think so. If flying bullets didn't take you down, I doubt a blubbering woman's tears could do it."

He brought her hand to his lips and kissed her knuckles. "You aren't just any blubbering woman, Katherine Callahan."

He rose, the words he spoke spurring him to action. No, she wasn't just any woman. She was unique and beautiful and important to him. He would find the pig who was attacking her and take him down if it killed him. Double-checking his Glock, he headed for the front door. "Call the cops. I'm going to look around outside. Lock this door and do not answer for anyone except me, got it? Oh, and for Christ's sake, stay away from the windows."

She nodded, followed him to the door, and dutifully locked it after him. The gray lady appeared as he exited, taking a seat by the window, and Katie ignored her. Now was not the time to play 'Ghost Whisperer.'

Pacing, she chewed on a nail, occasionally peeking out of a window despite Jake's warning. After ten minutes, she was sure she'd walked a hole through the floor and chewed her finger to a stump.

What the hell is taking so long?

Another five minutes passed. Just when panic reared its ugly head, there was a tap on the door, followed by a smooth, deep voice.

"It's me." Two words. Words that were so simple yet

spoke volumes. Two words that alluded to a familiarity she wasn't sure she would ever have with another man.

It's me.

"Cops on the way?" he asked when he entered the house. At her nod, he continued. "Well, I found nothing, no tracks that I can see. Rocks surround most of the tree line, so the bastard's feet may have never touched the ground. Doesn't mean he isn't still out there, though." Walking to the kitchen, he grabbed a coffee cup. "We need to find this asshole. I'm going to call my brother, Jed, to have him dig into Aman Bailey's background. Could be something there." He stared at her, deep in thought. "This guy has it bad for you, but my gut tells me he wasn't trying to kill you. At least, not today."

He poured his coffee, then rubbed his brow. "We were wide open out there. Helen Keller could have made that shot. It's almost as though he was deliberately trying to miss us and that, believe it or not, is not as easy as it seems." He took a sip from his cup. "This guy knows guns. Military maybe? Cop?"

She shrugged. "Got me. All I know is that I thought that was it, lights out. It terrified me, thinking about my dogs, my family. How the hell would they take another death?" She looked at him, her eyes inspecting every angle of his face. "You saved my bacon out there. One of those bullets was close enough to damn near part my hair. If it wasn't for your quick thinking..." She stopped and looked down at her hands, hands that shook and trembled despite her efforts to calm them.

He squeezed her shoulder. "It's over now. Thank Jesus that Darby left so early for her folk's house. I think a few rounds hit the apartment." They walked back to the living room, dogs at their heels. "I have to make some calls. Besides the locals, I want my guys here. Those bullets came from a high-powered rifle, probably an AR-15. A weapon like that has a long arm, so stay away from the doors and windows." He hesitated, a gleam in his eyes. "Of course, I'm just offering suggestions, Ma'am. I'm not telling you what to do, because I understand that you are a law-abiding American with no criminal history. A free woman, legally an adult who boldly paves her own road."

Katie frowned, unamused.

He arched a brow, and his mouth curved upwards. "But just this once, in the interest of my sanity, can you keep your head down until we make sure this guy is gone?"

She rolled her eyes. "Anyone ever tell you you're a wiseass? Anyway, don't give it another thought. I have no intention of becoming a moving target, like a duck in one of those penny arcade games. I will stay put, Agent Devereaux, until told to do otherwise." She ended with a mock salute, then plopped back down on the couch.

"That's my girl," Jake said, smiling.

The gray-haired lady, present for the last few moments, nodded her head in approval, then vanished.

After Jake contacted his office, asking for agents, he called Sully.

"Jesus, Jake," Sully said. "What the hell is happening here?"

"Damned if I know. I think we can safely conclude a few things, though."

"I'm all ears, boss. You have a theory?"

"Not so much a theory as a summary," Jake explained. "We know that someone is targeting this girl—ran her off the road, left a three-foot copperhead in her mailbox, broke into her home. Now, the fucker is taking shots at her.

Whoever he is, he's escalating." Jake paused, his expression darkening. "Does this shit have anything to do with the bones we found? If it does, is the rosary a calling card? And what's his end game? I have no clue yet, but we need to shut this scumbag down. Like yesterday."

Before they ended the call, Sully promised to be over as soon as he checked on Gus and stopped by the office. The formation of the Task Force was nearly complete, but they still needed to sweet-talk someone in Quantico into giving up office space to use as a base of operations. Sully was also working on developing a contact list of supervisors for outside agencies. As liaison for the Task Force, his job was to keep the various department heads informed of any progress. Since several agencies were lending their officers, Jake believed their supervisors had a right to be apprised during the investigation.

In addition to the Rangers and the surrounding FBI field offices, the Park Police assigned a man to the case. The current rumor from the law enforcement grapevine was that Katie's friend, Patrick, discovered she was a target and called in a few favors. The last chore on Sully's list was to check the National Missing and Unidentified Persons System, or NamUS, hoping someone had reported their victims as missing. Otherwise, they may never know the identities of the bodies found on Sugarloaf.

Jake walked back to the living room and found Katie sitting cross-legged on the floor with Chance and Blue. With a groan, he sat down next to her.

"Not as agile as I used to be," he said good-naturedly. "Ok, so here's the plan. I think we need to get more aggressive in our investigation. For starters, we need a search dog."

Katie lifted a brow and nodded her head toward Blue.

Jake frowned. "No, I don't think so. Blue has an impressive track record, and under any other circumstances, we may have taken advantage of that. But using him would mean bringing you, his handler, out in the open. I'd rather not put you further in this guy's crosshairs. The locals have a K-9 tracker with a decent record. And Sully will be here soon with some crime techs and agents. I think we stand an excellent chance of collecting some useful evidence."

Katie nodded in agreement.

"In the meantime, I need a lead on who you think is targeting you: enemies, jealous friends, ex-lovers? Anyone in your life angry with you or who gives you a bad vibe?"

Katie just stared at him. An enemy? A person angry enough to kill her? Could she have someone who loathed her that much that they wanted to see her dead?

"Honestly, no one comes to mind. I get along famously with my co-workers at George Mason, and I've no issues with anyone at the Smithsonian. Socially? The only person I see regularly is Darby. And you."

Jake hesitated. "What about this Park Police guy? The one sending an officer to our Task Force? What is he to you?" He raised a brow, but there was something else there. It wasn't concern or curiosity. It felt more antagonistic, suspicious.

"Pat? He's an old friend. I met him years ago when I was just starting with A.A.R.F." At his skeptical glance, she added, "It isn't like that, Jake. At all. He is happily married and old enough to be my father." Under her breath, she mumbled, "Jealous much?"

Jake heard her but feigned ignorance. "Ok, so let's start

with old boyfriends then. How did things end? Any history of abuse there?"

How awkward, talking to Jake about her romantic history. Over the last few years, her dating life amounted to just dalliances, nothing serious. Then she met Kyle Walker and was introduced to her least favorite term regarding relationships: 'it's complicated.'

She hated those words. They were words people used to excuse an unhealthy partnership. Her history with Kyle was that and much more: unhealthy, tense, controlling. How much could she share without divulging the actual reasons he left her? Kyle wanted a lackey, not a woman who could think for herself. He had trouble dealing with her career as an anthropologist and was envious of her success with her search dogs. Her independence and intelligence threatened him, causing him to belittle her ideas and discredit her accomplishments. But the biggest issue between them was that Kyle refused to accept her psychic abilities.

"My last relationship lasted about five months," she began. "I met Kyle Walker at the University. The college hired him to work in the I.T. department as tech support. A whiz with computers and a genius at more programs than I could count, he did freelance work and accepted their contract." She rubbed her forehead, the memories bittersweet. "When we first started dating, it was magical. He was cute, funny, adventurous. He had no family and very few friends, so I became the center of his universe. It was all very flattering, really. Then, about three months into the relationship, he changed. It was subtle at first, but eventually, he became overbearing and possessive. Over-the-top, bat-shit crazy possessive, and I was suffocating." Katie looked down at her hands, reluctant to share such a personal and painful period in her life. "The Kyle I knew changed into a bitter and cynical man, obsessed that I would leave him."

She rose and began to pace. "His paranoia grew wings, and things went from bad to worse. He believed every man I met wanted to bed me, even accused me of sleeping with the head of my department, a sixty-five-year-old grandfather of eight." She tipped her head, lost in the memories. "When Kyle begged me to quit my job at George Mason, I refused. In retaliation, he sabotaged crucial data related to a dig commissioned by the Smithsonian. He trashed my computer and destroyed all of my notes."

Jake walked to the fridge, took out two bottles of water, and handed her one. "Wow. I'd say that qualifies as a shitty relationship. Bet he was chock full of excuses to explain his behavior, too."

She nodded. "You're familiar with the type, I see. Oh, yes, Kyle was full of excuses. Said he was crazy in love with me, that the thought of another man lusting after me made him nuts. I couldn't live with that kind of insanity, you know? But he begged and groveled and promised he would change. Fool that I was, I believed him."

Jake sipped his water and patiently waited for her to continue. When she didn't, he prodded.

"Ok, so what happened? How did it end?"

The last day Katie saw Kyle was the day she told him everything. He had noticed, for the umpteenth time, that she often stared off into space, seemingly at nothing. When he questioned her on this, the final day, she laid it all out. She completely, naively, trusted that love would conquer all.

Katie explained her Empath ability, her gift of seeing the dead, even confessed that it wasn't an empty wall she'd been staring at but her deceased grandfather. She left nothing out, and in the end, he'd lost it. He called her unstable, told her she was hallucinating, and needed help. Then he ran, literally ran, out the door, and she'd never heard from him again. That was five months ago, July 28th, to be exact.

But she couldn't reveal all those details to Jake.

"It was his idea, I suppose. We got into a disagreement about truth and trust in a relationship. I believed in truth. Him, not so much. So he left. No note, no goodbyes. I reached out several times, but he ignored me." She sighed. "It's for the best. I grew weary of his need for constant reassurance."

Jake snorted. "What an asshole."

Katie's eyes widened, surprised by his reaction.

"Seriously, no offense," Jake explained, "but you were dating an asshole. Anyone who would let you go…" He let the rest of his thought dangle, its implication enough.

She smiled, eyes twinkling, and grabbed his hand. They sat there, holding hands for a moment. Then, squeezing his fingers, she joked, "You always shoot from the hip, don't you, Agent Devereaux?"

"Just call 'em as I see 'em, Ma'am." When she let go of his hand, he felt naked. Cold.

She took a sip of water and continued. "There was no animosity, though. He just skedaddled. He didn't even have the decency to tell the University he was leaving." Hesitating, she said, "You mentioned that I should include anyone who gave me a bad vibe." When he nodded, she said, "There is someone. A person I met, just recently, who makes my skin crawl."

Puzzled, Jake looked at her. "Who?"

Rubbing her arms, she shuddered. "That guy at the lab? The one you put on the case? Now, *that* guy gives me the heebie-jeebies."

Tucker Simon.

∽

December 21st, Fredericksburg, VA

The Apostle finished cleaning his AR-15 rifle, reloaded it, and put it in its case. He had been home for an hour and was still exhilarated. Closing his eyes, he could envision it —first her confusion, then the stark terror as bullets danced at her feet.

Bitch.

He walked to his bedroom and gingerly laid on the bed. His back was raw, the open wounds still fresh. And it was all her fault.

It began with the dream. He couldn't recall it in its entirety, but the parts he remembered lay etched into his brain, spinning on a continuous loop. As he lay there now, trying to erase the memory, the lewd images gained strength, seeping into his marrow, determined to torture him with their depravity. And, though loathe to relive the dream, it owned him now.

Helpless, he surrendered to the memory.

She was angelic, ethereal. So beautiful that it hurt to look at her. When she came to him, to his bed, she wore nothing but the frilly, lavender panties he had taken from her drawer. Oh, he knew what she was—a succubus, a sinner, a disciple of Satan. But she had bewitched him, tricked him with sorcery or voodoo or other dark magics. And, like the whisper of a temptress or the seduction of a siren's song, he could not resist her call.

She walked closer, and he cramped with need. The rhythm of her swaying breasts mesmerized him. She was captivating, stunning—a luscious forbidden fruit, ripe for the picking.

Shamed by his visceral reaction, he cried out in this dream, this nightmare, for salvation, for the power to refuse her. But there would be no relief from this torment.

And so he succumbed. In this dream world and under the purview of the holy ones, he ravished her. Hard and fast, in the sanctity of his bedroom, he took her. Brutally, thoroughly, with no conscious thought, save one... he had to have her, or he would die a thousand deaths.

She was carnal and savage, and he awoke feeling as though it were the best sex he'd ever had.

Then, slowly, reality floated in, like a feather on the wind or the soft kiss of an ocean sunrise. Once fully awake, he checked his surroundings. His bed was a mess, the blankets in disarray, the sheets stained with his seed. Furious, the extent of her treachery became clear. She had enticed him, made him do vile, immoral things, things he should never do, even in fantasy.

Especially with her.

In time, his fury gave way to remorse. He was unclean, even though his sins played out in a dream. The answer lay in atonement, for only self- punishment would bring redemption. Skulking to the root cellar, he dropped to his knees, curled his fists, and pummeled his face. Blood and saliva flew as he punched and pounded, trying to demolish the filth.

After the blistering assault, his swollen hands could no longer form a fist. A river of blood gushed from his nose, the coppery taste settling in his throat, gagging him. He dabbed at his split bottom lip as his tongue probed for loose teeth. Absently, he wondered if the vision would ever fully return to his left eye.

Exhausted but in need of more penance, he removed his shirt, chose the thickest whip he possessed, and laid open his back.

An hour after his visit to the cellar, left eye still puffy

and nose throbbing, he found himself at her house, hidden in the tree line.

Rifle snug against his shoulder, he'd waited.

She had invaded his dreams and manipulated him into fornication. One day soon, he would orchestrate her ultimate punishment. She would know his name, face his wrath, feel his whip. But until that day, he would toy with her.

Bang, bang goes the gun! See her fall! Watch her run!

The Apostle shook off the morning's memories and got up from the bed, aching, aroused, and thoroughly disgusted with himself. He had let erotic thoughts take control of his mind once again. It was as if her magic still lingered, the way a fine perfume clung to the air long after its mistress had gone.

Enraged, he grabbed a container of rubbing alcohol, undressed, and stepped naked into the tub. Raising the bottle overhead, he held his breath and let the liquid flow down his back. Alcohol skipped over dozens of open, weeping lacerations, leaving a trail of fire in its wake. Clenching his teeth, he shut down his mind and focused on just one thing—revenge. Soon the games would end, and she would, at last, understand why.

Why she was the Chosen one and he, the one to watch her die.

CHAPTER THIRTEEN

The days following the shooting were a blur. Once again, teams from various agencies swarmed Katie's home. Some faces were unfamiliar, some she recognized from the B&E investigation. Crime scene technicians cordoned off the property, scouring for bullet casings and footprints. They took measurements, snapped photographs, and drew diagrams. Their professionalism impressed Katie, and she made a mental note to mention it to Jake.

Though unable to locate the firearm involved, investigators discovered seventeen spent bullet casings, all identical and fired from a large caliber, semi-automatic rifle. Firearm experts would examine the impressions left on these shells, caused by the firing pin, to narrow down the make and model of the weapon involved. Once identified, the Integrated Ballistics Identification System, or IBIS, could compare digital images of spent casings to other crime scenes.

Ballistic scientists would also inspect the projectile itself. The unique striations produced on a bullet as it exits the barrel of a firearm provides crucial information. Examiners study the lands and grooves, or rifling marks, imprinted on the round to identify the weapon used. In this case, rather than the gruesome task of digging a bullet out of a body, they could collect several slugs from the property's poplar trees to examine.

Katie, needing something to do, brewed an insane amount of coffee and baked dozens of cookies for the many investigators invading her home. She found herself, at times, crawling too far into her mind, resenting her role as hostess to plainclothes detectives, officers dressed in SWAT uniforms, and lab techs in coveralls.

She wanted her life back. Then, ashamed of her self-pity, she'd scratch her way back to the surface, back to reality. These people were working tirelessly to help her. The least she could do was feed them—including her new friend, Bane.

Bane was a scary but gorgeous black and tan German Shepherd. The one-hundred-and-ten-pound police K-9 was focused, well-trained, and intimidating. He went to work immediately, picking up a scent that started at the tree line and continued toward the back of the house. His excitement built as he concentrated on an area dense with trees, vegetation, and boulders that led straight to the Rappahannock. Bane lost the trail right around the river's edge, assumingly because the perpetrator used both rocks and water to cover his scent.

"Well, it was worth a shot," Jake said as they stood outside. "And although the dog didn't find him, we did locate a lot of spent shells while Bane was on point. We also found a few footprints and some partials by the rocks. Figure the guy stood on the rock line, using height to his advantage." His expression darkened. "We will get this guy, Kate."

"I know," Katie acknowledged, "but until then, I need to take some steps to protect myself. An alarm system for one. And I want to learn how to shoot so I can get a permit to carry." She paused. "I may even take a kickboxing class."

Jake grinned. "Atta girl. And don't forget, I will be hanging my hat in Darby's apartment for a while. We can take the Suburban to Quantico during the day and come back together at night. As for the alarm system, I'll reach out to my brother. Jed has contacts with security companies all over the country. We can get you an affordable system, both for here and the apartment. I'll make the call."

Katie thanked him, then looked toward the house. A giant piece of plywood covered the gaping hole that had once been the guest room window—the room where Jake would have been if he hadn't heard her leave that morning. She shivered and sent up a silent prayer. They had to find this guy. Fast.

~

December 25th, Christmas morning

When Jake came into the kitchen, Katie was sitting at the small table with a cup of coffee, staring into space. Her hair was in a high ponytail, her face freshly scrubbed. Purple smudges cast shadows beneath both eyes. Though still in lacy pajamas, she wore a short, blue robe.

"Thank you, God," Jake mumbled, rolling his eyes to the heavens. He couldn't afford the distraction a nightie would create.

"Did you say something?"

"Um, no, just talking to myself. Look," he said, walking to the kitchen counter, "I know how much this sucks. Not exactly the Christmas you were planning, is it?" He poured a cup of coffee and took a seat next to her. "I'm sorry this is happening to you, sweetheart, but we need to figure out our next move. It's important that we be five steps ahead of this son of a bitch."

"Don't you think I know that?" she said, harsher than she intended. "This maniac is dictating my life. I'm living in fear, unsure of what he will do next, and I absolutely hate it." She twirled her coffee cup and continued. "Today, I was planning to go to my refuge, my happy place, to celebrate Christmas. I was so excited at the prospect of seeing my people." She put her head in her hands. "Now, I'm questioning whether I should go at all. Am I putting my family at risk if I go to Falls Church?"

She stood, brought her cup to the sink, and turned to him, frowning. "On the one hand, I don't want this bastard to win. I don't want him preventing me from living my life. But is my anger or pride going to affect the people I love?"

"I won't let anything happen to your family, Kate. You will have your Christmas." Jake paused. "I'd like to go with you if that's ok. I'll stay outside, keep an eye on things. The car will be an excellent vantage point to monitor suspicious activity, anyway."

She chuckled and rolled her eyes. The sound of her laughter warmed his heart. "Don't be a dunce. You will not sit in the car, Jacob Devereaux. Do you seriously think I'd allow that?" Not waiting for a response, she continued. "You will come as my guest, my plus one. Callie's gonna freak. But what about you? It's Christmas day, for pity's sake. I don't want to mess up your plans."

He was, for the first time in a long time, embarrassed by his dull social life. He had no plans because he had few friends. His family was across the country, and he wasn't going to fly over two thousand miles, in the middle of a serial murder case, for a baked ham. But, if he told her he was planning on watching a 'Twilight Zone' marathon with a few beers and a couple of tuna sandwiches, she'd think he was pathetic.

"Um... my plans sort of fell through. Last-minute stuff, so I'm free today. I would love to spend Christmas with you and your family."

Katie walked to the table, ruffled his hair, and said, "It's a date! I'm off to pack a bag since I promised Grams it would be an overnight trip. I hope that's ok with you?" she asked. When he nodded, she continued, delighted despite her current circumstances. "I have a carry-on that should fit both of our things if you want to share. Less to haul that way." The thought of sharing a bag with their intimate things sent a delicious shiver through her body.

While she ran upstairs to pack, Jake debated whether to call Sully. He was curious about where they stood with the Task Force and hoped to get the ball rolling in the next day or so. He also wondered if the M.E. completed Aman's autopsy report.

Still, it was Christmas Day, and Jake hesitated to bother his partner. Smirking, he took out his phone, anyway.

The hell with it. The kid's single and most likely has a date with a tuna sandwich himself.

"Hey, Sully," he said when the Agent answered on the third ring, "Devereaux here. I just wanted to reach out about the Task Force. We good to go?"

"Hey, Jake. Yeah, we're all set. I'm heading over to the office later today to make sure everything is in place. I have the first meeting set up for Thursday morning at nine."

"Great. I appreciate your hustle on this. How about the autopsy on Bailey? Any news?"

"Not yet, though they promised to have a report generated in the next twenty-four to forty-eight hours. I guess they're pretty swamped. A lot of deaths this time of year."

"Unfortunately, that's true. Well, keep me in the loop." Jake hesitated a moment, then added, "Oh, and Ian? Merry Christmas, buddy."

~

A few hours later, Jake and Katie were ready to go. They loaded up Chance and Blue, then headed to Jake's townhome in Arlington.

"Thanks for agreeing to stop by my place," he said. "I just need to grab some overnight things and check on my roommate. He doesn't do well alone, and I've been neglecting him for the last week or so. Sully was good enough to check on him, made sure he was staying away from the stove and was well fed. But I can't help but feel guilty for being away so many hours."

"Of course," Katie said, "No worries, it's early yet. So, tell me about this mystery man. Gus, was it?"

"Right." Jake smiled. "He's an ornery old coot. Not especially social and a horrible conversationalist, but he's got a good heart. Don't take it personally if he acts a little stand-offish at first. He takes a while to warm up."

Katie chewed on that for a moment. *Who was this guy? And why did Jake feel responsible for him?*

"Maybe we should bring him with us. To Falls Church, I mean. I hate to think of him spending Christmas alone."

The corners of Jake's mouth quirked a bit. Shaking his head, he said, "Trust me, you don't want Gus anywhere near your holiday table. You should see him eat. It's embarrassing."

Fifty minutes later, they turned into a lovely neighborhood in Arlington, a gated community complete with a clubhouse, pool, and beautifully kept homes. Jake pulled up to a three-story, slate-gray townhouse with maroon shutters. A corner unit, it was a pretty home with one townhome next door and a shared drive.

"Is this it?" Katie asked. "It's darling. Love the colors."

"Thanks. Yeah, it's a nice house in a low-crime area. My next-door neighbor, Mrs. Smith, is a gem. She bakes me an apple pie on the third Sunday of every month. Don't ask me why it's always the third Sunday, though," he said with a smile.

"Uh, back up a minute," Katie said dryly. "Your neighbor is Mrs. Smith. And she bakes you pies. Apple pies."

Jake chuckled. "Crazy, huh? True story, though. C'mon, I'll give you a quick tour and you can visit with Gus while I pack a few things."

Katie followed him into the home, her stomach queasy. Gus was an important part of Jake's life. What if the man didn't like her?

When they entered the foyer, Jake called out, "Hey Gus! I'm home!" The house, a split-level, had one set of stairs leading down and another going up. Just beyond the foyer was a small, tidy living room. Its bare walls, leather sofa, and huge wide-screen T.V. screamed 'man cave.' Aside from a quaint leather trunk that doubled as a coffee table, there was no other furniture in the room. The flavor of the décor was function, not fashion.

"Gus? C'mon, man, I know you're pissed that I haven't been home, but I brought a guest. The least you could do is come on out to meet her."

Several minutes passed until Katie heard distinct movement from the lower floor. Footsteps? Someone was coming up the stairs, but with difficulty from the sound of things. Their steps were slow, heavy.

Poor thing, Katie thought sadly, *the stairs must be a challenge.*

She chewed on a fingernail, waiting. When Gus finally came into view, she gasped, then playfully punched Jake in the arm.

"This is Gus?" she asked. "Your roommate?" Shaking her head, she sighed. "That's a Bernese Mountain Dog, Jake."

He grinned, slapping his leg to call the dog. "Kate, I'd like you to meet Gus. Gus, this is my friend, Kate Callahan."

She quirked an eyebrow. "Let's see if I've got this straight. This is the 'ornery old coot' who has a problem staying away from the stove? The same Gus who is a 'horrible conversationalist' and has no table manners?"

Jake grinned. "Hey, I never said he was human. And if I were you, I wouldn't leave him alone at the dinner table." A twinkle in his eye, he added, "He also steadfastly refuses any attempt at conversation, although he sings pretty well."

As if aware they were speaking of him, the enormous black and brown dog plodded over to Katie, put his snout on her thigh, and moaned in a low key.

She fell in love instantly.

"Well, he's adorable. And I insist that he come with us. I'll not leave a D-O-G at home, alone, on Christmas."

Still grinning, Jake said, "You know, he's bright, Callahan, but as far as I know, he hasn't mastered his A.B.C.'s. No need to spell in front of him."

Frustrated, she blew out a breath, her hair flying skyward in the breeze. "Just get your damned clothes, Devereaux." Stroking the dog, she whispered in his ear, "Nobody likes a smartass."

∾

They left Arlington, all three dogs packed in the back of the Suburban, and headed to Falls Church. The dogs were freakishly well-behaved and, following the usual canine greetings—to include a few rounds of enthusiastic butt-sniffing—they were content to lie down and enjoy the ride. It was a brief trip to Grams, so Katie thought it best to get a few things out in the open.

"Before we get there, I think I should prepare you for some family dynamics," she said. "You will adore Callie and Ryan. They are a breeze to get along with and more than hospitable hosts. And Grams will spoil you rotten for the next twenty-four hours. She's the best."

"Oh-kay," Jake said, drawing out the word. "Why do I feel like there is a 'but' in there somewhere?"

Katie sighed. "Unfortunately, there is. And that 'but' would be my older brother, Finn. I never told you about our history and the reasons he moved away to Leesburg."

Patiently, Jake waited as she gathered her thoughts.

"In 1996, when I was just six years old, I was swimming in the family pool. My dad was home but inside on a business call. Daddy was an Investigative Reporter and seemed to be forever on the phone, following leads. Ryan was napping, and my mom and Callie were out shopping. Finn was outside with me, watching me in the pool. He was thirteen at the time."

Jake listened, a knot forming in his gut. He knew where this was going.

She shrugged. "I was a crappy swimmer, but things were going ok. I remember having a blast, loving the sun, the water." She cocked her head, eyes closed as if trying to capture a serenity that had long since fled. "It was a perfect day, I had the pool to myself, and it was summer vacation. Finn was on a lounge chair, reading a comic book. I remember losing my volleyball in the air and watching, horrified, as it skimmed the surface and landed in the deep end. Finn had already retrieved it twice before, and I knew he would be angry with me. So, deciding to fetch it myself, I moved beyond the rope and into the deep end."

She looked down at her hands and picked at a fingernail. "So, there I am, three-foot nothing and crossing into water seven or eight feet deep, hanging onto my noodle. You know, that Styrofoam thingy that kids use in the pool? Anyway, next thing I know, the noodle pops out from beneath me." She turned, studying his profile. He was such a handsome man. "Once I lost the only thing keeping me above water, that was it."

"Damn," he said, "that's horrible. How long before Finn got you back to dry land?"

"Not soon enough, I'm afraid. I tried so hard to call for him, but my words were lost, just ripples buried beneath the water. I could see him, though. His back turned from the pool, house phone to his ear. I felt like I could almost touch him, you know? And yet, I continued to drown. To die."

He turned and stared at her. "To die? What the hell do you mean, to die? Are you saying you came that close to dying?"

She sighed. "I'm saying that I died; no respirations, no heartbeat. When Finn finally realized what was going on, I'd been underwater for at least five minutes. I shouldn't be alive, Jake. The doctors told my folks it was a legitimate miracle."

She gazed out the window, recalling the weeks following the incident. Relating the story was strangely cathartic, like ripping the band-aid off a wound and finding it nearly healed. "I was in a coma for over a week. Brain trauma from a lack of oxygen meant months of rehab. I missed the first month of school and needed a tutor until October."

Stunned, Jake felt an overwhelming sorrow for her family, for what they must have endured. And he sympathized with Finn. After Jake's horrific incident years ago, he could relate.

"Holy crap," Jake said, "that's intense."

"It gets worse, unfortunately. A few weeks after it happened, my dad died in that plane crash. He was on his way home from his field office in Texas when the jet he chartered went down. He and Finn had been having some serious issues right before his death. I remember there being incredible animosity, on both sides, after the drowning. That day affected so many lives."

She pulled her jacket tight around her middle, warding off a chill. "Finn feels guilty that he wasn't able to save me before I died. I think he also carries with him the burden of knowing that my dad died before they could patch things up."

Jake took her hand. "Christ, I don't know what to say here."

She shrugged. "For the last twenty years, Finn has been a somber, angry, and distant man. Being around family was an agonizing reminder of the past, so he moved to Leesburg. I've tried to speak with him, to get him to forgive himself. He was a kid, for God's sake. I know that it was an accident. I just wish that he did."

They drove the remaining moments in silence, each lost in their thoughts. Katie wished she could divulge more to Jake about that day, and the years in between, without fearing his rejection. Jake hoped to find the words to relate a secret of his own, to explain how one horrific day changed his life forever. He knew it was unfair to listen as she poured her heart out without reciprocating and giving something back. But what if she thought him a terrible person? What if she heard his story and recoiled in horror? He knew he couldn't handle that kind of rejection from her.

They pulled up to a two-story brick Colonial with a circular driveway in front and a two-car garage to the side. The yard was pristine; the landscape dotted with various plants, shrubs, and trees. Katie explained to Jake that this was not *the* house. Grams thought it would be inhumane to expect the children to live in a home that produced their most horrific memories. But she also feared that pulling the children away from their friends could cause a sense of isolation. Compromising, she sold the old home and purchased this one. It was in the same school district and just a few miles from the original. Uncle Tim's house was still within walking distance, but now he was in the opposite direction.

"Wow, this is nice," Jake said. "Distinguished looking. I've never been a fan of brick homes, but this is sharp."

They unloaded all three dogs from the Suburban and let them run around for a minute to stretch their legs. As they watched them, Katie's phone rang. It was not a number in her contact list.

"Hello?"

"Hello, Ms. Callahan? It's Pete Stanley, from Pete and Sons towing?"

"Oh, hello, Mr. Stanley. Merry Christmas."

"To you as well, Miss. I hope you don't mind the call on Christmas Day, but I know how anxious you were to get the Denali back, and wanted to let you know we finished her up this morning. Hired me a new mechanic, and the two of us got here at the crack of dawn to get her done. You can come by to pick her up anytime. Not today, though, if you don't mind. I expect the Missus would have my hide if I skipped out any longer on the Lord's birthday."

"I understand. I'm grateful that you worked so hard to get my car fixed. If it's ok with you, I'd like to pick it up tomorrow?" She gave Jake a pleading look and whispered, "can you take me?" He nodded.

Pete agreed, and she told him they would stop by in the afternoon, on the way back from Falls Church. She hung up, and they walked toward the front door. Within a few feet of the entryway, Katie halted abruptly, nearly sending Jake into her back.

"Oh, shoot, I almost forgot! Nicodemus."

"Nico, who?"

Smiling slyly, she asked, "So... how does Gus feel about cats?"

～

Dinner was amazing. Callie outdid herself, preparing a juicy turkey with all the trimmings and her famous home-made cranberry relish. Dessert was pumpkin pie, macaroon cookies, and the cheesecake Katie supplied. After dinner, they sat in the living room, bellies full, sipping on coffee. Jake, Tim, and Ryan talked sports, while Callie's friend, Stacy Egan, hung on Ryan's every word. Stacy was a pretty, cheerleader type brunette, who, even though a few years her junior, was Callie's best friend. Grams sat knitting, joining in when the conversation turned to football.

Katie, Trish, and Callie ignored the sports talk, and instead, caught up on their lives. They chatted about Callie's class schedule, Trisha's pottery business, and Chance and Blue's training. They reminisced about high school classmates and prom dates and tried to decide who their favorite character was on 'Game of Thrones.' The four dogs lounged by a stone fireplace, with Nicodemus nestled safely between Romeo's front paws. It looked like a Norman Rockwell painting; a loving and warm family holiday, adored by many, envied by some.

And then there was Finn.

Sullen, moody, and withdrawn, he sat alone at the kitchen table playing a game on his phone. He'd barely said two words during dinner and provided only one-word answers for anyone foolish enough to engage him in conversation.

After stewing about it for hours, Katie excused herself and went into the kitchen, watching him quietly from the doorway for a moment before speaking.

"Um… hello? Earth to Finn." When he looked up, she smiled, walked to the table, and grabbed the back of a chair. "Are you planning on joining the family anytime soon?"

His eyes went back to his phone. "Leave me be, Kate."

She pulled out the chair and sat down heavily. "Leave you be? Really? What's up with you?"

Finn ignored her.

"Tell me the truth, bud," she said. "Why did you come today? You barely spoke at dinner, and you've been curt and rude to our guests. Now, you're holed up, sulking, on the other side of the house. What, exactly, is your problem?"

Finn growled and blasted to his feet, the chair he was sitting on falling backward. His handsome face flushed, his mouth a tight line. Katie, fuming, jumped up as well, mimicking his stance. It was as though they were two prize fighters, ready to talk smack and bump chests.

"I don't know what you people want from me," Finn snapped. "Your sister rode my ass to come here, so here I am. I've listened to your conversations, eaten your food. I've even played the 'one big, happy family' game." He shook his head. "Afraid I'm tapped out, Kates."

She stood there, stunned. *My God, who was this man? How did he become so bitter?*

Speaking through clenched teeth, she said, "You're tapped out? You don't know what we WANT from you?" Angrier than she thought possible, she snarled, "We don't want shit from you, Finn. It would be nice to have our brother back, though. You know, the decent human being that we remember? Not this grouchy S.O.B. before me. The chip you've been wearing on your shoulder is getting mighty old, brother." Shaking her head, she continued, "Callie went through an awful lot of trouble to get us all together, to make this a nice Christmas for everyone. But you have your head so far up your ass you can't see it!"

The ferocity of her temper shocked her. She knew she needed to rein it in but couldn't seem to stop herself. A proverb, one she'd heard many years ago, mocked her.

'Anger is a condition in which the tongue works faster than the mind.' Well, fuck that! She was so mad, she didn't much care how fast her tongue was moving.

Jabbing a finger toward his chest, she snapped, "I'm the one who died, Finnigan. I was the little girl in a coma for over a week; the child who woke up one morning and learned that her father was dead. It was me who had to endure months of grueling rehabilitation and homeschooling." She gritted her teeth, her rage building. "And I was the one who walked into that bloodbath all over the fucking kitchen! So, if anyone should be a nasty, moody son of a bitch, it should be me!"

He stuck his hands in his pockets, his face pained, voice a mere whisper. "You have no clue, Kate. About anything." His eyes glazed as his mind played a scene of long-ago memories and heartache. "I swear to God, I wish I'd never picked up that phone extension. If I hadn't, you would never have drowned, and I would never have had to confront Dad about that fucking phone call. You almost lost your life, and Dad is dead. All because of me."

"Look, Finn, if you are going to start on... Wait. What? What the hell are you talking about? What phone call?"

Jake walked in just then, forehead creased in concern. "Everything ok in here? Just a PSA... noise carries far in this house."

Finn gave him a blank look, then stormed down the hall to his bedroom. Katie exhaled and looked at Jake, forlorn. "That went well," she said sarcastically.

Rubbing his neck, he said, "Don't beat yourself up, Red. He came here looking for a fight. Why don't you go back to the living room with your family? I'll let the beasts out for a bit and be right back."

She trudged back to the living room, replaying the words Finn threw at her. *He was just a kid. What the hell could he have confronted Dad about? Work, maybe?*

Whatever the issue was, she was sure of one thing—the confrontation between Finn and her Dad was monstrous, ugly, and life-changing.

Jake followed the dogs around outside, throwing them an old frisbee he'd found by the front door. After what seemed like a thousand tosses, he threw the disc one last time to Blue, who jumped up, hit it with his snout, and sent it careening into the row of cars in the driveway.

Jake glanced at the array of vehicles and noted with interest the last car in line, a white Ford pickup with

Virginia tags. Gut tightening, he walked around the truck and peered inside. He spotted a map, an old water bottle, and a Heritage Pride ball cap on the front seat. Heritage was the name of a high school football team in Leesburg.

This truck was Finn's.

Unnerved, he surveyed the backseat. There, on the floorboard and in plain sight, lay an AR-15 semi-automatic rifle.

CHAPTER FOURTEEN

"Whoever brings ruin on their family will inherit only wind, and the fool will be servant to the wise." Proverbs 11:29.

"Where's Finn, Kate?" Jake was doing his best to remain neutral and unconcerned, despite the pit in his stomach. His recent discovery just veered the investigation into a whole new direction. He needed to talk to Finn, and he wanted to get a good look at that rifle.

"Um, I'm not sure. He's probably hiding in his room, pouting. He used to do that when we were kids." Katie was back in the kitchen, wiping down the counters. "I would advise against trying to smooth things over yet, though. It's too soon for him. He hasn't played 'diva' long enough."

Jake grabbed a chair, flipped it around backward, and indicated for her to take a seat. When they were both comfortable, he spoke again.

"Sweetheart, I need you to tell me everything you know about your brother. His home life, hobbies, love interests. And exactly how long this 'thing' between you two has been going on."

Troubled, she said, "I'm not sure I like where you are going with this, Jake. Yeah, Finn is an enormous pain in my ass, but he's harmless."

"Are you sure about that?"

"Of course, I'm sure. He's my brother. 'The blood of the covenant is thicker than the water of the womb.' Are you familiar with that saying?"

"I've heard of it," Jake answered. "Not clear on its meaning, though."

"It means…" She paused, gathering her thoughts. "Look, Finn is just, well, Finn. He mopes, he pouts, but then he gets over it, and everything is just peachy. Grams says he was always like that. He had a difficult time when he was younger."

Jake frowned, then raised his hand as if a pupil in a classroom. "Difficult? Difficult as in acne and puberty, or difficult as in playing with matches and pulling the wings off butterflies?"

She stood and shot him a reproachful look. "Not funny, Mister. Let's just say he had an exceedingly shitty start to life. He isn't my parent's biological child. That's what I meant by the blood of the covenant. Sometimes, who we choose to call family is not blood." She opened the fridge and stared blankly at the contents, not knowing what she hoped to find. A change of topic? An ounce of courage? A place to hide? Closing the door with a sigh, she continued.

"My folks tried to get pregnant for years without luck. Eventually, they gave up, deciding to adopt instead. Before Finn came to be with us, he lived through a string of neglectful, abusive foster parents. We got to him just in time, I think. Saved him." She bent down and scooped up Nicodemus. "When he was six, they finalized the adoption. A year later, my mom unexpectedly got pregnant—with twins, no less. Isn't that how they say it goes, though? As soon as you give up trying, surprise!" She smiled at the irony.

Jake was reeling. *Talk about your plot twists,* he thought, stunned. *Finn was adopted?*

"Look, don't get mad, but could it be that Finn is jealous of all the attention that you received after your accident? Or maybe he blames you for feeling so shitty about what happened?" He raked a hand through his hair.

Open-mouthed, Katie just stared at him.

"Are you aware," Jake pressed, "of the vehicle he drives? Or that he owns a firearm?"

Cursing softly, Katie snapped, "You're kidding me, right? Are you suggesting that my brother is behind all the horrendous things that have happened? The road incident and the snake? The break-in and freaking sniper shooting? Is that what you are hinting at, in your not-so-subtle way, Agent? You know, if it weren't so insulting, it would be laughable." She put the cat down and slammed her hands down on the table.

"Ryan owns a firearm. Kyle owned one, too. Hell, you own a firearm." She vehemently shook her head. "You are way off on this one, Jake. I would stake my life on it."

Jake furrowed his brows, unwilling to back down. "And what makes you think you aren't doing just that?" He stood and bent forward, resting his arms on the chair. "Look, we should at least consider the possibility, given the circumstances. All I want to do is talk with him. No accusations, no pressure."

She pushed off the table, offended that he would dare entertain such a notion. "This is insane." Glaring at him, she snipped, "Fine, if it will ease your suspicions about him, be my guest. But I hope you're partial to humble pie, Devereaux, 'cause you're going to get a belly full of it."

Jake's phone rang, temporarily halting their disagreement. He walked to the foyer and answered.

"Devereaux."

"Hey, boss, Sully here. Sorry to bother you during Christmas dinner, but I'm at the office, and there have been some intense developments I thought you'd like to know about."

"Sure, no problem. Shoot."

"Ok, well, we have a probable hit on NamUS for a missing couple. A woman named Laura Dixon and her father, Henry Wurster, went missing in June of this year. The reporting party is one Benjamin Dixon, Laura's husband. The report states that Henry visited a sister in Tampa, and Laura went to pick him up from Dulles International. Benjamin Dixon received a text late in the evening on June 25th, indicating that she arrived safely at the airport. That was the last time anyone's heard from her. Baltimore PD found her car weeks later, stripped, in the parking lot of an abandoned warehouse."

"And you think they relate to our case how? There are plenty of woods between Dulles Airport and Sugarloaf Mountain. Just saying... that'd be quite a distance to travel to dispose of a few bodies, right?"

Sully clucked his tongue. "True enough. But there have been no other reports that have popped up. And there is something in Laura's history that stood out to me."

Jake sighed. Sometimes Sully could be maddening. *Ahh, youth.*

"Well, spill it, Junior. Don't leave me hangin'."

Sully grinned. Now and again, it was fun to torture his boss. "It seems Laura Dixon has a daughter. Which means..."

"She was a mom." Jake finished for him.

"Right, but that's not the best part. According to the

report, she was also in a horrific car accident years ago that required an extensive surgical repair on, guess where?"

Jake digested that information. "Her right wrist. Ok, that fits, at least for two of the three sets of bones. We will want to interview the husband; maybe get something we can use as a DNA comparison."

"Right. I've also been working on compiling all the info we have to date to give to Eric Gibson. He's agreed to do the profile for us. With any luck, we will have a working theory in a few days. Also, I spoke to Jed. His sources have never heard of Aman Bailey. And when I ran the guy's name through the legal system, I could find no wants, no warrants, and no arrests. Man has never had so much as a parking ticket." He paused and added gleefully, "Oh, and Jed said to tell you you're a douche for not calling him yourself."

Jake chuckled. "That sounds like my brother. Anyway, glad to have an expert like Eric Gibson on board. On my end, I have a few more names for you to check out, Finn Callahan and Kyle Walker. Priors, ViCap, you know the drill. Finn is Katie's brother, adopted at age six, and Walker is her ex. There's nothing concrete on either of them, but it's worth a look. I will text you the details when we get off here."

Jake rubbed his forehead. "I'm also going to get someone from the bureau to babysit Kate while we go to Baltimore to interview this husband. I don't want to leave her unguarded. Not sure how all this shit fits together, but no sense taking any chances."

Since it was closer to leave for Baltimore from Falls Church than travel back to Quantico, they agreed to meet at the Dixon home at 10 a.m. the next morning. Jake turned to walk to the kitchen and nearly stepped into Katie, who stood quietly behind him. He considered her posture—hands fisted on her hipbones, eyes unblinking.

Cringing, he muttered, "Oh, crap."

She slid up to him, so close he could see the tiny lashes at the corner of her eyes. Her hair smelled sweet, like a garden of wildflowers; her skin, like honeysuckle and something else, another flower whose name escaped him. Her face was flushed, her lips a rosy red. Her brows snapped together, and she tilted her head.

"So, I need a babysitter now? Is that right, Agent Devereaux?"

Damn, but she's pretty, was his first thought. His second was trying to figure out how fast he could backpedal.

Shrugging, he offered a weak attempt at humor. "Is that what you heard? Well, no wonder you're upset. But no, that's not what I said, not what I said at all. 'Babe is it,' that's what I said. Like you're da' bomb, the cat's pajamas. A babe." When her frown deepened, he said hurriedly, "So, it's a compliment, Red. 'Babe is it.' Get it?" He grinned, a smile that was so exaggerated, and an explanation so pathetic, she almost laughed. Almost.

"Really, Jake? Do I look like a moron to you?"

Uncomfortable, he said, "No, of course not." He brushed back a lock of hair from his forehead. "Listen, Kate. I won't blow sunshine up your ass or bullshit you with rainbows and unicorn kisses. Someone is trying to hurt you, maybe even kill you. And this fucker knows where you live. You must see the logic in not being alone right now."

"I know that, Jake. I'm not stupid, nor do I have a death wish. What I do have is a plan. I will buy a gun and install an alarm system, might even take some self-defense classes, as we discussed. But what I will not do, what I refuse to do, is run. This prick chose the wrong girl to fu

—" She stopped herself from completing the obscenity and took a calming breath. "I understand that you are trying to protect me, but this is MY life. I get to decide what is, or isn't, right for me."

It was as if she were a bullfighter, waving a red flag in front of him. Frustrated and angry, sure that he'd never met such a stubborn woman in all his life, he snapped. "I am leaving for Baltimore in the morning. We have a viable lead on the identity of the female and older male we found on the mountain. But I will not leave until I know you're safe, and I don't give a fat rat's ass if that, in any way, offends you. Hate me all you want, but at least you will do it alive, and not as some damned ghost."

She froze. Why did he say that? Did he believe in spirits, or had he somehow figured out her secret? Did he see the Gray Lady, as she had come to know her? Unsettled, she turned and walked back to the kitchen, Jake at her back. Her family was in the living room and close enough to the foyer to overhear their conversation. She still hadn't told them the events of the past few weeks and feared an awkward confrontation. She would tell them in her own time, on her terms.

"Ok, ok. I get where you are coming from," she said, facing Jake. "But do you know how embarrassing this is to me? At least when it's you that is hovering, it's more like," she hesitated a second, "more like we are together. People don't stare or feel sorry for me. They aren't afraid to be around me. But if you insist on assigning a bodyguard…" Inspired, she dropped her argument and said, "How about if I went with you? To Baltimore, I mean? Callie and Ryan can take care of the dogs, and Darby will still be at her folks for another day or so."

He shook his head, but she stopped him. "Think about it. It makes perfect sense, Jake. I can help with DNA collection at the Dixon home, and you won't have to pull anyone off the Task Force to 'babe is it' me."

He snickered. Walking closer, he was immediately hit with her scent again and recognized it now. Gardenias— her skin smelled like honeysuckle and gardenias. "Okay, fine. But you need to listen to me, Kate. No standing on the 'I'm a free woman' platform. I don't want to hear how independent you are or how this maniac will not change your routine. You will do what I say, when I say it, or I will take your sweet little ass right back home. Deal?"

She nodded. "Deal." As she headed back to the living room, she mumbled, in a mocking tone, "Do *what* I say *when* I say it. Overbearing, egotistical Neanderthal."

Jake heard, and he smiled.

Festivities winding down, Grams, Callie, and Stacy headed up to their respective bedrooms, slightly drunk and noticeably exhausted. Tim, Trish, and Romeo said their goodbyes, driving the few blocks away to their home, while Ryan headed out to his hospital shift. Jake and Katie sat comfortably in the living room, each with a slice of cheesecake and an Irish coffee. The Gray Lady popped in and out, occasionally wringing her hands but still frustratingly silent.

As for Finn, no one had seen him for hours.

"Do you think he's still here?" Jake asked aloud.

"I have no idea. He didn't say goodbye, although sometimes he does that; just slips out into the night, like a ninja or a cheap date avoiding the check."

"Well, I need to talk to him. For real, Kate. If nothing else, we can mark him off the person of interest list."

Katie exhaled loudly, and with enough exaggeration so

that Jake would get the message. She knew Finn. Yes, he could be quirky and eccentric, maybe even a bit intense. But he loved his family and would never cause them harm.

"Look, I know you believe in dotting your I's and crossing your T's. It's that kind of diligence that makes you an excellent investigator. But you have to trust me on this one, bud. You're barking up the wrong tree."

"I get why you don't want to go there, Kate, but it's just good practice to look at…"

She jumped in, annoyed. "Let me finish. Yes, Finn legally owns a gun. So does a third of the population in Virginia. And he drives a white truck, but the one that ran me off the road was different. Older."

"Maybe," Jake said, unconvinced, "but victims can get descriptions of suspects and vehicles wrong, especially in the heat of the moment. Look, if there's nothing there, there's nothing there. A conversation doesn't cost a dime."

"Ok," she said, eager to change the subject, "you win. But I insist on being there when you talk to him." She scooted back on the sofa. "So, Agent Devereaux. I gave you something, and I think it's only fair that you return the favor by answering a question."

"Ask away," he said, feigning a confidence he didn't feel.

She cleared her throat. "Why are you alone?"

Coughing, he nearly choked on his cheesecake. "Beg your pardon?"

"You heard me. C'mon Jake. You're a gorgeous guy, one with a stable income, a lovely home, and an adorable dog. So why isn't there a Mrs. Devereaux?"

Great, Jake thought.

He knew this conversation would come up. He just hoped it would be later, rather than sooner. "I could ask you the same thing. Beautiful woman, brilliant and single, with two great dogs."

She stared at him, unblinking.

"Ok, ok. I will give you the sanitized version." He put his plate on the coffee table and sighed. "There was an incident several years ago, a shooting that didn't end well. The woman I was dating at the time, the person I thought was the 'one' could handle neither the shooting nor the shrapnel that it left behind. Ever since then, I've shied away from any significant relationships. Women have a hard time understanding the job and the bag of shit that often accompanies it."

Katie was quiet for a moment. She knew what he went through every day, could sense what his life was like—the triumphs and the horrors, the joys, and the sadness. She could feel it all, but she could never tell him that.

He wouldn't believe it, anyway.

"What happened?" she asked. "It must have been something huge, frightening, even life-changing."

Jake scrubbed his face with his hands and swept back his jet-black hair. He was reluctant to tell her the truth but feared that if he didn't share this part of him, this chink in his armor, she would never truly trust him.

Sensing his distress recalling the memories, she grimaced. "Never mind, I'm sorry. I have no right. It's raw and personal and a guarded part of your life, a piece of your history that should be shared only with someone you trust implicitly."

"Someone I trust, huh?" he said with a wink. "And what would you say if I told you I found that someone? A special someone who's kind and beautiful and brave beyond measure?" He reached for her hand. "A sexy and brilliant woman, blessed with the most amazing green eyes I've ever seen, and kissed by a crown of crimson hair." He searched her face and whispered, "A lady who challenges me and believes in me and, literally, steals my breath away. So, what if that's the person I want to confide in?"

Katie gaped at him, stunned. *Me? He's talking about me?* Her stomach felt queasy, her limbs shaky. Suddenly, the world was full of possibilities.

He's talking about me!

He leaned in closer and gently grasped her face with both hands, eyes fixated on hers. Murmuring something she couldn't quite make out, his eyes drifted to her lips, and she knew. She held her breath in anticipation, her heart beating wildly. Tentatively at first, his lips brushed hers in a caress as old as the ages. The contact was gripping, electric. She kissed him back, and he grew bolder, probing the recesses of her mouth and the sweetness of her tongue. When they finally parted, she sighed, head back and eyes closed.

He ran a thumb over her lips and whispered, "Katherine Callahan, I could fall crazy in love with you."

Eyes still closed, she smiled. "Then my evil plan is working." She leaned in for one more of those mind-blowing kisses, then slid farther away from him. She couldn't think straight when he was so close, and she wanted a clear head.

"So, you were telling me about the shooting?"

"Yeah, I guess I was. Fair warning, though, Kate. After you hear this, you may feel entirely different about me."

"Try me, G-Man. You'd be surprised by how open-minded I am."

He stood and walked to the living room window, staring out into the darkness. "It was eight years ago, February 14th, Valentine's day. I was working with Metro D.C. when my partner and I caught a case involving a planned contract killing. We were staking out an apartment complex in a particularly shitty area of Logan Circle. The guy we were watching, Mario, was a known drug runner, busted a dozen times on possession with intent." Jake sighed, a man haunted by his memories. "We received a tip Mario was shooting his mouth off at a local bar, telling anyone who would listen that he wanted his wife dead, inquiring about a gun-for-hire. Our police informant swore that he overheard Mario wheeling and dealing with some big-time mafia goon, a suspected hitman. The information seemed legit, so we staked out the apartment, waiting for the killer to materialize. Weeks later, we still had nothing— not so much as a fart in the wind coming from that place."

He turned from the window to find her leaning forward, hands in her lap, engrossed in his story. "We were about to give up when, at 2 a.m. on the day of the incident, we heard an ungodly scream, followed by the sound of someone running down the fire escape stairs. It was Luciana, the suspect's wife, and she was carrying their eighteen-month-old baby boy." He frowned. "Funny. I can't seem to remember the kid's name now. Anyway, she was going full tilt toward the center of the courtyard, yelling for help and waving the biggest, baddest kitchen knife I'd ever seen. She was completely out of control, screaming that Mario was trying to kill them. I remember thinking, 'Jesus, lady. I hope to God you don't trip—you will put that knife right through your kid.'" He took a deep breath and stuck his hands in his pockets.

It was his 'tell,' an unconscious behavior people turn to when bluffing or dealing with something uncomfortable or unpleasant. Katie's tell was chewing on her bottom lip; Darby's, running her mouth faster than her brain could catch up. Callie, when upset, used a tone of voice that became almost sanctimonious.

And Jake's tell? His hands always found his pockets.

"Next thing we know, Mario comes flying down the stairs, a raging lunatic waving a semiautomatic, 9mm handgun and ordering her to stop. Spinning wildly, eyes frantic, he finally spotted us. And then the weirdest thing happened. He directed his screams toward us, begging us to 'do something.' Which, frankly, made no freaking sense because we WERE doing something… we were trying to prevent him from slaughtering his family." Jake stopped speaking and plopped on the couch.

"You can stop now; I get it," Katie said. "You, or your partner, were forced to kill Mario to save his family."

He rocked his head. "No, that's just it. It was more fucked up than that." He searched her eyes, unsure if he was looking for a sign that he should stop or seeking the courage to continue. "We identified ourselves and ordered him to drop his weapon, begged him to drop it. We did everything by the book, Kate. Everything. But the stupid bastard refused to comply. Instead, he lifted the gun and aimed it straight at his wife and child. We were out of options."

He dropped his head and folded his hands, as if in prayer. "We lit him up."

She patted his shoulder. "Devastating, but justifiable. My God, Jake, he would have killed his family. You had no choice."

Jake frowned. "There's more. As soon as we dropped him, we heard the wife. She was celebrating, dancing in place, laughing. It was the most evil, demented sound in the world, one reserved solely for the criminally insane. We started toward her, not sure if she was nuts, hysterical, or both." His eyes filled with the memory. "She gnashed her teeth, screamed, then raised the knife above her head. It happened so fast, a split second. There was no time to react." He dropped his head once again and whispered, "No time."

Katie sat there, stunned. Was he saying what she thought he was saying?

He shrugged in resignation. "The baby. She plunged the knife in his throat so deep, it damn near decapitated him. He was DRT... Dead Right There. We wrestled the knife away from her before she used it on herself or us. God help me, but some days all I can see is that little boy, and I kick myself for letting the bitch live." His eyes seemed to clear, and he said, "Nicholas. That was his name, baby Nicholas. Anyway, we found out later that the entire scene was a setup. She was certifiable, believed her husband and son were servants of the devil or some such bullshit. And Mario? That poor bastard was just trying to save his son, and I blew it. A little boy is dead, Mario is dead, all because I assumed too much. I took a leave after the shooting, went back to Montana to figure out if I still wanted to be a cop." He bowed his head in defeat. "But there was never any other option for me. I'll always bleed blue. Once I realized that, I got back on the horse, so to speak. Only this time, that horse belonged to the Bureau."

Katie placed her hands gently on his cheeks, lifting his head. "You listen to me, Jacob Devereaux. There was nothing, I repeat, nothing, that would have changed the outcome of this tragedy. That child's mother was insane, and you are not responsible for someone else's mental health. And Mario? Tragic, but you made decisions based on the facts presented. Good God, Jake, who wouldn't have taken him out? A man pointing a gun, threatening a woman and a child?" She lightly kissed both of his cheeks and said, "I don't know how a woman who professed to love you could hold you accountable for this terrible thing, but rest assured, that's not me. Never me."

He scooted closer to her on the couch.

"You know, you're pretty great. It terrified me to tell you about that shoot, wondering what you would think of me. I was afraid that I would become less of a cop, or a man—hell, maybe even less of a hero—in your eyes. And that would destroy me. So, thank you, Professor Callahan. You are a good friend." He shot her another over-the-top, sexy wink.

She cringed. *Friend? Oh, hell, no*!

"You're welcome, Agent Devereaux." She hesitated, not sure if she was bold enough to do what she had wanted to do since that kiss. What if he rejected her? She smiled, knowing she would try anyway.

"No guts, no glory, right?"

His face was blank, her meaning a puzzle to him. "Huh?"

Standing, she extended her hand. "C'mon, friend. I have a pillow on my bed with your name on it. God help you if you snore."

Smiling, he took her hand and teased, "I think I'm really gonna like this friend thing."

Shivering, the Apostle crouched several yards away from the house, watching her people. Using binoculars, he monitored the home's activity, unaware of how long he'd been there. Minutes? Hours? Days? Long enough to feel the burn and sting of frostnip. He couldn't turn away, though, even as he knew that he should leave. He risked not only discovery but hours of personal hell and torment, just watching these cretins. This mission was, perhaps, his most important one yet. Surveilling his targets, planning his next move, strategizing. He had something huge in mind. Something that would finally strike fear, dread, and heartbreak to the one who had altered his destiny and destroyed his life. Tomorrow would mark the start of a relentless campaign; one meant to shatter her peace, crush her spirit, and extinguish her future.

He was coming for her. Soon.

CHAPTER FIFTEEN

"Wake up, sleepyhead. We need to get moving."

Katie cracked one eye open. "Time's it?" she murmured.

Jake rubbed her shoulder and pulled her close. "Almost seven. It's going to be a long-ass day."

She nestled in closer to his warmth, her cheek on his bare chest. Sighing contentedly, she smiled as she recalled their night together. It was unexpected, tender, and sweet.

In short, it was perfect.

As if reading her mind, Jake grinned. "I don't know about you, but I think this friend's thing is the bee's knees. I mean, I've had pals before, but this..." He stopped, a twinkle in his eye. "Remind me again. Just how many times did we 'make friends' last night?"

Eyes still closed, she gave his ribs a nudge and whispered, "Hush now, I'm still basking. It's better for me when you're not yapping."

Jake snorted, playfully tickling her side. He rolled over her, supporting his body weight with his elbows. "Well, I heard a lot of noise last night, but I don't recall any complaints." Nuzzling her neck, he growled, "But maybe you need more convincing that our friendship is solid."

Now it was Katie's turn to laugh. She squealed as he chomped at the sensitive flesh below her earlobe. She was enjoying this banter, relishing in it. Reversing their positions, she rolled on top of him, crossed her arms, and laid her chin on her forearms.

As if her clouded vision suddenly cleared, she whispered, "You know, this has never happened before."

Teasing, he gasped, "You've never had sex before? Well, don't I feel like a jackass."

"You ARE a jackass," she said dryly. "No, dummy. I mean this, playing, teasing, having fun. You know, afterward?" Embarrassed, she said, "I know, I know. I sound like a dork. I'm just not sure how to express it." She flipped her hair out of the way and smiled. "Not making sense, am I? I'll just shut up now."

He raised a hand to her cheek, and she rested her face against his palm. "No, you make perfect sense, Red. I feel it too. It's different. It feels healthy, genuine, even honest, I think." Smiling brightly, he said, "But, just to be sure we are both on the same page, maybe we ought to, you know, give her another go." He wiggled his eyebrows, lifted his head, and found her lips.

And so, for the next thirty minutes, they became 'friends' all over again.

～

They headed down the interstate toward Baltimore, Jake behind the wheel of the Suburban. They were a bit behind schedule, though he couldn't regret the reasons that had them running late. He glanced at Katie in the passenger seat.

"You look amazing. I don't know why you keep futzing with your make-up and hair. You'd be gorgeous bald, in rags, and without a drop of face paint."

"I'm a train wreck, Devereaux. I told you my hair took forever to dry. Now, it looks like a curly, used mop." She sighed. "Whelp, can't do much about it now, other than cover this mess with a hat."

"Do it, and I'll shoot you," he deadpanned. "It looks wild and free and breathtakingly beautiful." He gave her a smirk. "The 'do' stays."

Katie grinned and threw the cap she was holding onto the backseat. "Fine. But don't come crying to me when the 'do' attacks, wraps around your throat and swallows your soul."

"I'll take my chances, Callahan."

It amazed her how happy and complete she felt, despite her current circumstances. She'd been run off the road, threatened, and shot at. A crazy person was trying to hurt her, maybe even kill her. And yet, here she was, grinning like a fool.

Insanity.

Still smiling, she said, "I saw Callie this morning. She agreed to pick up the Denali for me with Ryan and bring it back to Grams. That way, we can just grab it when we come back for the pups."

Jake froze, and his eyes widened. They had made love in her grandmother's home, a house brimming with Katie's family members. And, if memory served, they weren't exactly what one could call silent lovers.

He glanced at her, a blush creeping up his neck. "So, um, about last night. Did Callie mention anything? Like about us?"

Katie stared at him for a minute, confused. When comprehension finally dawned, she burst out laughing.

"Oh, my God! Are you embarrassed that my family knows we slept together? That's adorable!" Taking a breath, she smirked, "Jake, honey, my people know I'm not a nun. I'm twenty-eight years old. I think they can handle the fact that I'm sexually active." She smiled and grabbed his hand.

Clucking his tongue, he said, "If you're sure. I just don't feel like throwing down with Finn or Ryan if they feel the need to protect your honor."

Grinning, she said, "Finn or Ryan? Babe, the one you should be worried about is Callie. You hurt me; she'll kick your ass."

An hour later, they pulled up to an old brick home with a gated back yard and a manicured lawn. A 'For Sale' sign hung at the property's edge, with 'Contract Pending' affixed to it in bold lettering. They spotted Sully's car in the drive as they made their way to the front door.

"Watch my lead, darlin'," Jake said, his hand on the small of her back as they navigated the multi-colored pavers. "We need to make Dixon feel comfortable before we gather any personal effects of the wife."

Katie rolled her eyes and muttered, "No shit, J. Edgar," under her breath. Jake grinned and rang the bell. The door opened, and a little girl of about nine or ten years old stood before them. She was a beautiful child, with golden curls and almond-shaped eyes.

"Hello, young lady. My name is Special Agent Jacob Devereaux, and this is my friend, Kate Callahan. We're looking for your dad. Is he at home?"

The child turned and called out, "Dad! It's more police people to see you!" They looked beyond her as a short, balding man, with a slight paunch and sad eyes, hustled to the front door.

"Come in, come in. I was just talking to Agent Sullivan in the kitchen. I'm Benjamin Dixon, by the by."

They shook his offered hand and introduced themselves. Ben led them through a narrow foyer, into a vintage-looking kitchen. Cherry red appliances, stainless steel fixtures, and a commercial gas stove gave the room a Sixties vibe. Sully, seated in a retro, red-striped chair at a chrome table, stood when they entered the room. Looking around, Katie couldn't help but think of Darby—she would love this kitchen.

After declining the offer of coffee or water, Jake dug in. "Mr. Dixon, I'm sure my colleague has explained why we are here?"

Benjamin nodded. "Yes. I understand that remains found on Sugarloaf Mountain could be my Laura and her dad?"

Solemn, Jake answered. "I'm afraid so. We are trying to gather as much knowledge as we can about your wife and her father, Henry. It will help us determine our next step and, hopefully, bring us closer to finding answers. We have tests that we can perform, ways to extract DNA from their personal effects to analyze and compare their genetic profile with the victims we discovered on Sugarloaf. Do you understand all that, Mr. Dixon?" When Benjamin nodded, Jake removed a small notebook from his jacket pocket and flipped through the pages. "I have here that your wife was in a rather serious car accident years ago?"

Benjamin's head bobbed up and down. "Yes, it was a terrible time for her. Laura had a serious liver injury that required hospitalization. She also shattered her wrist and underwent several operations to repair the damage, keeping her out of work for months."

Jake shot a glance at Katie, who nodded imperceptibly.

Sully cleared his throat, his hands fidgeting at his sides. "I, um, explained to Mr. Dixon that we could use something as simple as a toothbrush, or strand of hair, to aid in identifying the remai—uh, the identity of the people involved."

Sensing Sully's discomfort, Katie jumped in. "Mr. Dixon, I promise we wouldn't trouble you about this if it weren't necessary. DNA analysis is the best way to determine if it's your family we found on that mountain. I understand this is difficult for you, and I cannot fathom your pain. But to solve this thing, to get you the closure you so desperately deserve, we need your help. In cases like these, any dental and surgical records you can provide to us are invaluable. And, with your permission, we can also gather the items Agent Sullivan mentioned from their possessions."

What she didn't say, dare not say, was that she had no doubt the bones on the mountain belonged to his wife and father-in-law. Katie recognized the middle-aged woman in the family pictures that lined the hallway. It was the same woman who stood silently on the mountaintop and visited her in the lab.

Laura Dixon.

Benjamin showed Katie upstairs, where the bedrooms and bathrooms held all manner of DNA, then excused himself to make some phone calls. Jake and Sully remained in the kitchen.

"Well, what do you think?" Sully asked. "The ages of the vics match, as does the wrist fracture on Laura. And the estimated time of death given by Katie lines up with when they went missing. We may actually get a slam dunk here, I.D. wise anyway."

"Yeah, I admit it looks promising, Junior. But let's wait until we get those records before we start dancing naked in the streets. Myopic vision always has a way of biting a fellow in the ass."

Upstairs, Katie quietly collected the toothbrushes, combs, and razors that belonged to Laura and Henry, then headed to the bedrooms. It was a grim task, the knowledge that father and daughter would never again walk these halls weighing heavily on her mind.

Just when you think you have it all, you discover you have nothing, she thought sadly.

The moment Katie entered the master bedroom, Laura appeared by the bay window. The powerful emotions Katie experienced the first time she'd seen her were noticeably tamer, but the spirit remained unable to move on. Henry Wurster, on the other hand, was nowhere in sight. Katie assumed he had been ready to leave this earth and found his peace.

"Hello again," Katie whispered. "We have to stop meeting like this."

Bemused, Laura smiled. Katie sat on the bed, careful to avoid any abrupt movement. Laura's presence seemed stronger than it was previously, perhaps because of familiar surroundings. Whatever the reason, it gave Katie hope that she could finally communicate.

"You must forgive me," she said quietly, "I seem to be just awful at this whole thing. As hard as I try, I can't seem to break through the veil."

Laura's image flickered for an instant, disappeared, and then returned. She raised her arm and pointed at a small vanity by the bedroom window.

"You want me to look through your desk?" Katie asked.

Laura nodded.

Katie hurried across the room and rummaged through the vanity drawers. Hopeful, she dug through the small desk, searching for something, anything, that could help identify Laura's killer. All she found was a tube of lipstick, a notepad, and a chewed-up pencil.

Confused, she turned back to Laura. "I don't understand. The lipstick? Or did you want me to find the notepad?"

Laura pointed to the vanity again, so Katie removed the paper and pencil and sat down. Her idea was to shade the top sheet of paper with the pencil's edge, hopefully uncovering an imprint of the last words written on the pad. Instead, the moment she sat down, she felt disconnected, dizzy. Her head pounded, sweat formed on her upper lip, and her hand seemed to develop a mind of its own. Eyes closed, a kind of trance took over as she scribbled feverishly on the paper. She didn't understand what she was writing; she only knew that her hand was working through Laura.

Several moments passed until Katie finally felt the grip that had overtaken her subside. When she opened her eyes, Laura was gone. Looking down at the paper, she gasped when she read what she had written:

'He took us, killed us. Evil in cowboy boots.'

Under that, she had written, 'Lies. Not of God.'

Katie stared at the message, comprehension unfolding like a morning glory in the sun's brilliance. With Laura's help, she had discovered the best way to communicate with the dead.

Automatic writing.

The entire way back to Gram's, Katie was silent. The

enormity of what had happened at the Dixon house was not lost on her. Automatic writing could very well be the key she had been looking for all these years. Yes, she needed to test the theory several more times to be sure. But it was a promising start.

"You ok, sweetheart? You are awfully quiet over there." Jake said.

"I'm fine. I was just thinking about the case. How much further to Grams? The dogs are probably going nuts."

"Thirty minutes, I think. Why don't you rest for a bit? You look beat."

Nodding, Katie had just closed her eyes when 'Sister Christian' pealed from her purse.

"Hey, Cal pal. What's what?"

"What's what is that the shit has hit the fan over here. We got trouble, Kates. Serious trouble."

Katie clutched her neck. "Why? What's happened?"

"Only everything," Callie said flatly. "Ryan and I went to pick up the Denali, so we asked Stacy to stay here and help Grams with the dogs until we got back. I wasn't exactly comfortable leaving the old girl here alone with all the animals. Stacy agreed."

"I agree, too. Three dogs and a cat can be a handful. So what's the problem?"

Callie remained silent, so Katie asked again. "Callie, what is it? Is Grams ok?"

"No, no, she's fine. But when Ryan and I got back, Stacy was gone, along with Chance and Nicodemus. We looked everywhere, Kates. Drove around the neighborhood, called Stacy's cell phone. I guess it's turned off because it went directly to voicemail." She drew in a ragged breath. "There's no sign of them."

"That is weird. Well, don't freak out. Stacy may have

just gone home, and Chance and Nic are probably nosing around the neighborhood, getting into trouble, no doubt."

She heard her sister's intake of breath, with a subtle hitch that only Katie understood. Callie was on the verge of tears.

"That's what we thought, too, but Stacy's car is still in the driveway. And when we left, we fenced the dogs in the backyard with the gate latched. Now, the gate is wide open, and Chance is missing. And Nicodemus? Well, he loves to be outside, but you know he never leaves the yard." She took another shaky breath and said, "It's like they all vanished, Kates. They're just gone."

Katie shot a nervous look at Jake. He mouthed "what?" to her and pulled over to the side of the road.

"Could Stacy have taken Chance for a walk?" Katie asked, not waiting for a response. "You know, Nicodemus could be hiding inside, or maybe he followed them out of the yard. I'm sure there's a logical explanation." She shifted in her seat, trying to stay calm. "We're about a half-hour away. Once we arrive, we'll form a Callahan search party. Don't worry, Shadow, we'll find them." They said their goodbyes, with Callie promising to keep looking. Katie ended the call, then burst into tears.

Stunned by the sudden change in her mood, Jake gathered her in his arms and waited until her sobs quieted. Brushing a tear from her cheek, he reached across her lap and pulled some Kleenex out of the glove box.

"Here, take these." Handing her some tissues, he joked, "They're not even used or anything."

She took the offering. "Thanks." Sniffling, she added, "I don't know where that came from. I'm not usually so emotional or panic-driven, especially without first knowing if there is something to panic about."

"So how 'bout you tell me what's going on?"

When she finished detailing the call, his expression darkened. They were both thinking the same thing—there was no such thing as coincidence.

"We'll go there and pull out all the stops, search all night if we have to. But I won't bullshit you, Kate. If Stacy truly is missing, then this situation just got a whole lot scarier."

She nodded, a sense of foreboding creeping up her spine. Something sinister was brewing, something that they may not be able to stop. And worse, it was all her fault.

If I'd just been honest about the threats against me, they would have been a lot more cautious. Idiot!

As soon as they pulled up to the house, Jake noticed Finn standing beside his pickup truck with Callie and Ryan. Blue and Gus were sitting next to Katie's Denali, seemingly waiting for their humans to come back and fix things.

Frowning, Jake said, "I wonder why Finn came back. You think your sister called him?"

Katie shrugged. "Who knows? If she were scared enough, she would."

They exited the Suburban and joined the group. Callie, face tear-streaked, clutched Ryan's hand while Finn stood a few feet away, posture tense and expression reserved.

"I take it from the look on your faces you didn't find anything," Jake said.

Callie rubbed her eyes. "Nothing. We rechecked the neighborhood, even went to Stacy's place just to see if she had a friend pick her up." Callie chewed on her thumb. "Although, seriously? Why the fuck would she leave her car if she was going somewhere? And she wouldn't just up and go, anyway." She pulled her hair back and secured it in a ponytail. "She wouldn't have just abandoned Grams like that. Hell, she knew Ryan was coming back with me after we picked up the car. That alone would have been enough to keep her here."

Ryan rubbed his chin, a faint blush on his handsome face. "We talked about maybe going out for cocktails tonight, just the three of us. She, um, she seemed excited to go."

Jake raked his hair back, the late afternoon sun accenting its deep, vibrant color. Katie knew he was worried, but he fought hard to keep that concern hidden.

"Ok, here's what we do. First, I need to speak to your grandmother. We need to know when, exactly, was the last time anyone saw Stacy or those animals. Callie, I want you to call all your mutual friends, see if anyone has heard from her. Try her family, too." He nodded toward Ryan. "I need you to canvass the neighborhood, buddy. Go door to door and see if anyone has seen them. There is a playground not too far from here. School is out now, so there may be some folks you can question."

Jake squinted a look in Finn's direction, his distrust of Katie's brother worn on his face like a bright neon sign. "I will call the locals and get the ball rolling for a missing person's report. Finn, you're coming with Katie and me. We'll take Blue and turn this area inside out until we come up with something."

Finn mumbled "swell" under his breath, then went to his truck to gather a heavier jacket and his Heritage Pride ball cap. Katie paced, trying to ignore her stomach as it flipped. Her belly felt like a free-falling elevator, plummeting blindly into the unknown. Every nerve in her body was on high alert as her gut twisted. There were so many riddles in this mystery, so many questions. But the one thing she knew for sure, the one thing she felt deep in her bones, haunted her.

This would not end well.

They searched for hours without luck. Methodically, they checked every road, every cul-de-sac, every wooded area within a five-mile radius. Blue would pick up a scent, follow it, then circle right back to where they started.

They spoke to several people along the way, none of whom recalled seeing Stacy, Chance, or Nicodemus. Daylight was waning, the temperature dropping to near freezing digits. Defeated, they met up with Ryan and started the trek toward home, intent on resuming their search in the morning. As they shuffled back, Jake used the time to question Katie's oldest brother.

"Finn, I couldn't help but notice your pickup. Sweet ride. What year is it?"

Finn looked startled for a moment, polite conversation the furthest thing from his mind. He rubbed the back of his neck as they walked. It was Finn's tell.

"Um, it's a 2018. It's a work truck, so I had some alterations done—custom stuff, like a built-in toolbox and a rifle rack. I removed the back seat and replaced it with shelving for feed and stuff. I own a ranch; animals gotta eat." He said the last defensively as if Jake were questioning his vehicle modifications.

"Rifle rack, huh? You a hunter?"

"Not particularly," Finn said, "but I have animals that need protecting. Predators come in all shapes and sizes, Agent Devereaux."

Jake thought about that for a moment. As much as he disliked Finn and his moody behavior, his reasoning made sense. There were many predators out there, ones who walked on four feet and those who used just two. Jake's father kept several firearms on his property for the same reason. Satisfied for the time being, he made a mental note to check with Leesburg P.D. to see if they'd had any run-ins with Finn that were off the books.

As they rounded the last bend on their journey back, Gram's house came into view. Gone almost two hours—cold, tired, and hungry—they trudged toward the warmth and security of home. Within a few yards of the front door, Katie's senses ignited. She could feel the shift of energy, the imbalance of the universe. Her skin prickled, and gooseflesh rose on her arms. Something sleek and gray darted in front of them, hair coated in blood.

Nicodemus!

"Oh, my God! Nic!" Katie cried. "What happened to you, baby?" Nicodemus, growling softly, cowered behind a grouping of Boxwood shrubs. Kneeling before him, she coaxed him out of hiding and pulled him into her lap.

"That's a lot of blood," Jake said, looking around. His senses were on high alert as well. "You find any wounds?"

Katie's voice shook, and her hands trembled. "No, I... I don't think this is his blood. I can't find a cut or anything. His skin seems intact." She carried him inside to the kitchen and sat him on a towel on the counter. Ryan came up beside her, giving the cat a more thorough exam.

"Nothing," he said. "There's nothing here. No signs of internal bleeding, no fractures or lacerations. I don't know whose blood this is, but it's not Nic's."

Jake ran a hand down the cat's back, more in comfort than in examination. "I'm going outside to look around. Maybe there's a blood trail we missed or something. You guys stay in here and warm up. I'll be back in a few."

"I'm going with you," Finn said hurriedly. "Extra set of eyes and all that."

Surprised, Jake nodded, and they headed out the door.

Once out of earshot, Jake turned to Finn. "I think whatever happened, wherever your cat picked up that blood, occurred while we were out searching. We hiked damn near five miles and never picked up a blood trail. Now, just as we return, Nicodemus shows up covered in the stuff." He zipped his jacket to his neck. "And I find that too damn convenient. Let's rework the area, starting in the backyard and working outward."

They headed toward the rear of the house, Jake taking the right side of the property and Finn, the left. Fanning out, they worked in a semi-circular pattern, moving toward the vacant, wooded lot just beyond the backyard fence.

Fifteen minutes into the search, a horrified scream echoed through the brush. Running full tilt, Jake stumbled over a tree root, catching himself just before he fell. Heart pounding, he sprinted the last few yards to Katie's brother, who was standing at the foot of a tall tree, his eyes raised toward the heavens. An overpowering scent filled Jake's nostrils, and he tilted his head back, mimicking Finn's posture.

"Jesus Christ," he whispered.

It was as if Jake's words were a portal, an opening for Finn to react. Without warning or fanfare, he jerked his head to the side and violently retched up his last meal. Jake continued to stare at the tree, stunned, his mind frantically trying to reconcile what he was seeing.

Behind them, a sudden, piercing scream splintered the air. It was a primal cry, a shattering of the heart so profound, all that remained was the tattered shreds of the soul who owned it. He whipped around, his eyes finding hers.

Fuck!

The torment on her face was like a sucker-punch square in the gut. Running to catch her before she collapsed, he grabbed her around the waist, supporting most of her weight.

"Dammit, Kate, I told you to stay put! Shit!" Softer now, aware of the harshness in his tone, he added, "Jesus, I wish you didn't have to see this, baby."

Gasping, her hand covered her mouth as she fought another scream. In disbelief, she digested the scene in front of her—a body, grotesquely hanging from a tall Chestnut tree, its limbs suspended ten feet in the air by a crude rope. The head lolled to one side, its neck and chest soaked in blood. There was a gaping wound at its throat where pieces of tissue, bone, and flesh escaped from the near-decapitating injury. Below the still form, blood fell in a macabre rhythm to the dry leaves below, each splash thrumming a ghoulish tempo.

And coiled like a serpent around a nearby branch, a set of thick, emerald-colored rosary beads.

"Oh, God, no!" she croaked, her voice guttural, husky. "Chance!" Her limbs finally gave out, and Jake gently lowered her to the ground. "Please, Jake, help him! Cut him down!"

He squatted down beside her, arm around her shoulder. "I got him, honey. We'll get him down." He kissed the top of her head and turned to Finn. "Do you know if your grandmother has a ladder?"

Finn nodded dully.

"Ok, I need you to get it for me." Trance-like, Katie's brother ignored him and turned back to the tree.

"Finn! Buddy! I need you to focus here. Just get the ladder, ok? Get me the ladder."

Finn, eyes still transfixed to the body hanging before him, blinked rapidly. Finally, he backed up, turned on wooden legs, and walked stiffly back toward the house. Jake sat on the ground, arms around Katie, gently rocking her as she wept. The anger inside him grew, his rage threatening to detonate with the slightest spark. He would not rest until he found the son of a bitch responsible for causing this woman, his woman, so much pain. And when he did, God help him.

He was going to kill the fucker.

CHAPTER SIXTEEN

"The evil deeds of the wicked ensnare them; the cords of their sins hold them fast." Proverbs 14:32.

The Apostle trotted happily to his mailbox, anticipation thrumming through his veins. Opening the hinged door, he pulled at the package wedged inside. The sender was a business by the name of The Spiritual Soldier. He was introduced to the company, an online military shop specializing in religious merchandise, while serving in the U.S. Army. Reading the name of the addressee, he chuckled. His alias was unremarkable yet clever—painstakingly chosen and well-thought-out, just as everything he'd orchestrated in his life.

Those years in the Special Operations Unit constituted perhaps the best, most memorable years of his life. He thrived on the respect and adoration the uniform commanded, excelled at the weapons and combat training he'd received, and relished in the absolute power bestowed upon him to crush an enemy. But now, years later, his were loftier goals with a higher purpose.

A responsibility, in this existential world, to answer His call.

He ripped open the shipping envelope, and five brightly colored strands of rosary beads tumbled into his palm. Thick and polished, they marched in line, strung together using the same nylon fiber manufacturers used for parachute cords. Those fibers, called paracord, had the smooth texture and tensile strength necessary to complete his work.

The success of a man's work is measured by the tools he employs. His father had taught him that.

He placed the beads back inside the package and returned to the house and the task before him. On his kitchen table lay the simple keys to his genius: a yellow legal pad, dozens of Post-it notes, and several freshly sharpened pencils. A meticulous note-taker, he subscribed to the theory that preparation and organization were paramount to success.

Today, he was especially creative, exceptionally flawless in his thinking. His ideas invaded his consciousness, overpowered his mind. He scribbled a few thoughts in the margins of a nearby sticky note, lest his notions escape him. Hungrily, he devoured the countless doodles, the poetry, the in-depth steps to ensure success. Hours of challenging work that, he was sure, would finally bear fruit.

The pages that littered the polished tabletop were random thoughts, inspirations too essential to ignore but too new to include in the plan. Given time, he would try to assimilate those scattered thoughts into his plot. In the meantime, he did not doubt the direction of his agenda.

If you aim for nothing, you'll hit it every time.

Standing, he gazed at the whiteboard that stood against the far wall. Pictures of his Chosen covered every inch of the 72 x 40-inch mobile board. Images taken as she relaxed by the fire, ate dinner, undressed. He studied the photos, tilting his head to the side like a Cocker Spaniel. A delicious idea took shape, one that hadn't occurred to him before; an idea that would prove most fitting when he was ready for the last act of this mission. He pulled one note from the table, read it, and placed it on the board. He needed to make his next move before his Chosen had time to regroup. Right now, she would be knee-deep in mourning.

Dogs, he thought bitterly. *Filthy beasts, the lot of them. Loyal only if they received a warm bed, a meal, and a roof over their big, fat heads.*

He would never understand why anyone would choose to own such a disgusting animal. No matter. The canine served its purpose.

He imagined her reaction, the agonized screams that would echo off the trees when she spotted the beast. In his mind's eye, he could see her crumpled and broken form, curled on the ground beneath her. Beaten, defeated, possessing neither the will nor the strength to stand.

It was a glorious vision.

He felt a dull, throbbing ache between his legs. His pants grew tight as his zipper strained to accommodate his pulsing erection. He needed release, an outlet, to assuage this torment. And he knew just where he would find it…

In the perky little brunette locked in his root cellar.

~

December 28th

Two days following the death of Chance, Katie found herself back in the lab, working feverishly on the remains. As painful as it was to forge ahead, she knew the key to finding this maniac and saving Stacy was to gather as much information as possible. She'd positively identified Laura and Henry, thanks, in part, to Tucker Simon. Katie admitted that, although he still made her skin crawl, he had worked diligently to match both victims to their dental records. Laura's medical information from the hospital, complete with x-rays of her wrist injury and the subsequent repair, sealed the deal. And while they sent out the DNA collected for comparison, they would not receive those results for weeks, maybe months. She was confident enough in the medical history data, and her visions, to make the call on a positive I.D.

Pinpointing the cause of death, on the other hand, was proving to be a challenge. Extensive decomposition of both individuals meant Katie could not examine tissue or skin samples for clues. However, she found that Laura had sustained a fractured hyoid bone perimortem. Whether that meant she was strangled to death or strangled to unconsciousness, then killed in some other fashion, was impossible to tell.

She'd had more luck with Henry's remains. There was an incised injury, one made by a very sharp, non-serrated knife, on the anterior surface of the fourth cervical vertebra. The wound must have caused tremendous bleeding, judging by the placement and depth of the incision. The smooth contour showed the victim's head was held in place, presumably by an attacker that came from behind. In addition, the injury was deeper on the right side of the bone than the left, which suggested that the killer was probably left-handed. After gathering all she could from Laura and Henry's remains, she turned her attention to the third victim.

He was a young male, probably late twenties to early thirties in age. Using Katie's findings, Lydia had begun the process of recreating his facial features. So far, the nose, lips, and facial muscles of the 3-D reconstruction were complete. Next, she would 'flesh' the face or add clay until the tissue depth and individual bone contours, such as the ridge of the brow, were comparative to the skull's landmarks. Determining specific physical characteristics, like eye and hair color or whether he wore glasses, was impossible to know for sure. For these, Lydia would make a few educated guesses.

Katie was eager to view Lydia's progress and planned on visiting her this afternoon. Meanwhile, with Chance dead and Stacy still missing, she felt an urgency to examine the young bones and, hopefully, determine his cause of death. As she worked, her thoughts drifted to December 26th and the cruelty of it all. The image of Chance hanging from that tree played over and over in her mind— just thinking about the fear and pain he must have gone through made her heart ache and her stomach burn. What could she have done to make someone that angry with her? Angry enough to torture a defenseless animal?

The jokes on you, Callahan—everything until now was just a dress rehearsal for the grand finale, a rousing 'fuck you' from the universe!

Jake had been incredible, though. After getting Katie back inside, he climbed the ladder to take a closer look. Several phone calls later, an investigative team arrived to process the scene. They took samples and many pictures, then bagged and tagged the rosary beads. Afterward, he and Sully removed Chance from the tree, wrapped him in a soft blanket, and carried him to Finn's truck. Later, they would dig a grave and bury him on Katie's land by the river.

The sound of 'California Dreamin' on her cell brought her back to the present. Stepping away from the table, she removed her gloves and grabbed her phone from her tote bag.

"Hey Darbs," she said, "you're up early. Everything okay?"

"I'm fine, hun. The question is, how are you? You sure you should be back to work so soon after everything that's happened?"

"I'm okay. I'd much rather be here, feeling like I'm doing something, then sitting home wringing my hands. I can't change what's happened, but I can damn sure try to prevent it from happening again." A note of sorrow crept into her voice. "Maybe to someone else I love. Stacy is still out there somewhere, in danger. I can feel it." She bent down and removed her left shoe, her fingers massaging the ball of her foot. Standing still for several hours did not make for happy feet.

"I'm worried too. And I'm so sorry about Chance. I don't know how you are functioning right now." Sniffing, she added, "I'm gonna miss that boy. Anyway, I'm at the house watching a guy install the alarm system. Holy high-tech, you gotta use a thumbprint to get through the door. Cool, right? As soon as he finishes, I'm heading out to pick up some groceries. Do you need anything?"

"No, thanks. Jake and I will stop on the way back from shooting practice. He is lending me his revolver, and I need to learn how to operate it."

Darby groaned.

"I know, I know," Katie responded. "Doesn't exactly thrill me either, but I need to protect my family from this psycho. Speaking of which, I have a proposition for you. And please, don't say no until you hear me out."

"Okay, Kates, but I warn you. It's been a long time since someone propositioned me. Things could get complicated."

Katie laughed. "I'll keep that in mind. I wanted to let you know that Jake will be staying at the house with me for a while. There's no telling what this scumbag's next move might be or who he will target. That said, we would feel so much better if you were with us. I've asked Callie to move in, too. Safety in numbers, right?" She searched her brain to find the most convincing words. "Look, we have enough bedrooms, so space is not a problem. Please say 'yes,' Darbs."

"So, you told Callie then? Your family? About everything that has been going on with you I mean?"

"I did. They took it surprisingly well." Katie paused. "Except for Callie. Man, she flipped out. And not because she might be in danger, but because I am. It took a lot of explaining, cajoling, and ass-kissing to get her to calm down."

"I bet," Darby grinned, "She's like a tiger, protecting her cub."

"Anyway, Ryan needs to be close to the hospital, so he and Grams will stay with Uncle Tim at his cabin." She paused for a minute, then added, "I know this is a pain in the ass, and I'm so sorry that this dirtbag is affecting your life, too. But unfortunately, he knows where I live, where my family lives." She lowered her voice, speaking softly. "Stacy is still missing, Chance is gone, and I've had more than one occasion where I've 'felt' this idiot watching me." She held her breath, afraid that her friend would give her an argument. Instead, Darby sounded relieved.

"I think it's an awesomely cool idea. This entire thing has me spooked." Pausing for a moment, she added, "Speaking of spooks, have you told Jake about you know what yet?" When Katie remained silent, she continued, "He's a good guy, Kates. He's not Kyle. I think he deserves to know the truth."

"What's that, Darbs? Crap doodles, you're breaking up! Poor connection, I guess. Well, gotta run! Later, 'gator!"

"Poor connection, my ass! Katherine Mary, don't you dare hang—"

Katie ended the call and smiled. Darby would kill her when she got home. Stepping back to the bones, she was examining the tenth rib of the young male when she heard someone enter the lab.

"Well, gracious! I didn't expect to see you here today. Such a vision of loveliness, too, and it isn't even 9 a.m.! Aren't I the lucky one?" Tucker Simon waggled his eyebrows and slithered up next to her. Looking at the collection of bones, he sighed. "Not much to see, is there? No DNA available for comparison, no bullet holes, no identifiers. This poor bastard will probably remain a 'John Doe' for years."

Katie looked up from her work, a sour expression plastered on her face. She really disliked this man.

"Tucker, I don't believe that to be true. All bones tell a story once we know how to read them. If we can determine what killed him, we are that much closer to linking this death to the other murders. How this man died can give us insight into how this killer thinks and what is and isn't important to him. Investigators are working on compiling a list of young males reported missing in the last six to eight months. Hopefully, we can use the physical characteristics we've discovered here as a guide to determine potential matches."

He shook his head dramatically, his 'Jefferson' eyeballs crawling up and down her body. Even without speaking, he made her extremely uncomfortable. It was like being in a confined space with an insect. A cockroach, maybe. Or a centipede.

Something creepy, quick, and revolting.

"If'n you say so," he said sarcastically. He glanced up at the lab door, then slid to the opposite side of the table, facing her. "Anyway, I'm glad you came in today. There's been something on my mind I've wanted to discuss with you privately, without your watchdog Devereaux in the room." His eyes pierced hers, lips curled in disgust. When he spoke, his voice dripped with contempt, his words a menacing whisper. "If you *ever* embarrass me like that in front of my boss again..." Snarling, he hissed, "I didn't come this far in my career, work my ass off night and day, only to watch it get fucked up by a silly little cunt like you!"

Spittle pooled at the corners of his mouth, along with what appeared to be the remnants of an egg and cheese sandwich. Katie's hand went to her throat, shocked by the venom in his voice and the threat that it implied.

Just then, the lab door slammed open, and their heads snapped up in unison. Jake stood at the doorway, face red, hands fisted at his sides. For a moment, he merely glared, the silence deafening in the still of the lab. Finally, he spoke.

"Kate, please leave." She blinked, a deer caught in the headlights. "I mean it. You need to go," he said, his jaw tight. When she remained motionless, he spoke quieter, his eyes never leaving Tucker's face. "Please, Red, step out for a minute. Things are about to get ugly in here." His fists clenched and unclenched as if he were itching to get his hands around Tucker's throat. A vein bulged at the side of his neck, the blue line pulsing with every heartbeat. Katie had never seen him so angry. She acknowledged that, given the circumstances, now might not be the best time to lecture him about the whole 'knight in shining armor' routine. Besides, Tucker worked for Jake; he deserved whatever punishment Jake would dish out. Decision made, she pushed off the lab table and quietly made her way out the door.

Tucker watched her leave, his mouth dry, his bowels in spasm—there was an excellent chance that he would shit all over his chinos.

"Jake, man, listen. I don't know what you think you heard, but I swear—"

"Save it, asshole!" Jake snapped. "You just blew your only chance at a career here. You're done, fired. You have exactly ten minutes to pack up your crap and get the fuck out of my building. If that clock hits 9:14 and you're still here, we will need Professor Callahan to identify your remains."

Tucker's hands shook, and his face paled. He started to say something, but the warning in Jake's eyes stopped him cold. Imperceptibly, he nodded and turned to leave.

"One more thing, dickhead."

Tucker froze.

"If I ever see you anywhere near Professor Callahan, her family, or this institution again, I promise you—I will rip off your head and shit down your throat!"

Tucker's head bobbed up and down, his feet virtually flying out of the room and down the hallway. After he was out of sight, Katie stepped back into the room. Jake stood stock-still, respirations rapid, face still flushed.

"Do I even want to know what went on in here?" she asked.

"Mr. Simon is no longer in our employ. I made it clear that he is to stay away from here, from you, or face the music." Jake smirked at her. "I believe he understood."

"Oh, I've no doubt," she said, amused. "You know, you don't always have to feel you need to save me, Jake. I've dealt with many Tucker Simons in my life. It's not always pretty, it's not at all pleasant, but I've handled it. Still, I'd be lying if I didn't say I'm glad you gave that creature his walking papers. Thanks."

Jake walked over and put his arms around her. "You're welcome, pretty lady." Eyes twinkling, he said, "I do feel obligated to defend your honor, and not just because you look amazing naked." He bent down for a long, sweet kiss. Then, bringing his mouth next to her ear, he murmured, "You don't know it yet, Katherine Callahan, but you are falling head over heels in love with me."

Katie snorted. "You think so, do you?" She brought her lips back to his and murmured, "You're awfully sure of yourself, Agent. Do you think you can just hold me close, kiss me senseless, and I will be putty in your hands?"

Grinning into her lips, he whispered, "Countin' on it."

Jake left the lab and headed for the Task Force meeting, a thousand thoughts weighing heavily on his mind. Chance's memorial service was scheduled for later that afternoon, and he knew it would be difficult.

Difficult? Hell, it would be a shit show. How much more can Kate take?

Kate had been chased down, shot at, her sanctuary violated. And now, her beloved dog was brutalized and murdered. He and Sully buried Chance by the river, near his favorite 'pee tree,' a wooden cross marking his grave. Katie would get a stone for him eventually, but until then, the cross would serve as a remembrance.

Since her entire family would be at the memorial service, Jake thought it would be an excellent time to re-interview each of them. Experience told him that Stacy's disappearance was not voluntary and, although the local

P.D. was interviewing Stacy's family and friends, they still had no solid leads.

The key was in Kate's past. People who wandered in and out of her life, bitter co-workers, ex-lovers. Someone out there held a grudge against his lady.

His money was on her ex, Kyle Walker.

He had put out an 'attempt to locate' in the neighboring areas. A BOLO, or 'be on the lookout,' would require more evidence of involvement in a crime. And so far, his investigation into the man had turned up nothing. Walker was a ghost, with no activity on his cell phone, no contact with friends or family, and no withdrawals from his bank account in months. One of three possibilities struck Jake; the guy was very cunning, independently wealthy, or dead.

The Task Force meeting was more than productive. Attendees included behavioral specialist Eric Gibson, Maryland State Police Lieutenant Frank Blake, and an investigator from the D.C. Park Police. Sully and two men borrowed from another FBI field office were also in attendance. Eric was ready to share his profile of the suspect, bringing them closer to understanding the mind of this killer.

The law enforcement officials gathered around a long table, in a generously sized office, a large bulletin board at the front of the room. Jake stood at a dais with Eric Gibson.

"Good morning, gentleman. I appreciate you all coming out today and look forward to working with you. Before we get started, a gentle reminder that you are not to answer questions outside this room, nor release any info to the media, unless cleared by command. We can't afford a panic, especially since we still don't know what the hell we're dealing with here. The individual responsible is dangerous, shrewd, and escalating in the frequency and viciousness of his attacks. Our latest and probable victim is a woman named Stacy Egan." He looked around the table at the group before him: all fine men, all top law enforcement officers dedicated to public safety. If anyone could find this bastard, it was this team.

"I know that Sully filled you in regarding the connection with Professor Katherine Callahan and this perpetrator. We've provided each of you with a synopsis of both the timeline and forensic evidence found at the various crime scenes. This suspect is cautious and well-prepared. The physical evidence we have gathered is, to put it bluntly, shit. A few hairs and fibers, ruled out as belonging to either the victims or their family members, were found in the Dixon vehicle. We also pulled a partial palm print off Professor Callahan's dresser. Other than that, this guy has left nothing of himself behind. The best evidence we have might be his calling card, the rosary beads. If we can identify where he got them, we can contact the vendor. Hopefully, they maintain a current customer list. These rosary beads aren't the delicate little things Father O'Malley, or even your Nana, pray on. We believe they are custom or military-grade. Maybe even home-made."

Jake took a breath and continued. "The man to my right, Eric Gibson, is one of our best behavioral specialists. I will turn this meeting over to him to share his insights about what makes this killer tick. Eric?" Jake swept his hand to the side in introduction, then took a seat at the head of the table. Eric stood behind the podium, shuffling his notes.

"Good morning, everyone. I know time is of the essence, so I'm just going to get started. If you need clarification of any details, feel free to jump in." He adjusted his reading glasses and began.

"As you may or may not know, there are twenty-five to fifty serial killers active at any given time. Their uniqueness of motive, signature, and psychopathy helps us define and differentiate one from another. Most serials have a particular victim or type that they favor. Take Theodore Bundy, for example. He confessed to killing over thirty women, most of them pretty brunette co-eds. John Wayne Gacy targeted youthful men and boys, many of whom were runaways or homeless. Jack the Ripper preferred prostitutes. This guy? He's all over the map. Aside from his calling card, the rosary beads, there is no pattern as far as victimology. But when we factor in Professor Callahan, we can see a clearer picture. It seems he cares more about targeting her than the pleasure of the kill itself."

He turned a page in his notes. "I believe this suspect is a loner, one who has minimal contact with people outside of his victims. He's white, aged twenty-five to forty, with above-average intelligence. He may have worked in the military or law enforcement fields. His employment records will be spotty, though, as he believes himself to be superior and most jobs beneath him. Most likely, there is a history of physical, mental, or sexual abuse at home. He may have had no interaction with police, or he could have a lengthy juvenile record. It would not surprise me to learn that, in his youth, he displayed aspects of the Macdonald triad. This theory describes three distinctive behaviors that may be predictive of extreme violence, or even serial killer tendencies, later in life. These behaviors include bed-wetting, a fascination with fire, and animal cruelty or torture. Now, that doesn't mean that someone who exhibits these behaviors will kill. Rather, the theory is a kind of guide or benchmark we can use in conjunction with other methods of evaluation." Gibson stepped away from the podium and paced.

"I would describe this killer as organized, a planner. He is also a narcissist and a sadist, displaying a true anti-social personality, complete with a lack of sympathy or remorse. He cannot know what his victims feel because he is incapable of empathy. Bizarre delusions, or even hallucinations, could very well be a part of his daily life."

Eric took a sip of water and continued. "His signature, the rosary beads, tells me he has a deep affinity or connection with religion. Someone in the clergy may have abused him, or he could be clergy himself. He may even believe himself to be God." A hand raised in the back of the room.

"So, what are you saying here, Eric?" Frank asked. "Is this guy loco? The wheel is spinnin', but the hamster's dead? Or is he just an evil son of a bitch?"

Eric walked back to the dais and rested his forearms on the surface. "Maybe all the above, Frank. I can't attest to his sanity without a psych evaluation, but I can tell you about killers in general." He looked around the room. "There are distinct types of serial killers. Some base their kills in sadism, some in sexual gratification, others kill for personal or monetary gain. This guy is a Visionary. He believes it is his duty to punish, to teach, or to kill anyone who is an offense to himself, the world, and perhaps, to God. Evidence from the autopsy shows that Mr. Bailey was on his knees for an extended period. Again, this harkens back to the theory that there is a religious component to these crimes." He resumed pacing. "So that's what I know, what I've gleaned from the information we've gathered. What I don't know, aside from who or where he is, is what triggered him. Some event occurred recently in his life and acted as a catalyst. We figure out *what* that was, and we figure out *who* he is."

Jake spoke from the front of the room. "Eric, is it your theory that this perp has never had an intimate relationship?"

"Not necessarily. In fact, he may have had romantic interests, but his partners would find him cold, controlling, perhaps even sadistic—both outside and inside the bedroom. I sincerely doubt that he has had the same lover, male or female, for over six months."

Okay, that still leaves Kyle on the table, Jake thought.

He got up, shook Eric's hand, and thanked him for his input. The officers spoke amongst themselves for a few more minutes, comparing notes. The medical examiner's report and Kate's findings were in the case files in front of them. Aman Bailey died of strangulation by ligature; the manner of death ruled a homicide. Deep lacerations to his back and the sides of his face, though disturbing, did not contribute to his death.

Katie determined that Henry Wurster died from a knife wound to the throat, probably carried out by a left-handed individual. The fractured hyoid bone on Laura Dixon's neck meant her cause of death was strangulation. As far as the last set of remains, the examination was still ongoing.

Jake spent the rest of the day compiling notes, evidence and studying the victimology of this case. All roads led back to Kate.

Laura, Henry, Aman, Chance, and now possibly... probably, Stacy Egan, had become targets of this killer. Laura and Henry were likely just victims of opportunity, caught in the wrong place at the wrong time. The suspect needed a vehicle, and they were unfortunate enough to cross his path. But what brought him to Dulles Airport?

The other victims were all connected, in some way, to Kate. But how did this guy know her? He'd run her off the road, burglarized her home, left a snake in her mailbox, and shot at her with a high-powered rifle.

He killed her damn dog, for Christ's sake, Jake thought angrily.

Now, it was likely he'd taken a close family friend. Katie and anyone important to her had a bullseye on their back.

Jake checked his service weapon and adjusted his holster. The winds had shifted. He could feel it in his bones, feel the change. A showdown was coming. Soon.

CHAPTER SEVENTEEN

"But in the end, she is bitter as wormwood. And as sharp as a two-edged sword." Proverbs 5:4.

"Please, Mister! Lemme go… I swear I won't tell!" When there was no answer, she yelled louder.

"C'mon, you psycho, Norman Bates wannabe! Let me out of here!"

Stacy sat on the dusty floor, legs crossed, hands chained behind her. She'd been here for days, listening to her maniac captor spouting scripture while he beat her senseless. The bastard had taken her clothes, save bra and panties, theatrically incinerating them in a wood stove in the corner.

Freak!

She studied her surroundings as she'd done a hundred times before. Aside from a tiny window on the far wall and the door at the top of the steps, there was no exit. Earlier, she thought she'd heard metal doors clanging in the darkened room to her left but couldn't see beyond her six-by-eight-foot area. Shackled for hours, pins and needles danced mercilessly from her shoulders to her fingertips. Although both legs were free, her torso was chained to a metal Lally column that stood sentry in the claustrophobic space.

Why is he doing this? What the hell does he want?

Hurting and exhausted, physically and mentally, Stacy's anger grew. She had never been one to shy away from a fight, her smart mouth notorious for getting her into a jam. She took great pride in her ability to deliver a healthy dose of sarcasm with a salty tongue.

"You know, Stace, someday your mouth is gonna write a check your ass can't cover," Callie once admonished. Then they'd laughed, imagining the poor bastard on the receiving end of her tirade. Stacy's eyes teared as she remembered that conversation and wondered whether she would ever see Callie again.

Fuck this dude... No way I just roll over and die!

The heavy thud of boots descending the stairs caused her breath to hitch and her pulse to quicken. She closed her eyes, took a calming breath, and prepared herself for battle.

"Time to rock-and-roll," she whispered, gritting her teeth. "The asshole cometh."

The Apostle stepped off the bottom stair, amused.

Feisty little bitch.

She was either unafraid or quite skilled in the art of deception.

Probably the latter, he thought bitterly. *A consequence of the company she keeps.*

He paused for a moment to admire his work. The woman's face was bloody and bruised, her nose swollen.

Snot trickled from her nostrils, a thin veil of mucus settling comfortably on her upper lip. Despite her smart mouth and bravado, the wet stains down both cheeks were telling. Though he would not bed her, the sight of her aroused him. He walked to the long table against the wall and selected his tools.

Eyeing him warily, she exhaled through pursed lips—a meditation trick she'd learned in yoga class—and tried to center her mind. It proved an impossible task in the face of such terror.

Shit, shit, shit! All right, girl, just breathe!

Taunting him, she hissed, "How does it feel, tough guy? Beating on a woman half your size?"

His hands stilled, and his back stiffened.

"Does it make you feel powerful? Superior?"

Jesus Christ, Stacy, shut up! Do you really want to die today?

She knew the risks she faced mocking him; she just couldn't seem to stop herself.

"Hey, you! Yeah, I'm talking to you, putz! What's your deal, anyway? Did your momma not hug you enough? Are you Schizo? Impotent? Oh yeah, I bet that's it," she snarled. "You can't get it up without beating the shit outta someone smaller than you." Shaking her head dramatically, she added, "Pathetic piece of crap."

The Apostle turned from the table and glared at her. After several moments of tense silence, he smiled. It was a gesture that turned her blood to sludge and sent her stomach to her knees. His eyes, the curve of his lips, revealed everything.

She'd gone too far. The realization slammed into her like a freight train.

A steady, piercing howl started deep in her throat, the sound echoing against the walls of her prison. Here, in the bowels of this dungeon and devoid of an audience, all hope of rescue vanished. The truth peeled away, layer upon layer, until it lay raw and naked before her.

She would die today.

The last thing Stacy Egan saw before he began his blistering, physical assault was his vacant eyes... and the thick rosary dangling from his pocket.

Ten minutes later, the Apostle stood over the lifeless, blood-soaked body crumpled at his feet. He was exhausted but exhilarated... and horny as hell. Grunting with need, he quickly unzipped his jeans and freed his engorged member. Staring at the body before him, he stroked himself, his perverted fantasy taking wings. His breath quickened as his excitement built, his rhythm changing from slow and focused to urgent, frantic. When release came, he shuddered, spilling his seed onto his unrecognizable victim. Grinning, he licked his lips, spat on her face, and snickered.

"Impotent enough for ya, bitch?"

"Holy crap cakes!" Katie said excitedly. "His hyoid is fractured!" She let out a low whistle, then rolled the tiny bone between her fingers.

Earlier, she'd re-examined the skull to check for injuries missed by Tucker Simon. It would not have surprised her to find he had deliberately sabotaged the results just to make her look bad. During that re-examination, she'd found a slight depression in the skull's occipital region not previously noted in Simon's notes. The injury meant the victim had taken a fall, or someone had cracked him hard enough on the back of the head to cause a skull fracture.

What happened to you, buddy?

She noted no sign of remodeling, the body's method of

repairing injuries to the bones. Since that healing process takes place one to three weeks post-injury, this fracture occurred at, or around, the time of death. The depression itself was shallow, round, and about an inch and a half in circumference. The edges were smooth, the fractured splinters close together. Those splinters, called bone flakes, were found on bone still living when an injury occurred. But did the blow to the head cause his death, or was he strangled, just like Laura Dixon and Aman Bailey? Though she couldn't prove it yet, Katie's instincts said that the skull fracture incapacitated the victim, allowing the perpetrator to execute his prey more efficiently.

Preoccupied with the examination, she failed to hear footsteps approaching. The light touch on her shoulder caused her to jump.

"Jesus Christ, Jake! You scared the pants off me!"

He leered at her, a wicked grin on his handsome face. "If only, Callahan. If only."

Playfully, she elbowed him. "What's up? I thought you had the Task Force meeting today?"

"I did. We just wrapped up, so I thought I'd bring you a copy of the profile. The behavioral specialist, Eric Gibson, gave us a good deal of insight about this killer. Cliff Notes version? Eric believes this jerk is a sociopath, deeply obsessed and delusional, who thinks you've wronged or disrespected him in some way. He believes himself to be omnipotent, holy, even a disciple of God. The truth? I like Kyle Walker for this."

She frowned, and he cupped her chin with his hand. "I'm sorry. I know this isn't what you wanted to hear." Brushing aside a strand of her hair, he said, "Crappy few weeks for you, huh Red? Tell me straight. You doin' okay?"

Katie smiled, wondering again how this guy was single. "I'm still digesting your reference to 'Cliff Notes.' That went the way of the dinosaur." She laughed good-naturedly and continued. "I'm okay, thanks. Just doing some obsessing myself, trying to identify these remains. Oh, and working on this." She handed him a piece of paper addressed to George Mason University. "I'm taking a leave of absence. I'd like to devote as much time as possible to this case, but, more importantly, I want to keep my students and staff members safe. If my presence endangers them, I shouldn't be there right now. This man has already taken shots at me. What if he shows up at the school? I can't take that risk. I can start teaching again when we catch this bastard."

Jake's features visibly relaxed at the welcome news. It would be difficult, if not impossible, to protect her in such an open setting. He grabbed her waist and pulled her close. "Anyone ever tell you you're pretty terrific?" he mumbled.

"All the time," she teased. "See how lucky you are?" Grinning, she continued. "Anyway, the other news I wanted to share is that Darby and Callie have agreed to stay with us. Uncle Tim is taking Grams, Ryan, and Trish to a cabin he owns in the mountains. It's off the beaten trail, but only a few miles from the hospital where Ryan works. At least they'll be safe for a few days." She snapped her fingers. "Oh, and the alarm system Jed arranged is being installed as we speak."

She reached over the table to pick up a bone. "But the most important news of all—drumroll, please—is that this victim sustained a hyoid fracture just like Laura Dixon's. I also found a depressed fracture at the base of his skull. Dollars to doughnuts, he was hit on the head initially, then strangled."

"By rosary beads," Jake said, no question in his tone.

She nodded. "A good bet, but I have a few more things to look at to be certain. Tunnel vision can be a rabbit hole in forensics. You know the old saying… 'crowded elevators smell different to little people.'"

He burst out laughing. "What the hell does that mean?"

Smirking, she explained, "Just that we need to look at every angle here, every aspect. Things aren't always black and white, so we can't afford to assume anything."

Kissing her softly, he said, "Point taken. I'll be back in a few hours to pick you up. We can hit the shooting range and the grocery before heading home for the service. We may even have time to go over some simple self-defense moves after the range." He bent forward and spoke directly into her ear. "Goes without saying, Red, but be careful. Anything seems hinky or out of place, you call me."

"Geesh, you are a pocket full of sunshine today," she joked.

He stroked his thumb down the side of her face. "Monsters are real, baby. And they don't just dwell in dark alleys or under children's beds. Trust no one."

At 3 p.m., Katie stood at the threshold to the tiny room Lydia called her 'Face Space,' an area so small, Katie was sure she had closets that were larger. But the forensic sculptor found it cozy, quiet, and convenient. She had a stool that swiveled, and the narrow diameter meant that all her tools were within arm's reach.

"Knock, knock. Okay if I come in?"

Bent over the small table, her back to the door, Lydia turned and said, "Sure! I was just putting on the finishing touches. I still need to decide on his hair and eye color, but I think we have a decent working model. Wanna take a peek? It's a damn shame. He was a handsome guy."

As Katie walked through the door, her phone rang.

"Hey, girlfriend. What's up?"

"Guess where I am?" Darby said, annoyed.

"I'm guessing it's not a club with killer drinks and a hot waiter."

"Not even. I'm in a freaking tow truck. The VW broke down on my way to the supermarket. Of course, it had to be on an isolated, dark-ass road, too."

"Oh, no! Are you okay? Do you need me to pick you up?"

"No, thanks. Gabriel will run me home after we drop the car off at Pete's."

Katie paused. "Gabriel? Who's Gabriel?"

"Oh, he's the new mechanic working at Pete and Sons." Her voice a whisper, she added, "He's cute. I think Pete hired him after Aman, well, you know." Her words hung in the air, the conversation taking a heavy turn.

"Yeah," Katie said, "I guess he would have to hire someone. Just sucks to know the reason."

"That's the truth. Actually, this new guy recognized your name," Darby said. "Gabriel was the one who finished the work on your car."

"Oh, right. Pete mentioned a new mechanic." Katie chewed on her lip. "I'll see you at the house then. And Darby? Be careful. I was on the receiving end of some brilliant advice earlier today. Trust no one."

After ending the call, Katie turned back to Lydia. "Sorry about the interruption. I'm juggling so many balls lately, I could get a job in the circus."

Lydia laughed. "Don't I know it. I feel like all I do is bounce from one task to another. My condolences, by the way. Jake told me what happened to your sweet dog. I hope my work helps us find this maniac." She turned back toward the table. "Anyway, you ready? The hair and eye color may be off a bit, but you should be able to get the generic version of our John Doe here."

Katie stepped fully into the tiny room, anticipation causing her stomach to flutter. They may finally get a picture out to the public, a photo of this poor man—a man who, so far, had no name. Lydia wiped her hands on a small towel lying on her lap and scooted the chair back, away from her cramped workstation. The man without a name filled Katie's vision. She noted the shape of his eyes, the fullness of his mouth, the way his chin jutted forward, strong and regal. At once, the room spun, her stomach rebelled, and she vomited all over her brand-new shoes.

Lydia jumped up. "Oh, my God! Katie!"

Katie wiped her mouth with the back of her wrist. Her face was deathly pale, and her hands shook, her knees quivered. An old western saying, one she'd read years ago, jumped into her thoughts.

You never hear the shot that kills you.

Her brain scrambled to process what she was seeing.

Never hear the shot? Hell, I never even knew the gun was loaded.

"It's my ex, Kyle. Kyle Walker." Katie shook her head in disbelief. "How could I have not known? How could I miss this?" Remembering, suddenly, that she was not alone, she croaked, "I'm so sorry. If you'll excuse me, Lydia, I need to use the restroom. I'll grab something to clean this up."

"You will do no such thing. I'll page someone from maintenance to take care of this. Why don't you go splash some water on your face while I call Jake?" She squeezed Katie's hand. "How tragic. I truly am sorry for your loss."

Katie left Lydia's station and shuffled, dazed, to the restroom. Once inside, she rinsed out her mouth, washed her face a dozen times with paper towels, and tossed her ruined shoes into the garbage. Thankfully, she always carried running shoes and work-out clothes in her tote.

She clutched the bathroom sink, thoughts racing, and studied her reflection in the mirror.

Kyle was the man on the mountain!

She'd been holding his bones for weeks, going through the motions, examining what was left of him.

Dear God, her mind screamed, *you held your ex-lover's remains in your hands!*

Sliding down the bathroom wall, she hugged her knees, rocking on the tile floor. Tears flooded her face, her grief at war with a niggling truth—Kyle could not be the killer.

They were no closer to finding a suspect than they were at the beginning of this nightmare. Head in her hands, she looked up as the sound of the door creaking open reached her ears. Jake quietly came to her, lifting her to her feet.

"Christ," he whispered. "I'm sorry, Red. All this shit landing on you is so unfair."

Katie wrapped her arms tightly around his neck, as though clinging to him would keep her from falling. "All those horrible thoughts I had, all the rage. I believed him a coward, a man who ran out on me without looking back. I cursed him for months. Jesus, Jake... he was dead the whole time." Sniffling, she choked out, "He died because of me, because he loved me."

"No," Jake said, "not because of you. It's because of a psychotic killer who has a thing for you. And I swear to God, I'm gonna make this bastard pay when we finally meet." He escorted her back to the lab to get her things. Now, more than ever, he was determined to get her to the range. If forced to wield a gun, her aim must be true. Her life could depend on it.

~

After some practice shooting and a kickboxing lesson, they made a quick stop at the grocery store and arrived in Fredericksburg an hour before the service. Katie shot well at the range, and Jake gifted her with the weapon she'd practiced on, a Smith & Wesson, .38 Special, double-action revolver. He also provided extra ammunition, a pocketknife, and a small canister of pepper spray. She was grateful but overwhelmed.

"Bud, I appreciate all of this. Truly, I do. But, don't you think it's a little, I don't know, overkill maybe? I feel like Inspector Gadget. Or Rambo."

Jake frowned. "I was going for 'The Terminator.' Look, forewarned is forearmed, right? We know this guy has been out there for months, killing people connected to you." He shifted closer. "This isn't a dress rehearsal. We're live, game on, with bases loaded and bottom of the ninth. And that revolver? It's just become your new best friend."

She nodded, knowing he was right but sad that this was what her life had become—checking closets, jumping at shadows, fearing strangers.

This crazy person is slowly taking my life away!

She pushed back her shoulders and furrowed her brows. *Screw that!* He would not take any more. She would do whatever she could to get her life back.

Even if it meant using her new best friend to stop him.

They stood in a circle by the river, heads bowed, and hands joined, reciting the Lord's Prayer. Katie wasn't sure if that was custom for a canine funeral, but it felt right. For now, a cross draped with Chance's collar served as a grave marker. A permanent stone was on order, inscribed with his name and a small photo on the front; the back would have a picture of the Rainbow Bridge, the span that many people believed led their furry friends into heaven.

Along with Katie and Jake, Callie, Ryan, Finn, and Trisha were part of that prayer circle. Grams was at home fighting the flu, so Tim stayed behind with her. Sully intended to stop in later this evening to help Jake re-interview the family. The only one unaccounted for was Darby. Katie looked back toward the house, wondering where she was. Her friend had called from the tow truck hours ago. Worried, she tried her cell phone. Darby picked up on the first ring.

"I know, I know. I'm sooo late for Chance's service. I'm sorry, Kates, but I got held up. I'm only about five minutes out, so try to stall."

Katie was so relieved to hear Darby's voice that she didn't bother to ask what had held her up. The group filled the time spent waiting with various prayers. Some were for Chance, others for Aman's soul or Stacy's safe return. The last prayer was for Kyle. Although Katie had never been an overly religious person, she found herself talking an awful lot to God lately.

The problem was, she wasn't sure He was listening.

When Pete and Sons' tow truck pulled into the driveway, Katie breathed a sigh of relief. From her vantage point, she could make out two figures sitting in the cab as the truck idled. Excusing herself from the group, she walked to the front of the house and, uneasy, waited for Darby to exit the vehicle.

C'mon, Darbs, shake a leg.

The driver's side door opened, and a man stepped down from the cab. Lazily, he moved around to the passenger side, opened the door, and offered Darby a hand. They spoke for a moment before Darby turned and made her way up the driveway. The man smiled at Katie, raised a hand in greeting, then inched the truck down the drive and vanished from sight.

"Howdy ho, girlfriend," Darby said. "Sorry I'm late. What did I miss?"

Katie worried her lip. "Was that him? That Gabriel guy?"

Darby's cheeks flushed. "Yes. Dreamy, right? He showed up just in the nick of time, too. The car took a crap in an area with absolutely no cell service. Then, bingo, like some kind of superhero, there he was. He hooked up the VW, then took me back to the garage to have a look."

Katie raised her eyebrows.

"A look at the car, smartass," Darby joked. "Not that I would have minded if he checked under my hood, you understand." She wiggled her brows and grinned. "Anyway, he thinks it may be the alternator. He will let me know before he starts the repairs. Do you think you could bring me to work tomorrow?"

Katie nodded, and they walked happily to the backyard, arm-in-arm. There was a fleeting thought, though, that tickled the recesses of Katie's mind. For weeks, the sense of foreboding shadowing her was content to sit silently in the background. Now, it was a cacophony, a persistent, jarring noise that thundered in her ears, daring her to reveal its true meaning.

Following the eulogy, they stood in a circle, each lost in their thoughts and memories. It was bitterly cold, a frigid breeze bouncing off the Rappahannock and chilling them to the bone. Katie cleared her throat, aware that they'd said all they needed to say.

"Okay, guys, how 'bout we move this party inside? I have some great food and a fabulous selection of craft beer waiting for us." She let go of Jake's hand, turned, and felt a shock wave so fierce, it nearly leveled her. Her hand went to her throat as she gasped for breath. Fighting denial, she locked eyes with the spirit who floated before her.

Oh, sweet Jesus! No!

An ear-piercing, terrifying scream split the air and, confused, she wondered where it came from. It was a gut-wrenching, heartbreaking wail reserved for only the deepest of pain.

She pitied the poor creature who'd made it.

Seconds later, the universe began its familiar tilt; its rotation halted, axis askew. She thought she heard Jake calling her name, but the roar in her ears had become deafening. Her brain hammered relentlessly inside her skull until finally, mercifully, the ground rushed up to greet her. And just before the black shroud descended, Katie understood.

CHAPTER EIGHTEEN

"Give her some space!" Jake yelled angrily. "You're damn near suffocating her!"

The group surrounding the form on the ground moved back as one. Darby—never one to remain calm in a crisis —danced in place and babbled about head trauma and spinal injuries. Callie, in a crouch and face ashen, grumbled incoherently about Jake and his attitude. Finn and Trish remained silent.

Ryan, the only one conscious with actual medical training, knelt beside the patient.

"Katie, can you hear me?" Ryan asked. "C'mon, Kates, open your eyes."

He checked her pulse and found it rapid but strong. Her respirations were easy, her pupils equal and reactive. She stirred, and a collective sigh resounded from the group.

Jake, speaking softly, took her hand. "Baby, you okay? Come on, Red, wake up. We're freezing our balls off out here."

Katie stirred, opened her eyes, and looked around. Six

furrowed brows, six worried faces, peered down at her. She
tried to sit up, but Jake held her in place.

"Whoa, girl, not so fast. You were out like a light. Just
take it slow."

Ryan nodded. "He's right. Take a moment to get your
bearings." A beat later, he teased, "Frostbite's taken hold
anyway, so we pretty much can't feel shit."

She shook the cobwebs out of her head and, with the
help of Jake, sat up. Her gaze locked with Darby's.

"It's time, Kates," Darby whispered. "They deserve to
know."

Still shaking, Katie nodded. "You're right, Darbs. Let's
go inside, and I'll try to explain everything." Her eyes
found Jake's. "But fair warning, FBI guy… this is a game-
changer. I'm about to unleash a cyclone, and I only pray
that we have the strength to weather the storm."

≈

The group sat in the living room, waiting for Katie and
Jake to enter. They whispered amongst themselves, drinks
in hand, speculating about what she would reveal. Only
Darby had an inkling of the truth about what had
occurred outside. She had never heard a scream as visceral
as the one that originated from her best friend.

"Maybe it's a breakdown," Trisha whispered. "After all,
she's gone through some tough stuff. And knowing that
someone's after you? Man, that would shake the fruit off
anyone's tree."

"No, that's not it," Callie said, biting her thumbnail.
"Her mind is as sound as any of ours. But she isn't well,
not physically anyway. Her face is pale and, not for
nothing, she could travel the world with that baggage
under her eyes." She stood and paced the room. "No, this

251

has something to do with her ability to feel what other people feel—good, bad, or otherwise." She stopped mid-step and placed her hands on her hips. "I suspect that someone in this room is in a bleak place, and Katie has picked up on it."

Glaring at her family, she tapped her foot and waited for someone, anyone, to fess up. "So? Which of you is it?" Callie asked. "Who here is in so much freakin' pain that they're killing my sister?"

Finn stood and waved his hands as if he were warding off an argument. "Whoa, hang on a minute, Callista. You're telling us that not only can Katie feel what others feel, but that those feelings can hurt her? Even kill her?" He rolled his eyes. "Horseshit. Look, I agree that something is off here. She looks wiped, and I think she's lost weight she could ill afford to lose. But to claim that this is all due to some mumbo-jumbo, hocus-pocus, new age crap?" He took a pull of his beer. "Nope, sorry. I ain't buying it."

Callie huffed. "Well, I guess it's a good thing I don't give a flying fuck whether or not you buy it, isn't it?" She aimed her finger at his chest. "Face it, Finn. There are things about Kate you couldn't possibly understand. And you want to know why?" She paused, her eyes narrowing. "Because for the last few decades, you didn't care enough to find out!"

Finn turned bright red, his handsome face contorting with anger. Callie glimpsed a flash of something else in his eyes. Pain? Contrition? He stretched his arms out in front of him and, with obvious contempt, slowly clapped his hands.

"Well, there it is, folks! My little sister has finally gotten the chance to say what she's been itching to say for the last twenty years." His voice dripped with sarcasm. "Tell us the truth, Callie… how'd that work out for you? Feel better?"

It was Darby's turn to stand. "Enough, both of you! Geez Louise, do ya'll ever stop?" She was uncharacteristically perturbed. "There is so much more going on here than either of you understand. Slinging mud and throwing stones won't help anyone. And honestly? This isn't about either of you. Your wounded egos and short-sighted opinions aren't worth a bucket of worm spit right now." She set her hands on her hips. "This is about Kate. She's in hell right now and deserves our support. So, just this once, can't we all play nice?"

Katie stood in the sunroom, head resting against the windowpane, watching a red-tailed hawk circle its prey. Jake stood behind her, arms around her waist, his chin resting on her shoulder.

"You ever wish you could fly, Red?" Jake asked. "I do. Sometimes I wish I could soar right out of this town, this state, Christ, out of this world. Just you and me. We would fly to our own Eden, a place where no one could touch us, and everything came easy."

Pensive, Katie said. "That sounds wonderful, Jake. I'd fly anywhere with you, and I mean that. To me, Eden is wherever you are, which is why I'm terrified to tell you the truth. I don't think I could bear it if I lost you before we ever really started."

Jake spun her around to face him. She kept her head down, afraid to see what was in his eyes.

"Look at me, sweetheart." When her head remained bowed, he took a finger and gently lifted her chin. "Red, look at me. Do you not understand how much I care about you? I promise that nothing you say will make me walk; nothing you divulge will cause me to turn away from you. I'm in it for the long haul."

With a smile that never quite reached her eyes, she said, "What if I told you I was a lousy dancer?"

"Same here. Two left feet."

She shrugged and raised her brows. "I can't carry a tune."

He chuckled, a deep, hearty sound. "Lady, dogs howl and children weep if I so much as hum. Try again."

She laughed and took a deep breath. Grabbing his hand, she led him out to the living room where the others waited. If she had to do this, she didn't want to do it twice. They would all hear the truth together.

Several pairs of eyes looked up as Katie and Jake walked into the room. Darby gave a reassuring thumbs-up, Callie held her breath and Finn tucked his hands in his pockets, defiance plastered on his face. Ryan just looked... lost. Jake took a seat on the sofa arm, reached out to squeeze Katie's hand, then gave her a wink.

"First off," she began, "I'd like to apologize for scaring the bejesus out of you earlier. I think once you hear what I have to say, though, you'll understand what happened and why I collapsed." Her fingertips drew circles on her temples, her head still throbbing. "This will be difficult to hear and even harder to believe, but it's time I came out of hiding."

Sighing, she crossed her arms, hugging her abdomen. "Shortly after I drowned, I discovered that there were things I could do—weird, paranormal-type things. Abilities that defy explanation and normalcy."

Struggling to find the words, she looked directly at Jake. "You know that feeling you get when you enter a place where evil has lived? Like taking a tour of the death camps of Germany, or visiting a museum dedicated to Pearl Harbor?" She scoured her mind, trying to simplify something so complex. "Standing where the Twin Towers once stood, or touching the shackles that bound a person into slavery? A location so saturated with haunted memories, the air feels like lead, and you find yourself overcome with sadness? That's how it is for me—every damned day."

Speaking about her gifts, out loud and in front of an audience, was more difficult than she'd imagined. "When I awoke from my coma," she explained, "I awoke with a psychic ability called clairsentience. It's the ability to sense, to experience, what other people are feeling. Think of it as an Empath on steroids. I can detect powerful emotions in people, pets, and places. Those impressions, those feelings, affect me emotionally, sometimes physically. Happiness, sadness, anger, and fear. Some days, it's overwhelming."

"Kates," Callie spoke up, "it's okay. I think we all knew you came back to us, um, changed. It just seems that this Empath business is taking a greater toll on you than we imagined."

"There's more, Cal-pal." The gray lady had made an appearance, standing with stooped shoulders by the kitchen door. She seemed to be as rapt as the rest of them, anxiously awaiting Katie's next words. Walking to where Callie sat, Katie kneeled in front of her and took her hands.

"Being clairsentient is only one part of my gift. The other, more frightening part, is my ability to see the dead."

Callie gulped, eyes wide.

Katie's fingers caressed her sister's clenched fists. "I've been seeing dead people my whole life, Shadow. Family members, like Granddad, Uncle Jimmy, and Aunt Gert. I'm not sure why, but Mom and Dad have yet to appear to me. Many, many others have, though. Like Mr. Perry, the nice old man from the general store, and that little boy, Robbie, from fifth grade. You remember… the one who died from meningitis?" Whispering now, she continued. "I've also seen Laura Dixon, our homicide victim, over the last few weeks. And now, there seems to be an older woman with gray hair sticking to me like glue." She paused. "In fact, she's here with us now."

Six heads turned to look behind them. Then, as if on a swivel, they slowly eyed the four corners of the room. Jake turned back around first, his eyes piercing hers.

Stunned, Ryan said, "Jesus, way to bury the lead, Kates."

She ignored him and continued. "She's standing by the kitchen door. I'm not sure, but I think she's waiting for something. Or someone." Still kneeling, Katie sighed. "I can see these spirits, feel what they feel. I just can't seem to figure out how to communicate with them."

Hurt, Callie rasped, "Why wouldn't you tell me this? Shit, Kates, don't you trust me?"

Frowning, Finn admonished, "Come on, Callie. You're not helping."

"Bite me, Finn."

Katie jumped in before her brother could react. "Oh, honey, of course, I trust you. It's just a lot, you know? Only Nana, Darby, and Kyle knew everything. And when I told Kyle the truth, he left me, or so I thought. After that, I've been hesitant to share what I can do." She stole a glance at Jake and saw that not only was he still there, but he appeared to be listening.

It's the little things, she thought wryly.

Callie nodded in understanding. "I get it. I do. But I want you to know that you can tell me anything. I'll always have your back."

Katie squeezed her hand, tears threatening to fall.

My God, how can I do this?

"I know, Shadow. And I will always have yours. But what just happened, who I saw, is devastating. It's the reason I fainted outside, the reason I screamed." She sat on the couch between Callie and Ryan, still clutching her sister's hands.

"I saw someone outside," Katie said. "Someone we all loved, very much, and hoped to see again."

Fear, then awareness, flashed in Callie's eyes. Feverishly, she shook her head.

"Jesus Christ, don't! Don't say it, Kate… don't fucking say it! I can't. Seriously, I can't." Her lips quivered; her face contorted in pain. A steady stream of tears slid down her cheeks to the delicate curve of her neck.

Jake jumped up, a knot forming in the pit of his stomach.

Voice shaking, eyes brimming with unshed tears, Katie gazed at her twin. "I'm so sorry, Cal. I don't know how, when, or even where it happened, but it was her—it was Stacy. The image was just a flash, but the Empath in me can confirm how it felt." Katie took a deep breath. "It felt unbelievably bad, Shadow. It felt… deadly."

"Feel like talking?" Jake asked, concern lining his face.

They were standing, once again, in Katie's favorite room, gazing out to the wintery scene before them. A light coating of snow had fallen, dusting the hanging branches and wooden cross that marked Chance's grave.

"To be honest, I'm not sure what I feel. My sister is upstairs on her bed, inconsolable, and I put her there. Maybe I should have just waited until Stacy's body is found so we could be certain. But what if it takes weeks? Months?" She dropped her head. "What if it's like my mother, and we never find her?"

Jake rubbed his neck, then stuck his hands in his pockets. "We'll find her. If I'm sure of nothing else in this case, I'm sure of that. This prick would never hide her too well; he gets off on the discovery. You need to stop beating yourself up about shit this asshole does, Red. It's on him, not you."

"Is it though, Jake? Is it really?"

His cell rang, and he sent the call to voicemail. "Listen, maybe we approach this from another angle. You can see the dead, right? So, we concentrate on opening a communication channel. If you can talk to Stacy, maybe we can find out what happened and where she is. Maybe even who killed her."

Harsher than she intended, she barked, "Don't you think I've tried that? Jesus, Jake, I've spent my life trying to talk to those who have passed, to pierce that veil. And I've never been able to do it." Hesitating, she added, "Until Laura Dixon. You know, I saw her earlier. I was upstairs, getting the DNA for comparison, and she was in her bedroom."

"Oh?"

"She directed me to her vanity and a notepad." Katie faltered, believing that saying these words aloud would send him screaming for the hills. "I sat down and started writing. But it wasn't my thoughts, wasn't even my hand. It was Laura's. She spoke through me, writing her messages with my hand."

Stunned, Jake asked, "So, sort of like using a Ouija board to talk to the dead?"

Surprised he'd even known about that, she answered,

"Exactly. I communicated with her through pencil and paper. It's called automatic writing."

He nodded thoughtfully. "Well then, there's only one thing to do. We need to set you up with a pen and paper, so when this gray lady or Stacy makes an appearance, we'll be ready."

Katie agreed. "I guess that's our best bet. Although, honestly, I'm not even sure it will work again. This way of communicating may have more to do with the strength of the spirit coming through than my abilities." She sighed heavily. "The gray lady is gone for now. I need to check on Callie. Be back in a bit."

He watched her walk up the stairs, then headed to the kitchen to return Sully's call.

"Cal? Okay if I come in?" Katie stood by the closed door, hands shaking, listening to the soft sobs, and shuffling footsteps as her sister crossed the room.

The door cracked open, and Callie stood awkwardly at the threshold. Her eyes were bloodshot and puffy, her cheeks wet with tears and mascara. She sported a bright, red nose that coordinated nicely with the blotchy pink spots covering her neck and chest.

We Callahan's have always been ugly criers, Katie thought.

"I think we need to talk, Shadow."

Callie opened the door wide, and they walked to the bed holding hands. Seated, Katie began.

"I need to know that you will be okay, sweetheart. I can't imagine how hard this is for you. If something happened to Darby…" There was no need to state the obvious.

A sliver of hair lay plastered to her wet face, and Callie yanked the errant strand back. Sniffling, she said, "You're sure about this, Kates? There can be no mistake? Maybe it's a premonition of the future, something we can change?" The desperation reflected in her eyes was heartbreaking.

"I wish that were true, Cal. I wish it like a child wishes birthday ponies and Santa Claus and happy endings were true. But I don't have warnings or premonitions. I have visions of the dead. And I saw Stacy Egan, as clearly as I see you." A tear ran, unnoticed, down her face. "Forgive me, but someone's hatred of me has cost us a friend. Your friend. And that's just so messed up."

Callie wiped fresh tears from her face. "This is not your fault! Promise me you understand and believe that. The psycho bastard that killed Stacy, slaughtered the others, crucified sweet Chance, is the only one responsible for this nightmare." She sat up taller, apparently deciding that she'd wasted enough time grieving for now.

"We need to find her. The idea of Stacy alone, sprawled on the ground or buried in an unmarked grave, with rodents or bugs or…" She dropped her head, unable to complete the thought.

"We will find her, Shadow, I promise. And we will find the sick creep who killed her. Trust me?"

"Always, Kates. Always."

～

"How's she doing?" Jake asked when Katie returned to the first floor. He was sitting at the kitchen table, leafing through papers tucked inside an open manila folder.

"She's a train wreck. I've convinced her to take a nap. It's killing me to see her like this, Jake."

He walked over and put his arms around her, holding

her tight. "I know, love. But we are getting close. I spoke to Sully, and he tells me they've tracked down the supplier for those rosary beads. It's an online military outfit, called The Spiritual Soldier, whose clientele consists mainly of devout servicemen and police officers." He stood and stretched his back. "They're sending us rosary samples so we can physically compare their stock to the beads we have in evidence. Unfortunately, because of the sometimes-sensitive nature of work their customers provide, the company strives to protect confidentiality."

"Meaning what exactly?" Kate asked.

He grabbed a bottled water from the fridge. "Meaning they don't keep client records, so we have no clue who patronizes this place. I can't blame them, really. If classified information gets out about Special Ops soldiers or undercover cops, it could get ugly. I have some of my team digging into felony crimes with a religious connection. Hopefully, something pops."

Finn walked into the kitchen just then, a somber expression on his face. He looked from Jake to Katie, then back again.

"Ryan said you wanted to talk to us all again about our lives, our past. There is something that I need to share with you both, something that will hurt my family, but it needs to be said." He looked through dark lashes at his sister. "And Kate, you especially need to hear it."

More secrets, Katie thought. *Perfect.*

The room grew smaller, the air thicker, as she waited for Finn to tell his tale. Her palms were damp, and dread pooled in the pit of her belly. She doubted she was strong enough to face more unwelcome news today, more sorrow.

For the first time in a long while, she wanted to flee. She prayed that the floor would open wide, drag her in, and swallow her whole.

I'm trapped! Boxed in and slowly suffocating!

Finn was oblivious to her torment. "My truth began years ago, July 12th, 1996, the day that you died, Kate. Mom and Callie were out for the day. Ryan was upstairs asleep in his crib, and Dad was in the den, supposedly working on his next big investigation."

Finn's voice held a trace of resentment when he spoke of their father. Anxious, Katie waited.

"You were in the pool, and I was on the patio lounge chair, ostensibly keeping you safe," he said bitterly. "The phone rang, and I picked up the outside extension so as not to disturb Dad. I wish I hadn't done that."

"Take your time, Finn," Katie said kindly.

He studied his calloused hands, struggling to stay on point. "I'm okay, thanks. Anyhow, it turns out Dad had already picked up the house phone. I never even had the chance to say 'hello.' I know now that I should have hung up, shouldn't have eavesdropped, but I did. I turned my back from the pool, grappling with what I was hearing. I was so wrapped up in the conversation, in that damned phone call, that I forgot I was supposed to be watching you. How does that even happen?" Finn's voice cracked, and he looked close to tears. Katie went to him, but he waved her away.

"Please, you need to hear this." His sad eyes searched hers, mentally begging her to challenge him, to stop this. He would have given anything to keep this truth from tumbling through his lips.

She remained silent.

Grudgingly, he continued. "Dad was whispering to the person on the other end of the line. It was a woman, a woman who, I knew, was not Mom. They spoke as though they were comfortable, close. I'd never heard her voice before, and I remember wondering if this was a neighbor, co-worker, or editor."

He clenched his jaw. "Soon, though, the bullshit started. The giggling terms of endearment; the declarations of love. They talked about what they were planning to do to each other, with each other, when next they met. It was disgusting."

Jake looked at Katie, wondering what she was thinking. Discovering your father had been unfaithful was a bitter pill for anyone to swallow.

Finn pulled out a chair and sat at the table. "It felt like I got punched in the gut. I couldn't listen to that shit anymore, so I hung up the phone. And when I turned back to the pool, you were gone." He inhaled sharply. "No, not gone. Underwater. Terrified, screaming for help, I dove in and dragged you out. Dad called 9-1-1, and we started CPR." He rubbed his eyes as if the action would stop his tears. "I've always blamed Dad for putting me in that position, and I've always hated myself for not protecting you."

Katie struggled to absorb all that he was saying.

"While we stood vigil at the hospital," Finn continued, "I pulled Dad aside and told him that once you were out of the woods, medically, he had to tell Mom everything. And if he didn't, I would. Funny, I'd barely started high school, and yet I found myself responsible for two deaths."

Katie looked at him, puzzled. "What do you mean?"

"Just what I said, two deaths. Yours and Dad's."

Katie shook her head. "That's bullshit, Finn. You're not responsible for what happened to me. It was an accident. And how could you possibly be responsible for Dad's death? He died in a plane crash."

Finn nodded. "He did, but I gave him an ultimatum. I think he was on his way back home after breaking things off with his mistress. Why else would he have left when you were still in rough shape, looking at weeks and weeks of rehab?" He raked his hand through his hair. "No, he got on that plane because of my threat. He had no choice but to end the affair, and on his return flight, the plane went down."

Sensing his pain, Katie said, "You need to stop punishing yourself, Finn. None of this is your fault."

"But it is, Kate, don't you see? I was the one who put him on that plane." Dropping his head in his hands, Finn croaked, "I killed Dad."

CHAPTER NINETEEN

October 27th, 1997

*"Even a child makes himself known by his acts, by whether his
conduct is pure and upright." Proverbs 20:11.*

The woman, hyperventilating, paced the wooden floor.
"What are we going to do?" she mumbled to no one
in particular. "Dear God, what do I do?" Narrowing her
gaze, she studied the child standing in front of her and
whispered, "Why would you do this?"

The boy shrugged, head down, and continued to count
the nails in the floorboards. Forty-six so far—or was it
forty-seven? He'd lost count, her shrill voice piercing
through him like a thousand swords. Towering over him,
arms flapping madly, she reminded him of Ursula, the evil
sea witch from "The Little Mermaid." He chewed on the
corner of his thumb, embarrassed.

Mother is such a tool!

Grabbing his shoulders, she gave him a jerk, her
lipstick-stained teeth and sour breath mere inches from his
face. "Look at me when I'm talking to you, young man!

Don't you get it? You killed someone! They could arrest you, charge you with murder! Send you away forever!"

She shook, on the verge of hysteria. "Oh, God! Think!"

She needed a plan. Mind racing, she rubbed her temples and tried to avert her gaze—from her child, from the blood, from the form lying face down on the pretty linoleum floor. But like witnessing a gruesome tragedy, it was impossible not to look. She felt as though she were a character in a story, playing a scripted part meant for someone else; a nightmarish role, intended for another woman's child. But the proof danced in front of her, waving its grotesque arms, daring her to circumvent the truth.

Her son took a life.

Out of options and sickened by her nonchalance, she said, "We need to get rid of her, dispose of the body so no one will ever find her. If there's no corpse, there's no evidence of death." She glared at the boy, a child still years away from puberty. "Are you listening to me? Jeremy!"

The boy raised his head, eyes angry, cold, and black with contempt.

She believed that the eyes were the windows to the soul —the doorway or portal to measure a person's true character. But when she looked into the boy's eyes, her boy, all she saw was darkness and evil. It was terrifying.

As if blinded for years, her vision suddenly, painfully, cleared. The truth was unspeakable and repugnant, but if she were to save him, save them, she needed to face the truth.

He was a monster.

"Come," she said, sounding much braver than she felt, "help me. We need to make this look like a break-in, a robbery gone horribly wrong. Be careful not to touch anything. Wrap a towel around your hands, then go upstairs and steal something. Money, jewelry, I don't care. I'll destroy the living room, make it look like a struggle occurred, and we will take her body far from here."

Her level-headed tone disgusted her. *How am I not screaming right now?*

Jeremy climbed the steps to the second floor while the woman, in a daze, ransacked the living room. Afterward, they dragged the body to an oriental throw rug, placed the murder weapon—an ordinary steak knife—on the victim's chest, and secured her using duct tape found in a kitchen drawer.

Admiring their efforts, the boy grinned. The dead woman was rolled up nice and tight in the multi-colored carpet, like a burrito or a Chinese egg roll. Suddenly, he was famished.

A cry shattered the stillness of the house, and the woman gasped. "Oh God, Jeremy, the baby! Didn't you see the baby when you were upstairs?"

Stumbling toward the stairs, she looked up. Standing on the landing was a toddler, hands fisted at his sides, his ear-piercing screams deafening. Upon seeing the strange woman staring up at him, his cries grew even louder. She tried to shush him, to soothe him as she ascended the staircase, but he continued to screech. Reaching him, she scooped him up, holding him tightly as he kicked and twisted. His little hands pushed against her face, desperate to escape. Tears falling, she sat him down in a hallway closet.

"I'm sorry, little one," she whispered, shutting the door.

The baby's muffled cries echoed throughout the house, throughout her mind, as she fled down the stairs to the freedom of the outdoors. Still weeping, she backed her sedan up the driveway and popped open the trunk.

Good God, what was she doing?

Her son, callous and impassive, stood yawning at the front door. He was a mentally unstable child who, she knew, should be locked away. She hated herself for covering up his crime, hated her cowardice. But he was all she had in this world, and she must protect him. To lose him would be to lose her heart, her soul.

Herself.

After loading the body, they drove in silence. The woman, mentally revisiting their actions, navigated the unfamiliar Virginia roads. Consulting a map, she searched for a secluded area to dispose of the woman's remains. Jeremy played with a loose string on his Batman t-shirt, occasionally staring out the window, seeing nothing. He didn't know what all the fuss was about; they didn't even live in Virginia, for Christ's sake. No one would suspect them; no one would look for them. If it were up to him, he would have left the lady crumpled on the kitchen floor. He wondered who would have found the body.

That would have been cool to see... all guts and blood and stuff.

They finally pulled into what looked like an abandoned park. Remnants of rusted barbecue grills, forgotten dumpsters, and weathered picnic tables littered the landscape. Beyond that lay a thick copse of trees, still green with foliage. She angled the sedan into a small clearing, pulling in as far as she dared, and looked around. Satisfied that their surroundings adequately camouflaged the car, they went to work.

The dead woman, though trim, was tall, making it difficult to carry her through the narrow, densely treed area. Adding to the challenge was that her 'partner in crime,' the person who held the other end of the body, was an eleven-year-old child. Still, they managed to half-carry, half-drag the form until safely inside the woods.

The boy stayed with the body while his mother, heart-pounding, walked the mile or so back to the sedan. She was half-expecting to see a dozen police cars surrounding the park, lights blazing, and guns drawn, but the area remained empty. Crouching, feeling like the felon she was, she opened the trunk and removed a shovel and a pair of gloves. After another look around, she sprinted back to Jeremy and the dead woman in the rug.

It took her nearly three hours to dig a grave deep enough to cover the corpse. While she worked, the boy sat on an old tree stump, happily squishing a colony of ants with a stick. When finished, they hurried back to the car— her on shaky legs, him waving his ant-squishing stick like a lightsaber.

As she drove, she stole furtive glances at him, shaking her head between sobs. Oblivious, Jeremy played with his stick and whistled a merry tune, paying little attention to their surroundings. He had no idea what road they were on or where they had just buried that lady, and he didn't much care. At that moment, there was only one thing on his mind. He turned to his mother, sighed dramatically, and said, "I'm hungry. Can we get ice cream?"

His relationship with his mother changed forever that day. The boy could see it in her eyes… disgust, disappointment, fear. Her drinking escalated, and her behavior became more erratic, the bills forgotten, appointments missed. The boy suspected she was self-medicating with anti-anxiety drugs purchased from the sleazy landlord next door.

Jeremy went hungry most days, simply because she stopped preparing meals. He missed more school than he'd attended and was forced to repeat the sixth grade. When he turned thirteen, the Texas Department of Family and Protective Services received an anonymous tip regarding his welfare. His mother's binge drinking, drug use, and irresponsible behavior became well documented. Eventually, authorities removed the boy from the home and placed him in the foster care system.

He spent two years with a young couple and their three children until, following an accusation of sexual assault by the couple's eleven-year-old daughter, social services removed him. The following year would see him placed with three more families, each arrangement shorter than the last.

His final placement proved to be the proverbial 'straw that broke the camel's back.' Deacon Billy Ray Porter was a strict, God-fearing man; his wife, Jolene, a mouse of a woman who believed that behind every good man was an obedient wife. By the time the boy came to them, he was sixteen years old and full of 'piss and vinegar,' as Billy Ray would say. Within a month of arriving on the deacon's doorstep, the couple made it their mission to exorcise the child's demons. The first lesson took place following the discovery of a pornographic magazine tucked beneath the boy's bed.

On the day that would mark nearly two years of corporal punishment and penance, Jeremy hurried up the stairs after school to the solace of his bedroom, his fortress. Soon after slamming the door, a voice bellowed from the first floor.

"Hey! Git your ass down here, Boy! Pronto!"

Jeremy slowly descended the stairs, wearing a bored expression, daring his guardian to knock the chip off his shoulder. He detested the Porters, his school, his life.

Billy Ray bared his teeth; the yellow tobacco stains an

ugly reminder of his two-pack a day habit. "You got any idea what your Momma found in your room today, son?"

Jeremy's eyes narrowed, his face chiseled in stone. "She's not my mother, dickhead. And I don't give two shits what she found. Bitch shouldn't be snooping through my stuff, anyway." He shrugged. "The fuck I care what she found."

"You best watch your tongue, boy," Billy Ray hissed, his face just inches away and breath reeking of cigarettes and rum. "You have the devil in you, Jeremy. God as my witness, you do. And those demons inside you, they's fightin' for control of your soul." Reverently, he whispered, "I can see 'em, son. Clear as a bright summer's day, I can see 'em. Just but one way to send 'em back to Hell, where they's come from; just but one way to save your soul." Snarling, he commanded, "To the basement with you! Punishment and penitence will free your soul!"

For the next twenty-two months, they subjected the boy to daily lessons. Locked in closets, denied food or water, made to kneel for hours at a time while praying the rosary. When he continued to resist, Billy Ray introduced The Punisher, a bullwhip so powerful, it inflicted broad welts and lasting scars. When that wasn't enough to tame Jeremy's tongue, the deacon took a razor blade to his face. Its purpose was to carve channels into the flesh by his ears to purge the soul. According to the Porters, all necessary to get 'deep under the skin, where the demons live.'

Billy Ray and Jolene kept the boy hidden, home-schooled, and isolated in a virtual hell for close to two years. Then, on his eighteenth birthday, when the state's monthly checks stopped, they threw him out. With nowhere else to go, he enlisted in the Army.

Many weeks after he'd left home, the police discovered the badly decomposed bodies of Deacon William Ray Porter and his wife, Jolene, in the basement of their home. Beaten and strangled, their killer had posed the bodies in prayer at the base of an altar. Billy Ray's decaying fist held a whip and a rosary, a startling juxtaposition of the beliefs he espoused and the truth behind the mask. Authorities questioned Jeremy about the slayings, but a lack of evidence and an alibi provided by his birth mother resulted in no charges being filed. The killings marked the second such unsolved murder in the area.

The first involved a woman in her thirties, a woman by the name of Samantha Norman.

Several years later, Jeremy's visit with his mother would sow a seed of jealousy and hatred—a seed that would grow, continuing to thrive until it blossomed. He had learned the truth and marked the Chosen one for death. Justice would be his.

He was the Apostle.

CHAPTER TWENTY

E arly the next morning, Jake woke up alone, the enticing smell of fresh-brewed coffee calling his name. He pulled on a pair of faded blue jeans and headed downstairs.

"Hey, beautiful," he said, placing an arm protectively around Katie's waist. He kissed the top of her head, inhaling the sweet smell of her skin. The early morning sun shone through the checkerboard curtains, its brilliant rays bouncing off her hair. Outside, the vibrations of a low-flying helicopter rattled the dishes in the sink—a novice pilot, no doubt, enjoying his or her new toy.

Jake walked to the cabinet and took down a mug. "You okay, Red? That was a heavy load Finn dumped on you last night."

"I'm not sure how I feel. There are so many unanswered questions. Daddy had an affair? For how long? And who was the woman?" She hugged her arms to her chest. "I wonder if my mom knew about it. To her, my dad was the sun and the moon and everything in between. It would have killed her to know he didn't feel the same."

Jake shook his head. "If I had to guess, I'd say no. Your father died shortly after your accident, right? Probably wouldn't be much time for anything, much less confessions of infidelity, before he took that plane ride."

He gathered her in his arms, and she dropped her head on his shoulder. In his embrace, she felt safe, loved, whole. So, why was it then that the closer they got to solving this case, the more she feared their relationship was doomed?

Knock it off, Pollyanna, she scolded herself. *We've got enough drama.*

Jake kissed her head again and walked to the sink. The thumping of helicopter rotors still echoed in the kitchen, forcing him to shout. "I'm going to the office to check in with the team. Over the last few days, Sully widened the investigation parameters to include unsolved homicides with a religious component. He went back as far as fifteen years ago, and I'll be damned if we didn't get a hit." Rinsing out his coffee mug, he twisted to face her. "Some preacher and his wife. The crime occurred in Texas, though, so if this is our guy, he's using an extensive hunting ground. With most of these fuckers, you can set your watch by a specific area they prefer. Geographically, they love familiarity, but these victims died of asphyxiation, and they found rosary beads at the crime scene. Worth a look, right?"

"Here's hoping," Kate said brightly.

How awful, she thought, *to hope that someone's murder would benefit her.*

Contrite, she said, "Callie's a mess, so I think I'll stay with her. I also want to be here in case the gray lady comes back."

Jake's phone sounded, and, plugging a finger in his ear to dull the chopper noise outside, he answered.

"Devereaux."

"Mornin', boss," Sully said. "Hate to be the bearer of shit news, but it looks like we have another victim, a female found in a clearing just off Route 29." He exhaled, the weight of the world on his shoulders. "She was beaten pretty badly, Jake. Some guy having car trouble found her lying there, out in the open, mere feet from the road's edge. Fucker isn't even trying to hide them anymore. There were marks on her neck and rosary beads in her hands. The level of cruelty, of savagery..." He let the words trail off. "I'm sending you the picture I received from the locals, but I warn you, it ain't pretty. We have a State Police bird flying a grid now, searching the area. Never know, the scumbag may still be out there."

Jake's jaw clenched. "Well, that explains the chopper circling overhead the past hour. Damn, Ian, I think I know who this young lady is but send me the picture, anyway. I'm coming in to make a few calls about this Texas couple killed all those years ago. We might want to talk to the detective in charge of that case. Hell, maybe we take an overnight trip down there."

"Roger that. You still want me to come over today to help re-interview the Callahans?"

"No, I've got it. I'll meet you at the office."

Katie stood, barely breathing, as Jake ended the call. She'd heard enough of the conversation to understand its significance. They'd found another body.

Stacy.

He read the fear in her eyes. "I know what you're thinking, Red, but don't go there yet. Wait until I get the preliminary and a picture of this latest victim. Otherwise, you're gonna drive yourself crazy."

"We both know how this turns out, Jake. As horrific as it is, I'd much rather find her than spend my life wondering where she is."

"I know." Jake's lips touched hers. "I need you to promise me something, Kate. Promise me you will not leave this house. I can't do my job if I'm worried that you are bait for this asshole."

She held his gaze. "You know I can't make that promise. While I have no plans to leave, if something comes up, if Grams needs me, then all bets are off."

And so, the spark was lit, and the fireworks began. Jake, on edge, argued that her leaving for any reason was tantamount to suicide. Katie countered that, although she didn't have a death wish, she would not hide if her family were in danger.

"I'm sorry, Jake, but my word is important to me. I won't make promises I may not keep." She shrugged a shoulder and quipped, "You want guarantees, buy a toaster."

Jake swore under his breath. "You are, without a doubt, the most exasperating woman I've ever known."

They stood toe to toe, staring each other down. Jake's hands fisted at his sides; Katie's rested at her hips. Neither looked ready to give an inch.

Callie entered the room, picking up on the tense atmosphere. She eyed Jake up and down as if deciding whether he was worthy of her counsel.

"Agent Devereaux, if I may be so bold," Callie started. "I'm sure in your line of work you are exceptional at staring contests. Biding your time, waiting for a suspect to crack, is probably a key interrogation tactic. But standoffs? I'm afraid my sister invented the game." Smirking, she added, "She makes a living playing with dead things; she can out-stare a corpse."

His lip quivered a bit, and he coughed to cover his smile. "Yeah, no kidding. She's also a pain in my ass." Callie grinned and made a beeline to the coffeepot.

Jake cleared his throat. "Look, I'm doing my best here. I'm trying to be a supportive, understanding, twenty-first-century man. But this is as real as it gets. I can't lose you." He took her hand in his. "I'm no superhero, Kate. I want to protect you, but you gotta help me out here."

She rubbed his hand with her thumb. "You spend your life protecting people. I get it. And whatever is happening here between us, I'm in, body and soul." Grinning, she added, "Despite your sometimes chauvinistic, archaic thinking. But the bottom line is that shit happens, and all I can promise is I'll do my best to stay safe, okay? Are we good?"

"Better than good. Anyway, while you are here, staying at home, I'm sure," he raised his eyebrows in a mock warning, "Sully and I are heading to Laredo. I want to check out the murder of that Deacon fellow and his wife. It's about a five or six-hour flight from D.C., so I may be gone overnight."

"Laredo? Yes, it's at least five hours. I know because my dad had an office there. It was where he was coming from when his plane went down. Hmm. What do you think, FBI guy? Coincidence or small world?"

Jake winked. "You know how I feel about coincidence."

"Right." She cleared her throat. "So, when do you think you'll hear about the body they found? I have to see her for myself, Jake. I have to know. Stacy was family."

"I understand, but if it's as bad as it sounds, you don't want to see it. Let me check it out first, okay? Any question of identification, I'll show you the pictures. Deal?"

"Deal."

Their goodbye kiss lasted several minutes. Katie fought back an irrational fear that fate had cursed this relationship from the start, and instead, closed her eyes and savored the moment. When they finally parted, she had just one thought on her mind.

Good God, but Jake Devereaux knew how to kiss a woman!

❧

Darby sat in a kitchen chair, stirring her bowl of oatmeal. "You realize we are just a few days away from the New Year, right, Kates? It's weird. Time seems to be standing still, yet here we are, on the verge of a new year. A new year where we are still monkeying around, waiting for this psycho asshole to make a move." She blinked back the tears. "I'm scared, Kates. I love you so much, and I'm afraid I will lose you."

Katie hugged her friend fiercely. "I'm not going anywhere. We will get this bastard." She kissed Darby's cheek. "We will grow old together, girl, just you wait and see." Katie swallowed, her fear and uncertainty crippling her resolve.

You're so full of shit, Callahan. You have no idea when, or even if, this nightmare will end.

Fifteen minutes later, Darby and Callie left the house to run some errands. Darby needed to open her store, even if just for a few hours, if she wanted to pay this month's bills. Christmas had always been a profitable time for the shop, and now that it was over, she hoped her after-holiday sales would further boost her business. Callie agreed to drop her off on the way to Uncle Tim's cabin to visit with Grams.

"You sure you don't want to come with?" Callie asked Katie. "I don't think we should leave you here alone."

"I'll be fine, Cal Pal. I promised Jake I would stay put if possible, and besides, I'm not alone. Believe it or not, Finn is still here, nosing around in the garage. I'm just going to hang out, maybe play with the dogs, and visit Chance's grave. His marker's finished, you know; I just need to figure out which direction to place it. Toward the river, maybe? Obviously, though, I have to wait until this rain stops before I do anything." She smiled warmly. "I'll be fine. And who knows? With any luck, the gray lady will appear, and we can finally get some answers."

She watched Callie and Darby pull out of the driveway. The steady rhythm of raindrops dancing on the roof interrupted the quiet of the house. Bone tired and numb, Katie felt as though she were a thousand years old. The magnitude of all that had happened, in such a brief period, was jarring.

Blue sat quietly at her side, his presence comforting. It was as if he understood the frightening, bizarre events dominating her life and sympathized. She stroked his back, the soothing motion helping her sort through the chaos in her mind. The sound of Charlie Puth singing, 'One Call Away,' made her jump.

"Hey, Red," Jake said. "Just checking in. You doing okay?"

"I'm fine. I was just waiting, impatiently, for the rain to let up. I'd like to visit Chance's grave."

"Well, just be careful. You still carrying the mace in your pocket like we talked about?"

"Yessir, Agent Sir," she said sarcastically. "You need to chillax, dude, before you get all wrinkled up. Folks will think you are my creepy uncle instead of my over-protective boyfriend."

"Yuck, yuck. Hysterical. You finished, Seinfeld?" He grinned, then continued before she had a chance to respond—his momma didn't raise a fool.

"Things are moving quickly. This case may be about to break wide open." For the first time, he sounded optimistic. "I just got off the phone with the medical examiner. They compared the sample rosary we received from that online company, The Spiritual Soldier, to the ligature marks on Aman's neck. It looks like a match. If the pattern of these beads also matches our latest victim, it's a slam dunk."

"Have you seen the body yet? Is it her?"

His silence told her all she needed to know. She dropped her head, defeated. Though not surprised, a tiny piece of her still hoped that somehow, she was mistaken about the spirit she saw, that they would find Stacy alive.

"I'm afraid so, sweetheart. There's no question in my mind that it's her." He left out the part about Stacy being beaten so severely, her face was almost unrecognizable. "This bastard is an animal. I pray to God she was unconscious for most of it."

Katie's eyes remained dry. She doubted she could shed a tear right now, even if Jesus himself commanded it.

What the hell's the matter with me?

"I can't imagine how hard this is for you, Red," Jake soothed, "but it would have been unbearable had you seen the photograph. People should remember loved ones as they lived, not as they died. Hang on a second, sweetheart."

She heard him cover the phone, silencing a discussion in the background.

Jake came back on the line. "Kate, weird question, but was Stacy engaged?"

"Engaged? Not that I know of. Her heart has always belonged to my brother, Ryan. I think she was waiting for him to notice her, to make the first move. Why?"

"I'm sending you a picture, but only of her left hand. She's wearing a ring on the fourth finger. Looks like a good-sized rock to me."

Katie pulled the phone away from her ear and waited for the picture to download. A few seconds later, the image emerged. Squinting to see the details, she enlarged it, and bile rose in her throat as she recognized the ring.

"Hello?" he called out. "Did you get it?"

"Oh my God, Jake," she whispered into the phone, "it *is* an engagement ring, but it isn't Stacy's. I think it belonged to my mother. How is that even possible?" Legs shaking, bracing herself, she eased down to the sofa. "What the hell is going on?"

After hanging up with Jake, Katie sat at the kitchen table, paper and pencil in hand. So much was happening so quickly, she thought it best to write it all down. Perhaps there was a pattern, a common denominator, within the facts. She drew a line dividing the paper into two columns: one column for what they knew, and one for what yet remained a mystery. Starting on the left, she began.

"Okay, boys," she said, addressing Blue and Gus, "what do we know?" Her voice broke the silence of the house, jolting her. "We know that there's someone, probably a male, definitely a wanker, who's been stalking me. It isn't Kyle or Finn, so could it be Tucker?" She nibbled on the end of her pencil. "We also know that whoever he is, he hates my guts and has been stalking me for months." Her mind was whirling, reviewing the possibilities.

She held up her fingers, tallying each point. "He's been to my house, so he knows where I live and, we can assume, also knows my routine. He can use a gun and shoots very well. He's physically fit, at least strong enough to transport a body a respectable distance away." She scribbled, then looked at the dogs at her feet. "Are you guys getting all this? What number was I on?" Blue and Gus remained stubbornly silent.

She continued. "It's also clear that this guy knows about forensics and crime scene investigation. Intelligent and cunning, he thrives on the havoc he creates." She chewed on her pencil again, wishing Callie were home. Her sister had a much better grasp of psychopathy and aberrant behavior than she did.

Leaning down, Katie spoke directly to Blue. "And the kicker, pal? He had my dead mother's engagement ring." Blue chuffed and put his head on his paws. "How did he come upon that? She's been gone for over twenty years."

Moving to the right side of the paper, she said, "As for what we don't know ... um, we don't know a lot. Why is he doing this to me? Why now? Did he kill Laura and her father out of necessity or out of malice? Who is he, and how do we stop him?"

As she wrote, she sensed another being in the kitchen with her. The gray lady stood to the side, hands folded, a resigned look on her face.

"Well, hello," Katie said. "I've been waiting for you. I think it's time we had a chat, don't you?" She smiled and lifted the pad and pencil. "I've found a way to talk with you, but I'm afraid I'll need your help. It's called automatic writing. Simply put, you say what you need to say through me, using my hand on the paper as your voice. Do you think you can do that?"

The woman nodded.

Katie closed her eyes and tried to clear her mind. Picking up the pencil, she put the tip to the pad and, almost immediately, began to write.

And she didn't stop for a long time.

When Katie became fully aware, thirty minutes had passed, and sweat covered her body. Staring down at the paper, a collage of initials, partial words, and doodles jumped off the page—a random array, floating like a word salad. She felt a pang of disappointment as she scrutinized her work. In her mind, the entire process should have been a lock, a sure thing; apparently, she was wrong.

Shocker.

Walking to the fridge, she grabbed a soda. It would take some time to decode this jumbled and nonsensical mess.

Flippantly, she muttered, "What am I? A cryptologist?" Gus yawned.

She sat down and studied the page. The first thing she deciphered from the patchwork of lettering was a place. Texas.

That state sure is popular in this investigation. But why?

Katie's only connection with Texas was her father's second office, and she'd never even been there. As an investigative reporter, he'd uncovered many sketchy backroom deals and exposed several corrupt officials.

Could something in Daddy's past have started all of this?

Scanning the writing, she could make out a few phrases, like "in danger" and "death will come." As for the rest, she was at a loss. There were circles, a partial name that looked like "Em," and a year, 1986. Within a circle appeared to be more initials. J. S.? Or was it T. S.? Her stomach dropped.

Could it be T. S. for Tucker Simon? Good God, is it possible that he, the weasel with the Jefferson eyeballs, could be the killer?

"Hey, Kates," Finn said, walking into the kitchen. "I just wanted to make sure we are cool after, well, after yesterday. I'm sorry I never told you about Dad. I guess I figured there wasn't any point, really. It's ancient history and would serve no purpose except to hurt you."

Katie smiled. "No worries, I appreciate your honesty." She hesitated, not sure of how much she could tell him. "Some decent leads have developed in the case. Jake is looking at a few murders that occurred over a decade ago in Texas, strangulation deaths involving rosary beads." Raising her brows, she said, "What I am about to tell you is strictly confidential, Finn. They found Stacy's body along Route 29 this morning. She was wearing an engagement ring on her left hand. I think it belonged to Momma."

Finn gaped at her. "Mom's ring? Are you shittin' me? Damn, what the fuck?" Massaging his neck, he added, "Poor Stacy."

She nodded, then showed him the paper in front of her.

"Then there's this. I tried communicating with the gray-haired lady, and this is what I came up with."

Finn examined the page. "I've no idea what this means. Initials? A locale? And what is 'Em'?"

Katie shook her head. "Not sure. Emily or Emma, maybe? My writing sucks."

Finn spoke the words aloud and understanding finally dawned. "Crap, I don't think it's 'Em,' Kate. I think it's the letter 'M'."

She looked at him blankly.

Pacing, he said. "The name of the woman on the other end of the phone on the day that you died? I'll never forget that name as long as I live."

"I'm not following, Finn. What does a phone call have to do with any of this?"

He stepped forward, his eyes pained. "The woman who called that day. Her name was Meredith."

"Oh, God!" Katie said, connecting the dots. "So, the gray-haired lady is…" She couldn't seem to finish the words.

"Yeah," Finn said coolly. "I think your ghostly sidekick is Dad's mistress."

CHAPTER TWENTY-ONE

"It is mine to avenge; I will repay. In due time their foot will slip;
their day of disaster is near and their doom rushes upon them."
Deuteronomy 32:35.

The time was upon him. The Apostle grabbed his gear, all packed neatly into an L.L. Bean equipment bag. His breath quickened, and his heart thrummed, its cadence rapid and strong. The thought of his mission's finale, the ending in sight, elicited mixed feelings. He was ecstatic, of course. Elated that she, that strumpet and offense to God, would finally get her due. But there was also a twinge of disappointment. Soon, the game would be over. He would need a new target, a fresh and wicked sinner, to satisfy his calling. There was no scarcity of miscreants and trespassers on earth, no shortage of human garbage. He just needed to find them.

Mulling over the logistics of his current plan, he conceded that it was prep work that helped realize his goal. Because of his foresight, he had cleared the path by eliminating any obstacles.

Case in point: The Crowleys.

The Crowleys, an elderly couple, one nearly blind and the other daft, had made their home in the very place he needed to be. The place where the ending, and the only logical conclusion to this mission, must occur. A decrepit duo, dispatching them would be less than challenging, like shooting fish in a barrel. Knowing that the odds weighed heavily in his favor almost made him reconsider his plan.

Almost.

He giggled heartily; the sound resonating in the empty house. Who was he kidding? This was his destiny, an integral part of the grand design, and he loved being such a principal player. No, he could never reconsider.

The Crowleys must die.

If he had one regret, it was that Devereaux would not witness the Chosen One's end. Unfortunate, but that would be a risk that only an amateur would take. A rock song, one that spoke of not always getting what you want, popped into his head.

No matter. He would always have what he needed—power, position, purpose.

Still, he couldn't help but feel disappointed, knowing her FBI lover would miss the finale. Perhaps he would document Katherine's Splendor, take a few photos as she drew her last breaths. It would be the metaphorical 'final dagger' to the agent's aching heart. Vivid, graphic images depicting his love suffering and dying, images that would burn forever in his mind.

How delicious, he thought.

He took one last look around at what was his home for so many months. Satisfied that he'd removed any evidence of his existence, he locked the door and, whistling that Rolling Stones tune, headed to his car. He would miss this house. Miss the view, the silence and, most of all, the isolated root cellar.

~

"Ok, let's take it from the top," Finn said enthusiastically.

Katie sighed. It was late afternoon, and they'd been over the paper she had written on a dozen times. They were no closer to solving the mystery of the initials or the dates than when they first started.

"I don't know, Finn, my penmanship bites. Is the 'Em' we see here an 'M,' as in Meredith, or could it be the first few letters of something else altogether? And what's this?" She pointed to some letters in the center of the page. "I can't figure out what that says, but I know I'm not acquainted with anyone who bears the initials J.S. But T.S.? That could be a slimeball by the name of Tucker Simon."

"Ok, so we start from there," Finn decided. "Tell me about this Simon character."

Katie started at the beginning, trying to give Finn an accurate picture of Tucker Simon; the suggestive leers, the nasty meltdown.

"Jake fired him, tossed him out on his ear," she said. "The fact that he seemed to know me, know my life, was most unsettling."

"Yeah, that's creepy. Where is this jackass now?"

"No idea. Last I saw him, he was crawling out of Quantico on his belly." She paused, then added, "But truthfully? I just don't see him as our guy. I've gotten some terrifying, very dark feelings relating to the person committing these crimes. With Tucker? All I felt was skeevy."

"Then we go with your gut. So, what else do we know? I'm positive that the name of the woman speaking to Dad that day was Meredith. He must have whispered her name a dozen times in that one phone call. Never got the last name, though." Finn's contempt for the woman was obvious.

"Right," Katie nodded, "although we don't know for sure that this spirit is Dad's mistress." She rubbed her temples, an attempt to stave off yet another brutal headache. Absently, she wondered if she had an undiagnosed medical condition that was slowly sucking the life out of her.

High blood pressure? Diabetes? A malignant growth choking her gray matter?

Almost predictably, the theme song from Jeopardy played on a loop in her head. Staring at Finn, Katie muttered, "I'll take brain tumors for a hundred, Alex."

"Excuse me?"

"Never mind. So, look, let's say we go with Meredith. What is the connection here? Why would she appear to me, trying to protect me? I didn't even know her."

Finn stuck his hands in his pockets and shrugged. "Maybe Dad sent her."

"No, I don't think so," Katie said. "That's not usually how this thing works. The dead I encounter either have a strong affection for me or have a chain, figuratively speaking, keeping them bound to earth. Some people call it unfinished business."

"Ok, but what kind of business? If this gray lady is Dad's mistress, is she connected to the killer? Did he kill someone she cares about? Does she know who it is and why he is targeting you?" He stretched. "Let's have another look at that paper."

Scanning Katie's notes, they bounced ideas off each other and compared theories. Katie was enjoying this time with her brother, although the reason for their collaboration didn't escape her. Pity that it took the loss of lives to bring him back into the family fold.

"I wonder what the date means?" Finn grabbed a mug from the cabinet. "You want one?" he asked, gesturing to the coffeepot. When she shook her head, he continued. "It says 1986. Maybe when the affair started?"

Katie shrugged. They had so many questions and so few answers. It was as though they were two silly dogs, endlessly chasing their tails. Round and round they went, with dizzying speed, only to come back to where everything started.

With Katie.

~

Jake and Sully sat on leather chairs in the Office of Criminal Investigations, Laredo Police Department. Investigator Adam Dempsey sat across from them, his workspace cluttered, his feet propped up on his desk. He had broad shoulders, a deep tan, and a large Stetson perched in his lap. When he introduced himself, his grip was firm, and his smile genuine. His soothing southern drawl, spurred cowboy boots, and neckerchief lent an authentic feel to this western lawman.

Nodding toward the boots, Sully grinned and rolled his eyes. "Do you actually use those spurs for anything, Adam?"

"Kickin' the butt of a visiting wiseass comes to mind," Dempsey deadpanned. Jake's laughter filled the room.

"So," Adam said, "I understand you're here about a double homicide that we worked several years ago. According to my supervisor, it involved Mr. and Mrs. William Ray Porter. That about right?"

Jake nodded. "Yes, Sir, it is. As I explained to your

Captain, we are investigating what appears to be the work of a serial killer. Our suspect has a distinctive signature and targets a specific subset, people directly connected to one individual. This individual, a young female, is the source of his obsession."

Dempsey frowned. "My Captain also tells me that the object of this guy's twisted obsession is someone close to you." At Jake's somber nod, he continued. "Well, I surely am sorry to hear that. Makes catching this son of a bitch even more personal. So, what can I help you with? I've taken a gander at the investigation report and, as far as clues go, there's not a lot there, sorry to say."

Sully leaned forward in his chair. "We were hoping we could speak to whoever handled the investigation back then. Sometimes, little details stand out that never made it into the report, like an impression or gut-feeling about the perpetrator."

Dempsey shook his head. "That's not possible, I'm afraid. The lead investigator on the case had himself a nervous breakdown several years ago. A run of rotten luck tipped him over the edge, starting with an off-duty shooting that killed a sixteen-year-old. The kid was far from innocent, had a rap sheet that'd wallpaper a room, but he was still a kid. Internal Affairs investigated, deemed it a clean shoot, but killing a teenager was a tough pill to swallow. Hear tell, it changed him. Near about six months later, he lost his only child, a baby girl, to cancer. The combination was just too much for the poor bastard. Last five years or so, he's been about half a bubble from plumb."

"Sorry to hear that," Jake said sincerely. "Shitty way to end your life, especially for someone dedicated to the service of others. I guess we'll go with the official report then. What can you tell us about the investigation and the conclusions reached?"

Adam handed each of them a copy of the report. "I'll give you a quick summary, but ya'll are welcome to take those copies with you. First things first, though—can't hardly work if your stomach thinks your throat's been cut." He smiled. "Have you eaten?" They shook their heads, and he buzzed his secretary, asking her to call a local deli for delivery.

Lunch ordered, Dempsey began. "Victims were William Ray Porter and his wife of twenty years, Jolene. Billy Ray was a deacon at Saint Mary's, a church on the outskirts of town. Rumor had it he was a fanatic, a real 'wrath of God' type fella when it came to his beliefs. Neighbors said that he was a strict disciplinarian, a true 'spare the rod, spoil the child' type of man. Unfortunately for his children, that rod was literal. He thought nothing of beatin' the tar outta his charges."

"He had children then?" Jake inquired.

"Foster kids. I heard through the grapevine that Jolene was barren, although I reckon Billy Ray coulda spread that gossip himself. He and the truth weren't exactly acquainted, if you get my meaning. In public, he could charm the dew right off the honeysuckle, but privately? Let's just say he was a man with little tolerance for failure. Sterility would be a weakness in his eyes." He stood and walked to the door. An instant after opening it, a young, heavyset woman jumped up from her desk to greet him. He handed her a credit card and smiled.

"Here you go, Nellie. When Casey delivers our food, you go ahead and put the bill on this card." He started to close the door, then added, "And be sure to give him a generous tip, will ya, darlin'? The kid is a hard worker." He shut the door, turned to his guests, and grinned. "We may be waitin' a spell. The delivery boy over at Martin's delicatessen ain't got the sense God gave a goose. All foam, no beer, if you get my meaning." Jake and Sully chuckled. "Casey Meyers is his name. Man, if stupid could fly, that boy would be a jet. Got gumption, though, I'll give 'em that."

Taking his seat, he began again. "Where was I? Oh yeah, Billy Ray. So, the Porters had themselves several foster children over the years. Billy Ray was one of them 'champagne taste and beer money' kind of folk. And cheap? Lord, the man could squeeze a quarter so tight the eagle would scream. Lucky for him, the State of Texas pays a handsome sum to those who take in a youngun'. They jumped at the chance to make a living from the downtrodden, taking in the children of the addicted, the insane, or the dead. Once their charges turned eighteen and the money stopped coming in, they'd toss 'em out of the house and take in a new, younger child. Greedy sons-a-bitches." As an afterthought, he added, "God rest, of course."

Jake stood and stretched his legs. "Sorry," he said. "Between the flight and car ride here, I've been sitting too long."

Adam smiled. "No apologies needed. Been there myself a time or two."

"So, what can you tell us about the murders?" Jake asked.

"Happened back in 2004. I was just coming up, so I didn't have actual hands-on during the investigation. But... you hear things. The scene was a horror show. The rookie first on location? Poor kid tossed his cookies after seeing the bodies, which makes me glad I wasn't there. Who knows? I might have lost my lunch, too." He shuffled the papers on his desk. "Original call came in from the church secretary over at St. Mary's. It seems that Billy Ray had missed services two Sundays in a row. She tried calling over to the house, but no one answered. At first, she figured they were away on vacation. Billy Ray only worked one Sunday a month, but he rarely missed a mass. So, after a few weeks of being unable to reach him, she called us." A light tap brought him to his feet. Nellie stood at the door, their lunch in hand. He thanked her, divvied up the order, and they ate while he talked.

"Best dang roast beef in the great state of Texas," he said happily. "Anyhow, that day, we dispatched a patrol car to their home. The Porters were in the cellar, shackled and kneeling at a make-shift altar, naked as the day they were born. Killer beat them senseless, too. Billy Ray was so busted up he was damn near unrecognizable. And Jolene? Broken, bloody, possibly sexually assaulted, but the autopsy was inconclusive. Their C.O.D. was strangulation by ligature, though not by the delicate rosary beads found in their hands. Never did find the murder weapon. There was also cat-o'-nine-tails wrapped around each of their wrists. A bench toward the back of the room held whips, ropes, and bibles. Creepy as fuck, if you ask me."

Sully was momentarily stunned by the profanity. Somehow, he never expected it from this genteel cowboy. "Did they like anyone for it?" he asked.

Dempsey took a giant bite of his sandwich. "No one we could charge. A person of interest was their foster child, a kid named Jeremy Sterling. The Porters kicked him out on his eighteenth birthday, a few weeks before the murders. Until then, patrol had visited the home several times on various complaints, including screaming matches and physical altercations. Not sure if the deacon smooth-talked his way around it, but nothing ever came of the complaints." He bunched up the wrapper for his sandwich and threw it into the wastebasket across the room.

"Score!"

Brushing some breadcrumbs off his shirt, he continued. "As far as the crime scene, it was clean. No DNA, no trace, nothing. And the icing on the cake? The kid had a solid alibi. His birth mother, Meredith Sterling, swore he was visiting with her in Baltimore. Come to find out, the boy up and joined the army on his birthday. He was fixin' to hit boot camp within the month, so Mom's official statement was that they wanted to reconnect."

Jake looked at Sully, both thinking the same thing. Jackpot.

"Do you know what Jeremy did in the army?" he asked.

Adam put on his reading glasses and shuffled a few more papers. Jake tried to follow along with his copy of the report. "Here you go. A few investigators kept tabs on him over the years, revisiting the case. Bobby, that was the original investigator, well, he always believed that the department missed something." He pointed out a section of the report. "Jeremy enlisted in 2004. The last time anyone checked on him was four years later when he re-enlisted. Which means he was in until at least 2012, unless they discharged him. Says here that he saw some combat in Iraq, maybe even spent time in Afghanistan. He was an expert marksman and could shoot the tick off a coon hound at five hundred yards."

Jake raked a hand through his hair. He tried not to get too attached to his theories. They needed more.

"You have an address for this guy? Or for his mother?" Jake asked.

"Nothing on him. As I said, the last anyone looked at this was 2008. He was still army then. I have a last known address for his mother, but again, you are going back a decade or better." He shrugged. "This is a cold case, gentlemen. You two are the first to ask about it in years. And unfortunately, once Bobby was out of the picture, the flame he stoked to keep the torch lit burned out."

Jake nodded. "We get that, too many cases and not enough cops. If we could get the mother's last known whereabouts, that would be great. Oh, and if you have a picture of Jeremy, that will help. If not, I'm sure I can get one from the DMV or the army."

"No need. There are a few in the original report, one from his time in the military. Expressionless, empty eyes, and sporting a rifle. Gives me the willies."

Jake looked over the photos. The one that Adam referenced showed a shirtless teenager holding an M-16 series semi-automatic rifle ... in his left hand.

Bingo.

Jake could hardly contain himself. He was itching to talk to Katie, to send her the photograph. They finally had a solid lead. The last known address for Meredith Sterling was an assisted living facility in downtown Baltimore. With any luck, she still lived there.

"We owe you, Adam. Big time. Your information has just blown this case wide open. With any luck, we will nail this guy. And not only for our case but for yours. Thanks so much." Jake shook the man's hand.

"Glad we could help," Adam said. "Do me a favor, fellas? Nail this son of a bitch, will ya? It's long overdue."

⌁

Finn and Katie sat in the living room, eyes glazed from inspecting the writings before them. They had been at it most of the morning but still had unanswered questions.

"I don't suppose the gray lady is still here somewhere?" Finn smirked.

"Nope, 'fraid not," Katie said.

Her cell phone rang.

"Hey, handsome," she said, "Give me some good news."

"I think I may have some," Jake said. "First off, that deacon and his wife were foster parents. The kid they took in enlisted in the army at eighteen, eventually climbing the ladder to achieve a special ops spot as an expert marksman. I'm looking at his picture now, one that shows him posing with a semi-automatic rifle. Want to guess which hand that gun is in?"

Katie digested that for a moment. "Judging by the excitement in your voice, I'm going with his left hand. What else do you have on him?"

"A few things, actually. According to the police reports, witnesses say Billy Ray Porter was abusive. He had a steady stream of foster children he took in; most say just for the monthly stipend. Neighbors allege that he wasn't afraid to smack them around to keep them in line, either. His last foster child, this army guy, was a prime suspect in the Porter murders, but he alibied out courtesy of his birth mother. The kid's name is Jeremy. Jeremy Sterling."

Katie froze. "Oh, God, Jake. I had a session today with the gray lady. I was in a kind of trance and don't recall all the details, but I took notes. There are dates, warnings, and a few initials. It's hard to read my unorganized writings, but Finn and I agree that the initials are T. S. or J. S. My first thought was Tucker Simon, but what if it's J. S., as in Jeremy Sterling?"

"Sounds like you've been busy, too," Jake joked. "I will send you a picture of this guy to see if you recognize him. Sully and I need to make a stop before heading home. This guy's mother, his alibi, was last living in Baltimore in a nursing home. Her name is Meredith."

Katie's heart started beating furiously. "This is it, Jake. I can feel it. I had the word 'em' written on the automatic writing paper. I was thinking Emily, but Finn swears it's Meredith." She hesitated. "Meredith is the name of the woman my dad was having an affair with. Coincidence or design, FBI guy?"

Jake grinned. "You know the answer to that, Red. I'm sending the photo now. Check your email."

Katie did, opening the file as soon as it downloaded.

"Oh, shit," she said, voice quivering as she got back on the line. "I know this guy, Jake. I saw him the other day, but he wasn't going by the name of Jeremy Sterling. He calls himself Gabriel. Gabriel Devine... Darby's new boy crush."

At 1:30 p.m., Finn and Katie were ready to take a break. They had been staring at the doodled paper, and at each other, for hours.

"I need to get back home to tend to the animals. Get some clean clothes and check my mail. How about we take a vay-cay from this crap and head on over to my place?" Finn asked, rubbing his neck to release the kinks.

"You go on ahead. I will be ok here for a few minutes. Callie and Darby are due back any moment, and I hate to have them come home to an empty house."

Finn frowned. "I don't feel good leaving you here alone, Kates. I'll just wait until they get home." When Katie shook her head, he quirked a brow. "No arguments. I'm not leaving you alone, so deal with it." Yawning, he added, "Man, this decoding shit has wiped me out. Lucky for me, I don't make a living at it."

Katie smiled and gave him a peck on the cheek. "Go lay down. I'm going to read for a while but call if you need anything."

She headed to the sunroom, and Finn padded upstairs to one of the bedrooms. Just as she sat down, her cell rang.

"Hey, Darbs," she said brightly. "You guys on the way home? So much has happened since you left. We have leads, girl—real, solid, honest to God, leads."

Darby hesitated. "Um, I'm still at the store, waiting. Have you talked to Callie? She was supposed to pick me up over an hour ago. I tried calling, but it went straight to voicemail. I thought maybe she went home first."

Katie's stomach flipped. Callie was, above all else, dependable.

And she's never late.

"No, she's not here. I haven't spoken to her since this morning." She worried her bottom lip. "I don't like this, Darbs. I'm calling Jake. Uncle Tim, too, since that's where she was headed. Just stay put, and I'll have Finn come get you."

She hung up the phone and shuddered, Spidey-sense on fire. Her head began its familiar beat, the approaching headache threatening to become a migraine.

It was an ominous sign. Callie could be in trouble. Deep, deep trouble.

Terrified, Katie raced up the stairs to Finn. The clock was ticking, and they were running out of time. She needed to find her sister. Fast.

CHAPTER TWENTY-TWO

"For the lips of a wayward woman drip like a honeycomb, and her mouth is smoother than oil." Proverbs 5:3.

For nearly an hour, he watched her sleep, wondering if she dreamed. Did she recognize the peril she faced? What he could do to her? He glanced around, appraising the dank surroundings. The scent of mold and dust filled his nostrils, and he sneezed several times. Spider webs glistened, caught by the waning rays of the afternoon sun beaming through the top window. He acknowledged that, though this basement was a good deal smaller than his usual work area, he had everything he needed.

The current object of his attention lay on her side, restrained to a cot he'd found in an upstairs bedroom. The duct tape over her lips silenced her voice, while a sunshine yellow scarf tied neatly across her eyes kept her in total darkness. Oh, he didn't much care if she saw him. In fact, he relished the moment when she would finally look into his eyes. But he was unsure how long the drug he'd given her would last, and he preferred that she was unaware of their location for the time being. Soon, when he gifted her back her vision, she would recognize these four walls and the house that surrounded them.

It was thrilling, really, like a game where only he knew the object, the rules, and the strategy for success. A game that only he could win. He took a seat in the corner and waited.

When Callie awoke, it was to an intense thirst and a headache so consuming, it rivaled her worst hangover. The pounding in her brain was relentless, a marching band clapping to its own beat inside the confines of her skull. She groaned, squeezing her eyes tight. There was a heavy odor in the air, vaguely familiar, that invaded her nostrils. Her mind was fuzzy, her mouth like sand. The sickly-sweet fragrance attacking her senses was making her stomach heave. She tried to lift a hand to her forehead, only to meet resistance. Panicked, she tried the other side. It, too, was bound. Clarity slowly drifted to the surface, and she attempted to roll to her side. But she was ratcheted down, immobilized against a crude bed whose springs jabbed painfully into her spine.

Blindfolded and gagged, the sensory deprivation magnified the tomb-like silence. The slightest brush of clothing, the faintest whisper of air, sent chills down her spine. Tamping down her rising panic, she attempted to reconstruct how she arrived here. Her memories were disjointed as she forced herself to recall the last few hours before she came to be here. For all she knew, she might have been here for days.

I was with someone. Someone close. Who?

Frustrated, she reversed direction in her mind. Rather

than try to figure out what happened directly before her capture, she worked back to the first coherent memory in her mind. Quickly, her thoughts went to Darby.

I remember being in the car with Darby, driving to Time and Time Again, trying to parallel park on the busy street.

Memories flooded her consciousness, firing in rapid succession; beeping her horn as she pulled from the curb, waving goodbye to Darby, driving miles away before limping to the shoulder just as her car stuttered and seized. She remembered getting out of the vehicle, lifting the hood, and having absolutely no clue what the fuck she was looking for. She was no mechanic; she could barely pump her gas or change a flat tire. Forlorn, with no cell reception on this desolate stretch of highway, she sat and waited.

What then? She wondered. *What happened next?*

The questions without answers wandered like nomads inside her brain, searching for a haven, a place to fit in. Bile gathered in her throat as nausea overtook her. If she didn't sit up, she would choke on her own vomit.

Using her tongue, she pushed against the duct tape sealing her mouth until, mercifully, the adhesive loosened. Feeling a sense of accomplishment, she exhaled forcefully, the blast of air causing a corner section of the tape to flutter upward. On inhalation, the edges gently settled back down against her lips. Moaning, she spoke through the side of her mouth.

"Hello?" she said, her voice low and weak. "Is anyone there? I need to sit up. I think I'm going to be sick."

Silence.

She tried again. "Seriously, I'm going to throw up. My stomach feels awful."

The fog coating her mind dissipated fully. Despite the silence in the room, she knew she was not alone. Another being shared this space with her, biding its time, watching.

She waited a few minutes, fear of the unknown sparring with outrage at the absolute audacity of the shithead who dared hold her captive. Eventually, anger won the battle.

"Hey!" she shouted, "Whoever you are! I'm gonna hurl, so unless you're a freak into the alluring stench of vomit, I suggest you get me upright!"

A voice, deep and threatening, growled from within the gloom.

"'For the anger of man does not produce the righteousness of God.' James 1:20. But I don't suppose you know of scripture, do you? Or of His Word?"

Callie held her breath, heart racing. *Scripture? Wow, I didn't see that coming.*

Sweat coated her palms, and her eyes moved frantically beneath the blindfold. Sounds and smells and touch seemed to be amplified, heightened. In this, her new reality, the world was void of everything but herself and the animal who took her.

As she lay there, afraid to move, to breathe, she recognized the odor that assailed her when she regained consciousness. The musky, sea-scented cologne saturated the air, reminding her of her grandfather.

Old Spice? Who even uses that anymore, unless you're like, a hundred.

After several tense minutes, she spoke. Her voice sounded tinny and high, with a false bravado that she had no illusions would fool her jailer.

"Scripture? The word? Call me crazy, but I seriously doubt that God would be onboard with kidnapping. Or with any of the other horrendous sins you've undoubtedly committed. And although the God I worship is compassionate and forgiving, that doesn't give people a license to act like assholes." She blew against the tape on her mouth, determined to break it free. "Going to church doesn't make you a good Christian any more than quoting His Word makes you a theologian. Just ask the people of Jonestown. Oh, wait, you can't—they're all dead, courtesy of a murderous coward who corrupted God's doctrine."

She sniffed indignantly, fighting to maintain her composure. She was scared to death. "Whatever you hoped to accomplish here, whatever your end game may be, it will not happen. I have friends, powerful law enforcement friends. And a huge, protective family that attacks when one of us is threatened. As a group, they are fierce, determined, and strong. They eat people like you for breakfast." She sounded as if she were running a marathon, her breath raspy and quick. There was a wet, slurping sound every time she spoke, the result of the tape over her mouth, making her reasonably sure she was drooling. "They are all searching for me as we speak. So, unless you want to die today..." She let the thought linger for a beat. "Let me go, and we'll forget this ever happened."

She heard rustling, then the sinister sound of heavy footsteps moving toward her. Her brain, though somewhat scrambled, understood the peril that she faced. She gasped as he yanked the blindfold from her eyes and ripped the duct tape from her mouth.

Once free of the chains of darkness, Callie's senses erupted. She blinked several times; the light flooding her eyes painful but welcome. Her mind flipped through the dim memories, desperate to solve the mystery of how she arrived here.

She recalled having car trouble and pulling off the road with difficulty, her brakes sluggish. Her cell phone's top corner mocked her with zero bars and a "no service" message.

Then what? A man, a man who dropped out of the heavens and offered me comfort, bottled water, and a much-needed tow. Oh, God, I remember!

I remember relief!

Relief when he pulled up behind her, convinced that it was her lucky day; relief that help had arrived, and her savior had landed... a cute guy with a quick smile.

Her very own guardian angel, sent from on high.

Heart hammering, her eyes struggled to focus on the massive man looming over her. His face contorted in anger, his pupil's slits of smoldering black rage. He had a thick whip wrapped tightly around one hand and a syringe in the other. And suddenly, she remembered it all.

He called himself Gabriel.

◇

"Finn!" Katie shouted, pounding on the door. "Finn, wake up! Something's happened!"

She heard the shuffling of feet inside the room before he pulled open the door. "What is it? What's wrong? Jesus, Kates, what the fudge?" He tucked his shirt into his pants and followed her downstairs. "What the hell happened?"

She wrung her hands and paced the living room. "Your sister is what happened. She was supposed to pick up Darby over an hour ago but never showed. No text, no phone call. Nothing. Uncle Tim says she never even got to the cabin. She planned to visit Grams there this morning." Katie's breath hitched. "Her location, her whereabouts, are unknown." Biting her lip, she said, "It's possible she's been missing for hours."

Tears pooled in the corner of her eyes. She grabbed the arm of the sofa for support and plopped down on the cushion. Rubbing her hands against her thighs, she looked up at her brother.

"Don't go jumping to the nasty," he soothed. "There could be a perfectly logical explanation to all this."

Katie wasn't buying it. "But there isn't. I have a bad feeling, Finn. Call it clairsentience, call it intuition, call it whatever the hell you want." She stood. "I need to call Jake, and you need to pick up Darby at the shop. She's stranded there right now."

Finn sighed dramatically. "Not a swell idea, Kate. Leaving you here while I fetch Darby is dangerous. We'll both go."

"No!" she answered sharply. "I need to stay here." His frown deepened and, placating him, she said, "Look, if Callie is in danger or had car trouble, or even just met a cute guy and went out to eat... whatever the reason is for her absence, the first place she will show up is here. And if I stay here, I can reach out to hospitals, police stations, impound lots... all without the difficulty I would encounter on the road. You know how archaic cell service can be in this part of Virginia." She smiled softly and held up three fingers. "Scout's honor, I will lock the door after you leave and open it to no one until you return. State-of-the-art security here, remember?"

Finn grudgingly acknowledged her reasoning and, grabbing his baseball hat, headed for the door. Turning to face her, he ordered, "Call Jake as soon as I leave. Don't forget to triple lock this door behind me and turn the alarm system back on after I'm gone."

"Aye, aye, Captain," she said with a wink and a salute.

He rolled his eyes. "Smartass."

After Finn left, Katie dialed Jake's number. She stroked Gus's head and waited for Jake to answer the phone. She feared he was already on a plane, his phone turned off. Just as she was about to disconnect, he picked up.

"Hey, Red, you caught me just in time. Sully and I are about to board our connecting flight. Everything ok?"

She groaned. "Not by half. I'm freaking out. I think Callie is missing, and I don't have a clue where to look for her."

"Slow down, babe. What's going on?"

Katie explained everything, leaving out the part that Finn was on his way to pick up Darby. She knew he would be angry that she was alone, and she didn't have the strength to argue.

"You all locked up over there? Everything secure?"

"Yes, Jake," she snapped, "I'm fine. It's Callie I'm worried about. You don't seem to understand that she's the most reliable person in the goddamned world. There's no way in hell she would leave Darby hanging." Katie felt the sting of tears yet again. "Should I call the police? Will they even do anything?"

"Leave that to us. Sully will call them and explain the reasons we need to act quickly." He covered the phone, quickly got Sully up to speed, and returned to the conversation.

"If she brought Darby to work, we know that she got as far as Stafford, right?" he asked. "Did she say anything before she left this morning? Any errands she needed to run, or friends she was going to see?"

"No, nothing. As far as I know, the only plan was to drop off Darby and visit Grams. She expected to be back here by late afternoon." She paused, then added, "Are you guys coming straight back here, or are you going to look for Meredith first?" She listened, annoyed at the sound of her own voice. She sounded needy, whiny. Helpless.

Wuss!

"What if something happened to her, Jake? I don't think I could bear it."

He cleared his throat, his voice steady. "Listen up, Red. Callie is a smart and strong lady, just like her sister. If she is in trouble, she can handle it until the cavalry gets there. And I promise you; we'll get there. Sully will follow the lead on Meredith Sterling on his own. As soon as we land, I'm coming straight to you. Count on it."

They spoke for a few moments more until they both heard the canned announcement for final boarding. Inexplicitly, Katie started to tremble, terrified to hang up. She had an irrational fear that to end the conversation would be to end it all—that this was to be their last goodbye, a pitiful close to a relationship that had barely begun. It was ridiculous, undoubtedly a stress-induced paranoia. But, try as she might, she couldn't shake the feeling. And it remained there long after the connection had ended.

Thirty minutes later, Katie was jumping out of her skin. She had walked circles around the house, called Callie's cell phone every five minutes, even tried to conjure up the gray lady a dozen times for help. Meredith, if that's who it even was, seemed to be AWOL. Katie hadn't seen her, or felt her, for hours.

Grabbing her jacket, she stuffed her cell phone in her left pocket and the house phone in her right. The dogs needed to go out, and she needed some air. The moment she stepped outside, the house phone rang. She snatched the portable out of her pocket and answered.

"Hello? Callie? Is that you?"

Static greeted her. She moved closer to the house and tried again.

"Callie? Is someone there?"

"Hello, ma'am? Can you hear me? I apologize for the poor connection. I'm still on the road, and service is spotty. This is Officer Noah Weber of the Falls Church Police Department. Are you Callista Callahan?"

Katie's stomach dropped. "No, sir, Callie is my sister. Is she ok? Did something happen?" A part of her felt relieved. If this cop was looking for Callie, that must mean they didn't find something horrendous.

Like a body.

"I don't know the answer to that, ma'am." More static sizzled in the line, but his words were clear. "We found her vehicle on the side of the road here in Falls Church. The keys were still in the ignition, and her wallet and vehicle paperwork were on the passenger seat. It appeared to be just a routine disabled motor vehicle, but the wallet and keys left behind have me concerned. Have you spoken to your sister recently?"

Katie tried to steady her heartbeat and slow her respirations. "No, I haven't, and I'm quite concerned. My friend, Jacob Devereaux, is an FBI agent and reported her missing thirty minutes ago. Callie left early this morning but never got to her destination. We've had no contact since then. You should know, Officer Weber, that this may be more than a run-of-the-mill disappearance."

As if a gate suddenly opened, Katie started rambling, throwing out facts and dates and random information. She was finding it difficult to finish one thought before spilling onto the next. It was as if all the ghastly things that had happened came rushing out, unchecked and unorganized.

This poor cop has no clue what the hell he just stepped into.

Finally spent, she asked, "Can you tell me if you found her cell phone?"

"No, ma'am, we didn't," he said. "No purse, either. Just the wallet with your phone number tucked behind her driver's license."

"Callie never uses a purse. She carries a wallet and puts her cell phone in a pocket." She thought for a moment. "Did it look like she was in an accident? I've checked all the local hospitals, but maybe she needed a trauma center?" Her voice sounded pleading, raw and desperate, even to her own ears.

"No, ma'am, there was no damage that I could see. I spotted some fluid, possibly from a brake line, beneath the car, though. As I've said, the only concern was that her wallet and keys were inside the vehicle. I'll see if I can pull up the missing person's report that your friend filed. Meanwhile, that stretch of highway is treacherous at night. We'll need to get her vehicle off the road. I can call our tow guy for you unless you have someone else in mind."

"No, that's fine. I have no preference at this point. I just need to find my sister."

"Ok, I will take care of it. Call me at the Falls Church station if you hear from her and Miss? Try not to worry too much. Most of the time, these things have a happy ending."

After ending the call, Katie dropped heavily onto the back steps, tears blurring her vision.

Jeremy, that crazy son-of-a-bitch, has Callie! She knew it, felt it deep in her bones. Noah Weber's words replayed in her mind.

Most of the time, these things have a happy ending.

But her instincts screamed that they were nearly out of time. And fresh out of happy endings.

She went inside to the bathroom and washed the tear

tracks from her face. Glancing up, she stared at the woman looking back at her in the mirror—eyes swollen, nose red, chest dotted with spots.

Like I said, ugly criers.

What was she going to do? It was at least two more hours until Jake's plane touched down in Dulles. If she had to sit here for even two minutes longer, let alone two hours, she would go stark-raving mad. Her pocket vibrated, 'Sister Christian' singing out from her cellphone.

Callie!

"Oh, my God! Oh, my freakin' God! Jesus, Callie!" she yelled into the phone, "you damned near scared me to death! Where the hell are you?" Her relief mixed with a tinge of annoyance. Wanting to hug her sister and never let her go was at war with wanting to kick her skinny little ass for making her worry.

There was a lengthy pause before someone spoke. It was a masculine voice, low, southern, and frightening in its intensity. "Callie can't come to the phone right now, Katherine. I'm afraid she's tied up." A dark snicker echoed on the line.

The hairs on Katie's neck stood at attention, and she struggled to breathe. Her heart raced, beating in time with the pounding in her skull. She thought her head would explode. "Who is this?" she growled. "Where is my sister? What have you done to her? If you hurt her, I swear to God…"

"Do not do that!" the voice hissed. "You do not get to swear to a God you know nothing about! Callie is alive, for now. But if you do not follow my instructions, exactly as I give them, I WILL kill her. But I think you know that, don't you?" After a few seconds, he said, authoritatively, "Katherine, I'm waiting. Do you understand?"

She swallowed the lump in her throat. Callie needed

her. She couldn't afford to fall apart now. "I understand. I'm not an idiot." She paused. "What do you want, Jeremy?"

She heard his swift intake of breath, followed by several seconds of silence. Finally, he spoke.

"Jeremy is dead," he said dully. "He died a long time ago. My name is Gabriel and I," his voice shook, "I am the Apostle."

"Congratulations, that's thrilling," she deadpanned. "Just tell me what the fuck you want, Gabe."

He growled into the phone. "Do not mock me, slut! I want you here, facing me, to fulfill your destiny. Our destiny." She could feel him struggling for control. "Come to where it all started. Come to the beginning."

"What beginning? What do you mean? I know we've never met before—I would remember an asshole like you." She rubbed her forehead. "You're speaking in riddles, Gabriel."

Careful, Kate, she scolded herself. *Don't push too hard!*

"Not our beginning, Katherine, but yours. Your rebirth, your sins, all started there; it is only fitting that there it will end." He chuckled and, in a sing-song voice, like a kindergartener with a secret, he whispered, "I know something you don't know."

A fleeting thought, like a fingernail tapping the surface of her brain, badgered her. A woodpecker, hard at work, trying to breach the roof of her skull.

Flick, peck, flick, peck.

The memory, centered on her hospitalization as a child, fought to scratch its way to the surface. It was the last piece of the puzzle, elusive and out of reach. She just needed more time to think. But Callie was out of time.

"The truth will set you free, Kate," he boomed. "But you must come alone and unarmed, or your sister will die."

The line went dead, and Katie closed her eyes.

Oh, God, Callie. Where are you?

And just like that, it came to her. The beginning, the accident, the strangers who visited her in the hospital. Strangers she had completely blocked from her memories, relegating them to an inaccessible niche in her psyche. Like a blind woman given the gift of sight, the shadows receded, and the curtain trapping her memories rose. Brilliant sunlight flooded the recesses of her mind.

Of course! Falls Church!

Falls Church, Virginia. She must go home, back to her childhood and the place where it all started. Back to the days where, in little more than a year, she died, was resurrected, and became an orphan. Back to the darkest time in her life.

Back to the beginning.

CHAPTER TWENTY-THREE

"For all have sinned and fall short of the glory of God." Romans 3:23.

"You need to wake up now, Callista," a voice whispered. "Company's coming."

Callie's mind swam through the fog, struggling to identify the speaker. Her eyes felt foreign, gritty, and hot, like flaming embers prancing over a bed of coals. The lids, impossibly heavy, fought to remain shuttered and safe, while the band in her head continued to pound out a familiar tune.

One step at a time, girl, she coaxed herself. *Open your eyes.*

Her eyelids fluttered, and a million tiny sparks, electric and hot, danced across her shoulder blades. Wincing, she rolled to her side and sat up, her fragmented mind working on the puzzle before her. She knew he had drugged her, but with what? Ketamine? Rohypnol? The memory bobbed and swirled in the distance, a buoy riding the tide. Frustrated, she tucked away the recent past to concentrate on more pressing matters.

Like survival.

She looked around, blinking furiously to clear her clouded vision. Confusion, then terror, sped through her as she tried to reconcile what she was seeing. The cot she'd been lying on earlier was gone. Instead, she sat directly on the icy concrete floor, crossed-legged and bare-assed. She swallowed loudly, the bile in her throat bitter and threatening. She was utterly, embarrassingly, naked.

Jesus, where are my clothes?

"You needn't worry about your virtue, Callista," he said, as if reading her mind. "It remains intact. Although, admittedly, it is tempting. You are a beautiful woman, but I have no intention of bedding you. It would be... inappropriate."

Callie's brain worked feverishly, trying to follow his words. *What the fuck is he going on about? And could he just stop saying my name?*

His voice felt intrusive, suffocating, like being engulfed by thousands of slithering insects whenever he spoke. Trying to gain control, she took in her surroundings through bloodshot, drug-hazed eyes. Then, like a tumbler releasing a lock, recognition.

Christ! I'm home!

The basement of her childhood home in Falls Church remained mostly unchanged. Her father's worktable was now against the far wall, and the current owners had added some shelving, but she had no doubt where she was. A rush of memories flooded her senses, a familiar nostalgia that temporarily comforted her.

Until she noticed the chains.

Blood thudded in her ears, and her heart kicked against her rib cage as comprehension collided with staggering disbelief. Metal clinked behind her, and she repositioned her body to get a better look.

She was shackled to a cinderblock wall by two thick chains that hung from a massive iron ring. One chain led to a steel manacle that encircled her ankle, the other to a metal band around her wrist. There was a large, medieval-looking padlock attached to each shackle by a rusty, horizontal bolt.

Oh, God, she prayed. *Help me!*

She tested the strength of her restraints. The chains clanged as she tugged, a hollow, haunting sound that echoed off the cement walls. She groaned when the sharp edge of the bindings cut into the flesh of her hand and foot. Her eyes moved from her ankle to yet another source of pain, a flaming, searing ache at her inner thigh that grew exponentially as her mind cleared. The offending area sat two inches from her crotch, the wounded flesh raw and raised.

No, not quite a wound, she thought. It looked more like lettering or some kind of inscription.

Lettering? Jesus Christ, he branded me? Like a fucking sheep?

Hyperventilating and close to hysteria, she squinted to make out the image. It looked rushed and amateurish, but the name scrawled across her leg was unmistakable. It was the name of her worst nightmare, a name meant to be emblazoned on her body until the end of time.

Gabriel.

Swearing, she looked up and locked eyes with her captor.

"I suppose I should explain," he said coolly.

～

"Callahan," Katie mumbled, *"you're such a dumbass!"*

The plan she had in mind was shortsighted and remarkably insane. A boneheaded move, a kamikaze run

315

destined for calamity, but she didn't give a damn. Her sister, her heart, was in danger. If the unspeakable happened, no amount of prayers or condolences or time would ever fill the vacuum Callie left behind.

I'd be lost without her. Without 'us,' there is no me.

Jake would not return for a few more hours. There was no way she could wait that long, no way she could withstand the torture of the unknown. Sticking her gun into her waistband—she wasn't *totally* crazy after all—she sat down and wrote a note detailing a scheme that, undoubtedly, Jake would hate.

Dearest Jake,
If you are reading this, then you are back home, safe, and sound.
Hallelujah! I, on the other hand, am in deep shit.
They say it's much easier to beg for forgiveness than ask for
permission. I just couldn't do what you wanted, Jake. The last thing
in this world I'd ever choose to do is let you down, but he has Callie.
He's threatening to kill her unless I come to him, alone and unarmed
(don't worry, I'm bringing a gun). We are meeting at our old home in
Falls Church. Back to the beginning, just as the bastard requested. If
I'm not back by the time you see this letter, send out a search party.
(I'm only half-joking on that. On second thought, I'm not joking at
all. Send freakin' help.)
I still haven't put the entire puzzle together, but I know the lady in
gray is my father's mistress and Jeremy's mother. I think she knew her
son was a psychopath and was trying to help me. But I have to say,
connecting the dots between him, Meredith, me, and my dad is making
me sick. If I think about it for too long, the possibilities terrify me.
Anyway, truth be told (and in classic Callahan fashion), I have no
real plan to rescue Callie. I suspect I will go storming in there, guns
a-blazing as they say, and get us both killed. But I'm out of options,
and I'd rather die on my feet trying to save her than live on my knees
praying for the chance to get her back.

One last thing I have to say to you before I go. Remember it, believe it, no matter what happens today. You are the best thing that's ever happened to me, Jacob Devereaux. Never have I felt so cherished, so protected, and so loved. Through my darkest days, you've brought me sunlight. When my burden was heavy and my legs too weak to stand, you've carried me. You've been my rock, my compass, my only constant while I've tried to navigate this shit storm that has become my life.

I am a better, stronger person because of you. Never forget that.

Be happy, FBI guy.

Always,

Kate

She folded the letter and propped it up on the kitchen counter. Gus lay sprawled out under the table, snoring loudly, an occasional tic making his right foot jump. At her side, Blue whined softly, seemingly waiting for an explanation to her somber mood. She squatted down beside him and wrapped her arms around his neck.

"You are an amazing dog, Blue-man, do you know that? I could never ask for a better companion and truer friend." Fighting off tears, she said, "Now you be a good boy, okay? I'm counting on you to watch over Grams and Nicodemus. They seem so lost without Chance." She kissed his nose. "You are too, though, aren't you, pal?" She sighed heavily, a thousand thoughts weighing on her mind. "Well, that makes four of us, I suppose, but we'll get through this. Together." He whined again and placed his snout on her thigh. "Aww, don't be such a negative Nancy, bud. With any luck, things will go smoothly, and I'll be back before you know it." She placed her cheek on his face and whispered, "Thank you for loving me." Then, taking

317

one last look around, she grabbed her keys and headed for the door.

I'm coming, Shadow.

⁓

When she got to her old neighborhood, Katie pulled into a forgotten playground a few blocks away from the house and surveyed the area. Several ornate benches, rusted and worn, lined an overgrown jogging trail. Empty swings, tarnished monkey bars, and a broken merry-go-round seemed to summon the ghosts of children past. On any other day, she may have felt a pang of nostalgia. Tonight, though, she looked on the scene without truly seeing it, her mind's only focus on saving Callie.

What now? I can't just run in there, half-cocked, so to speak. He'll be expecting that.

She needed a diversion, something that would lure him away from his sentry to give her the upper hand, the element of surprise.

Callie's cell phone! Call it, make him think you are still miles away.

With trembling hands, she picked up her phone, hesitated, then dialed Callie's number. She heard the phone connect and the ringing start. One. Two. Three. Four.

C'mon, dammit, pick up!

Five, six, and finally, a voice.

"Well, hello, Katherine. This is an interesting turn of events, wouldn't you say? Not only should you have arrived by now, but you seem to have misunderstood the terms of our agreement. You, in exchange for your sister. Perhaps I wasn't clear enough. Perhaps you need more convincing."

"Wait! It's not that! Listen, please! Just listen…"

But even as she said the words, she knew he had placed the phone down, although the connection remained. A second later, she heard a terrifying scream.

"Leave her alone!!!" Katie yelled into the phone, knowing he could not hear, yet compelled to try just the same. "Just stop! I'm coming, okay? I'm on the way!"

She heard a click as the line disconnected.

Oh, God, what have I done?

Sully sat in a large, comfy chair in Rosa Gonsalves' office. The Director of Nursing for Sunrise Horizons Nursing Facility in Baltimore, Rosa was a large, jovial woman with a quick smile and a hearty handshake. Caramel-colored skin, dotted with areas of hyperpigmentation, highlighted her apple cheekbones and slender nose. When she spoke of Sunrise Horizons, it was with obvious pride in the facility and love for its residents.

"I appreciate your seeing me on such short notice, Ms. Gonsalves," Sully began, smiling. "I know it's late in the day, and you'd just as soon be home having a nice meal with your family. I also understand that your time is valuable, so I will try to be brief."

Rosa laid a hand on her chest, momentarily dazzled by Ian's charm and winning smile. She nodded. "I appreciate that, Agent Sullivan. But here at Sunrise, we believe in helping one another. It is the only thing that separates us from the evil in this world. You mentioned you were seeking information about one of our patients?"

Sully nodded. "Yes, Ma'am. Her name is Meredith Sterling. I believe she is a resident here?"

Rosa shook her head sadly. "I'm afraid our Meredith is no longer here. She went to see the Lord, oh, sometime around June or July, I believe. Tragic woman." She dropped her head and discreetly blessed herself.

"I see," Sully said, disappointed. "Can you tell me anything about how she died? Was she sick?"

Rosa swiveled her chair to face her computer. "Just give me a moment. I'm afraid we have a lot of folks who pass on throughout the year. It is, after all, the final destination for most of our patients." She paused and then, almost defensively, added, "It's not like these people come here to get a new lease on life, you understand. They come here to die."

Sully nodded sympathetically. While she typed, he looked around the office. Dozens of pictures of residents and their families graced the walls. Absently, he wondered if Meredith was in any of those photographs.

"Here we go," Rosa said, "June of this year. It seems she died in her sleep, poor thing. She had multi-system organ damage from years of abusing alcohol, pain medication, and tobacco. Her health was frail from the moment she arrived."

"So, no autopsy, then?"

"No, we seldom have them here. These people are all chronically ill, Agent. Death, although not welcomed by all, is, nevertheless, expected and accepted."

"Understood," Sully said. "Do you know if she had any regular visitors? Family?"

"I seem to recall a son who would phone occasionally. He never visited, though, until the day she died." Rosa shook her head sadly. "You have to understand just how ill she was, Agent Sullivan. It wouldn't surprise me if she waited to die until she saw that boy again. Jerry, I believe his name was. I surely hope he gave her some comfort before she passed on."

Sully mulled that over. He doubted very much it was comfort Jeremy was giving his mother that day.

"Well, I've taken up enough of your time, Ms. Gonsalves," Sully said, standing. "Thank you very much for your kindness and hospitality." He nodded his head toward the wall. "There's just one more question I have for you. These pictures of your residents? I don't suppose you have any of Meredith or her son?"

"I'm sorry, I don't. Ms. Sterling cherished her privacy. She rarely ventured from her room and, I'm quite sure, would be upset with us if we'd paraded her photo for all to see. Time was not kind to her. It ravaged her mind and body, mercilessly. Broke my heart that she lived out her later years all alone, abandoned and forgotten." She held her hand out, and Sully grabbed it, shaking it warmly. She clucked her tongue. "You know, loneliness can cut you as cleanly and swiftly as the sharpest blade, Agent Sullivan. Meredith Sterling's boy will have a lot of sins to answer for in the afterlife."

Maybe, Sully thought. *But first, he needs to answer for his sins in this one.*

Jake was fuming, trying to work his way around a traffic jam on Route 95, just outside of Falmouth. He had another twenty-five minutes to get to Fredericksburg, and, admittedly, was antsy to get to Kate. She had sounded so scared, so lost, on the phone earlier. Since they'd landed, he'd been trying her cell and home number without luck, making him even more nervous.

Why wasn't she answering?

Just then, his phone pealed, causing him to jump a bit in his seat.

"Devereaux."

"Hey boss, it's me. Where you at?"

"Well, Sully, funny you should ask. Currently, I'm ass-deep in traffic, inching my way towards Fredericksburg. You finish up at that nursing home?"

"Yeah, that's why I am calling. I'm planning on meeting you at Kate's, but it will take me another hour and a half. Longer if I hit the crap you're hitting now, and I didn't want to sit on this info too long."

"Appreciate that. So, give me some good news, Junior. I could use a pick-me-up."

"Right. Well, I'm not sure how this all fits in, but Meredith Sterling is dead. She died sometime in June of this year. And get this—the day that she died, she had a visit from her long-lost son."

"Jeremy," Jake said, no question in his voice.

"Indeed. Sunrise's Director of Nursing said he was the one and only visitor Meredith ever had, although apparently, there were some sporadic phone calls. There was no autopsy done, though. Ms. Sterling's health was already declining when she came to live there. Convenient, don't you think? That bastard killed his own mother, Jake. I'd bet my life on it."

"You'll get no argument from me. The question is, why? Why, after all these years, did he feel compelled to visit her, compelled to kill her? I think when we answer that question, we blow this case wide open." Spotting an opening, he moved to the left lane and increased his speed. "I've been trying to reach Kate since we deplaned, and she isn't picking up. I'm going to change tactics and track down Darby. Hopefully, she knows what's going on."

"Roger that. You still want me down in Fredericksburg, or you want maybe I sniff around some more, retrace Callie's steps?"

"Nah, come directly to Fredericksburg. Who knows? Maybe by the time you get there, Callie will be home."

Hidden behind an old shed on the property, Katie stared in disbelief at the place she once called home. The yard was in shambles, its dead trees and dying shrubs standing guard against the dilapidated house. Empty planters lined the walkway, marching like soldiers toward the main entrance. The peeling paint and rotting wood of the exterior told of faded dreams and forgotten desires.

In a second-floor window, a gaping hole winked at her, the spidered glass creeping lazily up the pane. Gone were the feelings of welcome and love that the house had always radiated. Instead, a sense of foreboding and loneliness permeated the air.

Her reaction to the old house surprised her. It was disquieting to witness what had become of a home that once oozed energy and life. Despite the drowning and the horror of her mother's murder, this place held some of her fondest memories and shared many of her deepest secrets.

All that remained now was a ghoulish mockery, a parody of the ills that had befallen its residents.

She rechecked her watch and sighed. It was nearing 6 p.m., and although Jake would have already touched down at Dulles, it would still take time until he could get to Falls Church.

Time that neither she nor Callie could afford.

She scanned the home for any signs of activity. Preternaturally quiet, it appeared deserted, with neither sound nor light coming from within.

What now, Einstein?

Convinced that she was overthinking, that she needed

to act rather than plot, Katie crept forward. She decided an entry through the back door leading into the kitchen (*the kitchen that smelled like pennies*) would prevent her from being too exposed. Unless Jeremy were standing there waiting for the door to open, he would be unaware of her presence.

She hoped.

Staying low, she sidled up the back steps to the faded yellow door. She peered through the glass into the darkened kitchen, blind to what lay beyond the entrance. Moonlight bounced off the glass, making the large, looming shapes inside come alive.

What the hell is that? A table and chairs?

The furniture appeared to be shifting, moving, creeping closer to her position. An optical illusion, created by fear and light and perception, bent on scaring the bejesus out of her.

It was doing a damn good job, too.

She blinked several times, trying to clear her vision. Her hands shook as she hesitated above the brass doorknob. A sudden breeze caught the wind chimes dangling overhead, and she nearly screamed. Swearing softly, she inhaled through her nose, attempting to calm her racing heart.

Did he hear those musical notes? Could he sense her? See her?

Slowly, she tested the knob and felt no resistance. Sending up a quick prayer, she steeled herself and slowly opened the door.

CHAPTER TWENTY-FOUR

*"By faith, Abel brought God a better offering than Cain did. By faith,
he was commanded as righteous, when God spoke well of his
offerings. And by faith, Abel still speaks, even though he is dead."
Hebrews 11:4.*

"What in the Sam Hill is going on, Finn?"
Darby shifted in the passenger seat and
studied Finn's profile as he sat behind the wheel of his
truck. An icy mix had fallen, a steady rain mingling with
the occasional ping of sleet bouncing off the windshield.
Finn eased up on the gas pedal, unsure if the dark roads
ahead held the unwelcome surprise of black ice.

"Honestly? I have no fucking clue. No one has seen or
heard from Callie in hours. She was supposed to drop you
off and have a visit with Grams. She never showed."

"And Katie?" Darby asked. "Where is she? You didn't
leave her ALONE in that house, did you? Please tell me
you didn't leave her alone."

Finn winced. "Okay, I won't tell you. But I did. Look,

you have to understand…" His words were lost in his passenger's tirade.

"Seriously?" she yelled, fear and anger simultaneously jockeying for position. "Are you high? Or just stupid? What on God's green earth would compel you to do that, Finn? You know this asshole, this psycho, would love nothing more than to hurt her." She twisted further in her seat and glared at him. "Are you trying to get her killed?"

Cursing, he punched the steering wheel and slammed on the brakes. Instinctively, Darby braced her hand on the dashboard as her body pitched forward. He threw the vehicle into park and turned to her, furious. "Jesus Christ, Darby, how long have you known me? Do you really think I would do that? Don't you even want to know how we came to that decision, or would you rather throw me under the bus based on assumptions and half-truths?" He looked up at his mirror, checking for oncoming traffic. "The fact is that Katie had a compelling argument to explain why I should leave her in Fredericksburg. Excellent ideas, like coordinating a search grid with the help of her laptop or making phone calls with a landline. You know as well as I do that cell service is shitty during a storm. We needed to reach out to the locals, the hospitals, even the morgue with a phone that would actually work." Headlights from behind temporarily blinded him, and he put the car in drive. "We made a split-second decision based on the facts we had, so sue me if you don't agree with that."

Darby reached for his hand. "I'm sorry. You're right, of course. I don't believe for one second you would intentionally put my girl in danger. I'm just so scared, you know? I couldn't bear it if something happened to either of them. You Callahans aren't just my friends; you're family." She smiled softly. "Forgive me?"

Finn squeezed her hand. "Always." He cranked up the

heat and turned to her. "Now, what do you say we get back to Fredericksburg and see what Kate's up to?" He winked. "How much you wanna bet the two of them are in front of the fireplace right now, binge-eating popcorn and guzzling their third glass of wine." But even as he said them, the words rang hollow in his ears. His sisters were in trouble; he only prayed he got to them in time.

Pain throbbed with every heartbeat as Callie studied her lower leg. Her right foot, swollen and bruised from her toes to her kneecap, sat at an odd angle. She reached down to test the skin surrounding the bone and winced.

Gabriel sighed dramatically and shook his head. "'Carry each other's burdens, and in this way, you will fulfill the law of Christ.' Galatians 6:2. I apologize for having to teach you such a painful lesson, Callista. It was a lesson intended for your demonic sister that, regrettably, you had to bear. Never forget that the source of your discomfort lies solely at her feet."

Callie ignored his arrogance and continued to assess her injuries. Whatever Katie had said on that call enraged him. Wordlessly, he'd rushed to Callie's side and, with a heavy boot, slammed his foot across her unshackled ankle. Initially, she felt nothing. Her only clue to the splintered bone beneath her flesh was the sound—a sickening crack that shattered the silence of her nightmarish prison. Then came the hot, dizzying pain. She bit the inside of her cheek, refusing to allow him to celebrate her misery.

"Wow," she ground out, "it takes a big man to stomp on a defenseless captive. Remind me never to let you babysit my cat." She shook the hair out of her eyes. "I think you broke my ankle, tough guy. I need a doctor."

He studied her for a moment, amusement in his eyes. "And what makes you think I would care about what you need? When will you realize this isn't about you, little one? It never was. You are merely a means to an end; whether you live or die is immaterial."

She shuddered, finally grasping the hopelessness of her situation. She was like a slice of cheese wedged inside a mousetrap—nothing more than bait, a lure, to force her sister to play his stupid games.

Sorry, pal, not gonna happen. I'll die before I let you hurt her.

His presence was overpowering. Confined by her chains, she felt impotent and claustrophobic. How could she plan with him so near?

She needed space.

Sighing heavily, she said, "Okay, fine, got it. If I live or die means nothing. Demonic sister, a means to an end, blah blah blah. Whatever. But while the suspense is thrilling, waiting to see how your little scenario ends, can you at least pretend to be a decent human and get me some aspirin? Maybe an icepack?"

He seemed to consider this, then slowly nodded. "Yes. I suppose I could make you more comfortable." Smirking, he added, "I'll be right back. Don't go away."

Callie rolled her eyes. *Asshole.*

Finn parked in front of Katie's house, an unexplained urgency coursing through his body. Judging by Darby's silence and rigid posture, she felt it too. They hopped out of the truck, jogged to the front door, and entered the house.

"Kates? Where you at?" Finn yelled out. "I've got a special delivery for you! A cute little blonde who calls herself 'fun-sized' because she's too short for the rides at Disney!"

No response. They moved further into the house, through the living room, and into the kitchen. Toenails clicking on hardwood caught their attention. Blue, with Gus lumbering behind, greeted them.

"Hey, guys!" Darby said, reaching out and ruffling their fur. "Did you miss us? Where's Kates? Where is your human?"

Finn scanned the kitchen, his eyes finally resting on a folded piece of paper propped up on the counter.

"Uh, oh," he whispered. He scooped up the letter, skimmed it, and groaned.

"What?" Darby asked.

He handed her the note and watched the color drain slowly from her face. Taking out his cell phone, he scrolled through his contacts until he found Jake's number. His fingers shook as he hit send, mentally preparing himself for the tirade he knew was coming. Jake would be furious, and rightly so.

He should never have left his sister.

～

"What the hell do you mean she's missing?" Jake yelled into the phone. He was still making his way through a traffic nightmare and felt a million miles from Fredericksburg. "Jesus Christ, Finn, you had one job! What in the holy fuck made you think leaving her was a good idea?"

Darby heard Jake's tone through the speaker and raised an eyebrow.

Finn gave her a warning glance. "I know, Jake, I know. I messed up. But she had a convincing argument and promised to stay put until I got home." Exhaling, he added weakly, "But all of that doesn't matter, does it? Because I should have known better." Angry with himself, he snatched up the letter she'd written. "She left a note. Jeremy–slash–Gabriel–slash–whateverthefuck his name is, has challenged her. He's kidnapped Callie and wants Kate to meet him, alone and unarmed, at our old house in Falls Church."

Jake grunted. "Well, this just keeps getting better and better, doesn't it? And, dammit, she went unarmed?" As an afterthought, he added, "I don't suppose you have a clue how long ago she left?"

Finn closed his eyes, loathe to say what he feared aloud. "I have an idea about when she may have left, but you're not gonna like it. If it was close to when I went to pick up Darby, there's an excellent chance she's already in Falls Church. And even if I leave immediately, I won't get to her for at least an hour. As for being unarmed, don't worry; she specifically stated she has a gun."

"At least that's something. Fuck!" He raked a hand through his hair. "Okay, here's what we are going to do. I will swing around and head north towards Falls Church. I figure I'm about twenty-five minutes away from there, give or take. Text me the address, stay where you are, and keep trying her cellphone. I'll call Sully and get the local police out there as well. Goes without saying, Finn, but if you contact her, you let me know immediately. Comprende?"

Finn's voice cracked. "Got it. Just get there, Jake. I can't lose either of them."

～

Callie watched warily as her captor climbed the basement steps to the first floor. She was cold, hurting, and so damn tired she couldn't think straight. A part of her was tempted to just mind-fuck herself into a state of euphoria, pretend she was on a beach somewhere with a sexy novel and a frosty beer. But she was a Callahan, and Callahans don't wave the white flag—they burn it. She inched closer to the wall behind her, struggling to stand. A thousand nerve fibers in her ankle fired at once, nearly bringing her to her knees. White-hot shards of pain laced their way from her foot to her calf, the spasms shocking and violent. She bit her lip to prevent crying out, adjusting her stance so that all her weight rested on her shackled leg.

Jesus, help me! I don't think I can do this!

Sweat glistened from her brow as she scrutinized her dungeon, searching for a weapon, a key, salvation. Sawdust and rodent droppings blanketed the concrete floor. Several feet away, wooden shelves sat perched against the far wall, their various tools mocking her—hammers, saws, screwdrivers. All excellent weapons that meant nothing if she could not reach them. She studied the chains that held her and mentally calculated the distance to the nearest shelf. Even if she could walk, she estimated she would still be about three feet short.

It might as well have been a mile.

Dejected but determined, she continued to survey her surroundings. Above her, exposed beams held electrical wires and copper pipes. She turned her attention once again to the floor, expanding her search area to the limits of the chains. Hopping on one foot and using the wall behind to steady herself, she carefully inched from left to right, gaining additional vantage points.

Her eyes moved rapidly and with purpose, the knowledge that Gabriel would return at any moment urging her on. Crestfallen, she was about to give up when she spotted a shiny object amid the dirt and dust of the concrete floor.

Yes!

Keeping her weight on the uninjured foot, she bent forward, touching the ground. From there, she did a modified walkout, propelling forward on her hands and then following up with a one-legged hop. Each jump jangled the chains, and she worried that the noise would carry up the wooden steps to the first floor. In a matter of minutes, she reached her prize, nearly shouting with triumph.

The nail, at its face, looked harmless enough. She certainly couldn't kill him with it. But maybe she could slow him down a bit. Reversing direction, convinced the clanging chains could wake the dead, she returned to her previous position and looked around one last time.

Oh, shit! Handprints!

Heavy footsteps drew her attention from the palm prints she'd left on the floor to the narrow cellar steps. It was too late to crawl back, too late to smooth the scattered sawdust. She wished she'd had a few more moments to go over her plan, to strategize. But it was now or never.

Sitting with her back against the cold concrete, her skin irritated by the rough texture of the wall, she bowed her head.

"I'm back, Callista," Gabriel said. "I've brought what you've asked for."

She remained still, her breathing slow and shallow, mimicking sleep. Or unconsciousness. If this was to work, she needed him to believe she posed no threat. Stomach roiling, she tightened her grip on the nail tucked inside her hand, and waited.

Closer, asshole. Just a little bit closer.

"Callista!" he said forcefully, "do you hear? I've no time for games. Look at me!"

Through hooded eyes, she could see his shoes just inches away from her thigh. He lifted a leg and nudged her injured foot with the toe of his boot. She remained motionless, biting her lip to keep from crying out. He squatted beside her, his heavy cologne assaulting her senses. She fought to deny the overwhelming urge to retreat.

"Wake up!" he bellowed, his fiery breath fanning her cheek. He yanked on her chin and forced her head up. In that instant, Callie lunged, screeching as her fist flew toward his eye, the nail protruding from between two fingers. She felt a sickening yield as the object penetrated his lower lid, then the globe of his left eye, blazing a trail toward his temple. He fell back, landing on his buttocks and shrieking in agony.

"Bitch! I'll fucking kill you!"

Struggling to get up, he pressed his palm against the wound, attempting to staunch the river of blood. He screamed again, wildly kicking and slapping Callie's body as she lay curled in a ball.

"Harlot! Cunt! Who do you think you're dealing with? I am the messenger! You dare attack the right hand of God? I will end you!"

For most of her adult life, Callie had studied abnormal psychology. Murderers, rapists, pedophiles... it took a hell of a lot to shock her. But this? Never had she witnessed such fury.

It was beyond violent. It was lunacy.

He stumbled away from her, still moaning, toward the back wall. Bewildered as to why he wasn't currently beating her to death, she tracked his movements.

What are you doing? Where to, Cyclops?

Reaching the shelving, he grabbed a rusted coffee can and furiously shook out its contents. A handful of colorful, soiled rags tumbled to the ground beside his feet. Snatching up several scraps, he hastily folded them into quarters, creating a crude dressing. Next, he layered the folded squares on top of his eye, selected another filthy rag, and wrapped it around his head to secure the dressing in place.

"Oh, goody," she moaned, "Jack Sparrow's here."

He ignored her. Clearing his throat, he pushed back his shoulders and took several deep breaths. Callie watched, spellbound, as his demeanor suddenly changed from impulsive and reckless to composed, resolute. She worried her lip, the swiftness of his transformation more frightening than his outburst.

He turned toward her and, with a devilish grin, punted the coffee tin across the room. She flinched when the can found its target, the metallic ping echoing off the wall behind her. With measured steps, he walked to her, bent down, and whispered, "Now, you pay."

Grabbing a fistful of hair, he pulled her to her feet. She swayed and clutched at his shirt, her face inches from his. The outer edge of his eye was visible beneath the bandage, the flesh raw and bloody. Callie felt a fleeting sense of satisfaction.

I hope it hurts like hell, dickhead.

They stood there for a moment, toe to toe. Gabriel expected her to whimper, to shake with fear like all the others. But she did neither. Instead, her mouth curved into a sly smile, and she winked at him.

"Burn in Hell, Gabriel."

He raised an eyebrow and chuckled, impressed by her courage. Nodding his head in what could only be described as respect, he studied her for a moment. This person, this female, was unlike any he'd ever encountered.

Callie dared herself to believe that, perhaps, she'd make it out alive after all.

And then, without warning, he threw her to the ground. She watched a thin line of spittle escape from the corner of his mouth. He looked feral, crazed, a wolf stalking its prey.

He backhanded her, hard, across the face. An explosion of pain rained over her cheek as blood flew from her mouth. She covered her head with her arms, trying to shield herself from the assault. He drew back his boot and slammed his foot into her stomach, kicking her again and again. She felt her ribs crack and covered her abdomen with her forearm, struggling to breathe.

The last sounds she heard before blackness descended were her wheezing respirations… and the faint echo of footsteps overhead.

CHAPTER TWENTY-FIVE

*"For whoever wants to save their life will lose it, but whoever loses
their life for me will find it." Matthew 16:25.*

K atie wiped a clammy hand against her thigh and
stepped over the threshold of her former home.
Her heart slammed inside her chest, the thunderous beat
echoing in her ears. Pursing her lips, she pushed out a
breath and squinted into the darkness. Tension clawed at
her body as, for the hundredth time in the past ten
minutes, she questioned whether a sane person would
come here alone.

Probably not.

Although on the bright side, she thought grimly, *it's an
excellent backdrop for a horror movie. The only thing missing is a
moth and a lamb, and voila! I'm Clarice fucking Starling.*

The absence of light and sound was chilling. Ignoring
the instinct to flee, she closed the kitchen door in
increments, hoping to soften any protests made by the
rusted hinges. The gentle clack of the latch as it slid into

place was symbolic—the door was closed, the world shut out. There was no going back.

Inching into the kitchen, she blinked rapidly, trying to adjust to the gloom. Aside from a narrow beam of moonlight glinting off the faucet, the room was inky black. Sensory distortion, magnified by fear, left her feeling especially vulnerable. She dug her cell out of a pocket, hit the home key, and nearly groaned when she saw the battery was at twelve percent.

Dammit!

She flicked on the phone's flashlight and quickly scanned the layout of the room. A scarred oak table and three ladder-back chairs occupied most of the space to her left. To her right, distressed kitchen cabinets surrounded a porcelain sink and gas stove. Everything, from the linoleum floor to the deep walnut cabinets, had been replaced.

Of course, they remodeled, she reasoned. *Bloodstains are a bitch to remove.*

She pointed the light toward the back of the room and froze. A figure stood in front of her, tall, silent, and unmoving. She gasped, then relaxed her shoulders when she recognized the form: A string mop, tucked inside a metal bucket, standing guard in the center of the room.

Was it placed there deliberately? A poor man's alarm system for this shithead?

Whatever the reason, she was thankful that she'd verified her surroundings before moving on. Steeling herself, she tiptoed around the bucket and headed toward the living room.

She had a plan. In truth, it was more a guide than a plan. Handwringing did nothing to overcome worry, and inaction had never conquered fear. She believed that courage was born from a desperate desire to protect someone, rather than an innate drive to act. And, although scared to death, that terror could not hold a candle to the horror she felt at the thought of losing Callie.

She shined her light around the sparse living room, marveling that such a modest-sized home could feel like a mansion when searching for a killer. A dense, pungent odor tickled her nostrils, a lingering mixture of mothballs and arthritic cream. The carpeted floor was threadbare and faded, the result of years of sunlight beaming through the enormous front window. A well-worn sofa surrounded by two lazy-boy chairs dominated the room. Aside from a wooden sign that read, 'The Crowley's,' the walls were bare. The only other items of note were a floor lamp and a few throw rugs.

And cat hair. There was enough cat hair in the room to weave a sweater.

Moving on, she padded to the tiny closet and half-bathroom in the hallway. They, and the laundry room nearby, appeared as though they hadn't been used for weeks. The litter box and food dish near the washer looked untouched.

Strange. Wonder where the cat is?

She crept silently toward the staircase and bedrooms above, nervous sweat trickling down her back. When she reached the top of the stairs, she had a vivid flashback of her seven-year-old self, terrified and screaming for her mother. In her mind's eye, she saw herself frantically searching the bedrooms, yanking open the linen closet, finding Ryan. She started to shake, the memories overpowering, suffocating.

Move it, Callahan! It does no good to revisit history right now.

Robotically, she pushed on, marching from room to room and talking herself through it.

Left side first, to Ryan's room. Then on to Finn's, second door down. Just breathe.

Halfway down the hall, she paused, the disturbed air bringing her a fresh horror. It was an odor she'd experienced a thousand times; on excavations, with the search and rescue teams, in the lab. A sickly sweet, putrid scent, like spoiled fruit and rotten cabbage and alcohol, all rolled into one. It was intense, inescapable, and revolting.

It was death.

~

Jake tapped the edge of the steering wheel, anxiety and anger nearing a crescendo. He still had about ten minutes until the turnoff to Kate's former home. He flipped open the center console and, keeping his eyes on the road, began rummaging around for his secret, guilty pleasure... cigarettes.

He had quit smoking several years ago after finding a simple run had become a challenge. Still, like a security blanket or a safety net, he always kept a pack of smokes hidden somewhere in his car. The Marlboros he was searching for had to be three years old and staler than shit, but he didn't care. He needed something to prevent his mind from going to that dark place he knew so well. Cigarettes were as good a diversion as any.

His phone rang, and he checked the caller I.D. "Yeah, Finn, what's up?" he asked. "Tell me you got ahold of your sister."

"If only," Finn said sadly. "Darby and I are on the way to Falls Church now, though. Do you know if the cops arrived at the house yet?"

"No, not yet. The dispatcher on duty told me all her officers are responding to a three-vehicle accident involving multiple fatalities. I stressed that this was an urgent matter, possibly a life and death situation. They promised to get there as soon as possible."

"Jesus. I guess we hope she hasn't engaged with this Jeremy/Gabriel scumbag yet. Her cell is still going directly to voicemail. I've left several messages, as did Darby, but so far, nothing."

Jake grunted. "Same here. Listen up, if you get to the house before me, sit tight. I should be there in less than ten minutes unless I hit more traffic. Oh, and don't call me again unless it's critical. I'm silencing my phone, so I don't alert this asshole I'm there."

"Got it. And Jake? Be careful. This guy is a freaking powder keg waiting for a spark."

Katie stood in the darkened hallway, cupping a hand over her nose and mouth. The stomach-churning odor was emanating from her parents' former bedroom. She held her breath, opened the door, and fought a wave of nausea as the stench assailed her nostrils. Instinctively she stepped back, the smell so vile it seemed to coat her tongue and permeate her skin. She held the phone up to scan the room but found no light—the phone had powered down, its battery finally depleted.

Dammit!

She reached out and flicked stupidly at the wall switch, praying for a miracle. The room remained cast in shadows.

As if bringing in light would change what I know. Death lives here now.

She tiptoed into the room, confident that anything less would disturb the departed. Edging as close as she could without vomiting, she identified the silhouettes of two people on the bed. They lay side by side, a blanket tucked neatly around them. An orange and white creature wearing a green collar lay stiffly on the floor beside the bed. Within the shadows, Katie glimpsed two sets of rosary beads innocently dangling from the headboard.

She had her answer. The Crowleys were dead.

Jake took the Falls Church exit at a much higher speed than he should have and felt the Suburban tires skidding as he hit the brakes. His stomach dropped as he grabbed the wheel tighter, eased off the gas, and fought to bring the car back into alignment.

"Stupid asshole!" he hissed, pounding the wheel. "Pay attention!"

He had good reason to speed. The Falls Church dispatcher had called him back and let him know that, while an officer was en route to the scene, the cop was coming from some distance away.

Jake would arrive long before the locals. He only prayed he would get there in time.

Katie checked the remaining bedrooms upstairs and, finding them empty, crept back down the steps to the first floor. Pausing at the bottom of the staircase, she held her breath, straining to hear. Except for the occasional groan of the wind against the eaves, the house was silent. She swiveled her head, searching the shadows, but saw no movement.

There was just one place left that he could have Callie, one area of the house she'd always avoided as a child. It embodied the stuff of her nightmares, the unspoken dangers she was reluctant to face. It was the room she forbid herself to enter unless absolutely necessary.

The basement.

She rarely visited that musty, underground tomb in her youth. And not because it was teeming with ghosts, screaming to be heard. It was the creepy crawlers; insects, mice, and spiders, all threatening to wriggle down her neck, in her hair, or up her back. Now, as she approached the 'door of gloom,' as she used to call it, goosebumps pimpled her skin. She moved the gun in her waistband to the front of her pants and twisted the doorknob.

Jake was having difficulty finding the address. The road was unlit, each house looking the same in the black of night. There were very few homes that displayed a house number, so he resorted to finding one and counting up.

"C'mon, lucky fifty-four, where are you?"

He peered into the darkness at the structures lining the road. Squinting his eyes, he strained to decipher the numbers. *That looks like the number sixteen. Or is it an eighteen? Shit, why can't people put their damn numbers where you can find them?*

Frustrated, he called Finn for landmark help and continued to count.

Hang on, Red.

Dust motes swirled in a beam of light at the top of the basement steps. Squeezing the railing, Katie cautiously descended the stairs, aware that she was inching toward disaster. The heaviness weighing on her chest when she first entered the home had turned to terror.

This must be what Hell feels like... every turn, every step, bringing you closer to the belly of the beast.

A dangling thread of a spiderweb brushed against her face and clung to her cheek. She shuddered and slapped at it, then rolled her hands over her limbs, swiping at the imaginary bugs she knew were crawling on her body.

Get a grip, idiot. It's not real. There aren't hundreds of soulless insects burrowing deep beneath your skin, depositing eggs.

Not entirely convinced, she forced herself to keep moving, descending into the unknown. Halfway down the stairs, she peeked her head below the ceiling into the dimly lit room and spotted a person lying against the back wall. Horrified, she slapped her hand across her mouth and rushed down the remaining steps. Even from this distance, in poor lighting, she recognized the figure was female—fallen, silent, unmoving.

"Shit, Callie?" Katie whispered. "Shadow, is that you?"

The figure, naked and bloody, groaned. Oblivious to the danger, Katie stumbled across the room and fell to the ground, cupping Callie's face.

"Cal? Honey, can you hear me?"

Callie groaned again, but her eyes remained closed. Her copper-colored hair gathered limply around her shoulders, a matted mop of dirt and blood. Her bruised face was puffy, her lips chapped and caked with dried blood. She swallowed hard, hoping the saliva would soothe her parched throat, allowing her to speak. The effort to engage, to awaken from the safety of nothingness, was exhausting. She drifted back into the wasteland.

Katie brushed the hair from Callie's face and gently shook her. "Cal, sweetie, we gotta go."

Looking up, Katie examined the thick chains

imprisoning her sister. The bilco doors, and only other avenue of escape besides the cellar stairs, were to her left. Not that it mattered, though—they weren't going anywhere without the key that unlocked those chains.

Although she could not see him, Katie felt Gabriel close by. Her skin was alive, the back of her head awash with pins and needles. They were running out of time.

"C'mon, Shadow," Katie begged, "wake up. We need to get out of here, and I don't think I can carry you."

Callie stirred, her eyes half-open. "Ith that a crack 'bout my weight?" she asked around a decidedly fat lip. Her words were slurred and slow, but Katie understood them.

"Always the comedian. Can you sit up?"

A work lamp flicked on, and light flooded the space. Behind her, Katie heard a deep voice rebound off the concrete walls.

"Hello, Katherine."

Katie let out a breathy curse, then slowly stood. Her tongue felt too large for her mouth, her throat raw and dry. Senses heightened, breath quickening, she closed her eyes when he came up behind her.

"On. Your. Knees." He pressed against her, his voice low, his scent overwhelming.

She looked helplessly at Callie, weighing the possibilities. She could pull her gun, but he stood at her back, and she didn't know if he was armed. She had to face him, see what weapon he carried, before deciding on an action.

Callie was more alert now, her eyes somehow communicating resolve and strength, despite her fear. She rolled to her back and tried to sit up, sharp pain blasting her ribcage with every breath.

Katie lifted her hands in surrender and, giving her twin a wink, slowly dropped to her knees.

Gloating, Gabriel said. "At last we meet. I must say... you are much more attractive on your knees."

Katie snorted. "Yeah. Forgive me for not getting up, but after seeing the mess you've made of my beautiful sister's face, I'd rather not risk it." She paused. "So, tell me, Jeremy, what's the plan here?" His name tasted like venom as it fell from her lips.

"My name," he drawled, southern accent stronger now, "is Gabriel. I am the Apostle, God's most powerful messenger. Jeremy is dead."

"Oh, right, right. My mistake. Personally, you look more like a 'douche canoe' or a 'shit stain,' to me, but hey, what do I know."

He grunted, grabbed her by both arms, and forced her to stand. She turned to face him, hoping that he couldn't see the gun in her waistband. Ice pumped through her veins, and her breath quickened, his fury pinning her in place. Fresh blood trailed down his face from beneath the simple dressing that covered his eye. Katie felt a deep satisfaction knowing that it was, most likely, extraordinarily painful.

Good for you, Callie!

"So, Gabe," Katie said, "or should I call you Captain Gabe? Pirate Sterling? How about One-eyed Willie?"

Callie let out a nervous giggle and attempted once again to sit up.

He let go of Katie's arms and, hands fisted, leaned close to whisper in her ear. "Your tongue is sharp, demon woman. It's going to get you into trouble someday. But I suppose I shouldn't expect anything less from a Callahan."

"Ouch," Katie said, mocking him. "But seriously, Gabe. You know dick about my family and nothing about my life. Yet, for some demented reason, you've chosen to target me—a person with countless ties to the law enforcement community. You're not very bright, are you?"

Too far, Kates! Callie thought, trusting that another gift her sister possessed was telepathy. *He's a psychopath and a narcissist. Flattery, not ridicule, will disarm him.*

"I have a question," Callie interrupted, trying to defuse the bomb that Katie may have triggered. Her words remained garbled around swollen lips. "I've studied people like you my whole life: serial and spree killers, sadists, and fiends. Sociopaths have a type, a particular victimology, that they follow to get their rocks off." She pulled at a strand of hair stuck to her bloodied mouth. "History has shown a commonality of targets, like prostitutes, homosexuals, young brunettes—you get the picture. But your profile defies all the studies, all the experts." She pushed against the wall and, finally, sat upright. "And so, I'm curious about your selection process. Are all of your killings a bizarre form of revenge against my sister?"

Katie stopped herself from clapping. *Magnificent, Callie! Keep him talking!*

Gabriel squared his shoulders and moved around Katie to address her sister. "You will never understand my process, little one. Do you think all I do revolves around this cretin? This slut?" He threw a hand in anger toward Katie, his eyes narrowing. "She is but a minor player in the grand design." He pulled his shoulders back. "I am the Apostle. I plan carefully, I follow His word, I eliminate the plague that infects His creations. Yes, I targeted Katherine," he said, contempt in his voice, "but I have other names, other individuals that stain this earth. And I continue my quest for the Splendor." He grinned. "Perhaps, I will discover it today, with one of you."

He really is quite mad. Katie thought.

Watching him, she deliberated her options. Taunting and pushing might be risky, but he was a narcissist and loved to talk. If they could stall long enough, either help would arrive in time to save them, or he would relax his guard until she had a clear shot. He hadn't made a move to search her yet, probably because he was decompensating. His brain was firing in all directions, a runaway train speeding toward derailment, and collision was imminent.

Callie's eyes darted from Katie to Gabriel, watching the bitter interaction unfold. Vulnerable on the ground, she slowly wriggled up the wall to a standing position, her weight resting on her left leg. Extending an arm, she took Katie's hand in hers and squeezed, conveying a silent understanding of their dire situation. Katie squeezed back and stepped in front of her sister, shielding her from the man before them.

Gabriel paced, his hands behind his back as though preparing a lecture. "Is this room as you remember it, Katherine?" He asked, looking around. "From your childhood, I mean. I assume you have many fond memories of this house? And some not so fond, I'm afraid. Let's review, shall we?" His brows creased. "Hm, where shall we start? Maybe at the beginning, a perfect little prologue to this story. You remember, don't you?"

His demeanor changed, and, in a breath, he shifted from weird civility to unbridled rage. His face flushed, and saliva flew as he annunciated each word. "It was the day your selfish foolishness got you killed! The day you ruined my life!"

Katie blinked, confused. "What? That's absurd. How could my drowning affect you in the least? I don't even know you! None of us do!"

Gabriel sneered. "A series of events transpired after

that day, Katherine, events that altered the course of my life. Because of you, I lost the only person I ever cared for —the only soul on this earth that gave a shit about me!"

Katie's head spun, and her stomach heaved. The images in her mind came fast and furious; her time in the hospital, the woman and child who were present but never made it into her room. And her father—pacing, speaking in whispered tones, hurriedly ushering the mystery guests away. The memory taking shape was shocking and undoubtedly true. This maniac, this sadistic killer, was the product of her father and his mistress, the gray lady.

Gabriel was her father's illegitimate son... and their brother.

CHAPTER TWENTY-SIX

"We know love by this, that He laid down His life for us, and we ought to lay down our lives for the brethren." John 3:16-18.
"Fuck you, asshole." Katherine Callahan, 12-30.

Bingo.

Jake stared at the crumbling house in front of him, looking for movement. The home was in desperate need of attention, and from all appearances, abandoned. His brief conversation with Finn had given him a basic idea of the layout inside: kitchen, living room, half-bath, and laundry on the main floor, bedrooms with another two bathrooms upstairs. There was a full basement below the house and a small attic off the master bedroom.

He decided a systematic approach to the search—entering via the back door and clearing the rooms as he went through them, was his best bet. Years of training and experience screamed at him to wait for back-up. He was about to commit a rookie mistake, break a cardinal rule ingrained in every cop's head since the academy. He didn't care. Kate and Callie were in trouble. He crept toward the rear door, gun drawn.

Rules be damned… nothing would keep him from entering that home.

~

Katie knew she was hyperventilating and struggled to control her respirations. Behind her, Callie was fighting as well, the mental and physical pain colliding in a thunderstorm of emotions. She squeezed Katie's hand and whispered, "We got this, Kates."

"Welcome to the truth, sisters."

Katie drifted toward the center of the room, putting as much space between her and Callie as possible. She wanted a clear shot, as far from her sister as possible if she used her weapon. Gabriel's rage was building.

Placing her hands on her hips, Katie moved her fingers to the side of the gun, keeping contact with the steel. "And what is the truth, Mr. Apostle?" She asked snidely. "That you killed Aman? Stacy and Chance? My God, Gabriel, you've killed so many people. The Crowleys, Laura Dixon, and her father, even your foster parents. You are responsible for so many deaths."

As predicted, Gabriel brushed past Callie and stalked toward Katie, getting within inches of her face. "More than you know," he snarled. "Take your lover, for example. This would be, what? Six months ago?" Katie said nothing, conveying her contempt with an icy stare. Flustered by her silence, he pushed on. "Y-yes, I recall it well. All it took was a well-placed hit to the back of the head as he was leaving your house. Within a few hours, he was on Sugarloaf Mountain, unconscious, a rosary around his filthy neck. Dying."

Listening to him drone on and on, a sinister lilt to his voice, Katie had a strange, momentary urge to chuckle.

Where are we? Bizarro world? Trapped in an episode of 'Scooby-Doo,' forced to listen as the bad guy recants his evil deeds? If so, where the fuck is Shaggy when you need him?

"Is he talking about Kyle?" Callie gasped, bringing Katie back to the present. "Did you know this, Kates?"

"Yes, once our forensic artist completed the facial reconstruction." Glaring at Gabriel, she said bitterly, "It must have been such a challenge for you, strangling an unresponsive man. What's your next trick? Picking off babies? The elderly? Oh, wait, you did that one already when you took out the Crowleys, didn't you? Outstanding."

Gabriel scowled and grabbed her face, his fingers digging painfully into her cheeks. "Careful, Katherine. You wouldn't want to see the finale before we've completed all the acts, would you?" He pulled a phone from the pocket of his jeans and started snapping close-ups of her face. "I plan on sending these to your lover, Devereaux, so that he can relive this day over and over. Unfortunately, I couldn't document the others for you: the cheerleader, the mechanic, that mangy dog. More's the pity." He let go of her and smoothed a hand down the side of her face. "I'm especially proud of the very first one, though. It was my masterpiece, created when I was just a boy. That was, hmm, in October of '97, I believe."

"Jesus Christ," Callie whispered hoarsely, her heart splintering into a thousand pieces. Tugging on the chains imprisoning her, she screamed, "I'm going to fucking kill you!"

Katie's knees buckled, and she struggled to remain upright. "Mom? You killed our mother?" she croaked, finding that revelation impossible to absorb. Her mind flashed back to Stacy and the ring found on her finger. "Of course, you did," she said thickly. "That's how you ended up with her engagement ring. But why? What could she have done to a little boy that signed her death warrant?"

Gabriel turned and casually walked to the back table. Eager to begin, he was growing bored with the conversation. His Chosen One would soon be in her own hell, a torment borne in his mind, meant to produce the ultimate punishment. He selected a navy-blue rosary and turned to face her again.

"Enough! All you need to know is that I was protecting my birthright. Our visit to your mother to expose the truth was, frankly, disappointing. Once Meredith explained that I was Rowan's son and rightful heir, Eileen lost it. She called mother a liar, told us to leave, even threatened to call the cops." He grinned wickedly. "So, I stabbed her. Repeatedly, if memory serves." He stared hard at Katie, a feral look in his eyes. "Do you understand now why you are the Chosen?"

She looked at Callie, then back at Gabriel. "No, I don't. I mean, I can see you're a bowl full of crazy, so I suppose trying to wrap my head around your way of thinking is impossible. But just for shits and giggles, how about you explain it to me."

Gabriel bared his teeth, agitation growing. "If you never drowned, never died, then Father would still be alive. His guilt over your accident destroyed him. Honestly, Katherine, how have you come so far in this world with such a simple mind?"

Aware of his increasing anger, she stayed silent.

Pacing again, Gabriel's voice rose. "Father believed redemption lay in severing ties with my mother, which meant severing ties with his eldest son. Collateral damage, you see." He stopped moving and pointed at Katie. "And that, dear sister, is what put him on a plane that crashed and burned. Your foolishness, your reckless behavior, put him on that plane!"

Katie swallowed hard, trying to tamp down the urge to lash out. He was irrational, and no amount of pleading, no avenue of approach, would change that. Still, how could she let those accusations go unanswered?

To hell with it... taking the high road is overrated, anyway.

Voice trembling, she said, "Let me get this straight. My father had an affair with another woman, an affair that produced an illegitimate child. He continued to live this double life for years, behind the back of his adoring wife, consequences be damned. And yet somehow, ignoring his part in any of it, you blame his death on a six-year-old drowning victim?" Hearing the words aloud was surreal.

My God, he truly is insane.

Switching gears, aware his madness defied reason, she said, "You realize the police are on the way, right? You've left a trail of ghosts, a body count of people I love, and the cops know all about it. You have two options here, Gabriel; leave now, save yourself, or stay and wait for the calvary, fully armed, to bust in here. Your choice."

Disregarding her, he marched toward Callie, wrapping the rosary around his hands. He would choke the life out of her while his Chosen watched.

Shit, shit, shit, he's going for Callie! We're out of time!

Hands shaking, Katie pulled her gun. "Hold up, asshole," she rasped, sounding braver than she felt.

Jake had taken her shooting a few times, and in each session, her aim was true. Squinting her eyes, she followed his movements with the barrel. "Back away from her, nice and slow." She began moving toward Callie's position, intent on shielding her once again.

Gabriel lifted his hands and smirked. "Well, well, well.

Bravo, Sister, how very clever of you." His hands were clenching and unclenching in the air, as though he were waving to a toddler. It was unnerving.

Katie stood in front of Callie, gun trained on her target, and contemplated her next move. Sweat pooled under her arms and above her lips. The rage that emanated from Gabriel made her stomach heave, and she swallowed the bile burning her throat.

"Kates," Callie whispered, "tell him to unlock me. We need the key to these padlocks."

Katie nodded imperceptibly and addressed Gabriel. "Keys. Where are they?"

"In my back pocket," he said, shrugging. "Which means either I dig them out, or you come and get them." His face remained neutral, but his eyes shone as if he held the secrets to the universe.

What do I do?

If she got too close to him, he could overpower her. But, if she let him dig around in his pockets, he could have a weapon.

Too close is just too dangerous. I'll let him dig and pray he is unarmed.

A faint thud overhead fueled the hope that help had arrived. "Get on your knees and place your hands on your head." She wanted his hands in one place, both to monitor his movements and to end his constant waving.

It was pissing her off.

Gabriel dropped to his knees gracefully, as if he had performed the task a million times, and indeed, he had. Genuflecting was part of his adoration routine and an essential part of his identity as the Apostle.

"Good," Katie said. "Now, using just one hand, find the key and toss it to me."

Callie's ears perked up as gooseflesh rose on her limbs.

She heard movement upstairs as well. *Please, hurry!* She thought desperately. *I have an awful feeling about this, and I'm not even an Empath!*

Gabriel smirked and nodded. The time was now, his work completed. A brief feeling of sadness washed over him, knowing that in a few minutes, his mission would be over. He watched the women closely, debating who he should neutralize first. One held the gun, while the other held the most potent weapon of all—vulnerability.

Eeny, meeny, miny ...

Comfortable with his decision, he made his move.

Jake, tactical flashlight in one hand and gun in the other, crept through the kitchen and foyer. After clearing the living room, he moved to the bottom of the staircase. As he climbed, the pervasive odor of death filled his nostrils. Stomach rebelling, there was only one thought on his mind.

Please, God, don't let it be them!

Logically, he knew that the stench of decomposition takes time; bacteria need to breakdown, while gases need to build up. But that thought brought little comfort to him. He wouldn't be satisfied that Kate was still alive until he found the source of the smell.

Finding the first two bedrooms empty, he crept to the open door at the end of the hallway. White slivers of moonlight spilled through the tattered curtains at the window, their rays illuminating the headboard resting against the sill. His heart tripped as he stepped inside the room, the outline of two bodies noticeable atop the bed. The bright beam of his flashlight landed on an elderly male, and Jake released the breath he was holding.

Two old-timers. And a cat? Probably the homeowners, possibly transients, but definitely not Kate or her sister.

He moved the light over the rest of the room, stopping on the shimmering rosary beads hanging from the bedpost. Rage boiled in his veins as he made a vow to this couple and every other victim of this gutless killer; he would see this man caught, or he would see him dead.

At the moment, Jake preferred the latter.

It happened in a flash, a microsecond, with no time to react or defend. Katie could have had the instincts of a Navy SEAL, or the agility of an Olympic gymnast, and still wouldn't have seen it coming.

Gabriel, on his knees, had one hand on his head while the other reached into his back pocket. He jumped to his feet in one swift movement, lowered his head, and charged at Katie.

Oh, God!

His shoulder plowed into her abdomen, bringing them both to the ground at Callie's feet. Katie grunted and bit her lip, the bitter taste of copper bathing her mouth. Gun still in hand, she twisted and bucked, struggling to roll to her side. Gabriel mirrored her movements, his body pinning her legs, his grip like a vice around her forearm. Grunting, she worked to wriggle free, her breaths coming in quick bursts. Callie's screams and the dull thud of her uninjured foot kicking Gabriel's side floated in the air around them.

Snorting with effort, he began a slow crawl up Katie's body, oblivious to Callie's obscenities or the blows her bare foot landed on his head. Katie, too, noticed none of it, furiously working to keep the weapon out of Gabriel's reach. His revolting scent surrounded her, a vile mixture of sweat and musk and moral decay.

They started a slow roll, each grappling for the gun. Callie continued howling, pulling against her chains, the metal clang of iron echoing off the walls. Gabriel stretched, reaching for Katie's right hand, yanking at the gun. His fingers fought hers for the trigger, the barrel twisting and turning in all directions.

A deafening blast, followed by a piercing scream, rocked the room.

Jake was still in the bedroom that held the bodies of the Crowleys when the first scream penetrated the silence. Instinctively he spun, sweeping his gun and flashlight in an arc. The cry he'd heard was muffled and distant, but he knew it originated from inside the house. Descending the stairs two at a time, he missed the last few steps and landed on the first floor with a thud.

Cursing, head low, he crept through the main level, straining to hear. The scuffling and yelling intensified as he made his way down the hall, and he increased his pace. Passing a door to his left, the crack of gunfire rumbled beneath his feet, followed by a heart-stopping wail. Commanding himself to use caution, he backed up, slowly opened the door, and eased down the wooden steps.

Nothing could have prepared Jake for the sight before him; two people, on the ground, bathed in blood. One was raging, screaming, cradling the still form beside her. Running footsteps drew his attention momentarily from the women to the back of the basement.

Sterling!

Gabriel glanced back at Jake, smirked, and ascended the steps that led to the bilco doors and freedom.

"Freeze, FBI!" Jake yelled, his gun aimed at the fleeing man.

Gabriel kept climbing.

"I'm not going to warn you twice, Sterling. Give me a fucking reason!"

Ignoring him, cackling like a lunatic, Gabriel scrambled up the remaining steps. As he was pushing on the metal doors, Jake fired once, the round hitting the fleeing man in the upper thigh. Screaming in agony, Gabriel exploded through the exterior doors and vanished into the night.

"Fuck!" Jake swore, running toward his suspect. He was not about to let him go.

"Jake, please!" A desperate voice cried. "She's hit bad! Help us!"

Torn, Jake cursed once again and ran back to the women, simultaneously dialing Sully's number. Putting the phone on speaker, he bent over and, for the first time, noticed the severity of the injury.

Oh, Christ!

Sully picked up on the third ring, and Jake gave him a brief report. "We need everything you have sent to this location, Ian. Cops, paramedics, everything. I have two victims, at least one gunshot wound, and a suspect on the move." Voice cracking, he added, "It's bad, Sully. Step it up."

Dropping to his knees, Jake gently touched her neck. Her skin was clammy, a weak pulse tapping below his fingertips. There was a puncture wound above her breastbone, pumping out a steady stream of red with each heartbeat. He slapped an open hand over the hole, then quickly checked her breathing. Noisy, wet gasps escaped her lips while blood continued to pour from her chest, oozing through his fingers and spilling down her side. He looked at her face, horrified to see that blood was now bubbling from her nose and mouth. Her back arched slightly, and her eyelids fluttered.

"Jake!" her sister cried. "Do something!"

Repositioning his hand, he quickly scanned the basement for something, anything, he could use to stem the bleeding.

C'mon, c'mon! He thought wildly. *Think!*

Her breathing had become faint, nearly imperceptible. There would be no last-minute reprieve, no comforting words to ease the sting of the inevitable. She coughed, a foamy mix of blood and fluid flying from her lips. A single tear slid down her face as her eyes bounced between them, pleadingly, knowingly.

She was dying.

"No, no, please!" Jake whispered. "Stay with us!"

Frantic, helpless, he looked up at her whimpering sister and reached out a free hand. They stayed like that, hoping, praying... holding each other's hands as if the mere touch, the human contact, could triumph over death. He continued to apply pressure to the gaping hole above her breast while her sister spoke words of encouragement, championed her zest for life, begged her to hang on.

"Stay," she whispered fervently. "God, I'm so sorry. It should have been me! Please, stay! I don't think I can live without you!"

The distant sounds of sirens and car doors slamming broke the night. Daring to hope, they stared at the dying woman and willed her to live. But her skin had turned to ice, with a pallor reserved only for the dead.

Jake swept the hair away from her neck, once again feeling for a pulse. The bleeding had slowed to a trickle, as her chest rose once, twice, then was still. Her head lolled to the side, her gaze fixed and unseeing.

Huddled together on the floor, they held her, sobs wracking their bodies.

It was over.

In the shadows of the cold cellar, an eerie glow surrounded them, the brilliant light luminous and self-originating. It seemed to engulf them, protect them, become them. It was warm and inviting and... beautiful.

It was the Splendor.

CHAPTER TWENTY-SEVEN

Three months later, Fredericksburg, VA

Wearily, she ascended the steps, taking off her windbreaker as she climbed. Her tank top, damp with sweat, clung stubbornly to her body. The easy jog she'd planned had morphed into a four-mile run, her chaotic mind seeking a mundane task. The monotony of running had become the best avenue to a short-lived peace.

Reaching the hallway, she started to tiptoe past her sister's bedroom as if her quiet footfalls could silence the ache in her heart. The room held an echo of memories she could not bear, and entering would only cause more pain. She understood this, knew it like she knew the earth was round, and the tides would rise.

She entered anyway.

It had become a sacred place, a shrine to the dead. Moving to the oversized dresser, she toyed with a few baubles, a framed picture, a strand of pearls. A bottle of French perfume sat next to the jewelry box, and she dabbed the liquid on her wrists. Eyes closed, she inhaled, trying to capture the scent of its owner.

Her shoulders sagged, and she sighed; a fragrance meant little without the person who wore it.

For three months, the guilt of being alive had waged war with her gratitude for survival. She tugged on her ponytail and shook her head, her hair tumbling around her shoulders. Gazing into the mirror, blind to her reflection, she picked up a brush and combed through the thick waves.

Her eyes drifted to her chest, and the elastic bandage wound tightly on top of her tank top, compressing her breasts. The wrap dug painfully into her ribs, and she struggled to release the binding, wondering, for the thousandth time in weeks, why she bothered.

He still had not come.

Movement caught her attention, and her head snapped back to the mirror—a flicker of light, a kaleidoscope of color, and finally, the woman she ached to see.

She smiled, and the luminous image in the mirror smiled back.

"Hello, Shadow," Katie said.

"Kates," Callie rasped, turning away from the mirror to face her sister. "I was wondering if you'd come."

Katie smiled again, warm and genuine.

Callie had missed that smile. "Oh, Kates," she whispered, "I miss you terribly. I don't think I can live this life without you." Tears filled her eyes. "It's like getting sucker-punched in the gut. A piece of me, an enormous chunk that defines not just who I am, but who I hope to be, is gone."

"I know, Shadow. It wasn't in my plans either, but I wouldn't change a thing. Not if it meant keeping you safe." Katie's image flickered. "I'm so new at this, Cal, and am still learning how to manifest on this plane. I can't stay long, I'm not strong enough yet, but I am curious. How did you end up with my gifts?"

Callie shrugged. "It was when you crossed over, I think. When you…" she hesitated, "when you left, Jake and I became bathed in a bright light, a brilliance that emitted a warmth I didn't know existed. That light, I believe, carried with it your special gift. I can only assume that, as your twin, I was pre-disposed to absorb it." Raising a brow, she grinned. "So, it turns out psycho-boy was right about something. The term he used for it was the Splendor. Anyway, it seems I've inherited your ability to see the dead. So far, I've seen Stacy, Nana, and a shit ton of people I don't even know. I still haven't figured out how to control who I see or how to shut it all off. Your ability as an Empath, though, didn't transfer over, and I'm grateful for that." She cocked her head. "Still, I seem to have the same difficulties interacting with spirit that plagued you. Worse, I think. All I can do is see them." She paused. "Except for you. Very curious."

"The mysteries of the gifted are endless, Shadow. Now, as for psycho-boy," Katie chastised, "do you want to tell me just what you think you're doing? I see what's going on here, Cal. The long runs, using a wrap to, um, to flatten your chest to look like mine, wearing my work-out clothes. You're trying to bait Jeremy, aren't you?"

Callie shrugged. "He ran out of that basement like his ass was on fire, but we all know how much he hated you. Jake and I figured he would stick around for a while, see if you were truly gone. We deliberately avoided placing an obituary in the paper. Jake even put out a press release saying you were in 'critical but stable' condition. If only." Saddened by the thought, she continued. "When that didn't work, we came up with another plan. Well, I came up with a plan. Jake wasn't too keen on the idea, so I thought I'd spare him the details."

Katie flickered again, her image becoming more transparent. Fatigue was gaining ground.

"I'm running out of time, Shadow. I need you to stop this foolishness and listen to Jake. If Jeremy is out there, lurking, then you are in terrible danger. I'll watch over you, become *your* Shadow, but I can only do so much from this side. Promise me you'll reconsider."

Callie stepped closer, fighting an urge to hold on to Katie to keep her here. "I'll take all the precautions, be extra careful. But Kates, I need to track this bastard down. He has taken too much from me to let this go. He has to pay."

Katie shook her head sadly, fading to nothing more than a wisp of smoke. As she left, Callie heard her say, "I love you, Shadow. Don't do anything stupid, you hear?"

Callie was attempting to unfasten the safety pins securing the Ace wrap on her breasts when the doorbell chimed. Cursing, she grabbed a flannel shirt and headed down the stairs.

This better be good.

When she got to the front door, she peeked out the small window, noting the back of a man's head—a head full of wavy, black hair. Sighing, she tossed the flannel shirt on the kitchen counter and opened the door.

The first thing Jake noticed when he entered was the ridiculous wrap across her chest. Then the suitcases lined up like soldiers next to the stairs. He raised his brows.

"Going somewhere?"

"I am," she said. "These were Kate's suitcases, stored

in the basement. I figured I might as well use them for my trip. Her luggage was always better than mine, anyway."

Jake frowned. "Do you mind if I ask where you're off to? Not being nosy, but you do realize that a killer is still out there, right? One who is extremely pissed off at you and your family."

"Of course, I know that. I blinded the fool in one eye. And you, by the way, shot his ass. I'm willing to bet he isn't too fond of you, either."

"I shot his leg, not his ass," Jake said impassively. "And I hope to God he does come after me, though I doubt he will. He doesn't have the stones to face me. But you? You and your family could be in genuine danger."

Callie tugged at the elastic bandage on her chest. "Which is the exact reason I'm leaving. I'm heading to Montana to see Jed."

Jake spun her sideways and began fiddling with the safety pins. "You're going to my brother? To P.I.P.P.S.? What in the world for?"

Jake released one pinned side, and Callie turned to give him access to the other. "Well, it's a funny story. My original plan was to hire him as a private investigator to help me find Jeremy. I realized that, even though I have a doctorate in psychology, I know next to nothing about starting a manhunt. Sure, I could profile him and get into his head, but I have no clue how to track him. Did he buy a car or a plane ticket? How about his credit cards? Has he used an ATM or made any phone calls?" Jake interjected, and she held up a hand. "Before you say anything, yes, I understand the FBI can do all the things I mentioned to track him. But so far, he's a ghost, no pun intended." She threw her hands in the air. "And honestly, how much longer will this case be a priority for the FBI? It's been three months since Katie died. Eventually, they will have to move on. But a P.I. will stay on the case if there is a paycheck involved. So, I called Jed and made him a proposition."

Jake rolled his eyes. "Oh, this should be good." He released the last pin, freeing her breasts from their elastic prison, and she groaned in relief.

"I offered to pay him to teach me the ropes. And you know what? He did one better than that—he offered me a job."

Jake smirked. "Jed always did go for one-upmanship. So, when are you leaving?"

She folded the ACE wrap. "Not for a few weeks. I still have some loose ends to tie up."

"And what about your family? The house? Blue?"

"I don't believe Gabriel has any real interest in my family. But just in case, they will stay out at Uncle Tim's cabin for a while longer. They know what I am doing and are concerned about me, of course, but they also understand why I need to do this." She walked to the counter and picked up a bottle of water. "Blue is coming with me. Jed was kind enough to offer us the small apartment over his garage until I can find a place. As far as the house, Darby has agreed to move in until I return. I couldn't bear to sell, and besides, I'll need a place to stay when I come back to visit. I plan on renting out her apartment for now; the extra income will help pay some monthly bills."

When Jake's eyes narrowed, Callie stood taller. Her posture, the tilt of her head, even the sheen of her hair, were all reflections of Kate. He wondered why he'd never noticed the similarities before.

"Seems like you have it all figured out," Jake said dryly. "Your family is safe, you've discovered a way to keep the house, and Darby won't be alone." He moved closer, and she backed up a bit. He was an imposing figure.

"There is just one person you forgot while you were keeping everyone else safe," he growled. "Who will watch over you?"

Untroubled, Callie wandered over to the suitcases and picked one up. "I'm not worried, Agent. I plan on being extra cautious, and don't forget, Jed will be there." She watched concern flicker over his face.

Eager to change the subject, she blurted, "I saw her, you know."

Jake swallowed hard. Ever since Callie told him of her newly found ability to see the dead, he wondered if this day would come. The moment the two of them shared at Katie's death, and the bright light that enveloped them, was magical. Even a skeptic could sense that something unique and life-altering had happened during those moments.

"I see," he said, voice shaking. "How did she seem?" What he really wanted to ask was if she was happy. But he nixed that question as ignorant and weak.

"She was good. Accepting of her fate, but worried sick about me." Callie smiled sadly. "Some things never change."

"Well," he said, "I, for one, don't want her to have to worry about any of this shit. She should be running in a field of wildflowers or playing hop-scotch with a dozen children or having tea with your Nana." He picked up the other two suitcases that sat by the stairs. "So, in the interest of her sanity and peace, I'm coming with you to Montana. You were important enough to her that she gave her life; the least I can do is see that she didn't die in vain."

Callie clucked her tongue. "You know, I'm a big girl,

Jake. I can take care of myself. I think I proved that point in that basement."

"Yes, you did." Jake scratched the back of his head, ill at ease. "Look, I just want to nail this guy, be the one to slap the cuffs on the bastard, okay? Or, if there is a God, be the one to blow his fucking head off. I'll take a leave of absence from the bureau, and we'll track this scumbag down. Together."

Callie shrugged. "Suit yourself, Devereaux. I won't stop you if that will soothe your inflated sense of responsibility. But understand this—I plan to see this through, do all that I have to do, to catch this maniac. And I'm not too particular whether it's dead or alive."

Jake smirked. *Oh yeah,* he thought. *Beauty, brains, and attitude. She is definitely Katie's sister.*

~

Sheridan, Wyoming, 130 miles south of Billings, Montana, 10 a.m.

He stood at the steps of St. Michael the Archangel Church, admiring the manicured lawn and ornate stained-glass windows. The church was one of the older buildings in the area; its wooden door and stone walls a testament to its simplistic beauty. He tipped his head back and inhaled, the warm spring air filling his lungs. Dust caked the tops of his loafers and clung to his sweat-stained shirt, but he didn't care.

It was good to be alive.

Of all the places in all the world, God had led him here, so close to his target's family.

When one door closes...

It was only a matter of time before they met again. He

would seek his revenge. All he needed to do was bide his time and wait.

He had become accustomed to waiting... had become quite good at it, in fact.

The faint scuffling of hurried footsteps caught his attention. Smoothing his collar, he turned, a relaxed smile aimed at the approaching figure.

"Hello, and welcome, Sir!" the young man said. "I believe we spoke on the phone? I'm Charles, Charles Ryan —but you can call me Charlie." Gushing, he stuck out a hand and smiled, his braces and acne scars a testament to his youth. "We've been waiting for you. The entire congregation is eager to meet you!"

The stranger shook the boy's hand. "Well, then, let's not keep them waiting. Tell them to gather in the vestibule! Tell them to fear no more!" He adjusted the patch that rested over his left eye.

"Tell them Father Gabriel is here."

ACKNOWLEDGMENTS

Many people in my life contributed to the making of this book. To my husband, Mark, and children, Jennifer, Brian, Jared, John, and Jordan, thank you for understanding my dream and tolerating my sometimes-neurotic behavior. A tremendous shout out to Jordan, web designer extraordinaire and sounding board during our many "creative mind sessions." Gracias, hija.

To my mom, Mary, your endless support and uncanny ability to spot grammatical mishaps has saved my bacon more than once. Thanks, Momma.

Thank you to my cousin, Brian Quinn, for his patience with me and his enviable talent of knowing just what I wanted in a book cover. Bravo.

A special thanks to my lifelong friend, Mary Hoffman. You believed in me when I was fresh out of faith. Thank you, my dear friend.

And finally, to my best friend, Lisa. You were my rock when I needed strength and a beacon of light in the darkest storms. Your grace and courage in life, and your dignity in death, inspire me. I am a better person because of you, and I will love you forever.

PREVIEW: THE DISCIPLE'S FURY

I hope you enjoyed reading *The Apostle's Fury* as much as I enjoyed writing it. The Callahans have become family to me, and I appreciate you visiting with us. So, as Darby would say, grab a cup of coffee, sit a spell, and keep reading for a brief description of what lies ahead in the second book of the series, *Shadow Sisters Book Two: The Disciple's Fury.*

Callie Callahan has seen enough heartache to last a lifetime. Kidnapped, beaten, and tortured by a madman, she lives with the horrific memory of watching her twin sister die. Now, months after Katie's death, Callie's mission to find the man who took so much leads her to Montana—and Jed Devereaux—renowned private investigator and brother of Katie's boyfriend, Jake.

FBI agent Jake Devereaux has had heartaches of his own. The woman he vowed to protect, the best and brightest light in his life, died at the hands of a sadistic killer. As Jake's guilt over Katie's death grows, it ignites a fire in his belly that puts him on a path toward vengeance and redemption. Teaming up with Kate's sister, Callie, the

373

two embark on a journey to track down a killer and bring him to justice.

Dead or alive.

~

In a heavily wooded area just outside Ten Sleep, Wyoming, a group of hikers uncover the lifeless body of a middle-aged male, naked and propped against a juniper tree. The victim's head tilted at a peculiar angle; a bloodied bandana wound tightly around his neck. Milky eyes, wide open in fear, stared sightlessly ahead, privy to secrets known only to the dead. Next to the corpse, creating a macabre sense of normalcy, sat a basket of red apples and a can of black bean soup.

Shortly after arriving on the scene, authorities recognized the deceased as Arthur Sinclair, a local high-school math teacher. Several years earlier, police were called to investigate a brutal assault against Mr. Sinclair that left him fighting for his life. In one of the most gruesome atrocities to visit the quiet little town of Ten Sleep, an unknown individual, or individuals, attacked Arthur, bludgeoning his head with a crowbar. Following the vicious beating, the perpetrators raised the stakes from assault and battery to attempted murder by repeatedly hacking his neck with a butcher knife.

Luckily for Arthur, a passerby witnessed the violence and intervened before his attackers could decapitate him. After spending weeks in critical condition, he eventually made a complete recovery.

This time, he would not be so fortunate.

Investigators processed the front of the body and, after noting the crimson blotches of livor mortis peppering Arthur's abdomen and legs, prepared to move him from beneath the juniper to examine his back. A young officer, barely two months into his law enforcement career, hung his head, crestfallen, when directed to reposition the body for further examination. As a rookie, he was still navigating through an unspoken rite of passage… the lowest in rank suffered the most dreadful assignments.

Groaning at the prospect of touching the waxy, rigid cadaver, the cop, nonetheless, grabbed Arthur Sinclair by the legs and pulled. The back of the dead man's head skipped cruelly down the tree before jerking to the side, rolling off a shoulder, and landing with a thud to the Juniper leaves beside him.

Then, as if in a horror movie, the head began a slow roll, coasting like a child's ball to the feet of the young policeman.

The rookie cop vomited all over the crime scene.

Gabriel Devine was pissed. His anger was a raging, living thing as, forced into hiding, he contemplated missed opportunities. It wasn't supposed to be this way. He was the Apostle, for Christ's sake— messenger of the Lord and the one-true messiah for humanity. And yet, he cowered in fear.

Fear of discovery, fear of retaliation for his deeds, fear that God would replace him.

His reign, he believed, was over. How could he continue his work, his destiny, to cleanse the world of the damaged and unholy? Forlorn, he'd almost given up. Almost. But then, like a beacon from the sky bathing him in light, Gabriel had found his salvation: an apprentice, a trainee, someone to mold and guide and teach.

The Disciple.

ABOUT THE AUTHOR

Want More?

For updates, bonus content, and special offers, be sure to
visit me at QuinnNoll.com and sign up for my newsletter!

Happy reading!

Quinn Noll
Writer. Poet. Dreamer.

Made in the USA
Middletown, DE
23 January 2021